OREGON
Brides

OREGON
Brides

*Three New Loves
Thrive in the Midst
of Tragedy*

Tracey Bateman

BARBOUR
PUBLISHING

But for Grace © 2004 by Tracey Bateman
Everlasting Hope © 2005 by Tracey Bateman
Beside Still Waters © 2006 by Tracey Bateman

ISBN 978-1-59789-626-9

This book is a work of fiction. Names, characters, places, and incidents are either products of the author's imagination or used fictitiously. Any similarity to actual people, organizations, and/or events is purely coincidental.

All scripture quotations are taken from the King James Version of the Bible.

Cover photographs © Connie Ricca/Corbis and © Gunter Marx Photography/ Corbis

Published by Barbour Publishing, Inc., P.O. Box 719, Uhrichsville, Ohio 44683, www.barbourbooks.com

Our mission is to publish and distribute inspirational products offering exceptional value and biblical encouragement to the masses.

 Member of the
Evangelical Christian
Publishers Association

Printed in the United States of America.

Dear Reader,

Oregon Brides includes three of my favorite heroines. Star, Hope, and Eva. All three are strong women who must overcome incredible odds to find romance and a strong commitment to Christ. One must discover that she is worth loving despite her past, one must sacrifice her life of privilege for her children's sake, and one must heal after a devastating attack.

I have always loved reading about real women who experience loss, tragedy, love and bad hair days—women who face challenges and overcome. God has given us built-in provision as we walk with him, a promise that all things will work together for good for those who love Him and are called according to His purpose. It is my prayer that as you turn the pages of this book, you are infused with hope and with the assurance that God will do abundantly above all you could ever ask or think—that he can turn your mourning into joy and give beauty for ashes.

May God bless you, may He heal your wounds, and give you peace.

Until we meet again,
Tracey Bateman
www.traceybateman.com

But for Grace

Dedication

To my pastors: Matt and Aimee Flanders
I pray that God will multiply and extend to you the abundance of
grace you've poured into my life over the past few years.
I love you both.

And to the lover of my soul, Jesus Christ.
Thank You for knowing my heart and for loving me at my most unlovable.

Chapter 1

Oregon City, Oregon, 1855

S tar Campbell grasped the smooth maple rail and forced her aching legs to climb the stairs. When her feet touched the landing, she breathed a silent prayer of thanks that morning had finally arrived. Wonderful, blessed dawn marked the end of another long night of dodging groping hands and avoiding leering eyes. Only a few more steps to go, then she could stretch her weary body on her cot and, for a few hours, dream of another life.

Pressing a fist to her mouth, she covered a wide yawn and proceeded down the dusty, wooden hallway until she reached the room she shared with her mother on the second floor of Luke's Saloon. She stopped short of entering as her mother's voice drifted through the closed door. "Luke, you promised."

Star frowned at the distressed tone. But it was Luke's response that made her draw back in horror.

His tone was gruff. . .mocking. "Come now, Greta. Be reasonable. You're too old to be of use to me anymore. Star, on the other hand—she'll draw those lumberjacks like flies to a rubbish pile."

Star stifled a gasp. Leaning closer, she pressed her ear to the door.

"She's so young and innocent. Please don't do this."

"Young?" A cynical laugh erupted from Luke. "She's seventeen years old. I should have put her to work two years ago. And as for her innocence. . .do you really think she doesn't know what you're doing every night while she's serving drinks and cleaning tables?"

Heat rushed to Star's face. Of course she knew. She hated it, but she knew.

"You've seen how the men ask for her." Luke's silky, cajoling tone made Star's skin crawl. She rubbed her arms. "They'd pay any price. Star'll be a gold mine. And you. . .well, honey, you wouldn't have to entertain anymore. I'll even put you in charge of the other girls."

Star shrank back as the words hit her with full understanding. Luke wanted her to join the other women? He wanted her to. . .to. . . ? Panic clutched at her heart and sucked the breath from her lungs. Mama had told her over and over that Luke promised she would never have to do. . .that. That all she'd ever have to do in the saloon was serve drinks and food.

Oh, no! I just can't. . . .

"I won't have it, Luke Harper!"

Star had never heard her mother raise her voice before, but the words came out in a startling near-scream. "I followed you to every dusty town and filthy mining camp between here and California. I've done anything you've ever asked of me so that my daughter would have a better life. You promised to send Star back East to school. Or have you conveniently forgotten that promise as well as all the others you've made?"

"She's too old for that now, and you know it. It's time the girl understands what she's destined for." He gave a short laugh, completely void of humor. "Frankly, I'm amazed you'd even consider another future for the daughter of someone like you."

"Star can have her pick of good men to marry if we send her someplace where folks don't know her. Kansas City, maybe. Or New York."

"She can't hide who she is, Greta, any more than you can. Or me, for that matter. What decent man will ever want her when he finds out what she is?"

The words wound their way around Star's heart like a tight, heavy chain. Mama had always told her she wasn't made for this life—that someday the right man would come along and fall in love with her. And Star had dared to believe.

Her mother's voice drifted with finality through the closed door. "I'm sending her away tomorrow. My little girl will never sell herself to any man. Do you hear me? Never!"

A stream of curses flew from Luke's lips. Star heard a loud slap, followed by a sickening thud. "After all I've done for you, this is the thanks I get?"

A gasp escaped Star's throat. How dare he? Nearly choked with fury, she reached for the door.

"Miss Star, whut you think you's doin'?" The deep whisper stopped her before she could storm in to rescue her mother.

Star spun around, coming face to face with Luke's servant, Samson.

"Luke just hit Mama!"

"Keep yo' voice down. You want the same thing your mama's gettin' in there?"

Pushing at the massive, restraining hand on her arm, Star took in a large gulp of air and muttered an oath. "Let me go," she hissed.

"Honey, you cain't stop that man," Samson said softly. "He gots a mean streak in him a mile wide. You only get yo'sef hurt."

"I don't care. Let me go!"

"I cain't let you do it." The giant black man swept her up in his arms as though she were a child.

Kicking and fighting to no avail, Star finally fell limp against him. All of the struggle sifted from her body, and she rested her cheek against his comforting chest. He carried her down the stairs, through the deserted main room, and into the kitchen.

Lila, Samson's wife and the hotel cook, threw down a cleaning rag and pushed out her lower lip indignantly. "Sam," she said, hands on her boyishly small hips, "what you think you's doin' treatin' Miss Star like she one of dem other women? Set her down."

Samson gently lowered her to a rough-hewn wooden chair next to the table. Leaning forward, Star wrapped her arms around herself. Great sobs wrenched her body.

"Whut's wrong, honey? Sam, whut da matter wit' Miss Star?"

Through a haze of disbelief, Star heard Samson quietly explain her situation to Lila. High-pitched whispers followed. Heavy boots thudded on the floor, then the kitchen door opened and closed.

In an instant, Star felt Lila's comforting arms embrace her, pulling her head against a warm breast. "There, now, chile. Everythin's gonna be a'right. Lila and Sam won' let no one hurt our gal."

She shook her head, trying to make sense of all that had just happened. "Why? Why would Luke do this?"

"Shh, don' you fret none. Sam's goin' right now to check on yo' mama, honey."

Relief washed over her. Samson would take care of everything.

Lila pushed a dry cloth into her hand. "Now you jus' dry dem tears, and Lila'll fix you a cup of tea."

Barely deciphering the woman's words, Star nodded, her gaze fixed on the kitchen door. Moments later, it swung open, and Samson stumbled across the room. Grabbing Star's arm, he lifted her to her feet and led her to the back door. "You gots to get outta here, Miss Star."

Fear clutched her belly at the tears streaming down the scarred face. "What is it? Where's Mama?"

"Oh, Miss Star, Luke done kilt her. I heared him telling that no-good Clem to fetch you to his office."

"No!" Star slipped through his grasp and collapsed to the floor. "Oh, no. No!" It couldn't be!

Samson hunkered down in front of her and took her face in his massive brown hands. "Honey, I knows dis be a hard thing. But if you stays here, now, you never gets away from Luke." He grabbed her arms and stood, lifting her with him. "Come on, now. Ole Sam'll get you outta here."

Helpless fury seeped through the pain and grief, bolstering Star's strength. Breaking free from Sam, she snatched up Lila's butcher knife from the counter and ran back toward the kitchen door. "I'll go to that snake's office, all right. But he'll sure wish I hadn't!"

"Put down dat knife!" Lila intercepted her, wrapping her long, bony fingers painfully around Star's wrist. "Sam's right. You gots to get outta here. You just get yo'sef in a heap o' trouble, fixin' to stick a knife in Luke. Is dat whut you thinks yo' ma'd want?"

"I—I can't just let him get away with it." Fog wrapped around her mind. Mama couldn't be gone. Lila reached forward and brushed away a strand of tear-soaked hair clinging to Star's cheek. "If Luke done kilt Miss Greta, you gots to go. You cain't help yo' mama now."

With a groan, Star let the knife clatter to the floor. She collapsed against Lila. Strong fingers grasped her arms and pushed her back. Black eyes stared firmly into Star's. "You ain't gots time fo' dis. Grievin' can come later, Miss Star. Sam, get her outta here."

Star had no strength left to fight as Sam once again took her by the arm and guided her toward the door.

"What do you think you're doing, boy?"

Star gasped and spun around. Clem, Luke's strong-arm man, made an imposing figure standing in the doorway. A scowl twisted his face, and his burly chest stuck out as though he were itching for a fight.

"Mister Clem," Samson began, "Miss Star here was jus' goin' out fo' a lil' while. I thought I best keep an eye on her."

Clem sneered and sized him up. "Miss Star ain't going nowheres, boy. Luke wants to see her in his office."

"'Dat so?" Samson shuffled his feet but kept his gaze fixed to the floor. As he did so, he inched Star closer to the back door. "When I opens de door you run lak de wind."

"What was that, boy? You talkin' back to me?" Clem pulled back his coat to reveal his pistol.

"No, suh. You knows I wouldn' do dat. I was jus' tellin' Miss Star she better go see Mister Luke like you says."

Fingering the Colt, Clem narrowed his gaze. His nostrils flared. "Move away, and let her by."

Samson took one step back as though he would comply. In a flash, he reached behind Star and flung the door open. "Go!" He gave her a shove.

She stumbled across the threshold and landed hard on the ground. Behind her, a gunshot rang out. Lila screamed.

Star looked back. Samson lay motionless on the wooden floor. A wailing Lila threw herself across his body. Her mournful cries rang out in the smoky, sawdust-filled air.

Oh, no. Not Sam. Star scrambled to her feet and took a step toward the kitchen, stopping at the sound of Lila's shrill voice. "Miss Star, you get outta here."

"You best stay where you are, girl." Clem stepped away from the door and started toward her. "I can give you the same thing he got."

Anger burned inside of Star. "Samson is twice the man you'll ever be, you stinking, murdering skunk!"

"Run, Miss Star!"

"Shut up, woman," Clem growled. With two fingers, he snatched a half-smoked cigar from his lips and tossed it to the floor, never breaking his stride. As he raised his leg to step over Samson's lifeless body, Lila grabbed his boot with both hands and pushed hard. He landed flat on his stomach, uttering curses.

Over his sprawled body, Star met Lila's dark, beseeching gaze. Star recognized the woman's silent plea. If she were caught, Sam would have died for no reason.

Clem recovered and scrambled to his feet. He sneered down at the black woman, his heavy hand poised to strike.

Through a veil of tears, Star pressed her fingertips to her lips. She extended them toward Lila as Clem's arm came down, sending the woman back to the floor with a thud. Resisting the urge to return to Lila's side, Star sprang into action and took off through the dirty alley as fast as her feet would carry her. She darted past the clutter lining the buildings and scattered in the street.

"You better stop right now, girly!"

Desperately trying to ignore the corset cutting painfully into her ribs, sucking the breath from her body, she ran on. Her lungs felt like they were on fire as she made her way around the nearest corner.

Star glanced over her shoulder. Panic welled up inside as she spied Clem closing the distance between them.

The walkway filled with pedestrians the nearer she came to the center of town. On and on she ran. Her feet landed hard on the boardwalk. *Thud. . .thud. . .thud. . .* matching the rhythm of her heart as it pounded in her ears. Without slowing her pace, Star glanced behind her. *He's going to catch me.*

"Oomph." She came to a jarring halt, slammed against a rock-hard chest.

Strong hands encircled her arms in a steadying grasp. "Whoa, there, young lady. Slow down. You running from a swarm of riled bees?"

Star glanced up into soft, teasing brown eyes. Her heart leapt into her throat. "Wh–what?"

"Are you all right?" he asked gently.

Terror washed over her, and she craned her neck, her eyes searching for Clem. He stood, hands on his hips, only footsteps away.

"Turn me loose," she said, her voice a hoarse whisper.

A frown creased his brow, and he looked closer as though studying her. "Are you in some kind of trouble?"

"Please, it's none of your concern."

"Better let the lady go, like she said."

Star gasped at the sound of Clem's voice. "Come along with me, Star. You don't want to keep Luke waiting."

"N—no. You leave me alone. I'm not going back."

The long scar along one of Clem's cheeks whitened in contrast to the rest of his face, which had turned red as he fought to control his anger.

"Miss, are you sure you don't need help?" the stranger asked, keeping his hard gaze fixed on Clem.

Still locked in the iron grip, Star's emotions riffled between relief and hysteria.

"This is none of your affair, mister," Clem growled. "Back off, and me and the girl will be on our way."

"It appears to me like the young lady doesn't want to go with you."

Star watched as Clem slowly fingered his pistol. With a gasp, she twisted her body, trying to break free. When the fingers tightened around her arms, she pulled back her foot and kicked hard at the stranger's leg. He let out a yowl and turned her loose.

Star darted past the man and ran as fast as she could, her ears straining for the sound of a gunshot.

When her aching legs refused to move another step, she ducked inside the livery. The smell of fresh hay and manure rose to her nostrils, causing her hollow stomach to churn. She made her way into an empty stall, hoping Clem wouldn't look that far if he was still following her. Shivering, she lifted a horse blanket from the shoulder-high partition between stalls and wrapped it around her body.

Still unable to draw a full breath, she gasped for air and wished she'd never begged Mama for a corset in the first place. Mama. The image of the precious woman who had given her life, who had raised her with tenderness and love, sent a wave of pain to Star's heart. How could the dearest, kindest woman in the world—her entire world—be dead?

The thought brought tears to Star's eyes and sapped her strength. Unable to stand a moment longer, she sank to the livery floor. She drew her legs to her chest, pressed her forehead to her knees, and gave in to her grief. When at last the tears were spent, she curled into a ball on the hay-covered floor and closed her eyes in hopeless defeat.

Despair cast a shadow over her heart. What was the point in running? She had nowhere to go. She had no friends other than Samson and Lila, and they couldn't help her now. Neither could she help them.

Weary and heartsick as she felt, suddenly nothing mattered. If Clem caught her and took her back, so what? What did she have to live for, anyway? Mama was dead. Star was all alone, with no money and no family or friends. And Luke. . . how could she have been so wrong about him? Anger coursed through her at the thought. She couldn't let him get away with murdering Mama.

The memory of Samson lying on the ground, dead from a gunshot wound, flashed to her mind, strengthening her resolve. Samson had died saving her from Clem. She couldn't let him down either. She would hide until she was sure Clem had given up looking for her. Then she'd escape once it got dark and she could slip out. She'd get away, all right. Away from the filthy saloons and men who wanted something from her that only her husband would ever have.

But escape would come later. . .after she'd rested and regained some strength. Star knew one thing for sure: If it was the last thing she did, she'd come back to Oregon City one day and give Luke what he had coming.

&

Rage simmered, then rose to a boil as Michael Riley matched the burly man glare for glare. He'd recovered from the girl's kick just in time to stretch out his leg and send "Clem" pitching to the ground before he could take out after her. The gun had flown from the man's hand and now lay in the mud, out of reach.

"Take it easy," he warned as Clem slowly climbed to his feet.

As a general rule, Michael preferred to mind his own business, but the one thing he couldn't abide was a man bullying a woman. Any woman. For any reason. Even one who had just booted the daylights out of his leg.

"Now look what you went and did, mister," the man said through yellowed, gritted teeth. "You let her get away again."

"Seems to me the lady needed to get away for her own protection."

The man gave him a slow, snide grin. "Don't let her pretty face fool you. That girl stole a load of cash from my boss, and he wants it back."

Michael narrowed his gaze, trying to read the expression on the man's face. "So why not go to the law?" He couldn't imagine the innocent-looking girl stealing anything, but he'd been fooled by a beautiful woman before.

"Well, the girl's like a daughter to my boss. He don't want her thrown in jail. Just wants what belongs to him."

The man strode the few steps to retrieve his pistol. Michael tensed, then breathed out as Clem retrieved a handkerchief from his pocket, wiped away as much of the mud as possible, and slipped the Colt back into his holster.

Clem cleared his throat. "Helping Star out was real gentlemanly of you, mister, but try not to interfere with things that ain't none of your business next time. That girl's trouble." He glanced up and down the street, then locked his squinty-eyed gaze back on Michael. "Ain't no sense trying to find her now. She's likely holed up somewheres, waitin' for dark."

Releasing a heavy sigh, Michael watched him go. Unease crept through his gut at the thought of what might happen to the girl once that rough character got his hands on her, but he ignored the discomfort and excused himself with logic. He'd done all he could. The girl was more than likely long gone by now anyway. As the man had said, she was probably "holed up" until nightfall. Nothing he could do about that now. He'd tried to help her, and she'd refused his offer.

A gust of wind blew across him, sending a shiver up his spine. Michael glanced nervously at the sky. If he wanted to make it home before suppertime, he'd better get the rest of Ma's supplies and head for the farm. The way those clouds were rolling in, he knew he was in for a rough ride home.

He couldn't keep his thoughts from straying back to the girl's luminous violet eyes as he strode toward the general store, made his purchases, then crossed to the livery to pick up his horse and wagon. Even as he tried to force away the image, another face flitted to his mind. Sarah. One smile from her painted lips was all it had taken for him to fall. And fall hard. Marriage followed shortly thereafter, and then the fighting began.

He could still hear her mocking voice the day she told him she was carrying his child. "I married you to get away from Charles." Tears of anger had flowed down her smooth face. "Now I'm going to lose my figure and be saddled with a brat. I wish I had never met you! Any life is better than this."

Sarah's death during childbirth had been a sort of poetic justice. She was free from the life of a farmer's wife. Free from raising a child she didn't want. Free from the life she'd led before.

Oh, he'd known what kind of woman she was when he met her, but his heart hadn't judged. He had truly believed she wanted to change, to straighten out her tangled life. He'd been wrong. Sarah had used him the way she used all men. The only difference was, he had been fool enough to put a ring on her finger and take her home to meet his mother.

The lessons he'd taken away from his disastrous, short-lived marriage had been hard learned. But learned well, nonetheless. He would never be fooled by another woman as long as he lived.

Stepping into the livery, Michael pushed away the troublesome thoughts. Sarah had been gone for five years, but each time he allowed the memories to surface, the pain cut through him as though it were yesterday.

"Morning, Mr. Riley," Mr. Carlson, the silver-haired liveryman, greeted him.

"Morning."

"Team's all hitched and ready to go, but that sky's not looking too friendly. Best wait till the storm passes."

"Thanks just the same. I think I'll settle up and be on my way." There was no telling how long the bad weather might last, and if he hurried, he might stay ahead of it all the way home.

"Suit yourself."

Michael handed the older man a couple of coins.

Mr. Carlson took the money and turned his attention to an approaching wagon outside the barn.

Michael walked to the back of the wagon and deposited his purchases among the other supplies he'd picked up the day before. Just as he started to climb into the seat, he heard a soft mewling sound coming from an empty stall. A kitten?

He grinned. Aimee had been pestering him for a kitten. Maybe it was time he surprised his little girl with the pet. Still grinning at the thought of his daughter's squeals of delight and strangling hugs, he opened the gate to the stall. The sight that met him stopped him in his tracks. That was no kitten curled up in the hay. The girl was even more beautiful than he remembered, though he wasn't sure how that was even possible.

Michael swallowed hard as she let out a soft moan and shifted. His first instinct was to turn away, get into his wagon, and ride off without giving her another thought. But something stopped him short of doing just that.

The innocence reflected in the wet lashes clinging to her tearstained cheeks and her soft, slightly parted lips melted his heart. Remembering the terror in her eyes, Michael knew there was no way he could turn her out and risk having her get caught. Whether she was guilty or not, he couldn't do it. And he had the strong suspicion God had led her to him in the first place. To what end, he hadn't the faintest idea; clearly, she needed help, and evidently God intended for him to provide it.

Gently, he bent and lifted her—blanket and all—into his arms. She moaned and opened her eyes. "You again," she whispered. "Please don't let him take me back."

"I won't."

A sleepy smile curved her lips, sending Michael's heart racing. He carried her to the wagon and laid her down among his packages. "Stay hidden," he said, raising the blanket until it covered her from head to toe. When he left the town behind, he could remove the blanket. But for now, he wanted to avoid the chance anyone would notice the dark-haired beauty asleep in the back of his wagon.

Shaking his head in annoyance at his weakness, Michael climbed up to the seat and flipped the reins. Would he ever learn to mind his own business where troubled women were concerned?

Chapter 2

C'mon."

Star woke with a jolt as strong hands closed around her shoulders and jerked her to her feet. The wagon rocked beneath her feet.

A scream tore at her throat. Clem had found her! With abandon, she began to kick for all she was worth. He was not taking her back to that saloon—not without a fight on his hands. She clamped her teeth down hard on his hand.

"Hey! Ow!" He turned her loose. "Simmer down, lady."

Star felt no sympathy for her attacker. If she had a gun, she'd shoot him dead without thinking twice about it. Blinded by panicked rage, she wheeled around, reared back, and belted him squarely in the jaw.

Giving him no chance to finish, Star shoved hard, and he stumbled back toward the wagon gate. Gasping to catch her breath, she ventured a glance at his face. His brown eyes widened as he teetered along the edge of the wagon before crashing down to the ground. *Him!* Realizing her mistake, Star clasped a hand to her mouth.

Bewilderment registered on his handsome face as he lay sprawled on the ground, rubbing his jaw. "I can't believe you—"

A loud clap of thunder reverberated across the sky. Star screamed, instinctively covering her head with her hands while another bolt of lightning reached from the heavens, splitting a nearby tree. A crack filled the air as half the tree toppled to the ground barely ten yards from where the stranger lay.

Staggering to his feet, he shook his head as though to clear it. He stumbled to the wagon and offered her a hand.

Expecting the hand to strike, Star shrank back.

"Do you want to be hit by lightning?"

Star hesitated. Again, lightning flashed, followed closely by a boom of thunder. A tingle raced up her spine, causing the hairs on her arms to stand up straight. She shuddered. Grabbing the proffered hand, she hopped from the wagon and rolled underneath just as the heavens opened, sending a torrent of rain on the already damp earth. She eyed the stranger.

He cupped his jaw, rubbing the spot she'd punched. He turned to her, capturing her with a steely gaze. Then he dropped his hand and scowled.

A knot formed in Star's stomach. It was probably just as well the storm made conversation impossible. She'd likely get an earful as soon as the skies quieted.

18

Rain dripped through the wagon bed and slammed into their makeshift shelter from the side. Miserable, Star lay in a pool of muddy water for what seemed like hours. When the lightning and thunder moved away and the storm slowed to a gentle rain, the stranger rolled out of the shelter and looked at her expectantly.

The water soaking into Star's petticoats drenched her to the skin until her teeth chattered. With a sigh, she crawled out from under the wagon.

"I–I'm sorry for punching you. B–but you scared me."

Eyeing her, he silently rubbed his chin and jerked his head, acknowledging her apology.

"What's your name?" She lifted her skirt and squeezed, sending rivulets of water to the rain-soaked earth. "I'm Star Campbell."

"Michael Riley." He glanced her way, then gave her his back. "You're not being very modest."

Star looked down and saw her pantalets clinging to her legs. Her cheeks grew hot. She unclenched her hands and let the skirt fall. "Sorry," she muttered. "Just trying to wring it out."

"Well, let me know when you're done."

Star cringed at the frustration in his voice. "I'm done," she said, not wanting to provoke him any more than she already had, though the skirt still hung heavily from her waist.

"Fine. I'm going to care for the horses." He walked to the edge of the road where the horses were hobbled with rope and tethered to another rope that was tied between two trees.

Star admired his careful movements as he approached the skittish animals. Speaking in low tones, he stroked first one, then the other. Moments later, when he walked back to her, he gave her a tight smile.

"We can be thankful the only tree hit was that one over there," he said, inclining his head toward the road ahead of the wagon.

She nodded. He regarded her as though he expected her to comment, but Star couldn't think of anything to say. He adjusted his hat and, with a shrug, made his way to the fallen tree. Each step was smooth and confident, inviting Star's admiration.

His irritation with her had been evident, but Star could tell he wasn't the type to be violent. She knew a lot about men, and she'd wager a night's tips he wouldn't hit a woman, no matter how she provoked him. Still, she didn't want to anger him, she wanted to help him—to repay the kindness he'd shown her thus far.

Star watched as he struggled to lift the tree. She joined him, grabbing hold of the other end.

"What do you think you're doing?"

"Obviously, you'll never get this thing out of the road by yourself," she said with a grunt. "I want to help."

Michael sent her a scowl. "Do you think we're going to lift the whole tree?"

Brow lifted, Star blinked. That was precisely what she'd thought. "What were you trying to do?"

"Come here, and we'll try to lift this end together. Maybe we can turn the thing around enough to get the wagon past."

Without a word, Star moved to his end of the massive half-tree.

"All right. On three, lift."

She did. But the monster refused to budge.

After three tries, they had made no progress whatsoever. Michael growled and gave it a sound kick.

"That must have really hurt that old tree." Star rolled her eyes. Men!

He gave her a sheepish grin, sending her pulse racing. "It made me feel better."

"What are we going to do now?" A knot formed in her stomach. "Y–you're not going back to Oregon City, are you?"

"Don't plan to."

Relief flooded Star, and she sank down wearily onto the tree.

Breathing heavily from the exertion, Michael straddled the trunk, facing Star. He yanked off his hat, revealing thick, reddish-brown hair plastered to his head from a combination of rain and sweat. Star tried not to stare, but she found the scruff of a beard lining his jaw only added to this man's appeal in a way that made her heart race.

"What were you doing, hiding in that stall?"

"What do you think I was doing?" Star retorted more sharply than she'd intended. She couldn't help but be bewildered by her reaction to this perfect stranger. Many men had tried to catch her eye over the last few years, but none had been successful. That this stubborn, difficult man could send her heart into a tizzy bothered Star no end.

Apparently taking no offense to the sharpness of her words, he simply nodded. "Don't you have any friends? Family? Someone who would have taken you in?"

"If I did, do you think I would have hidden in a barn and covered myself with a smelly, old horse blanket?"

"Are you always this sharp-tongued when people try to help you?"

Star bit back a retort. For now, she was at this man's mercy, and it was pretty evident he was tiring of her. "I'm sorry," she murmured. "I do appreciate your help. After I kicked you, I wouldn't have blamed you if you'd left me in that horse stall." She cut her glance to him. "Why'd you carry me out of there, anyway?"

His brow lifted thoughtfully. "I'm not really sure. Maybe God led me to do it." He shrugged. "Who knows?"

God? A thrill passed over Star's heart. *Oh, Mama, if only you could have lived to see that I was right about God. He does care about the likes of us.*

Tears sprang to her eyes at the thought of her mother. Never again would she lay her head on Mama's lap and feel gentle hands rubbing her hair. With whom would she share her secrets now? She longed for solitude so she could cry out her anguish.

"What's wrong?" Michael asked.

Star glanced up, noting the bemused frown on his face.

"Nothing," she replied, blinking back the tears clouding her vision. It wouldn't do to show her tears and elicit questions from him. She needed to distract him before he got nosy. Mustering the energy, she turned her prettiest smile on him. "Except that I'm so happy you stuck out your neck for me. Just think, I might have ended up being found by someone who isn't nearly as charming and helpful as you are."

With a short laugh, he sent her a dubious look. "Save your flirting. It's wasted on me."

Star's cheeks burned. So flattery only worked on some men.

She decided to change the subject. "Is your farm near a town?"

"Why?"

"I'll need to find a position somewhere."

He scrubbed a hand over his face and winced when it made contact with his jaw.

Star sucked in a breath. Hopefully, the painful reminder of her attack wouldn't break the peace between them.

"Hobbs is a couple of miles from my farm, but there isn't much to the town. We just built a church. My brother's the preacher." Pride shone in his eyes. "We'll use the building for the school too, soon as we find a teacher. There's a small mercantile." He gave her a wry grin. "Not much of one, but it'll do in an emergency. Let's see, what else? One of my neighbors is talking about opening a lumber mill, but he hasn't made up his mind yet. Joe Grafton's restaurant is always needing someone to serve the food, but Joe's a pretty rough character from what I understand. Keeps running off the help. I guess that's about it. Unless you know anything about blacksmithing or shoeing horses." He laughed at his own joke.

Star's heart sank. The only position available to her was to serve food? Exactly the kind of job she wanted to avoid.

"I—is that the only town nearby?"

" 'Fraid so. Other than Oregon City. But that's a good half day's ride." He sent a wary look toward the sky. "When the weather cooperates."

"Well, that's not an option, anyway."

"Didn't think so." He eyed her reflectively. "Do you want to tell me why that man was chasing you?"

Star averted her gaze to her fingers. Now what? She tried to think up a good lie, but as always, her mind went blank. She fumbled with her hands as the silence grew incredibly loud between them.

"Never mind. You don't have to tell me anything." Michael stood suddenly, swinging his leg over the tree. "I'd better hook the team up to a chain. Looks like ol' Pete and Dan are going to have to pull this monster out of the way if we're to make it to the farm by nightfall. I don't know about you, but I'm looking forward to the hot meal waiting for me."

Hot meal? Star's heart sank. Of course he must be married. He was at least twenty-five years old by her estimation. Someone would have snatched him up by now. She felt foolish, remembering her racing pulse when he'd smiled at her.

"How will your wife feel about you bringing a woman home?" she called after him.

"I doubt she'll care since I don't have a wife," he replied over his shoulder.

Star stood and followed him to the wagon. "But you said. . .well, then who is going to have a hot meal waiting for you?"

"My ma." Without looking up, he began to work with the team.

"Do you mean to tell me you still live with your mother?"

He shot her a quick glance and scowled. "No," he said in a clipped tone. "She lives with me."

Star groaned inwardly. Mothers could sniff out a woman of questionable character a mile and a half away. And they couldn't be sweet-talked, either. She'd be tossed out on her backside before she could say "Howdy do." Star muttered an oath.

"What did you just say?" Michael asked incredulously, straightening to his full height.

She repeated the word.

"Lady, you have a dirty mouth."

"Dirty? I only said. . ."

"I heard you, and don't think you can talk your way around this issue. I have a five-year-old daughter at home, and I will not have her exposed to such foul language."

Foul language? Star gaped at him. "Do you mean—?"

He stepped back, holding up a hand, palm forward. "Don't say it again."

He strode to the other side of the wagon, leaving Star to stare after him in bewilderment. She caught up to him, her long legs matching his, stride for stride. "What do you mean you have a daughter? I thought you said you weren't married."

"My wife died when Aimee was born."

"Oh," Star mumbled. "I'm so sorry."

He shrugged. "Don't be. She's not."

"She's not what? Dead?" Michael was sure an odd duck. Did he have a wife, or didn't he?

Michael took a step, then stopped as Star blocked his path. "She's not sorry she's dead. Okay?"

"I don't understand."

"She didn't want to live if she had to live with the likes of me. All right?" He took her by the arm and moved her out of his way. He grabbed one horse by the bridle and led the team toward the fallen tree.

Spurred on by insatiable curiosity, Star trailed behind him, refusing to be intimidated by his frustration. "Well, how could you possibly know that?" Confused by the whole conversation, she felt a measure of hope all the same. "Do you have the power to speak with the dead?" she asked in a hushed voice.

"What?"

"You know. . .the power to converse with the dearly departed." Star had visited a traveling carnival once where a lady claimed to have the power to tell the future and communicate with the dead. At the time, there was no one she especially felt the need to speak to—not enough to part with ten cents, anyway. Star gathered a deep breath, suddenly feeling foolish. But, if Michael knew how his wife felt about being dead, he must have been talking to her about it. "Well?" she asked, resting her hands firmly on her hips. "Can you or can you not speak with the dead? Or is your wife the only person you can conjure up?"

His jaw dropped, his eyes wide in horror. "What are you suggesting?"

Stung by his sharp tone, Star felt heat rise to her cheeks. "I just. . .well. . .will you help me speak to my mother?"

"How can I?"

Unbidden, tears filled her eyes. "She was. . .that is, she died recently, but I didn't have a chance to say good-bye." Her voice was a hoarse whisper. "If I could only speak to her one more time."

All the thunder left his face. He dropped the bridle and took Star's hands in his.

She eyed him warily and pulled away from the warmth of his touch.

He didn't try to hold her, but placed two fingers beneath her chin, raising her head gently until he captured her gaze. The kindness in the brown depths surprised her, confused her, and made her want to lay her head against his broad chest and unburden herself.

"Honey, no one can speak to your ma after she's dead. The Bible is very clear that to even try is sinful. Worse, it's an abomination to God."

"It is?" Star didn't want to be sinful or an abomination—whatever that was. She wanted desperately to be good. Ever since the night she'd learned about Jesus from an old drunken miner, she'd tried to be kind and obedient—to somehow make up for all the pain Jesus had gone through at her expense. She didn't own a Bible, had never even seen one up close, but, oh, how she wanted to please God. "S–sinful?"

He gave her a solemn nod. "I'm afraid so. Didn't you know that?"

Feeling foolish, Star felt her defenses rise. "Well, if I knew, do you think I'd have asked about it?"

"How am I supposed to know? So far, I've noticed you don't seem too concerned with what is or isn't right. You kick and punch perfect strangers trying to help you, you use foul language, and you raised your skirt when I was looking right at you. I'm not sure what kind of woman you are."

A gasp escaped her lips. "How can you say that? You don't even know me." An image of women turning away from her mama on the street flashed through Star's mind, igniting her anger. This man was no different from the people in town who crossed the street when she and Mama came anywhere near, people who never had a kind word for the likes of them.

Familiar resentment burned inside of Star until she felt she might burst. A torrent of words bubbled to her lips as she opened up and let him have it. With an eloquence she didn't know she possessed, Star released all the pent-up frustration she'd held onto for years. Frustration of being turned out of school after school when people—usually the very men who frequented the saloons—found out she was attending with their precious children.

The bewilderment on Michael's face gave her some measure of satisfaction as she told him just what she thought of his high-and-mighty attitude.

His brow furrowed when she called him a hypocrite. And his eyes grew stormy when she told him she'd met a huge grizzly bear with more kindness than he would ever possess.

Then the moment came when she knew she crossed the line. The words flew from her mouth before she could stop them. "And no wonder your wife would rather be dead than stuck living with an unfeeling, grouchy man like you."

Chapter 3

Michael felt the blood drain from his face. How could such beautiful lips utter the cruel words he had just heard? Pain knifed through his heart, and suddenly he felt weak. Unable to speak, he stared in stunned silence at the flushed face before him.

Her eyes grew wide and her hands flew to her mouth. "Oh, Mr. Riley," she said, her voice full of regret. "I don't know how I could have said such a horrid, horrid thing."

Michael grabbed a chain from the bed of the wagon and walked back around to the horses. "Forget it. It doesn't matter."

She trailed behind him. "Of course it matters. You've been nothing but kind and helpful."

He maneuvered around her to attach the chain. "And so far it's gotten me punched, kicked, bit, and a good tongue-lashing," he said bitterly. "You certainly know how to show your appreciation."

"You're right. I don't deserve your kindness."

The self-loathing in her voice melted some of Michael's anger. Some. But enough remained to keep him from falling for the quivering rosy lips and eyes luminous from the tears. He'd been taken in by such beauty before. This woman had been nothing but trouble since he'd met her. Her recent poisonous words solidified his suspicion that she was just as cruel as Sarah. Was there not a lovely woman alive who was lovely in spirit as well? Or must a man choose between beauty and grace? If a man gave in to the lust of the eye and fell for a pretty face, was it his lot in life to be saddled with a sharp-tongued shrew? Well, not him. That was for sure. If he had to marry the ugliest woman God ever made, he'd see to it Aimee had a decent woman to call Ma. A God-fearing, sweet-tempered gal who would love him the way a man needed to be loved.

Michael led the horses to the fallen tree and found a branch he hoped would be thick and sturdy enough to drag from.

"I—is there anything I can do to help?"

"No." He wrapped the chain securely to keep it from slipping. "Just stay out of the way. I've wasted enough time as it is."

From the corner of his eye, he saw her shoulders drop as she walked away. Guilt pricked him, but he brushed it aside in a moment of indignant self-justification. After all, he had left home two days before, expecting to sell a pig and pick

25

up enough supplies to last a few weeks. Everything had gone as smoothly as he could have hoped for until this slip of a girl had smacked into him. Now he was stuck with her—a foul-mouthed little heathen who, in all likelihood, would rob him blind in his sleep.

Fighting with the horses as they slipped around on the muddy road, Michael turned his full attention to the chore, all but forgetting about Star in the process. When the tree finally lay at the side of the road, he looked around. The girl was nowhere in sight. His throat tightened. Where could she have gone? A good thirty minutes had passed since she walked away, so she couldn't have gotten far.

He assessed the situation. There were only two choices for her: the woods or the road back to the very place she had run away from.

If he were a betting man, he'd wager a nickel she'd head back to town and try to find another way to avoid being caught. Most likely, another unsuspecting man would take pity on her before the day was out. Good riddance.

If she doesn't get herself caught first.

Frustrated, Michael yanked off his hat and wiped the sweat from his brow with the back of one hand. Why should he care if she walked all the way back to Oregon City and faced what she had coming for stealing? He wasn't wasting any more time on her. He'd hitch up the wagon and head for home.

He set about doing just that, trying to ignore his niggling conscience, until finally in frustration, he smacked his hat against his thigh and stared heavenward.

"But that girl is nothing but trouble, Lord," he argued. "Look what she's put me through in the few hours I've known her."

A leftover rumble of thunder in the far distance answered. He couldn't very well just leave her on the road alone—even if she did deserve it.

Releasing a heavy sigh, Michael climbed into the wagon. The girl obviously needed help—the kind of help only God could give her. Resolutely, he turned the horses to the road heading back to Oregon City.

Within a few moments, he spied Star ahead of him. She looked so fragile, walking between the trees towering above her on either side of the road. A protective urge tugged at Michael's heart, and suddenly he was glad he'd followed her.

Star glanced around.

Michael waved.

Jutting her chin, she turned back to the road and straightened her shoulders without slowing her gait.

Look, Lord, she's not even grateful I came after her.

Michael flicked the reins, and the horses quickened their step. Within a couple of moments, he was close enough behind her that the horses could have nudged her if they'd wanted to. He cleared his throat loudly, waiting for her to acknowledge his presence. She ignored him.

"Get in the wagon, Star. You know you can't go back to Oregon City. What about that rough character looking for you? Do you want him to nab you?"

"It's no more than I deserve for speaking to you the way I did."

Michael didn't try to cover his smile. He inched the wagon beside her. "Come on," he said, as though speaking to his daughter. "Let's go home."

"I don't have a home," she said with a sniff. Michael could see the tears creeping down her face, and his heart lurched.

"You can stay with us until you figure out what to do," he offered. Now where in the world had that come from? He'd planned to let her stay the night, then take her into the small, nearby town of Hobbs in the morning. He figured she could work in the restaurant.

"I don't take charity." She lifted her chin. "I'd rather go back and face Luke."

You'll take money that doesn't belong to you, but not a little kindness that's freely offered? He kept the words to himself. She had no idea he knew what she'd done. If there was any hope for her soul, he'd have to wait until she repented and confessed her sin on her own.

"Glad to hear it, because I'm not suggesting charity. You can work for your keep until you find something else."

That stopped her in her tracks. Her brow creased. "Listen, mister, I know you don't have a wife, but I'm not that kind of woman."

"I don't know what you mean," Michael replied, pulling the horses to a stop.

She eyed him warily for a moment. Her eyes grew wide, and a bright pink spot appeared on each cheek. "Oh."

Understanding dawned on Michael. He felt the heat creep up the back of his neck and knew his face was as red as hers. Where had the girl gotten such crude notions?

Are you sure I'm supposed to take her in, Lord? What about Aimee? I don't want this woman teaching my daughter sinful habits.

"All I meant was that my ma is getting on in years. She could use a little extra help around the place. And that's all."

"No, thank you. I don't deserve your kindness."

Michael expelled a heavy sigh at her dramatics. If she kept up the self-loathing, she'd end up in sackcloth and ashes before the day was out.

He hopped down from the wagon and reached out. "Come on. You know you can't go back to Oregon City. And you'd be doing me a mighty big favor if you come help Ma out."

She released a sigh and remained silent a moment as though weighing her options. Then she nodded. "All right." Avoiding his gaze, she accepted his hand and climbed up into the wagon. She scooted as far away as she could without falling off the seat.

Michael shook his head and climbed up beside her. Carefully, he flicked the reins and maneuvered the horses around.

As he headed the wagon toward home, anxiety gnawed at his stomach. How would he ever be able to explain this to his mother?

❧

"Wake up. We're home."

From a dream world, Star awoke to the soothing voice. Slowly, she came to consciousness, aware of her aching cheek. Her eyes flew open as she realized her head rested upon Michael's solid shoulder. She jerked away, heat rushing to her face. "Sorry," she muttered. "Why didn't you wake me up sooner?"

"I'm surprised you slept at all, the way this wagon bounced and slid around in the mud," Michael said with a chuckle.

Star held herself up primly and settled her hands in her lap. "Well, it's just not very proper for me to have rested my head on your shoulder like that. It's bad enough we didn't make it to your home before dark."

Star groaned inwardly. What would his mother think? Would she be like the town women, all propriety and no kindness? Probably. The very thought filled her with dread.

Michael leaned toward her, causing Star to shrink back. "Don't worry," he said in a conspiratorial tone. "I won't tell a soul."

Michael pulled on the reins, and the wagon slowed to a stop. He hopped to the ground and offered her a steadying hand. "Go on up to the house while I unhitch the wagon and put the horses down for the night."

Star's stomach tightened. "N—no, I'll wait for you." If she went to the door alone, the woman would send her packing before Michael even made it up to the house.

Michael shrugged. "Suit yourself."

A shiver slid up Star's spine as he led the horses to the barn, leaving her alone in the black, starless night. Nervously, she rubbed her hands up her arms. She hugged herself tightly for warmth, wishing for her shawl.

The overwhelming events of the day came rushing back. Everything she'd ever known was gone. She was orphaned, without a stitch of clothing besides what she wore on her back, and so little money in her pocket, she couldn't afford to buy any more. And here she was, at the mercy of strangers.

Oh, what had she been thinking? This Michael Riley could be a robber or a murderer. She might be worse off now than she'd been in Luke's greedy clutches. *And what if. . . ?* Star gasped at the wretched thought spinning around her brain. What if Michael didn't have a mother or a daughter? What if that was only a ploy to get her to come all the way out here?

Panic gripped her. She turned on her heel and fled into the night, back up the rutted road leading away from the house. She didn't care where she ended up, but anywhere certainly would be better than being stranded alone with a lying skunk like Michael Riley.

Star stumbled along blindly, praying for all she was worth that no wild animal would capture her scent and come to investigate.

She glanced around and screamed as a shadowy figure closed the distance between them. Without warning, her foot twisted painfully, and she lost her balance. The ground came up to meet her, and she landed with a squish on the muddy road.

Pain shot through her ankle. Star moaned, knowing there was no way she could outrun whatever was chasing her. She rolled over, prepared to fight off the attacker. Before she could put her hands up in defense, a furry body straddled her. Massive paws rested on her chest, pushing all breath from her body. She looked up at sharp, white fangs. Closing her eyes, she waited to become dinner for the beast.

A warm tongue lapped at her face.

"Cannonball, get your muddy paws off the lady."

Star's eyes popped open at the sound of Michael's voice. She took a closer look at the wild beast and nearly fainted in relief. Cannonball turned out to be a big, tail-wagging mutt. He licked her a couple more times, then let out a loud bark.

Michael laughed outright. "You made his night. It isn't often old Cannonball gets someone new to play with."

Star ignored his outstretched hand and struggled to her feet. But her ankle gave out, and she would have lost her footing again, if not for Michael's sudden, steady hand on her arm. "I wasn't playing with him. I was running away from him."

"Well, don't let him hear you say that," Michael said, amusement thick in his voice. "You might hurt his feelings."

Cannonball sniffed her hand, then gave it a lick, leaving a wet streak. Star pulled away and rubbed her palm on her skirt. "As if I'm worried about hurting his feelings," she huffed, pushing at the great mutt as he jumped up on her, nearly sending her back to the ground.

"Down, boy," Michael said sternly. His hand tightened around her arm, and he started to guide her back up the road toward the house.

Star sucked in a breath as she tried to step down.

"Did you hurt yourself?"

"My ank—foot."

"Put your arms around my neck."

"Th—that won't be necessary."

Michael released a heavy, frustrated sigh and swung her up into his arms before she could resist.

"I can walk!"

"I doubt it. And even if you could limp your way up to the house, it would take twice as long. As I told you hours ago, I'm hungry."

Star's stomach did a flip-flop at her closeness to this man. She tried to dredge up the anger she'd felt just moments before, but his warm breath tickled the arm she had slung around his neck for support, making it impossible for her heart to harden against him.

Excited by the new game, Cannonball let out a high-pitched bark and jumped up again, knocking against Star's ankle. "Ow! That's the worst dog I've ever seen in my life. Can't you make him stay off me?"

"Bad dog," Michael said, lowering his tone. "You're hurting Star. Now you stay down."

Miraculously, the animal obeyed.

"You know," Michael said, "if he scared you, you should have run to the barn instead of heading off down the road. You could have gotten lost if you'd run into the woods."

"I didn't think," Star muttered, unwilling to admit she had been running away from the man and not the beast, to begin with. A quiver rippled through her stomach. What would she find when they got inside?

This girl was nothing but trouble. Bad enough he had to explain her presence to his mother. Now he also had to try to explain why she was caked in mud from head to toe.

He knew better than to question God again. For some reason, this waif had been led to him. All he could do was try to find a way to help her.

Michael stepped onto the porch. Star sighed, her breath against his neck sending a rush of emotions through him.

Turning, he looked into her heart-shaped face. The lamp hanging over the awning cast a glow over them, making her hair shimmer in the light. Even with her face smeared with mud, her beauty shone through.

He lifted his eyes to meet her gaze. His breath caught in his throat at the fear widening her eyes. She was afraid of him? All he had done since he'd found her was try to help her. How could she even imagine he'd do anything to harm her?

He would have demanded an answer, but the door swung open. His mother stood at the threshold, wearing a relieved smile. "Michael, you're home! I was beginning to worry. My word, who have you got there?" She moved back.

"This is Star Campbell," he said, stepping inside.

"Y—you really have a ma?" Star squeaked out.

"Of course I have a—"

"What did you do to the poor child? She's covered in mud."

"It was that mutt. He—"

"Daddy! What took you so long?" Aimee stood in the center of the room, looking very much like a doll in her nightgown and lacy nightcap.

"Hi, sweetheart—"

"And a daughter?" Star began to sob.

Ma jammed her fists onto her round hips. "Now look. You've gone and made the sweet thing cry."

Michael's head whirled from all the questions flung at him. Star thought he had been lying to her? That explained her fear.

"Shh, Star. Everything's all right now," he said, wishing the wailing in his ear would stop.

"Come," his mother said. "Let's lay her down on my bed."

"She's filthy. How about the cot in the lean-to?"

"Don't be ridiculous," she retorted. "It's dusty and cold out there."

Michael sighed heavily. "She can take your room, and you can use the loft. I'll sleep in the lean-to for tonight."

Star let out another loud sob. "I can't take your bedroom, ma'am!"

"Nonsense. You'll just use Aimee's bed, and she'll hop in my bed with me. We gals can all share that one room, and Michael can keep to his loft."

"You can stop arguing over where to put me," Star gulped, "because I'm not staying."

"Of course you're staying," Ma said firmly, gentleness softening her voice.

"I don't want to be any trouble, ma'am. I've already caused your son more than his share."

Ma patted her arm gently. "Don't you worry yourself about any of that. Michael can take it." She cast her gaze upward. "Now, go set her down in a chair by the table, and I'll warm some water for a nice bath."

Star swiped at her nose with the sleeve of her dress, smearing more mud on the perky tip.

Fearful of sending her into another tizzy, Michael fought the urge to laugh aloud at the sight.

Ma turned her attention toward Aimee, who scampered around the room, trying to assess the situation. "Aimee, honey, you can sleep with me tonight, and we'll let our lovely guest sleep in your bed. How does that sound?"

"Okay."

Michael's mother scurried to the kitchen.

Aimee cast a shy glance up at Star. "Don't you wish sometimes you could just keep the mud on for a while? Grammy always wants me to wash it off right away."

Star sniffed and giggled. The sound captured Michael's heart. It was the first time he'd heard her laugh. The spontaneity was every bit as heartwarming as a child's.

"I've never been covered in mud until now," she admitted.

The little girl gave her a serious look. "How do you like it?"

Star's lips twitched, and Michael could tell that she was trying to keep her expression grave to match Aimee's. "Well, it's not too bad," she said. "But I think I prefer to be clean."

Aimee sighed. "I suppose it's because you're grown up." Her face lit with a grin. "I like being muddy better."

"Run along and do as you were told, sweetheart," Michael instructed. "Crawl into Grammy's bed. I'll be in to hear your prayers soon."

"Yes, Pa." Aimee bobbed her little head, wrapped a quick hug around Michael's leg, and set off to do as she was told.

"Sorry about that," Michael said.

"About what?"

"She's rather outspoken."

Star's lips curved into a soft smile. "I think she's sweet." She cleared her throat, her eyes downcast. "Mr. Riley, I'm sorry I doubted you."

Michael started toward the table. "You don't know me well enough to trust me yet. Let's forget about it for now, okay?"

Star winced when he set her down. Sliding a chair up close, he gently lifted her leg and propped her foot. "May I take a look at it?"

A blush crept to her pale cheeks. She nodded her assent. Quickly, she averted her gaze, which was just as well. His attraction for her was growing, and he didn't need the complication of being captured by her luminous eyes. He could either have a beautiful woman or a proper mother for his daughter. They just didn't come in the same package. For Aimee's sake, he had to be practical. If he had to throw on a blindfold every time he walked into the same room with Star, so be it. He wouldn't be hornswoggled again.

Grabbing her dress with both hands, Star inched the skirt upward, revealing tattered slippers. Michael could only wonder why she would wear such impractical footwear, but in this case, it was a mercy. Michael would never have gotten a boot off her foot without causing her undue amounts of pain.

Gingerly, he lifted her heel. Star drew a sharp breath. Michael glanced up. Her lip was captured between her teeth, and fresh tears of pain shimmered in her eyes.

"I know it hurts, but I have to get the shoe off."

She nodded. "It's all right."

Michael slipped it off as gently as he could, but knew from her furrowed brow and deathly white face, the pain was excruciating.

She let out a long, slow breath once he set her foot back on the chair.

Ma bustled to the table, carrying two heaping plates. "You both must be starving." She glanced at Star's foot. "What happened?"

"She twisted her, um. . .limb outside." Michael scowled. "Why did you think I was carrying her?"

Ma shrugged. "Well, how was I to know? I thought maybe you'd gone and found yourself a wife."

Feeling the heat scorch his ears, Michael cleared his throat. "No, Ma. Cannonball scared the daylights out of her, and she hurt her foot running away from the dumb mutt."

Ma scowled and set the plates down on the wooden table. "That animal. He's going to be the death of someone one of these days. I should've sent him packing long ago."

Michael couldn't help the grin playing at the corners of his lips. Ma had found the dog as a pup and insisted they take him in. She spoiled him more than any of them. Of course, he couldn't very well remind her of the fact, or he was liable to get a thwap on the head.

"Please don't send Cannonball away," Star pleaded. "It was really my own fault, anyway. H–he thought it was a game."

Ma's face softened, and she reached out a plump hand to pat Star's arm. "All right. He can stay." She turned her gaze to Michael and sharpened her tone. "But teach him some manners."

"Yes, Ma."

"Now, you two eat before your supper gets cold," she ordered. "I'll sit here and drink my coffee, and you can tell me all about how you came to find each other."

Star jerked her head up, sending Michael a silent plea.

Michael wanted to respect her obvious wish to keep secret the fact that someone was after her, but he knew he couldn't keep the truth from his ma. Not only was it the wrong thing to do, it wasn't possible. Ma could smell a lie from ten miles away.

He gave Star a reassuring smile and launched the tale.

"What were you running from, honey?" Ma asked when he finished.

Star kept her gaze on her plate.

Ma reached over and took the girl's hand. "It's all right, Star," she said gently. "You'll tell us when you're good and ready. Until then, don't you worry. You're safe with us."

"Thank you, ma'am."

"You must call me Miss Hannah. Everyone does." She stood and headed for the stove. "Now, that water should be just about ready. Son, can you go and get one of Sarah's old night shifts so Star can have a bath and get to bed? She looks exhausted."

Michael stiffened at the suggestion. He hadn't touched Sarah's clothing since he'd packed them away after her death. The thought of Star wearing any of Sarah's frilly things irritated him and brought back his suspicions. Were these two women cut from the same cloth?

Star glanced quickly at Michael. "I. . .really don't bother," she said. "I don't want you to go to any trouble because of me."

Ma waved away the protest. "Nonsense. It's no trouble at all. Those clothes are just packed away in an old trunk up in Michael's loft. Anything I own would wrap around your little body three times." She looked pointedly at Michael. "There's no choice."

She was right. The poor girl had to have something to wear. But he made a mental note. First thing in the morning, he would go to the mercantile in Hobbs and buy material for her to make some things of her own. As soon as she did, he would burn every last stitch of clothing Sarah had owned.

"Will you be all right in here alone for a few minutes?" Ma asked.

"Yes, ma'am," Star whispered, without looking up. Ma fixed her gaze back on Michael. She raised her brow, and he braced himself for the kind of tongue-lashing only Ma could give.

"Come onto the porch and help me carry in the washtub, son," she said pointedly, allowing for no objections.

Michael followed her outside. As soon as the door shut behind them, she whipped about, hands resting on ample hips.

"How could you make that child feel so unwelcome?"

Michael blinked in surprise at the attack. "Unwelcome?"

"You nearly refused to allow her to wear Sarah's things. Your wife has been gone for five years. It's high time you start living again. That sweet thing in there needs us, and I intend to make sure she feels just as welcome as if she were the president's wife. And so will you, or so help me I'll. . ." Her eyes widened, and she reached out to touch his bruised jaw. "Michael! What happened to your face?"

Still reeling from the onslaught, Michael laughed outright. Bending way down, he kissed her plump cheek with a resounding smack. "That sweet, helpless thing in there knocked me flat on my back. That's what. And you ought to see the bruise on my leg from the kick she gave me."

He couldn't help but enjoy the effect his words caused. Ma gaped at him, her eyes round as saucers. "She did that to you?"

" 'Fraid so." He grew serious. "Ma, the man who was chasing her told me she stole a load of cash from her guardian. I know God sent her to us, but we need to use wisdom so we don't get ourselves robbed."

Ma's eyes clouded with worry for a moment. She recovered quickly and gave a short, decisive nod. "If God sent her to us, He has His reasons. Thief or no, Star has a good heart. I can see it in her eyes. And we'll do all we can for her. Let's start by getting her all snuggled in for the night. Oh, no." She clapped her hand to her cheek. "I forgot all about Aimee. Finish pouring the water and go tuck her in. She's missed you something awful."

Michael grinned as they went back inside. He'd missed her, too. Steam rose up, clouding his vision as he poured the hot water into the tub. He only hoped God, and not a pretty face, had drawn him to Star. What if he had made a mistake bringing her into his home?

Chapter 4

Star snuggled down between soft sheets and a quilt. Feeling remarkably cozy and warm, she closed her eyes and smiled. Michael's mother was wonderful, she decided. The woman had provided her with a hot bath, helped her dress, then tucked her into bed as though she were a child.

The memory of her own mama tucking her in for the night came back as a faraway image in the recesses of Star's mind, but it quickly became as vivid as though she were reliving the past. She could almost feel the gentle hands smoothing her hair back from her face, could almost hear Mama's whispered dreams of someday leaving Luke and buying a small home of their own. A place where Star could go to school and play with other children. Tears formed at the corners of Star's eyes.

Oh, Mama, I never cared where I lived or whether I had other children to play with. All I ever cared about was you. But you don't need to worry about me anymore. I got away from Luke. He'll never find me—not until I'm ready to face him for what he did to you.

A wrenching sob rose and became a groan as it left her lips. Her stomach tightened, and her body shook violently as the anguish she'd suppressed throughout the day now came pouring out. She pounded at the soft bed with her fists. *Why did he have to kill my mama?*

He wouldn't get away with it. Somehow, she would make Luke pay for what he'd done. When the time was right, she'd go back to Oregon City; and if Luke had already moved on, she'd track him down like the animal he was. He'd get what was coming to him. If it was the last thing she ever did on this earth, she'd make him pay.

A floorboard creaked, pulling Star from her vengeful thoughts. She stiffened. Suspicion clouded every sense. She knew it! Michael Riley was a snake if she'd ever seen one—and she'd seen plenty—enough to know what he was after. What sort of a man entered a woman's room when his own mother and daughter were in the next bed?

She balled up her fist and waited. If he so much as laid a fingernail on her, she'd scream and blacken his eye.

The muffled sounds of bare feet moved closer on the wooden planks. Star's heart hammered against her chest. Slowly, the covers on the opposite side of the bed lifted, letting in the cold. Star frowned as the bed moved a little. But not much. Even if he were particularly careful, Michael's weight would have made more of a dent in the mattress.

Opening one eye, Star ventured a peek. Recognizing the little intruder, she let out a relieved laugh. Aimee lay so close, they were practically nose to nose. Her wide brown eyes—so like her father's—stared curiously back at Star.

"What are you doing?" Star asked the little girl.

"Grammy's snoring real loud," Aimee whispered. "Can I sleep with you?"

"Well, what if I snore, too?" Star teased.

The little girl seemed to consider the question. "Then I guess I'll go sleep in the barn with Cannonball." She let out a giggle. Star laughed at the joke, enchanted with the little pixie next to her. The child's face suddenly grew serious. "Miss Star?"

"Yes?"

"Did you come here to be my new mama?"

Star gasped. "Did your pa tell you that?"

"No."

A curious disappointment fluttered across Star's stomach. "No. I'm not going to be your new mama. Why do you ask?"

The little girl's face fell. "Because I don't got one. Most children do, you know. Only not me. Never had one. I keep praying and praying for God to send me a ma. I just thought maybe you were the one I prayed for."

Star knew she was no one's answer to prayer. She searched for comforting words to say, but could think of nothing suitable. She understood the pain of losing a mother, but at least she'd had seventeen years with hers. The poor child had never known a mother's love. "Well, if I was going to have a little girl, I couldn't think of a nicer one than you."

"I have an idea." Aimee's round eyes shone with the wonder of her brilliant plan.

"Tell me," Star said. But the child's next words nearly broke her heart.

"Let's pretend you're my mama. Just for tonight."

Star's breath left her lungs with a *whoosh*. "Oh, Aimee. I don't know if that's such a good idea." What would Michael think? He'd hit the roof if he thought she'd even entertained such a request.

Aimee's face clouded with disappointment. "Just until I fall asleep?"

"I've never been a mother, sweetie. I wouldn't even know what to do. How about if we pretend I'm your aunt or your big sister, maybe?"

A scowl darkened the moonlit face. "Never mind." The frown lifted as soon as it had appeared and her expression brightened. "Could you tell me a story?"

Star's heart sank to her toes. She only knew a couple of stories, and they weren't even close to suitable for Michael's little girl, though she'd heard them when she was a child.

"I don't know any," she admitted.

"Not even one?"

Star shook her head. "I'm afraid not."

"But didn't your ma and pa ever tell you any stories?"

"I didn't have a pa," she replied, hoping Aimee wouldn't press that particular subject.

The little girl's eyes sobered with understanding. "Like I don't have a ma."

"Yes."

"Do you have a ma?"

"I used to, but she passed away."

Aimee reached out and touched Star's face with her soft hand. "Mine, too."

Swallowing hard, Star fought back the tears threatening to begin all over again. She covered the pudgy little hand with one of her own, marveling at its sweet softness. "My mama had to work very hard to take care of me. She didn't have much time to tell me stories, but she tucked me in every night before she went to work."

Aimee sighed in obvious sympathy for Star's plight. "Grammy or Pa tucks me in, and they always tell me a story from the Bible. Want to hear one?"

Star made an effort to push away the sadness. "I'd love to hear a Bible story."

"Do you want one from the old part of the Bible or the new?"

"I thought the whole thing was pretty old."

A giggle escaped the tiny rosebud mouth. "You're funny."

She hadn't meant to be funny, but Star was glad her ignorance had brought the child some pleasure. Smiling, she brushed away a strand of golden hair from Aimee's cheek.

"I think you're pretty funny, too. So what story do you want to tell me?"

Aimee scrunched her nose, her brow creasing as though she were deep in thought. "Well, there was a man named Jonah in the old part of the Bible. He was swallowed by a fish. Do you want to hear that one?"

Star felt her eyes grow wide as she pictured a catfish large enough to swallow a grown man. Rising up on her elbow, she rested her ear on her palm and nodded.

Aimee sat straight up.

"There was this man named Jonah," she began, then frowned. "I don't know any men named Jonah, do you?"

"I don't think so, but I've heard of lots of men named John."

"There's some of those in the Bible, too. Want to hear about one of them?"

Star wanted to hear the fish story. "Let's finish the one about Jonah first."

"Oh, yeah." She grinned an infectious smile that Star couldn't help but return. "Well, God told Jonah to go to. . .to. . .Nin. . .Ninna. It was a town with very bad people who wouldn't obey God."

"Then why did God want to send Jonah there?" Star asked.

"I guess he was a traveling preacher, like the circuit riders that used to come around here until my uncle Hank started being the preacher regular-like."

"Oh. So God wanted Jonah to preach to the people in Ninna?"

"Yeah. Because they were really, really bad. Do you know what bad people do?"

"What?"

A shrug lifted the small shoulders. "Pa won't tell me. I just thought you might know."

Stifling a giggle, Star shook her head. After Michael's comments about her own conduct, she wasn't sure what "bad" was, either. She had the feeling, the way Michael had pounced on the word she'd used earlier, it wouldn't bother him a bit to set her straight when the situation warranted. "Did Jonah go to Ninna like God told him to?"

Aimee's mop of curls bounced as she bobbed her head. "But not at first. He got in a boat with some men and went the other way."

"I wonder why he would do that." If God ever spoke to Star, she'd be so honored, it wouldn't bother her a bit to do exactly what she was told.

"Pa says he was a scaredy-cat."

"What was he afraid of?"

"I dunno. Maybe he thought he might get scalped. I guess it's like the preacher that tried to bring a little religion to the heathen redskins last year. They didn't want to hear it, so they scalped him."

"That's awful!"

"I heard Uncle Hank telling Pa about it awhile back. Pa said some folks would just rather live in their sin, and maybe it would be better to leave the Indians alone. Uncle Hank didn't think so, though."

Star wondered how Uncle Hank had heard about it, but even more, she wanted to get to the part of the story where Jonah got swallowed by the fish. "So what happened to Jonah after he got into the boat and went the other way?"

Aimee leaned forward, her eyes wide. "God sent a big storm." For emphasis, she held her arms out as far as they would go. "And the other men were real scared because the boat was tipping over and they didn't want to drown."

Star placed her palm flat on the bed. Pushing herself up higher, she rested her full weight on her hand. Her stomach tightened with the intensity of the story. "Did Jonah fall out of the boat? Is that how he got swallowed?"

"They threw him out! Wasn't that mean?"

It certainly was. "Why would they do such a thing?"

"I don't really understand why, but Jonah told them to do it. He knew if he got out of the boat, the storm would stop."

"What happened after they threw him in? The fish came and ate him?"

"Yep."

A twinge of regret snaked its way across Star's heart. "Then he died? I thought he went to Ninna to preach."

"He didn't die."

"He got swallowed up by a fish, but he didn't die?" Star couldn't keep the cynicism from her voice. Obviously, Aimee heard it, for she stiffened her spine and jutted her chin defensively. "Pa says that's the miracle part about it."

"Oh."

Aimee gave her a gap-toothed grin. "There's always a miracle in Bible stories. Jonah stayed in the fish for three whole days. I wouldn't want to do that, would you?"

"Huh-uh." Star shuddered at the thought.

"But Jonah prayed and told God he was sorry. And God made the fish swim over to the ground and throw him up. And Jonah was so glad to be out of the fish that he went to Ninna."

"I should hope so." Though it seemed to Star a preacher, of all people, should have known better than to disobey God in the first place.

"After he preached in Ninna, the folks there told God they were sorry for being bad, and God forgave them."

"Just like that? He didn't punish them?"

Aimee shook her head. "Pa says Jonah was kinda mad about that part. He thought God should punish the people."

"Well, that's probably because he had just spent three days in a fish's belly and wasn't feeling too happy about things in general."

"Probably," Aimee agreed, a wide yawn muffling the word. She lay back on the bed, so Star did the same. "But Uncle Hank says when a person is really sorry for the wrong things they do, that God throws the sin away just like it never happened."

"He does?"

"Yes, and if you ask Jesus to live in your heart, He makes you His child. And then you get to be with Him in heaven someday."

Tears stung Star's eyes. Aimee's eyes had drifted shut, but Star shook her. "Aimee, what else do you have to do to live with God in heaven someday?"

A soft sigh escaped the rosebud lips. "You have to tell God that you believe Jesus is His Son."

"I do believe that." *With all my heart*. "And then what?" she prodded. "Aimee, what next?"

Aimee's eyes popped open and she gave another wide yawn. "You have to believe Jesus died for your sins and then came back alive."

"I do." Joy rushed to her heart and burst forth. "I believe it, Aimee. I really do. What next?"

Her eyes closed once more and she snuggled under the covers. "That's it.

Now you just have to be good."

"Oh, sweetie. Thank you. Thank you so much."

"Mmmm. . ."

Star smiled and reached forward, caressing the child's golden curls. She would have loved to hear another story, but Aimee's steady breathing indicated she had already fallen asleep. Leaning forward carefully, she pressed a soft kiss to the child's forehead.

Rolling onto her back, Star folded her arms behind her head and stared up at the ceiling. The story amazed and perplexed her. On one hand, God let a fish swallow Jonah to punish him, but he forgave the wicked people in Ninna. Aimee had said when a person was sorry for what they did wrong, God threw the sin away. But what if a person didn't know what was right? What then? Star's eyes grew heavy and a yawn opened her mouth wide.

One thing she knew for sure, she had landed smack dab in the middle of a family who knew right from wrong, where folks read the Bible, and even a five-year-old could recount the stories by heart. If there was anyplace to find out about God, this was it. She could have done a lot worse.

With a sigh, she rolled back onto her side, trying to find a comfortable position in the unfamiliar bed. Her good foot bumped against the injured ankle. Instinctively, Star swore at the shooting pain. With a gasp, she covered her mouth and squeezed her eyes shut. "I'm sorry, God," she whispered. "I didn't mean to say it ever again."

She glanced at the little girl lying next to her and expelled a relieved breath. By the child's even breathing, Star knew she couldn't have heard the word.

Star groaned. She'd better learn to stop saying that before Michael took her straight back where he found her. Or worse, he might just throw her out and let her fend for herself. Then she'd never get a chance to find out everything he knew about God.

❧

Michael stripped off his jeans and cotton shirt and stretched out on his bed. The memory of his daughter's version of Jonah still lingered in his mind. He grinned into the darkness and shook his head. *Ninna.* He'd have to set Star straight tomorrow. When he heard Aimee's little voice in Star's bed, he had fully intended to order her back to his mother's bed. But when he heard her ask if Star wanted to hear about Jonah, he couldn't help but listen.

He couldn't figure Star out. One minute she was cussing as well as any drunken cowboy he'd ever heard; the next, she was listening with childlike wonder to one of the earliest Bible lessons taught in a Christian home. The puzzling part was that she seemed genuinely interested. When he heard her agree to the story, he'd assumed she only did it to appease Aimee. From the sound of it, she'd probably never picked up a Bible in her life. If she'd ever been to a church meeting, which he doubted, she apparently hadn't learned much. While she was under his roof, he'd have to do something about her lack of understanding on spiritual matters.

An owl called to its mate from the tall oak outside of Michael's loft window. He turned his head toward the sound. The light of the moon filtered in through the glass, casting a glow on the hope chest below the sill. Sarah's trunk. Michael had lovingly crafted it as a wedding gift for his wife. Painstakingly, he had carved out her initials in large script across the middle of the lid. On either side of the initials, facing inward, he had carved a dove, each carrying a leaf in its beak. Even now, Michael relived the disappointment he'd felt back then—that the symbolism for a new beginning was lost on Sarah.

She'd been genuinely happy with the beauty of the trunk but had been less than thrilled with the Bible accompanying the gift. Michael had never once seen her attempt to read it. He remembered her teasing laughter when he mentioned the oversight. "What do I need to read it for? You quote the Bible constantly. Folks could mistake you for a preacher or something."

He swallowed hard at the memory. He had met her while staying overnight in Portland, after driving a herd of cattle to sell. Sarah had worked in the saloon next to the hotel. He had met her on the street, a bruised, swollen lip marring her otherwise perfect face. Michael had taken her to a restaurant and bought her a meal and was desperately in love before the last bite was eaten. In a moment of unaccustomed impulsiveness, he had asked her to marry him. After all, hadn't she cried and told him how much she wanted to change? How much she wanted out of the life she led?

Throughout their three-day journey home, Sarah had listened to his talk of God. She had agreed with everything. She knew all about God, she'd said, but had gotten down on her luck and was forced into her sinful life just to make ends meet. Now she wanted to return to her roots and become respectable once again.

Michael's hand balled into a fist. He had been fooled, plain and simple. He should have known better, but his smitten heart had so wanted to believe her.

The memories strengthened his resolve to remove everything of Sarah's from his home. He knew Aimee would probably want the trunk when she grew up, so he would keep it. Everything else would be burned. Except the Bible. Even in his anger, Michael knew he couldn't bring himself to destroy such a treasure.

A loud clatter drew him up straight in the bed, his heart pounding in his chest. What was that? He swung his legs around to the edge of the bed and grabbed his pants from the floor. Standing, he slipped on the jeans and buttoned them. He glanced at the Colt lying on the table next to his bed. After a moment's hesitation, he snatched up the gun. No telling what that noise could have been. Cannonball might have found a way inside, but the sound could have just as likely been caused by an outlaw up to no good.

Or it could be. . . *Don't let that pretty face fool you, Mister. That girl stole a load of cash from my boss and he wants it back. . . .*

Michael scowled as the words came back to haunt him. After he had saved her, brought her home, and let his daughter sleep in the same bed, Star was trying to rob him. Was there a woman alive, besides Ma, who could be trusted?

He looked down from the loft. A quick glance toward the bedroom confirmed the door was open. He inched down the ladder, ready to catch Star in the act. He wouldn't even wait until morning to take her into Hobbs and let the sheriff deal with her. He would be well rid of the little thief.

He stepped into the living area and, sure enough, there she was, stooped over by the cherry wood armoire his pa had built for Ma thirty years ago. Ma had insisted it was too beautiful to hide away in a bedroom, so the cupboard had always graced the main room of the house. It seemed only right that Ma bring it with her when she came to live with Michael after Aimee was born.

Anger boiled his blood at the thought of this girl going through his mother's things.

"What do you think you're doing?" he demanded, closing the distance between them in a few short strides.

Star gasped and spun around to face him. "Michael!"

He grabbed her by the arm. "Surprised?"

"Of course I'm surprised. Wouldn't you be if someone came sneaking up on you? I'm trying to find—"

In no mood to hear a pack of lies, Michael cut her off. "Save it for the sheriff."

"Michael Riley, turn that poor child loose."

Michael kept a firm grasp on Star's arm and faced his mother.

"Ma, I caught her red-handed trying to steal from us."

"N–no, I—"

"Don't be ridiculous," his mother snapped. "The girl wouldn't get past the barn with her injury. It took her ten minutes to get this far. And put down that gun. Have you taken leave of your senses?"

"Oh, Miss Hannah, I'm so sorry I woke you."

"Think nothing of it. Let me help you find whatever it is you were looking for."

Michael gaped at the two women, one contrite, eyes wide with fear; the other, his own mother, ready to help her loot the place.

"Ma—"

"You didn't even give her a chance to explain, so I don't want to hear anything you have to say. Shame on you for expecting the worst. Do as I said and let her go this instant."

Michael let go at once.

"Please don't argue on my account," Star begged.

Slapping his hand against his thigh, Michael glared at the girl. "Fine, tell me what you're doing skulking about the house at this time of night."

"I—I—"

Obviously, she was trying to think up a convincing lie. "Well? Make it good."

Her eyes narrowed, growing steely. He'd seen the same expression on her face just before she'd shoved him from the wagon during the storm. Instinctively, he stepped back.

"If you must know, I was looking for a candle so I could find my way to the privy! But I wasn't going to steal it, just borrow it."

Michael felt the anger drain from him.

Ma stepped between him and Star. "Let me help you outside, honey. It's a good thing you made noise and woke me up. I doubt you'd have made it ten feet alone, anyway. Gracious, is that my teapot on the floor?"

"Yes, ma'am. It fell off the cupboard and broke when I was trying to feel around for the candle. I'll find a way to pay you back for it. I promise."

"Nonsense. Accidents happen. Besides, it's as old as Adam. 'Bout time I bought another one."

Michael watched in bewilderment as his mother helped Star out the door. Guilt pricked him as he squatted down and started picking up the broken pieces. He knew for a fact how much his ma treasured that teapot. If he'd have been the one to break it, she'd have chewed him up one side and down the other; but for some reason, Ma had decided to become this girl's champion. There was nothing he could say or do to change her mind. When Ma got a notion in her head, that was that.

He disposed of the shattered teapot and returned to his loft. With a frustrated sigh, he sat on the edge of the bed and raked his fingers through his hair. The girl might be a heap of trouble and a heathen to boot, but there was nothing worse than being falsely accused. No doubt about it, he owed her an apology.

A grin lifted the corners of his mouth. He knew he could do better than an apology. Striding to the trunk, he lifted the lid. After rummaging through the clothing, he found Sarah's Bible. With a satisfied smile, he carefully closed the lid and walked into the bedroom. His little girl didn't stir as he bent and kissed her soft, round cheek and lifted the covers over her shoulders.

The front door opened as the women returned to the house. Quickly Michael set the gift on the table beside the bed and crept back to his loft, pleased with himself for fulfilling his duty. Not only to get that girl some religion, but he felt the gift equaled an apology. His assumption that she was stealing had been an honest mistake. Maybe Star wasn't stealing from them—this time, but she was *still* a thief. What else was he supposed to think with her sneaking around the house in the dead of night, looking through cupboards and such? He undressed for the third time that night and stretched out fully on the bed.

The glow of the lantern on the table made him smile. She'd see the Bible soon, and the light in her pretty eyes in the morning would be all the thanks he needed.

Chapter 5

It won't work, Michael Riley." Star plunked the Bible down on the table the next morning. She stumbled, trying to compensate for her injured ankle.

Michael's heart lurched as she nearly lost her balance. He reached out to steady her. Jerking away, she grabbed the edge of the table. Her knuckles grew white under the strain of holding her weight off the swollen ankle.

"What are you talking about?" he asked, stung by her reaction to his gift. He stood and grabbed a chair. "Sit down before you fall."

Red-faced and eyes blazing, she ignored him. "Only a low-down skunk would try to plant the Good Book in my room to make it look like I was trying to steal it!"

Ma set a plate of fluffy biscuits on the table. "Michael! How could you?"

"Now wait, you don't really think I—"

"Miss Star doesn't need a Bible, Pa. I'm telling her all about it, ain't I, Miss Star?"

In an instant, Star's expression softened. She turned to look at the little girl. "You sure are. I loved the story you told me last night. If I'm still around tonight, maybe you could tell me another one."

"You're not going anywhere, are you?" Aimee's soft brows drew together.

"That depends on. . ." Star turned her steely gaze back to Michael. "Well, that just depends."

"Pa, don't send her away!"

"Now look, you've gone and made the child cry." Ma gathered Aimee in her arms. "Of course Star isn't going anywhere, sweet thing."

"Hang on a minute, all of you." Still holding the chair he had offered Star, Michael lifted it a good two inches off the floor and let it clatter back down for emphasis.

"Sit," he ordered, this time taking her firmly by the arm. "You need to stay off that if it's ever going to heal."

Surprisingly, she obeyed.

Taking the chair at the end of the table, he set it next to her and turned her around. "Prop your foot up." Once she was situated, Michael sat back in his own chair. "I didn't plant that Bible to try to trap Star into stealing it." He looked from his mother to Aimee, then rested his gaze on Star. "It was meant as a gift."

Her lips parted as she drew in a quick breath.

Forcing himself not to stare at the softness of her mouth, he met her wide-eyed gaze. "My way of apologizing for accusing you of stealing last night."

"You were giving it to me?"

"I *am* giving it to you." Michael slid the black book across the table to her. "It's yours if you want it."

"Hmph. . .seems to me you were trying to bribe your way out of a real apology," Ma said.

Star grabbed up the Bible and hugged it to her chest like a dog hoarding a bone. "Oh, no. This is fine. I accept. No harm done."

Ma's face softened as her gaze rested on the girl. Lowering her plump form into a chair, she glanced up at Michael and gave him an approving smile. "Sit down and say the blessing, son."

A warm glow enveloped Michael at the almost tangible excitement on Star's face. Only when Ma insisted she eat did the girl release her death grip on the Bible, setting it reverently next to her plate.

Why couldn't Sarah have felt that way about it? he thought pensively. He berated himself. He had to stop comparing Star to Sarah. But it was only natural, he reasoned. They were exactly the same sort—women of loose morals and questionable character. Was there really a difference between a thief and a prostitute? Not according to the Bible. Sin was sin. Of course, he had to admit, Star's reaction to his gift gave him some hope that she, at least, was redeemable.

"Michael?" Ma's voice drifted through his bitter thoughts. "Did you hear what I said?"

"Sorry, Ma," he muttered. "My mind was somewhere else."

Ma released an exasperated breath. "I *said*, the new teacher's due to arrive in a month or so."

Michael looked up sharply. "Hank found a teacher?"

"Just got the letter last week. A woman from Kansas."

"Well, that's good news."

"Can I go to school?" Aimee nearly bounced in her chair.

"Sit still," Michael scolded, softening his words with a smile.

The little girl's face clouded over, but she obeyed. "Well, can I?"

"We'll just have to wait and see."

She let out a sigh and turned toward Star. "Wait and see usually means no. But I don't see why I can't go."

Star grinned. "I think your pa just means he's not sure how old you have to be to attend school."

"I'll be six pretty soon. And I already know my ABCs. I can even read if the words are little."

Star's smile fairly lit the room as she beamed at the child. "Already? You know what? I'd bet my last penny that by the time school starts, you'll be old enough.

Right, Michael?" Reaching out, Star smoothed Aimee's curls. The maternal gesture took Michael by surprise, and so did his pleasant reaction. But he knew better than to allow Aimee to grow too attached to their temporary houseguest. He'd have to discuss the matter with Star. Soon. Very soon.

"Michael?"

"Pa!"

Michael blinked and stared from one to the other. "What? Oh, yeah. Probably." He hated the thought of his little girl going off to school. How was it possible she was even old enough?

Tossing his napkin down on his empty plate, he stood. "Ma, I'm going into Hobbs. Need anything?"

"Nothing I can think of. What are you going to town for? You brought plenty of supplies from Oregon City."

Michael shrugged. "Just need a few more things."

"Can I go, Pa?" Aimee shot from her chair and ran to grab Michael's hand.

"*May* I go," Ma corrected.

Aimee glanced at Ma, then back up at Michael. "Grammy wants to go, too."

Ma shook her head and gave him a helpless smile. "I think she'd better get some schooling soon before there's no hope for her."

Swinging the little girl up in his arms, Michael cast a glance at his mother. "Have any plans for her today? I wouldn't mind taking her with me." While he hated to indulge his daughter too much, he'd missed the little tyke and they'd always made these short trips to town together.

With a wave of her hand, Ma dismissed them both and set about cleaning up the plates. "Go on and take her. If you don't, she'll just pout and be underfoot until you get back."

Michael set her down and gave her little rump an affectionate swat. "Go get your jacket. There's a chill in the air this morning."

"A'right, Pa," she returned, happily running to do as she was told. She grabbed her jacket from its hook by the door and shrugged it on. After buttoning her up, Michael offered his hand.

Aimee hung back, turning to Star. "You going to be here when I get back?"

"I promise." Star smiled with affection.

A grin tipped the child's lips. "Mrs. Merlin always gives me a sourball when we go to the mercantile. I'm going to ask for one for you, too. Let's go, Pa." Tugging on his hand, she led the way out the door.

❧

Mrs. Merlin's eyebrows rose in obvious curiosity when Michael asked to see dress goods. "Your ma feeling too poorly to come pick out her own material these days?"

Michael shook his head. "Ma's feeling right as rain. Thank you for asking, ma'am."

The older woman sniffed and pulled down two bolts of fabric—one, the ugliest brown muslin Michael had ever seen—the other, a gray piece he could only describe as matronly. Neither would do for a young woman with Star's creamy complexion and violet eyes. But how did he go about explaining that to the proprietress without giving her more information than she needed to know—information sure to be all over Hobbs before his wagon rolled out of town?

Aimee saved him the trouble, making Michael sorry he'd ever brought her along. "Oh, it's not for Grammy. It's for Miss Star. She don't have any clothes, and Pa don't want her wearing my ma's old things."

A pleased smile lit Mrs. Merlin's pinched face at the easily obtained morsel of information. "I see. And who is Miss Star?"

Indignation hit Michael square in the gut. The woman didn't even have the grace to direct the question to him!

"Pa brought her back with him from Oregon City," Aimee said matter-of-factly, her pink tongue sliding over her lips as she eyed a jar of sourballs on the counter.

With an elated smirk, the shameless woman twisted off the lid and offered the jar to the little girl. "Take one, and tell me about Miss Star."

Feeling his collar tighten like a noose around his neck, Michael reached up and loosened his top button.

"Miss Star is beyoootiful!" Aimee began enthusiastically, ready to tell everything she knew and then some. "When Pa carried her inside last night, I thought she was going to be my new m—"

Michael recovered enough to slip his arm around the back of his little girl's head and cup his hand over her mouth in the nick of time.

"He carried her inside?" Giving him a triumphant smile, Mrs. Merlin cocked an eyebrow and waited. Michael would have liked nothing better than to give her a sound piece of his mind but, aware of his daughter's presence, swallowed the words past a boulder-sized lump in his throat.

Resigned, he expelled a long, slow breath and relented. "The girl will be staying on to help out around the place. Ma's not as pert as she used to be and could use someone to take over part of the chores."

Mrs. Merlin continued to stare, a look of impatience on her face. "You carried her inside?"

"She had a little accident and couldn't walk," Michael said firmly. "And that's all there is to it."

The woman scowled, obviously not getting all the information she wanted. She let out a huff and turned her attention back to the bolts of fabric on the counter. " 'Bout how much of this do you want?"

Michael fingered the brown muslin, scanning the shelves until his gaze rested on a bolt of deep green muslin. *Pretty enough for a girl like Star.* Dropping the drab brown muslin, he pointed at the shelf. "Actually, I was thinking more of something like that—enough for a dress." He cleared his throat. "And some of that blue over there."

"Kinda fancy for hired help, I'd say."

"The girl has to have something to wear to church," he said, defenses raised.

"If you say so," she shot back, with a shrug that clearly indicated she had her own opinion.

Michael left the store a few moments later, carrying a bundle containing enough material for four dresses—one blue, the closest color he found to match Star's eyes; the green, because it was his favorite color; and the brown and gray, because Mrs. Merlin seemed to think they were more fitting than the material he had chosen. In no mood to argue, Michael had bought the whole bundle. At the woman's suggestion, he'd also plunked down money for material to make underclothes. He'd had to guess on the size for a pair of sturdy boots; but by the time he'd gotten that far, Michael was so fed up with Mrs. Merlin's questions and hints, he didn't care if they pinched Star's toes into tight balls or if they swallowed her feet whole. He just had to get out of that store before the busybody drove him crazy.

On the way home, Aimee chattered incessantly until her eyes drooped and she fell asleep against his arm. When he reached the homestead, Michael lifted her gently from the wagon seat and carried her up to the house. He stopped at the sound of a deep, booming laugh that could only belong to one person. He groaned inwardly. Andy had returned.

❧

Star's heart did a funny little flip-flop when Michael walked inside carrying Aimee in his arms. He stood tall in the doorway, staring at his brother, a scowl on his face.

Not fifteen minutes after Michael's wagon had rolled out of sight, his brother burst through the door, grabbed up Miss Hannah, and swung her around the room. Thinking he was an intruder, Star had grabbed a broom and would have whopped him a good one, if not for the look of pure joy on the older woman's face.

"Michael!" Andy's voice resonated throughout the house. "Good to see you."

Michael's scowl deepened as Aimee stirred and lifted her sleepy head. Her mouth popped open as she stared at Andy.

Star couldn't blame her for staring. The man stood well over six feet tall. His hair, the same reddish-brown color as Michael's, hung shoulder length in almost feminine waves. But there wasn't a thing feminine about the rest of him. Broad shoulders and a thick chest filled out his buckskin shirt, and with a bushy beard covering his face, he looked downright scary.

"Pa? Who's that?"

"Who am I?" Andy said. "I'm your uncle Andy, little girl. And I have a present for you."

"You do?" Aimee wiggled until Michael set her on the floor. She walked toward her uncle, eyeing him cautiously.

"I sure do. Traded a fine pouch of tobacco to a little Indian squaw to get it."

Star glanced at Michael. He definitely was not happy to see this brother. Curiosity piqued, Star wondered if they'd had a falling out or if Michael just didn't like people in general.

"Pa says tobacco's evil."

A grin spread across Andy's face. "That a fact?"

"Yes." Aimee wrinkled her nose. "And it's nasty, too. All that spittin' and stuff."

Andy threw back his head and let out a belly laugh that fairly shook the house. "Good thing I got rid of it, then, isn't it?"

He riffled through his saddlebags and pulled out an Indian doll. She wore a fringed buckskin dress and a beaded band around her straw head.

Aimee stared wide-eyed. "Is that for me?" she whispered.

"Sure is. You're not too grown up to play with dolls, are you?"

"No, sir." She reached out her pudgy hands.

"Where are your manners, young lady?" Miss Hannah asked.

"Thank you, Uncle Andy." She hugged the doll tightly to her chest, then gave him a puzzled frown. "How come you're my uncle? I only had Uncle Hank before."

That seemed to draw Michael out of whatever state he was in. He stepped forward and extended his hand to his brother.

Star breathed a relieved sigh when Andy clasped the proffered hand and grinned. Michael seemed to relax. There was obviously trouble between the two men.

"Uncle Andy is your uncle because he's my other brother," Michael explained to the little girl. "And he's been gone since right after you were born." His voice held the disapproval Star was learning to dread, but it didn't seem to bother Andy in the least. As a matter of fact, he let the challenge go and focused on his niece.

"That's a fact," Andy said with a nod. He grinned and reached forward to tweak Aimee's nose. " 'Course, back then, you were a wrinkly, squalling little thing and not nearly so pretty as you are now. You were just about as big as that doll, I'd say. Maybe a little bigger."

At the reminder of her gift, the little girl turned suddenly to Michael. "Where's the presents we brought for Star, Pa?"

Presents? For her?

Star glanced up into Michael's flushed face. He cleared his throat. "I bought a few things to get Star through the winter," he explained, the red on his face deepening and creeping up to his ears.

"I'll go get them." Aimee bounded from the house before anyone could say a word.

Star glanced down at the ill-fitting, pink satin dress she wore, one Michael had grudgingly allowed her to borrow from his wife's trunk. He must have loved the woman very much to have kept her things all these years. Star could only imagine how painful it must be for him to see another woman wearing them.

Truth be told, the gown wasn't exactly comfortable for Star, either. She'd never worn such a tight, low-cut dress before—nor satin. Ma had always insisted upon her wearing modest, high-necked, dark dresses revealing the least amount of her curves. Though Star had longed for the pretty things at the time, now she understood Ma was keeping her hidden to protect her.

An all-too-familiar ache swelled inside her heart. How she missed Ma. She struggled to push the pain aside. Lila had said there was a time for grieving, but now wasn't the time. Only in solitude could she relieve her sorrow through tears.

Aimee returned to the house carrying a fat bundle in her little arms. She shoved it at Star and bounded back toward the door. "I'll get the other one," she threw over her shoulder.

The other one? How long would it take for her to pay for this and start saving her money?

She turned to Michael. Looking everywhere but at her, he shifted his position and cleared his throat again. "Well, I best get to the chores. Looks like more rain is coming in soon." With that, he headed for the door, practically knocking Aimee over in the process.

" 'Cuse me, Pa," the little girl said, as he grabbed onto her to keep her from tumbling to the floor. Michael bent to give her a quick kiss on the head and was gone in a flash.

Aimee handed Star another fat bundle. "You'll like what Pa picked out." She scrunched up her nose. "Mrs. Merlin made him buy some ugly colors, too, but Pa says you can do chores in those and wear the pretty dresses to church and town and such."

"Your pa bought me dresses?"

" 'Course not. We don't have ready-made dresses in town. Mrs. Merlin don't think it's prof. . .prof. . ." Her brow furrowed as she tried to think of the word. Then she gave up with a shrug. "She don't think anyone would buy them."

Miss Hannah grinned. "Mrs. Merlin doesn't think it's profitable to have ready-made gowns in the store."

"Then what do you mean, I can wear them to church and for chores?"

"Pa got some pretty material for you to make you dresses. When are you going to start?"

Star's stomach turned over, and she thought she might fall off the chair.

How could she ever bring herself to tell Michael she didn't know how to sew?

She glanced at Miss Hannah. The older woman gave her an encouraging smile. "It's all right. Michael wouldn't have bought the things if he didn't think you needed them."

Wishing the woman had read her mind, Star felt her heart sink. She was just going to have to find a way to explain that she couldn't make the dresses. Sarah's gowns would have to do for her.

"I don't see anything wrong with what she's wearing now." Andy gave her a once-over and winked.

Feeling her face grow hot under his appreciative gaze, Star looked away uncomfortably. She'd seen that look before on the faces of dozens of other men, and she'd just as soon never see it again.

Miss Hannah stood. "You'll be wanting to take these things to your room so you can rummage through them. Let me help you in there."

"Want me to carry her, Ma?"

"No!" Star said, a little too sharply.

His brow lifted. "Just trying to be helpful," he said with a smirk.

"Thank you, but I—I can make it. Really. It's not hurting nearly as bad as it was before."

Miss Hannah slid an arm around Star's shoulders. "Lean on me, honey. Aimee, carry Miss Star's new things into our room, will you?"

Star drew in a sharp breath as she tried to step down on her swollen ankle.

Andy stepped forward. "Sure you don't want me to—"

"No!" Star and Miss Hannah said in unison.

He held his palms up in surrender. "Okay, okay, just trying to be a gentleman."

Throwing him a reproving look, Miss Hannah gave a disgruntled sniff. "Behave yourself, young man, before I turn you over my knee and whip the daylights out of you."

Andy chortled. "Aw, Ma."

"Don't 'Aw, Ma' me," she shot back, but her voice had softened considerably. "You just stay put until I get back. No telling how long till you up and take off again, and I haven't got my fill of you yet."

"Yes, ma'am," he replied, that big grin plastered on his rugged face.

Star was glad when they reached the safety of her bedroom. That man made her uncomfortable.

As if reading her thoughts, Miss Hannah gave her shoulders a squeeze. "Don't worry about Andy, honey. He's just a big young'un at heart. He don't mean anything he says."

"Yes, ma'am." But Star couldn't shed the uneasiness filling her. She'd seen enough big, good-looking men with funny ways sweep the girls right off their feet, only to leave the next morning, never to be heard from again. She didn't care for his kind, and she didn't like the way he looked at her—as though he had a right. Michael never made her feel uncomfortable or undressed in the way his eyes held their own appreciation for her looks.

Aimee dumped the first bundle on the bed. "I'll get the other one," she hollered and ran out the door.

"Well, you going to open these packages and see what my son brought you?" Miss Hannah eyed her.

Star couldn't help but feel the excitement of getting the new things, although they would do her no good unless no one minded if she wrapped the material around her like a shawl. She smiled at the thought of Michael's face, should she do just that.

"You're a lovely girl, Star. Especially when you smile."

Surprised at the sudden compliment, she didn't know what to say as she glanced up to meet the older woman's gaze.

Cupping Star's cheeks in her work-roughened hands, Miss Hannah seemed to see straight through to her very soul. "You're a good girl, honey. I don't know what trouble brought you to us, but I'm mighty thankful the Lord saw fit to bring Michael across your path."

Removing her hands, she let out a sigh and dropped to the bed beside Star. "We all have our share of troubles to muddle through. Sometimes we need to work things out for ourselves; but if the time comes when you feel the need to unburden yourself, you can come to me."

Again, Star was left speechless. Her throat tightened and her eyes stung. She kept her gaze directed to the packages spread out over the bed.

"Well, I'll leave you to open these by yourself," Miss Hannah said. She placed her hands on her thighs to brace herself and stood. "You feel free to use my sewing kit to fix yourself those dresses. Won't be able to do much else for the next week or so, with that ankle looking big enough to choke a horse."

Star lifted her hands in despair. Gathering her courage, she faced the woman. "Miss Hannah. . .I can't. I mean, I don't know how to. . ."

A puzzled frown furrowed the woman's brow, then changed to an understanding smile. "Why, you can't sew a stitch, can you?"

Dropping her gaze, Star shook her head.

"Well, there's nothing to it. Trust me, we'll whip them up in no time. By the time that ankle allows you to go to church, you'll be lovely as a picture in one of those pretty colors."

Church. Star's stomach nearly leapt with the joyous thought. She willed her ankle to hurry up and heal.

Chapter 6

Three weeks later, Star swirled around the main room of the homestead while Miss Hannah and Aimee watched with delight. The wide skirt of her newly made green muslin dress brushed against Aimee, nearly knocking her off her feet.

Laughing aloud, Star snatched up the little girl and danced her around the room. "Oh! Have you ever seen anything so pretty in your life?"

A giggling Aimee shook her head.

"Your grammy's a sewing genius!"

Breathless, Star plopped down in the wooden rocker near the fireplace. Unable to contain the emotions welling up inside, she hugged Aimee tightly until the little girl began to squirm.

Miss Hannah beamed under the praise. "Oh, now. You'll be sewing your own dresses in no time."

"You really think so?"

"Why, sure. Nothin' to it. Right after dinner, we'll start cuttin' out the gray material."

Aimee turned her pixie face to Star and wrinkled her nose. "I don't like the gray. Do you?"

Star pressed her lips together. She couldn't very well admit to thinking that material was about as ugly as the brown dress Miss Hannah had already made.

"Can't Miss Star make the blue dress first? Then she could wear it to church on Sunday."

Star glanced hopefully at Miss Hannah.

The older woman shook her head. "I think it best we let Miss Star learn on the gray material. What do you think, Star?"

Swallowing her disappointment, she nodded. She detested the gray, but Miss Hannah was right. No sense making a mess out of the pretty material.

Besides, now that her ankle was healed, she would begin all the outside chores in the morning. It had just about healed, and she'd tried to be too independent. As a result, she set back her healing and earned a thorough scolding from Michael. She already had the ugly brown muslin, but since there were more "every" days than special days, it was only practical to have two dresses to wear around the house.

A low whistle brought Star back to the present.

"You look as fresh and pretty as a summer forest." Andy's large buckskin-clad frame filled the door. His gaze raked over Star, making her feel undressed.

"Thank you," she mumbled, feeling the heat rush to her cheeks. Oh, what she wouldn't give for one chance to put that scoundrel in his place. But her mind went blank, and her hands started shaking every time he made an ungentlemanly or improper remark. The words she would like to say fled her mind, only to resurface at some later moment when she was alone with her thoughts. That did her no good at times like this.

"The dress is lovely, Star. You look very nice."

At the sound of Michael's voice, Star glanced up and smiled. "Thank you." The look of appreciation in his eyes thrilled her, reducing Andy's unwanted attention to a mere annoyance rather than a cause for concern.

"Is it already dinnertime?" Miss Hannah pushed herself up from her chair. "You boys sit yourselves down. I'll have your meal on the table in no time."

"I'll help." Star followed Miss Hannah to the stove, wishing she didn't have to walk past Andy to get there. She recoiled as he leaned in close enough to brush against her.

"Mmm, smell good, too."

Star sent him her best look of disdain. She was getting pretty tired of his comments. Over the past three weeks, he seemed to have gotten steadily worse—finding opportunities to brush against her, making comments that weren't at all fitting or proper. To Star, it was as though she were back at Luke's and putting up with leers and suggestions from the drunken patrons. She avoided contact with him as best she could and prayed he'd feel the call of the wild and be on his way soon.

"Leave her alone, Andy," she heard Michael growl.

"Jealous?" Andy's mocking voice shot back.

Holding her breath, Star waited for the answer.

"Of course I'm not jealous. But common sense can tell you she doesn't appreciate your so-called admiration, so why keep baiting her like that?"

Andy gave an unpleasant chuckle. "I think she does appreciate the attention."

"Andy. . . ," Michael growled.

"Now, come on. What do you really know about this girl? You picked her up off the street without even asking around about her. No telling where she came from." He gave a short laugh. "And unless I miss my guess, she's closer to my kind of woman than yours."

Star felt the heat rise to her cheeks and tears burned her throat. Was it that obvious where she had come from? A sense of helpless fury invaded her. How would she ever gain respect if one look at her convinced people she was no good? She would just have to do something about her looks—that was all.

Michael's sharp response drew her from her thoughts of a pinched hairdo and drab gowns.

"If you don't shut your mouth, I'm going to shut it for you."

A gasp escaped Star's lips. "Oh, no! They can't fight. Miss Hannah, do something."

"I'm putting a stop to this nonsense." Miss Hannah scowled and grabbed the broom from the corner as Andy and Michael slammed to the floor, a tangle of long arms and legs. "You boys stop it this instant," Miss Hannah bellowed, raising the broom up high and bringing it down hard on Andy's leg.

"Ow, Ma! Will you move away before you get hurt?"

"I will not. You two don't have any sense at all," she huffed. "You're acting like a couple of young'uns."

From the corner, a meek voice piped up. "I don't hit people, Grammy. And I'm a young'un."

Star's gaze flew to Aimee's wide-eyed stare and trembling lips. The sheltered child looked as though she would dissolve into tears any second. The weight of responsibility for being the cause of Aimee's pain pressed into Star's chest. She gathered a deep, unsteady breath.

"Michael," she pleaded. "Please don't fight to defend me. I'm not worth it."

The two men stopped midstruggle, and all eyes turned to Star. She swallowed hard, trying to choke back the tears. "Please. . .just stop."

Miss Hannah's heavy arm pulled Star close. "You're worth every punch, darling Star. But these boys know fightin' don't solve a thing." She glared at Michael and Andy. "Now, get up off that floor, both of you. You two weren't raised to settle your differences with your fists. Andy, keep your mouth shut about Star from now on. She's a decent, God-fearing child, and I will not stand for any more of your disrespect."

Andy rose to his feet and offered his hand to Michael. Star held her breath as he pulled Michael to his feet.

Bending down, Michael pressed a kiss to Miss Hannah's anger-flushed cheek. "I'm sorry, Ma. No more fighting."

"Glad to hear it, son. Now what about you?" She pointed the question to Andy.

Following Michael's example, he kissed his mother. "I reckon it's time for me to be pushin' on, anyway."

"Oh, Andy," Miss Hannah moaned. "Ya don't have to leave. I just want you to behave yourself like a gentleman."

"Now, Ma, it's not just because of this scuffle. You know I can't stay put for long. To tell you the truth, I'm headed East to scout for a wagon train, come spring."

"Andy, please," Star heard herself say, "I should be the one to leave. It will break your ma's heart if you go."

Giving her a lopsided grin, Andy bent at the waist in an exaggerated bow.

"That's generous of you, *Miss* Star, but it's time for me to go. Although, I'll sure miss the sight of your pretty face."

"Listen, Andy," Michael said, his voice conciliatory, "I'd like you to stay. I could use your help with the harvest and, as Star said, Ma's going to miss you something awful if you leave again."

Andy hesitated, then shook his head. "I'm not much good in the fields."

"Pa?" Aimee's uncharacteristically meek voice captured their attention. "Is everything okay now?"

Michael lifted her from the floor and held her close. "Pa's sorry for scaring you, Angel. Everything's fine and dandy."

"No more fighting?"

"Nope," Andy cut in. "Your pa and I made up like a couple of lovebirds. And your uncle Andy is ashamed as all get out to scare you like that. Forgive me?"

A grin split Aimee's precious face as she bobbed her head, allowing her golden curls to bounce on her shoulders. "They got any Indian squaws where you're goin'?"

"Probably." Andy chuckled and sent her a wink. "Got any particular reason for asking, or were you just wondering?"

"You think you could bring me another Indian dolly?"

"Aimee!" Miss Hannah scolded.

Michael scowled at his daughter.

Throwing back his head, Andy, emitting a belly laugh, grabbed the little girl from Michael's arms and lifted her high into the air. "You bet I will. You just wait. I'll find the prettiest Indian doll I can find and bring it all the way back here just for you."

Miss Hannah gathered a deep, unsteady breath. "Well, no need to leave on an empty stomach. You sit yourself down, and I'll bring your dinner in a jiffy."

Star's heart clenched as she watched the older woman lift her apron and swipe at her eyes. She would have appealed to Andy once more, but as she turned to face him, she found his steely gaze boring into her, all but daring her to speak.

Fear shot through her, and her knees threatened to give way. Eager to escape, she followed Miss Hannah to the kitchen area.

❧

Michael stood in the predawn darkness and watched as Andy mounted his black mare.

"I sure wish you'd reconsider leaving, Andy," he said, surprised to find he really meant the words. After a lot of prayer and soul searching, he'd repented of his attitude toward his brother and for the brawl.

"Thanks anyway, little brother," Andy said with an easy grin. "But I think we both know this is for the best. But you be careful with that girl. Something don't quite add up about her, and I have a feeling you might know what it is. I just hope you know what you're doing."

"I do," Michael replied tersely.

"Maybe you do, and maybe you don't." Andy's shoulders lifted in a shrug. "Anyway, it's none of my business. I'll be seeing you when the wagon train makes it back to Oregon next year. I hope that woman doesn't do the same number on you Sarah did."

"Let me worry about that." Michael lifted a hand in farewell. Irritation threatened to rise again as he watched his brother ride away.

Maybe he was a little jealous of Andy's easy way with women, of the way he seemed to understand certain types. Andy had been right about Star. She was a questionable woman, though he'd never admit it to his brother in a million years. The girl was trying, after all, and she deserved to be given a chance. It had been a couple of weeks since he'd heard one undesirable word leave her lips, and each night he'd seen the glow of her candle at the table as she read her Bible. Each morning when he asked her about the previous night's text, her face lit like the midday sun, and she enthusiastically recounted what she'd read. Yes, Star was trying. He had to give her credit for that. She had proven herself beyond his expectations. Her growth spiritually was nothing short of miraculous. Even Ma had commented on that fact.

And now that Star's ankle was completely healed, he greatly anticipated escorting her to church in the morning.

Chapter 7

Star felt the warmth of contentment envelop her, despite the chill in the Sunday morning air. Seated in the back of the wagon with Aimee, she was hard-pressed to contain her excitement at the thought of her first church meeting ever.

The little girl's lively descriptions of the people and town had her giggling like a child.

Apparently, Mrs. Merlin knew everything about everybody and used her mercantile as a lively gossip shop, so Star should be careful what she said when that woman was anywhere close by. Least that's what Grammy said—more than once, according to Aimee.

Old Mr. Cooper never made it past the singing before he nodded off. Uncle Hank had too many manners to holler at him and wake him up, though Grammy thought it would teach the old man a fine lesson if Uncle Hank did. The snoring was downright distracting, and someone should really do something about it.

Star sat mesmerized as Aimee's descriptions of the townsfolk painted vivid pictures in her mind. The beautiful new seamstress had only been in town for a few months, it seemed. Everyone thought she must be hiding a "teeerrrible" secret for a woman that pretty to be living alone and running her own business. According to Mrs. Merlin, the woman was making herself mannish and needed to find a good husband to take care of her. But Grammy said Miss Rosemary was a smart young woman, looking after her own interests.

"Honestly, Aimee," Miss Hannah huffed from the wagon seat. "Talk about something else."

Aimee gave Star a bewildered look, then shrugged. "I'll tell you all about the Simpson twins later," she whispered. "Mrs. Merlin says they need to find husbands too, but they're getting a little long in the tooth so the pickin's are getting mighty slim."

Star laughed out loud, gaining her a questioning glance from Miss Hannah. "Tell me about the church service," she suggested to divert the child's attention and hopefully keep them both out of trouble.

"First we all stand up and say the Lord's Prayer," Aimee said, her eyes brightening at the fresh topic. "I know it by heart. Want to hear me say it?"

"I'd love it," Star answered, not sure what the Lord's Prayer was.

"Our Father, which art in heaven, hallow be Thy name."

The little girl's nose scrunched and a frown furrowed her brow. "I wonder why the Lord called his father Hallow, don't you? Everyone knows God's name is God, and why didn't Jesus just call Him Pa, since He's His son?"

"I don't know."

"The word's *hallowed*, Aimee," Michael's deep voice said with a chuckle from the wagon seat. "It means holy."

"Oh." Apparently satisfied with the answer, Aimee turned her attention back to Star. "Ain't my pa smart about Bible stuff?"

Star couldn't deny it. Michael had become quite the teacher in the last few weeks, explaining scriptures she didn't understand.

"*Isn't* your pa smart," Miss Hannah corrected from her seat next to Michael.

"That's just what I was saying to Miss Star, Grammy. Pa sure is smart."

Miss Hannah shook her head. "I give up."

The rest of the trip to town was filled with laughter, and Star felt positively lighthearted until the wagon approached the white church and rolled to a stop.

Aimee hopped down and raced to join a small girl who was just climbing from her own wagon.

"Walk!" Miss Hannah called as Michael helped her down. "That child will be the death of me yet."

With a shaky breath, Star watched Miss Hannah walk toward the building. She knew she should hop down and follow, but nerves held her fast.

Wagons lined the small churchyard; and men, women, and children filed into the church, dressed in their Sunday best.

Star's stomach suddenly began to churn at the memory of folks, much like these, who turned away from her on the streets of Oregon City. Would she receive the same welcome here?

"Coming, Star?"

Michael's throaty voice brought her about to face him. Heat rushed to her cheeks as she accepted the hand he held out for her. "Sorry," she muttered, her stomach doing flip-flops from the gentle warmth of his touch.

"Don't worry," he murmured, leaning in close enough that his breath fanned her cheek. "You'll fit right in."

"I—I'm not worried." Star lifted her chin to emphasize her point.

A low chuckle rumbled from Michael's chest. "You ought to check out the Ten Commandments," he whispered, holding out his arm. "There's one there about lying."

Slipping her trembling hand through his arm, Star smiled in spite of herself. "Maybe I am a little nervous. One look at me, and everyone will know I'm different."

"You're right about that."

Taken aback, Star stopped midstep, jerking Michael's arm as she did so. "Is it really that obvious that I'm not like these folks?" she whispered, ready to turn around and run all the way back to the farm.

"Yep." Michael's brown eyes twinkled down at her. "If any of those girls had your beautiful eyes and curls as rich as molasses, they wouldn't be caught dead wearing that gray dress. And I noticed you pulled your hair back so tight, your eyes look like you'd have a hard time blinking."

So she looked plain. That's exactly what she had hoped to accomplish, wasn't it? But somehow, seeing herself through Michael's eyes brought her no pleasure whatsoever. As a matter of fact, she had the urge to yank the knot from her hair and let her curls frame her face. But Michael's next words brought her back to her objective.

"You look very respectable." He looked at her kindly, all traces of teasing gone from his handsome face. "And not one person in that church will have a reason to think otherwise."

"You really think so?"

Holding out his arm once more, Michael nodded. "I know so—unless, of course, the singing starts without us. It wouldn't do for the preacher's brother to walk in late with a pretty girl on his arm. That would set tongues wagging for sure."

Star grabbed his arm and fairly dragged Michael toward the church doors. "Hurry up, then," she insisted, filing away the "pretty girl" comment for another time when she could be alone with her thoughts and remember the pleasure of the compliment upon Michael's lips.

The fresh smell of newly cut pine filled Star's senses as she stepped into the church with Michael at her side. The room, which had hummed when they walked in, suddenly grew silent as people stopped to stare.

Dropping her gaze to the plank floor, Star took an instinctive step closer to Michael.

To keep her gaze averted among decent folks was a habit born of years of receiving haughty glances, looks she'd rather die than have to bear—especially today, when all she wanted to do was attend the church meeting, just like she belonged.

She didn't want to give Mrs. Merlin anything too juicy to share with her customers at the mercantile the following day.

Feeling the pressure of Michael's hand at her elbow, Star glanced up. He inclined his head toward a bench at the front of the church where Aimee and Miss Hannah were already seated.

Star swallowed hard, a sense of dread pressing on her already nervous stomach. She was going to have to walk all the way up there?

Michael dipped his head and spoke close to her ear. "We'll be there before you know it. Move one foot after the other."

Spurred on by his sympathetic tone, Star did as he bade. She made haste, keeping her gaze fixed on her destination. Once there, she quickly sat next to Aimee.

Michael took his seat at the end of the bench, next to Miss Hannah. Disappointment flitted across Star's heart. She had rather looked forward to sitting next to him. The disappointment was short-lived, however, as Aimee slipped her warm hand inside Star's, sending an overwhelming sense of contentment through her.

"That's Uncle Hank," the little girl whispered, pointing to the man striding to the pulpit centered at the front of the church. Unlike Andy, Hank's looks weren't too similar to Michael's. His hair wasn't the reddish-brown she admired so on Michael. It was plain orange, almost like a carrot. She had to admit he was almost as handsome as Michael; and when he found her gaze and smiled, she felt her heart warm to the kindness reflected in his clear green eyes.

He shifted his eyes and scanned the room. "Shall we stand and say the Lord's Prayer?"

Amid the shuffle of the congregation rising to its feet, Aimee leaned closer with a grin. "See? I told you."

Miss Hannah scowled at the top of Aimee's head, and Star felt compelled to place a finger to her lips to shush the girl.

As one voice, the members of the small church offered the prayer. Though she only comprehended part of their meaning, her pulse quickened at the reverence displayed in the hushed tones.

In this place she felt clean, as though perhaps it didn't matter quite so much that her mother had sold herself to men, and maybe it was okay that Star didn't know who her father was. And maybe, just maybe, she had finally found a place to belong.

As in a beautiful dream, Star floated through the service on a beam of wonder. The singing lifted her beyond anything she had ever experienced, causing her to positively ache with joy.

Though she had spent her life listening to lively, bawdy tunes in the saloons, she had never known the beauty of voices lifted in praise. She felt God must be sitting back in heaven and smiling at the wondrous sound.

And the preaching! How could one man take the Good Book and cause it to come so alive in a few short moments? Yet, that was exactly what Reverend Hank had done.

Over and over, Star allowed her gaze to drift to her open Bible so she might reread the text: *"Trust in the LORD with all thine heart; and lean not unto thine own understanding. In all thy ways acknowledge him, and he shall direct thy paths."*

In the weeks she had been reading the Bible, Star had never read anything so utterly comforting—that God was able to direct her path. And that's what He had done so far.

Though her heart still ached at the loss of her mother, and tears still flowed during moments of solitude, Star was learning to accept her circumstances and looked forward to her new lessons each day. She'd been learning the scriptures and had started to do some of the chores; and through it all, God had truly opened up a whole new life for her. She embraced each new day.

When the service was over, Star stood outside on the church steps with Michael, Miss Hannah, and Aimee. Star's mouth curved into a timid smile as the little girl proudly introduced Star to the preacher.

Hank smiled warmly. "I apologize for not getting out to the farm to meet you sooner, Miss Campbell."

"I—it's okay," she said, ducking her head and feeling perfectly unworthy to be standing before such a good man. "A man such as yourself has more important things to attend to."

"Well, I'd like to make it up to you." He glanced past her. "Ma, how about if we all go over and eat dinner at Joe's? My treat."

"Pay for a meal when we have perfectly good food at home?" Miss Hannah sounded scandalized. "You come on out to the farm, and I'll make you a nice home-cooked meal."

"Now, Ma," he said with a teasing grin. "You wouldn't deny your son the pleasure of showing off his lovely mother to the folks, would you?"

A blush stained Ma's weathered cheeks. "Oh, go on, sweet talker. Just like your pa." Her fond gaze belied her scolding tone. With a grumpy sigh, she shook her head and waved a plump hand. "All right then, but I have it from a very reliable source that the prices that man charges are plumb outrageous."

"Mrs. Merlin, eh?" Hank chuckled. "It looks to me like she's headed over there, so the two of you will have a lot to talk about next time you make a trip to the mercantile."

Michael chuckled, too.

"Shall we head over to the restaurant?" Hank asked.

"I still say it's nonsense to pay someone else to cook a meal when a body has two perfectly good hands, but if you insist. . ."

Michael and Hank grinned at each other over Miss Hannah's gray head.

The men each took up a place on either side of their mother, and Star grasped Aimee's hand, trailing after them.

Once they had crossed the dusty street, Aimee ran on ahead while Star hung back, enjoying the coolness of the autumn air as she surveyed the town. She passed the mercantile and the bank, then continued forward.

To Star's surprise, the door hung open at the next shop she came to. The sign above the door read *Rosemary's Creations*, and Star could only surmise that this was the seamstress whom Aimee thought lovely and the rest of the town believed had no business being single.

From within, voices carried to the wooden sidewalk.

"Well, I still don't think it's very proper for a young lady to be living out there with a widowed man and his daughter."

Star stopped in her tracks. Curious, she pressed herself against the building and peeked inside.

"I mean, what is Michael thinking?" The woman who spoke could have been eighteen or thirty. Star couldn't tell past the sour expression marring a face that might have been attractive, had she smiled. "A person would expect the preacher's brother to think a little more about keeping up appearances."

"I'm sure Mr. Riley knows what he is doing, and his mother is there, too," a quiet voice spoke. "And the young lady seems to be a fine girl. I wouldn't worry about the preacher's reputation if I were you, though it's awfully kind of you to be so concerned."

Star viewed her champion. Her blond hair was swept up into a chignon and netted at the nape of her neck. Star had trouble believing behind the gentle face lurked a "teeerrrible" secret as Aimee had disclosed earlier.

An unladylike snort left the other woman's lips. "But did you see how she sat next to Aimee and held her hand through the service?" She sniffed. "As though she was the child's mother. If you ask me, that girl is fishing for a husband and thinks Michael would be a good catch."

Star bit her lip to hold back a gasp. What nerve! She was hard-pressed to keep from stomping in there and telling that woman just what she thought of her opinions, and probably would have done just that if not for the soft voice drifting through the doorway.

"Anyone would be blind not to see that Mr. Riley is a good catch, but that doesn't mean every available woman is looking to catch him." The pleasant woman's voice had taken on a tone that Star could only describe as irritated. "Maybe we should wait until we get to know the new girl before we judge her too harshly."

"Well, there's no need to get snippy."

"I apologize, Mrs. Slavens. But Mrs. Barker will have dinner on the table, and she gets mighty upset if her boarders are late. So if the gown is to your satisfaction. . ."

"Oh, dear me, yes. It's lovely. I do appreciate your opening the shop for me on the Lord's Day. I could never have made a trip to Portland without that dress."

"It was my pleasure, I assure you. And I truly hope your mother's broken leg heals quickly so you may return to our fair town without delay."

"Why, thank you, dear," Mrs. Slavens returned, a flush of pleasure sweeping her pinched cheeks. "How sweet of you to say so."

"Coming, Star?"

Star jumped as Michael's voice called to her. Glancing toward the sound of his voice, Star caught his questioning frown from down the block. A blush burned her cheeks as she darted a gaze back inside the shop, praying they hadn't heard.

But they had.

Both women stood mutely observing her. Catching the haughty expression on Mrs. Slavens's face, Star jutted her chin and moved to join the Rileys, wishing for all she was worth that she hadn't stopped to eavesdrop in the first place.

Chapter 8

Tears slipped down Star's face as she forced her feet to carry her the two miles to Hobbs. Overhearing the conversation at the dressmaker's yesterday had confirmed what she'd known all along and refused to admit to herself. She couldn't continue to take refuge and charity from Michael and Miss Hannah one more day. Not when she ran the risk of besmirching Michael's good name by her mere presence in the house.

Lying awake, watching moonbeams dance across her bedroom ceiling, she'd made the decision to leave the security and warmth of Michael's home.

An hour later, after dressing in the drab gray dress and packing the even uglier brown, she waited until she heard Michael rise, start a fire in the kitchen stove, and head out to do chores. When the door closed behind him, she crept through the house and stepped into the cold morning air. Now, as she neared town, streaks of pink were just beginning to stretch across the gray sky, but even the beauty of awakening dawn did nothing to improve her dismal outlook.

She breathed only a small sigh of relief when the town loomed before her. She certainly didn't look forward to serving food to people like that hateful Slavens woman. But what other choice did she have? Even with her newly acquired sewing skills, she wasn't experienced enough to do it for a living. Except for serving food and drinks, she had no other skills to speak of. The saloon was out of the question, but the service at the restaurant the day before had been so poor, Star figured she could get a job easily and probably do a lot to improve the quality of the cafe.

Few people occupied the streets this early, but shops were beginning to open. A smile tipped Star's lips. Aimee had mourned for two days upon finding out she would have to wait another year to go to school.

Memories replayed in Star's mind. Memories of laughter, love, stories, and evening Bible reading. Michael and Miss Hannah answered question after question for Star. Her heart swelled with hope for her future; and although she felt a physical pain at the move away from the Rileys' farm, peace permeated her spirit.

"Trust in the LORD with all thine heart; and lean not unto thine own understanding. In all thy ways acknowledge him, and he shall direct thy paths."

A deep, cleansing breath lifted then lowered Star's chest. She trusted Him. Hadn't He guided her to Michael and Miss Hannah in the first place? Hadn't

He allowed her time to learn His holy Word? Of course she had a lot more to learn, but she almost never swore anymore. When she did, she immediately repented—even if there was no one around to hear the offending words. She was beginning to recognize that prick of conscience when she committed infractions. Like three mornings ago. Cannonball had jumped on her when she was walking from the henhouse with the morning eggs. She'd been so mad that he'd dirtied her freshly washed dress, she pitched three of the eggs, hitting the bewildered animal before she realized what she was doing and hurried into the house.

When Miss Hannah remarked over the fewer than usual number of eggs, Star had blurted out that this surprised her as well and perhaps the hens required more feed. Knowing that by not telling the whole truth, she was lying, Star went about the rest of her morning chores in miserable silence. At breakfast, when Michael asked her to say the morning blessing, Star burst into tears and confessed about the three wasted eggs and how she'd let her temper get the better of her. As penance, she offered her breakfast to Michael to make up for the extra two eggs glaringly absent on his plate.

Michael's lips twitched as he told her he thought four would be plenty this morning, but to try to control her temper and not throw their breakfast at Cannonball from now on.

Oh, how she had tried to slow her quickening pulse when he'd winked at her to let her know he was teasing. Even now, just picturing his gentle brown eyes, her heart picked up a beat.

Immersed in the sweet memories, Star almost passed the restaurant. Had she not smelled bread baking within, she might have missed it altogether. She stopped short at the door. Reaching forward, she tried to gain entrance, but the knob refused to turn. She knocked hard and waited, then knocked again.

"Who's down there?" an abrupt female voice called from somewhere above Star. "We don't open for dinner until eleven."

Star stepped back and tipped her head so she could see to the second floor of the building. "Wait!" she called as the shutters started to close. They opened again, and Star recognized Jane, the young woman who had served their inadequate meal the day before.

"What do you want?" she asked with a scowl.

Star's heart beat a rapid cadence within her chest. Oh, why did Jane have to be the nasty sort? Groveling for a job was going to be difficult enough as it was.

"Well?"

"I–I'm looking for a position. I thought there might be something available for me here."

"Why would you think that?" The hostility radiating from the girl could heat the coldest room.

Star's cheeks warmed. She knew she couldn't very well insult Jane's serving skills, so she just shrugged. "I don't know. I ate here yesterday and noticed how busy you were." She gave her best effort at a friendly smile. "Your customers surely were running you ragged. I—I thought maybe you could use some help."

Jane gave a sniff. "If you didn't like the service, you could have eaten at home."

"No! Th—that's not what I—" But it was too late. The shutter slammed, cutting her off midexplanation.

Stomping her foot in frustration, Star spun around and took a second to swipe the town with her gaze. Across the street, a man stumbled from the saloon. He boldly raked her with a hot look and tipped his hat in drunken approval, despite Star's plain attire and pinched hairdo. Thankfully, he didn't attempt conversation. Star shuddered, her mind replaying every night of serving drinks in Luke's Saloon over the past two years. She'd never go back to that! But what if she couldn't find a position somewhere? Panic exploded in her chest, sending tremors of fear and dread through her belly. Would she be forced to serve drinks again?

She dipped her head and prayed a quick, silent prayer for help.

"Why, hello."

Star jerked her head up in surprise. The seamstress stood only a few feet from her on the boardwalk, getting ready to enter her shop. Her lovely smile warmed Star immediately.

"Hello," she replied.

"Joe doesn't open for breakfast. As a matter of fact, he refuses to come to the door one second before eleven."

"Oh, I wasn't waiting for breakfast. I, well, as a matter of fact, I was hoping Joe might hire me. But his daughter—" Star's voice trailed as she gave a helpless little wave toward the upstairs window.

"Yes, I saw. . ." A look of sympathy crossed Rosemary's features, and she nodded. "My name's Rosemary."

"Star," she mumbled and waited for the raised eyebrow her unusual name typically brought.

Rosemary only gave her a pleasant smile. "What a lovely name. How about joining me for a cup of tea, Star? Jane obviously isn't going to inform her pa you're waiting to speak to him, so you'll have to wait until he opens for business."

"I—I don't know, I really should try to knock again."

With hands on her slender hips, Rosemary gave her a firm look. "Joe will be clanging away in the kitchen, preparing whatever he plans to serve later. You could knock until your knuckles bleed and never get an answer. Besides, you must give me the opportunity to make up for my unspeakable rudeness yesterday."

Heat sprouted to Star's face. "There's no need—"

Closing the distance between them, Rosemary slipped her arm around Star's shoulders. "Pshaw, of course there's need. I'd planned a little trip out to the Riley farm later to apologize anyway. This is ever so much better, because now I can treat you to a nice cup of tea, and we can get to know each other without an audience."

Overcome by the unaccustomed kindness from a respectable and beautiful woman, Star almost broke down and wept. Instead, she reined in her emotions, smiled, and nodded. "All right. I'd appreciate it."

"Wonderful!" Rosemary beamed as though she truly was delighted. Star felt she had no reason to doubt the dressmaker's sincerity.

Inside the snug little shop, Rosemary removed her gloves and rubbed her hands together. "Mornings are getting a bit chillier as the days grow shorter. I'll have a fire on in no time. Would you be a dear and get some water for the tea-kettle? The pump is out back."

By the time Star returned, a small fire burned in the woodstove. Rosemary beamed, her smile lifting Star's spirits and assuring her everything would be all right.

Taking the teakettle, Rosemary motioned toward a small straight-backed wooden chair. "Go ahead and sit down," she said. "The water will take a few moments to boil."

"Thank you." Star sat gratefully. The two-mile walk into town had tired her out more than she'd realized, and a hot spot on her big toe felt suspiciously as though it might become a blister inside the slightly large boots Michael had purchased for her.

Rosemary brought a stool from the other side of the room and set it down close to Star. "Now, tell me why you're looking for work. Did the Rileys turn you out?"

"Oh, no! Of course not!"

"I didn't think so, but I wanted to be sure."

Heat crept up Star's neck and warmed her cheeks once more. Rosemary obviously meant she wanted to be sure Michael hadn't turned her out for a good reason. As embarrassing as it was, Star couldn't blame her. "No, I just felt I could no longer accept their kindness."

"But weren't you staying there to help Miss Hannah? I was under the impression they hired you as sort of a housemaid."

A rueful smile tipped Star's lips. "Miss Hannah gets along just fine. She works circles around me. I suspect they only invented a position so that I wouldn't feel like I was accepting charity." As soon as she spoke the words, Star worried she might sound ungrateful and hurried to clarify. "Miss Hannah and Michael are the kindest, most generous people I've ever known, besides my own mother. I simply couldn't accept their generosity any longer." She glanced at Rosemary, silently beseeching the dressmaker to try to understand and not ask too many questions.

"I see. And does this sudden decision have anything to do with the conversation you overheard yesterday?"

Star averted her gaze to her hands. "I suppose," she mumbled.

"Honey, there will always be gossips who delight in speculating. Moving into town won't stop tongues from wagging about you."

Jerking her head up to meet Rosemary's gaze, Star regarded her earnestly. "Yes, but this way they are only talking about me, and they can leave Michael out of it."

"Oh. I see."

And Star could tell by the raised brow and knowing lift of her chin that Rosemary indeed saw much more than Star would ever have revealed had she not been so annoyingly transparent.

"And does Michael feel the same way about you?" Her eyes twinkled and a teasing smile curved her lips.

"Oh, no!" Star couldn't bear the thought of Michael's good name being dragged through the mud on her account. Better to spell it out right up front. Maybe Rosemary could pass along the information. "Michael is much too fine a man to fall in love with the likes of me. I—I heard him tell Miss Hannah he was going to begin looking for a proper wife for him and mother for little Aimee."

How her stomach clenched at the very thought of another woman filling that role. Despite knowing she had no business even allowing herself to think about it, Star had been unable to stop the dream of occupying that place in their lives. She heaved a sigh and glanced up to find Rosemary's sympathetic gaze studying her. Star cleared her throat. "So, you see, Michael has no idea how I feel about him. I have no intention of ever making a fool of myself and admitting it. I only hope it's not so obvious to everyone else."

Rosemary's pleasant laughter filled the air. "I have a knack for picking up on this sort of thing. Don't worry. Your secret is perfectly safe with me."

Star couldn't resist returning her grin. "That's a relief."

Steam lifted from the kettle, bringing an end to the embarrassing conversation. Rosemary stood. "I love tea. There's just something about a cup that cheers me right up on a gloomy day."

A couple of moments later, she returned with two dainty cups, each sitting primly on a matching saucer.

Star took hers and studied the hand-painted roses. "This is lovely."

"Thank you." Sadness darkened Rosemary's sunny expression. "They were my mother's. I inherited the entire set of china when she passed on."

"Oh, I'm so sorry. I lost my own mother recently. Sometimes I miss her so much, I think my heart will break in two."

"We will have to be there to support one another." Rosemary's gentle voice felt like a comforting embrace.

Swallowing back the sudden lump in her throat, Star nodded and sipped at her tea.

Obviously sensing her need for another topic, Rosemary gave a bright smile. "Well, now, have you found a place to stay?"

Star blinked at her. "Wh—why no. I hadn't thought that far ahead. I assumed if I got the job, I'd have a place to stay above the restaurant."

Rosemary gave a careless wave. "Honey, even if Joe had room upstairs, believe me, you don't want to live there."

Imagining Jane's scowling face, Star shuddered. Rosemary was more than likely right about that. "Then what do you suggest?"

A warm smile curved Rosemary's lips. "It just so happens that I have too much space in my room at the boardinghouse. I could easily move a cot in there for you. How about moving in with me and sharing expenses?"

Star's stomach sank, and she dropped her gaze to the cup and saucer in her lap. Her mind went to the few small coins in her bag. "I am afraid I don't. . ." Her cheeks warmed.

"Oh, don't worry about that for now."

Stiffening her back, Star regarded Rosemary with a frank stare. "I couldn't take charity, though I do appreciate the kindness."

"Don't be silly. You can't sleep on the street, can you?"

"I don't suppose."

"Tell you what: This place is such a pigsty, I can hardly find my shears. What if you clean it up for me? That would be worth at least your share of rent for a week."

Star cast a dubious glance about the spotless shop. Pigsty indeed. She regarded Rosemary frankly. "Why are you doing this?"

"Let's just say, if I'd had a friend when I first came to Hobbs a few months ago, things might have gone much smoother for me." Her lips tilted into a grin, and her eyes widened in mock horror. "Imagine a woman living alone and choosing to be an old maid! I declare, I simply *must* be hiding something!"

A giggle burst from Star at Rosemary's version of little Aimee's tale surrounding the dressmaker.

"I see you've already heard the rumors." The statement held no animosity, only a lacing of humor behind the husky tone.

"I'm sorry. If it means anything to you, I didn't put much stock in what I heard. I don't really think you're hiding anything."

The dressmaker's eyes twinkled in response. "One of the most important things my mother ever told me was, 'Sweetie, folks will always love to tell tales about anyone different. The most important thing to remember is never, ever give them a real reason to talk.'"

"Then it doesn't bother you what they say?"

A wistful sigh escaped Rosemary's lips. "I suppose it does sometimes. I don't have a lot of friends among the women of this town." She lifted her brow. "They keep me in business, so I shouldn't complain. So, what do you say? Help me for a few hours, and you can stay with me at the boardinghouse."

Reluctantly, Star accepted the kind offer.

She spent the rest of the morning sweeping up nonexistent dirt from the floor, wiping nonexistent dust from the shelves, and refolding perfectly neat piles of dress goods.

At eleven, she walked into Joe's Restaurant, determined not to take no for an answer.

≈

Michael muttered to himself as he pulled up to the restaurant and tethered the team of horses to the hitching post. Only the memory of Aimee's tears and Ma's insistence that he "not come home without her" kept him from turning around and leaving Star to her own devices. If the girl was so ungrateful that she could walk away without so much as an explanation, then as far as he was concerned, she could just work in a sweltering kitchen and serve beef stew to the townsfolk.

What did it matter to him? Surely he'd done more than God expected of him. He'd taken her in, bought her clothing. But the memory of her bright face when she'd tried on the green muslin gown reminded him exactly why he cared enough to put aside his plowing for the rest of the day and follow her into town like a loyal dog. Star's laughter lifted his spirits at least once every single day. Her beauty never failed to trigger a rise in his pulse—no matter how carefully she tried to conceal it. He didn't have the heart to tell her that, despite her efforts, she was still lovelier than the prettiest flower ever to grow.

For weeks, she had woven her life with his so tightly, he'd come to expect her presence as a matter of course. Like Ma and Aimee. He resented her absence deeply enough that he'd paced at breakfast, unable to eat, and then again at lunch, until Ma had insisted he come to town, find Star, and bring her home.

He hadn't had to be told twice. All the way to town, he'd practiced telling her how much they had come to care for her as part of the family and how Ma needed her there. But as he stepped toward the door to Joe's, his forlornness had changed to anger. He had no intention of begging her to come home. He was going to tell it to her like it was, and she'd better not argue.

What had she expected? That he would just let her go? That in a town the size of Hobbs, he couldn't find out from one stop at the mercantile where she was? Mrs. Merlin had delighted in telling him exactly what Star had been up to. Working! As a serving girl at Joe's!

"Good afternoon, Mr. Riley."

Snatching his hand back from the door, he turned to find Miss Rosemary smiling at him from her shop next door. He lifted his hat from his head. "Good afternoon."

"Are you heading into Joe's for a late lunch or an early supper?" Her eyes twinkled merrily, and Michael could have sworn amusement hung on her words.

"No, I'm looking for someone."

"Anyone in particular?"

"Well, yes. Of course." Michael frowned. Why did women have to be so nosy anyway? "I'm looking for the young woman who accompanied my family to church yesterday. I heard she's found herself a job at Joe's. I have to go and talk to her."

"Why not wait until her workday is over? You know how Joe is, Mr. Riley. If you interfere with Star's work, he might find it an excuse to fire her. And then where would she be?"

"It doesn't matter. I'm here to take her home anyway."

"Oh? And what if she prefers to live and work in town?"

Michael let out a snort before he could stop himself. "I beg your pardon for my lack of manners, miss, but why would anyone rather serve food for a man like Joe than be a part of a family?"

Rosemary tilted her head and regarded him evenly. "She isn't a part of your family, Mr. Riley. She knows that, and the folks in town know it. She's saving you from gossip. I must say, I admire her a great deal for it."

Gaping, Michael watched her speak and forced himself to assimilate her words. "So you're saying she left for my sake?"

"That, and because she just knew it was the right thing to do."

"It wasn't the right thing," Michael protested. "We need her."

"She doesn't feel that you do."

Michael scowled. "How do you know all of this, anyway?"

"Let's just say Star and I got to know each other pretty well this morning before Joe hired her."

"Well, I've known her for a lot longer than a few hours, and I say she'd be better off where I can keep an eye on her."

"I see. And are you prepared to offer her a proposal, Mr. Riley?"

"A proposal for what?"

She smiled pointedly.

Michael's neck warmed as her inference hit him smack in the gut. "Of course not!"

"Oh? Because she isn't the 'proper sort of wife for you and the proper sort of mother for Aimee'?" Her words rang with challenge. "It seems to me, for a man not willing to officially make her part of the family, you're awfully possessive."

Indignation burned within his breast. "That's my business, Miss. Not yours. Now if you'll excuse me, I'll collect Star and be on my way."

"Very well, Mr. Riley. Do what you feel you must. But please consider something first: Star has made arrangements to share my room at the boardinghouse, she is gainfully employed, and I'm guessing for the first time in her life she is feeling a sense of accomplishment. Perhaps if you would put her needs above your own, you would see that this just might be the best thing she could have done."

Resentment boiled inside Michael, and he fought to be civil. What would he expect from a woman who clearly chose to live and work alone? He'd never been one to put much stock in idle gossip, but perhaps in this case. . .

He jerked a nod toward her. "Thank you for your advice, Miss," Michael said tersely. "Good day."

But her words strung a trail of reason through his brain. Did Star actually *prefer* working at Joe's and living at the boardinghouse? He almost convinced himself to return to the farm and come back later after Star was able to leave for the day when he saw her. She came through the kitchen door, carrying a tray. His heart clenched at the sight of her. Sweat beaded her brow and strands of hair had come loose from her tight bun and framed her face in ringlets. Weariness showed plainly in her eyes and the slump of her shoulders. Michael could see she tried desperately to keep up with the yelling Joe in the back and the equally demanding customers in the dining room. "Hurry up, girl!" a man called across the room. "I ain't got all day!"

Rosemary's words of reasoning fled Michael's mind at the abuse Star was taking. He'd had all he could abide. In a few short strides, he reached Star and grabbed hold of her arm. "Come on, we're going home!"

She gasped and turned sharply. "Michael!"

Heat seared Michael's chest as a steaming bowl of beef stew slid down his shirt.

Chapter 9

Star stared in horror at Michael.

He winced at what must surely burn like fire.

"What are you doing here?" she whispered, though she doubted he could hear her through the raucous laughter filling the dining room—completely at Michael's expense.

"I came to take you home," he replied through gritted teeth.

Resenting his assumption that she would jump at the chance to return to the farm, Star nevertheless couldn't help the thrill she felt that he'd come after her.

He pulled out his handkerchief and uselessly rubbed at the mess down the front of his shirt. "Doesn't look like you're cut out for this kind of job anyway."

"I wouldn't have spilled the food if you hadn't pulled my arm and scared me half to death."

He glowered. "Is that so?"

"Yes," she snapped back. "I am good at serving customers. It's what I did at Luke's. . . ." She broke off and clamped her lips together. Clearing her throat, she then slowly forced herself to meet his inquisitive gaze.

"You didn't leave so much as a note."

The quiet statement sent a quiver through her stomach. "I know, and that was wrong of me. I should have explained."

Stepping closer, he towered above her, taking Star's breath away. "Explain now."

"Hey, girl! Is that my food your beau's wearing?"

The room erupted in renewed laughter.

Dread wormed its way through her stomach as Joe appeared at the kitchen door, obviously summoned by the noise.

"What's going on out here?" he demanded, then seeing Michael's shirt, he scowled. "Guess I just lost me another worthless serving girl."

"No, please!"

"It was my fault, Joe. I grabbed her arm."

The grizzled cook glanced from one to the other, grunted, and fixed his gaze on Star. "That's coming out of yer pay. Get back here and dish up another bowl. Harvey ain't gonna wait all day."

"Yes, sir," Star replied, her cheeks burning under the reprimand.

"Jane!" Joe bellowed. "Get out here and clean up that mess the new girl just made."

"Please, don't bother Jane. I'll clean it up in a jiffy—just as soon as I take Harvey a fresh bowl of stew."

"You got yer hands full. Or are you trying to tell me how to run my business? I fired the last girl because she thought she knew how to run the business better than me."

"Oh, no, sir!"

"Fine." He closed the kitchen door, but his voice slammed through the wood and filled the entire dining room as he hollered once more. "Jane! Get down here and clean up this mess!"

Never in all her years of serving food at Luke's had Star spilled anything on a customer. Now Michael had to go and make her look incompetent. She turned her glare upon him. Gathering a deep breath for control, she focused on keeping her voice calm. "I am sorry I didn't say good-bye. It was truly inexcusable. But as you can see, I have my hands full at the moment."

He scowled. "Would it interest you to know that Aimee cried because you left?"

"She did?" Oh, the darling child. Star already missed her terribly.

"Yes, she did. And Ma wants you to come back. She told me not to come home without you."

Star's heart sank. "Excuse me, Michael. I have to go and dish up another bowl of stew." Giving him no chance to protest, Star retrieved the dishes from the floor and headed into the back room.

Disappointment sang a bitter song inside her head. So he hadn't come to bring her back because he cared for her and missed her himself. He was simply doing his mother's bidding. At least Miss Hannah and Aimee loved her. Would it have made a difference if he'd come of his own volition? Perhaps. But Star knew God had led her to leave, had led her to Rosemary, and even Joe's, though she hated the job already and she had only been working for three hours.

When she returned to the dining room, Michael stood in exactly the same place she'd left him. "I need to speak with you," he growled.

A heavy sigh escaped Star's lips. "Michael, I can't talk now. You'll either have to wait or leave."

"Fine," he said with a stubborn tightening of his jaw. "I'll wait." He located an empty table and sat in a chair next to it.

Without another glance in Michael's direction, Star delivered the food to her disgruntled customer and caught up with the rest of her work. A good twenty minutes later, Michael still sat alone at the table, scowling.

She gathered a steadying breath and walked toward him.

"Now, let me explain," she said. "I appreciate your kindness more than you'll ever know, Michael. I know how blessed I am that God saw fit to lead you to me and that you saw fit to put me in your wagon and save me from Clem and Luke."

"Then how could you leave?" He glanced purposefully around the dining room. "I know we don't have a fancy home, but surely it's preferable to this sort of life."

"I suppose that depends on your perspective." Star's defenses rose a bit at his superior tone. "There's nothing wrong with a person putting in a hard day's work—even if that work includes serving food and cleaning up after people." She gave a short laugh. "That's what wives do all day. It's good, honest work."

"Is that what you think being a wife is? Just a lot of work equal to this sort of life?"

"That's not what I—"

But he gave her no chance to finish. He stood, towering above her. "I'll tell Ma you've made your choice. I hope you don't live to regret it." With that, he turned and strode through the room and left without looking back.

Tears pricked Star's eyes, but there was no time to allow them free rein as a half dozen more customers walked through the door and demanded her attention. Grateful for the diversion, Star immersed herself in keeping Joe and the diners satisfied. It was after eight when the last customer left. Star spent the next two hours cleaning the dining room, washing dishes, and restocking supplies for the following day. When she stepped outside, it was past eleven. She was weary to her bones, but satisfied that she'd put in a good day's labor.

Though the night was chilly, she couldn't help but enjoy the fresh air. She gathered a few deep, cleansing breaths.

"Star?"

She jumped. "Oh, Michael. You nearly scared the life out of me."

"Lucky for me you didn't have hot food in your hands."

"What are you doing in town? You must be dog tired."

"I came back in after supper. I brought the rest of your things."

"I brought everything that belongs to me."

"What about the Bible I gave you or the two pretty dresses you and Ma made?"

Star glanced at the ground. "I didn't want you to feel as though I took advantage."

"Who else is going to wear them?"

He had a point there. Star smiled and nodded. "All right. I'll pay you back as I'm paid."

Michael scowled. "We'll discuss that at a later time. As far as the Bible goes, that was a gift. I want you to have it."

Unable to refuse, Star nodded again. "Thank you, Michael. I'll take good care of it, and if you ever need it or want it back, I promise not to make a fuss."

With an exasperated sigh, Michael reached out and captured her chin between his thumb and forefinger, forcing her to meet his gaze. "I will never take that Bible away from you. Get that through your head. It's yours forever—or for however long you'd like to keep it."

"I'll keep it forever," she whispered, her heart beating so fast she thought she might pass out from the sheer joy of his soft touch. The way his eyes studied her face, the sudden intake of his breath as his gaze lowered to her mouth, made her legs go weak.

He released her chin and motioned toward the road. "Come on to the wagon, and I'll drive you over to the boardinghouse."

Fighting disappointment, Star slipped her hand inside the arm he gallantly offered. "How did you know I'm staying there?"

"Rosemary caught me earlier and explained that you were going to share her room."

He helped her to the wagon seat.

As she watched him walk around to his side and climb up, Star was struck by a painfully brilliant idea. She was never going to be the sort of woman Michael had in mind for a wife. Even if by some miracle he fell in love with her, once he found out about Mama and Luke and the real reason Clem had been following her, he would be horrified and never speak to her again. Rosemary was everything a man like Michael could want in a wife, and Aimee would adore her. After all, hadn't she already said Miss Rosemary was beautiful?

"Michael?"

"Yeah?" The wagon lurched forward as he flapped the reins.

Even in the pale light of the moon, his handsome face caused her heart to still and she almost changed her mind. But she bravely forged ahead at the thought of little Aimee and her need for a good ma.

"What do you think of Rosemary?"

"I hardly ever think about her at all. Why do you ask?"

"I don't know. Just wondering."

"I suppose she's a mite opinionated."

"But you like that. At least we've had some lively discussions."

"Well. . .I reckon that's true. What brought this on, anyway?"

"I heard from Rosemary today that the ladies' society is hosting a bazaar to raise money to build the new school next summer. That way, the church won't have to serve as the school, too."

"Yeah, Hank and I discussed it this evening while I was waiting for you."

"I'm sure Rosemary doesn't have an escort."

"You think Hank should ask her? As a matter of fact, that's not a bad idea. Ma's been pestering him something awful about a preacher needing a wife." He grinned. "Look at us, playing matchmakers."

Letting out a frustrated breath, she decided to take a more direct approach. "But, Michael, don't you think Rosemary's pretty?"

He shrugged. "I suppose she's pleasing to the eye. Come to think of it, I guess she's more than a little pretty, isn't she? I never thought of it before."

Star wasn't prepared for the pain his honest words would inflict, and she couldn't bring herself to go through with it. She'd planted a seed. Her part was done. Should he take the hint and invite Rosemary to the bazaar, Star would try her best not to let jealousy come between her and her new friend. Somehow she couldn't help but hope Rosemary would take a liking to the parson and leave Michael alone.

Michael gathered a deep breath as he watched Star walk into the boardinghouse. Mrs. Barker, the dragon who ran the place, stood at the door in her nightcap, clutching her dressing gown to her throat as though he might ravage her any second. Comical as that might be, Michael resented anyone refusing him access to Star. For the past weeks, he'd had the benefit of her company whenever he wished. And often when he didn't particularly wish, but at least there hadn't been this constant ache he now felt in her absence.

Just why he should feel this way about a girl like Star, he wasn't sure. He'd be a fool and a liar to try to make anyone believe he wasn't drawn to her beauty. She was an uncommon beauty, despite her obvious attempts to make herself plain. Why she was trying to make herself look like Mrs. Barker was beyond him. But there was more to it than merely a physical attraction. He looked forward to hearing about Aimee's antics from Star's animated lips. Ma did a fair amount of talking about his daughter's adventures, but not with the delight with which Star could weave a tale. Star spoke with all the love, pride, and indulgence of a doting mother.

A frown creased Michael's brow, and he urged the horses faster. A doting mother? Where had such an ignorant thought come from? Star. . .a mother. Beautiful, childlike Star who knew nothing about being a mother. Half the time, she seemed more like an older sister to Aimee. How old was she anyway? Eighteen? Well, that was old enough, he supposed. He'd been barely more than that when he married Sarah. But what about her manners, her swearing? He had to admit, though, it had been a long time since he'd heard a curse word fly past those beautiful, rosebud lips.

A war raged inside him the rest of the way home. On one hand, Star was a breath of fresh spring air. She filled his senses every waking moment and his dreams at night. She loved his daughter and the feeling was mutual. His mother felt Star could do no wrong and had come to the conclusion that if she'd stolen anything, it was with a right good reason, and Ma chose to forget it.

Problem was, Michael couldn't forget. If he didn't have an impressionable daughter to consider, things might be different; but for all of her softening and apparent spiritual growth, Star still hadn't opened up about anything in her past.

She hadn't confessed about stealing. The times he'd hinted at it, she'd quickly changed the subject.

Michael's heavy heart grew even heavier, and by the time he got the horses bedded down for the night and entered the house, he was convinced more than ever that Star couldn't be the woman for him. Though he strongly felt God had brought Star into their lives, he had to be realistic. No matter how his sentimental heart wished otherwise, she wasn't his. They had rescued her and introduced her to the Word and helped her understand fundamental truths about being a Christian. Now God had sent her out on her own like a baby bird leaving the nest. Would she fly or come crashing down and return to her life of thievery?

"Well? Where is she?"

Ma's demanding voice startled him. "What are you doing up?"

"Do you think I could sleep without knowing when Star's coming home?"

"As I told you earlier, she made her decision."

Ma heaved a sigh and plopped down in a chair by the table. "I had hoped she would change her mind and come on home with you. It's amazing how easily the heart attaches itself to another heart, isn't it?"

"I suppose." Michael knew better than to agree too readily, though Ma pretty much summed it up. His heart was attached to Star. It would be awhile before he was able to detach. It wouldn't do anyone a bit of good to let Ma in on that fact.

"Well, what are you going to do about it?"

"What do you mean? There's nothing else I can do. Last I heard, kidnapping is a crime."

"Aren't you just the clever one?" Ma's wounded tone shamed Michael.

"I'm sorry. I didn't mean to sass. But, truly, Ma, there's nothing we can do to keep her here if she wants to leave. She feels she needs to make it on her own."

"Hogwash. She feels uncomfortable living with a widower, his daughter, and mother. She doesn't believe we really need her, and all the funny looks she received yesterday at service made her feel like an outsider."

"What looks?" Michael scowled, indignation rising in his breast. Who had the nerve to give Star any *looks*?

Ma rolled her eyes. "You men don't notice anything unless it smacks you on the head."

"Rosemary said Star left for our sakes."

Ma nodded. "I figured as much. She doesn't want folks suggesting improper things about you."

Michael's neck warmed. "Who would think anything improper is going on with my ma and little girl in the house?"

"Just about everyone, I'd venture to guess. That's just the nature of things. I'm ashamed to say, I might think the same thing in their position. Star is a beautiful young woman, and you are a handsome and lonely widower."

"Ma!"

"Oh, now. You're a grown man. Don't play innocent with me. I know you're a decent man and would never take advantage of a situation like this. Anyone should know that after you married that floozy instead of just—"

"Ma. . ."

"I'm sorry. You're right. I shouldn't speak ill of the dead."

"You shouldn't speak ill of anyone, but that's not the point. Sarah was Aimee's mother, and I don't ever want Aimee to feel she has cause to be ashamed. I don't want to chance her overhearing the truth about her ma."

Ma reached over and covered Michael's hand. "You're a good man, son. I know God has a woman for you. You deserve some happiness."

Michael retreated inwardly, waiting. . . .

"I'd hoped that maybe you'd cast your attention toward Star."

Clearing his throat, Michael turned his hand over and squeezed Ma's. "She isn't right for Aimee and me."

"Why? Because she's beautiful? Or because she wasn't nursed on the Ten Commandments?"

"Because the only thing I know about her is that she's accused of being a thief, and I'm not convinced the man was lying."

"Then why don't you just ask her about it? If she admits to it, why, then you have proof that she's changed. If she denies it, then the man was lying."

"What if she's the one lying?"

Standing, Ma gave a careless wave. "Star couldn't tell a lie to save her life." She shook her head and chuckled. "Remember the other day when she pelted Cannonball with eggs?"

Unable to resist the sweet memory, Michael laughed outright. "Poor Cannonball was forced to have a bath. I don't think he'll ever forgive her."

"My point is that her conscience won't allow her to do anything that she feels is a sin."

Cynicism returning in full force, Michael snorted. "Maybe she doesn't feel stealing is a sin. Have you checked your valuables?"

Eyes narrowing, Ma shook her finger. "I am ashamed of you. You know that sweet girl would rather chop off her hand than do anything to hurt this family—or anyone else, I'd vow. You can deny that you care about her all you want, but I'll not have you implying anything improper about her character in my presence. You're so concerned with what Aimee might think of her mother, well, let me tell you, Star has been more of a ma to that child than Sarah ever could have been. It would hurt Aimee much more to hear her pa saying hateful things against Star than the ma she never knew."

Giving him no chance to apologize, Ma spun around with a surprising agility, given her girth, and stomped to her room.

Drumming his fingers along the smooth oak table, Michael felt the shame sear his heart. Maybe Ma was right. If he out and out asked Star if she had stolen from her guardian, would she admit to it? But if she denied the accusation, how could he ever believe her?

Chapter 10

Star slowly roused to the rumble of thunder outside her window. After enduring storms for three days in a row, she was becoming accustomed to nature's way of waking her. She rolled over, buried her face in her pillow, and wished desperately she could sink back into sleep and forget about her dismal life. Instead, she opened her eyes to the wet, gray morning that intruded into her room through the white lacy curtain hanging from the window.

Sunshine might have made facing a new day bearable. As it was, the only things she had to look forward to were rain and mud. . .more loud men and haughty women demanding that she move quicker than humanly possible. . .more insults from Jane. . .more yelling from Joe.

As if the stormy days weren't enough to douse her already drooping spirits, lack of sleep made her eyes feel gritty. Every single inch of her body ached, and she'd have gladly donated a week's salary for thirty more minutes of slumber. But sleep wasn't an option. She had to wash and dress, tidy up her section of the room she shared with Rosemary, eat a bite of breakfast, drop off her laundry with Mrs. Barker for the obscene price of one dollar a week, and get to work.

She'd always worked hard; but after one month of backbreaking, twelve-hour days serving meals at Joe's, she had to admit this was the most difficult task she'd ever undertaken. It might not be so bad if she could discern an end in sight. If she could dream for the future. But her dreams had died with her mother; and the days, months, and years stretched before her in gloomy premonition. There was no Prince Charming. No knight on a white steed. No castle. This was life and, tedious as it might be, she was making an honest, respectable living. Not what she'd choose, if she had a choice, but infinitely preferable to the life she would have faced at Luke's Saloon.

A sigh escaped as Star rolled onto her back and lifted her Bible from the table between her cot and Rosemary's bed. Daily time with the Lord was the only thing Star felt she had to look forward to, and she gave up extra sleep in order to receive that life-sustaining nourishment every morning before she left the comfort and warmth of her bed. She opened up to the Psalms and let the words of a man after God's own heart lead her, comfort her, and draw her into fellowship with her Shepherd.

Thirty minutes later, ready to face the rainy weather, she pushed aside the covers and began the process of preparing for the next fifteen hours.

By noon, Star realized she'd been kidding herself. Thirty minutes alone with God was nowhere near enough to keep from wishing she could slap Jane right across the face.

"Star, you forgot to take Mr. Gabriel his coffee." Jane's haughty accusations never failed to annoy Star. More so now that she realized the girl was trying to humiliate her at every turn. Star had come to the conclusion that Joe's employee problems weren't so much his fault as they were a result of his daughter's nasty disposition.

"I didn't forget to take him the coffee, Jane," she said, forcing herself not to grit her teeth. "I had to take Mr. and Mrs. Arnold their food before it got cold." She refrained from reminding the girl that it wasn't even her job to wait on the Arnolds. As was becoming a habit, Jane neglected her customers shamefully, forcing Star to take care of them. Star wouldn't mind so much if there were a legitimate reason, but it seemed the girl did it purposely so that she could make it appear Star was the one neglecting the restaurant patrons. Star desperately wanted to defend herself, but she was trying hard to heed the Bible's advice to "do good to those who hurt you."

"Well, don't blame me if Mr. Gabriel complains about you to Pa." With that, Jane flounced away.

Gritting her teeth, Star took the coffeepot and headed toward the dining room.

"Star."

She turned, steadying herself for another customer she didn't have enough hands to take care of. Her pulse quickened as she met Michael's gaze. He sat alone at a table in the center of the room. How she had failed to notice him, Star couldn't fathom, but she didn't take time to ponder the question. Her hand went instinctively to her head, and she smoothed back her hair in a futile effort to appear presentable.

"Michael," she said breathlessly. "What are you doing here in the middle of the day?"

"My ax handle busted. Came into town to get another one." He gave her a grin that Star could only describe as devastating. "I thought I'd stop by for a quick hello and a bite of lunch."

And to see me? Star forced the hopeful words from her mind before foolishly voicing them.

"How about my coffee, Miss Star?"

From two tables over, Mr. Gabriel's voice arrested Star's attention. Her cheeks flooded with warmth. "Excuse me a minute, Michael. I'll be right back to get your order."

"Take your time," he said softly.

"I'm sorry, Mr. Gabriel."

The jovial man gave her a broad smile, his attitude far removed from the impatience of a man who might complain to the boss about lack of service. "I hate to begrudge a young man the pleasure of conversing with a beauty such as yourself, but I need my warm cup of coffee on such a miserable day."

Wishing desperately that his voice didn't boom as loudly as the thunder outside, Star poured his coffee.

She turned back to Michael but couldn't quite bring herself to look him in the eye. "What can I get for you?"

He cleared his throat. "You can look at me, first of all."

Reluctantly, she did so.

"How are you?" His voice was so filled with genuine concern, Star couldn't help the tears that sprang to her eyes. She lowered her lashes, but not quickly enough.

"Why don't you come home? Ma can still use someone to help her out with the house and Aimee."

Briefly, she considered his offer—even allowed herself a split-second dream that Michael would fall in love with her, but a bellow from Joe brought her back to reality. "Star, get over here and pick up these orders!"

"I'm sorry, Michael. I have to go. H—have you decided what you'd like to eat?"

With a scowl, he ordered a steak.

Hurrying about her duties, Star didn't have a moment to breathe, let alone continue her disconcerting conversation with Michael. When she saw him rise and glance in her direction, she tried to go to him and say good-bye, but a customer stopped her.

His expression darkened in disappointment. She shrugged and smiled, then lifted her hand in farewell. With a reluctant smile of his own, he returned her wave, then stepped out the door, leaving a cavern in her heart.

"Forget about him." Jane brushed by her and spoke the words for Star's ears only. "He's not worth it. None of them are worth it."

Star finished taking the order, then followed Jane to the kitchen. "I don't know what you're talking about."

The girl snorted. "Don't try to deny being in love with him. It's written plainly on your face."

Star tried to appear nonchalant, but inwardly she groaned at Jane's words. Had she really been that transparent? Grabbing a tray, she filled the order for an impatient couple with twin sons. She remained silent, hoping Jane would let the matter drop, but Jane followed her back into the dining room and continued to bait her. "A man like that will never marry a girl like you."

"Leave it alone, Jane," Star hissed.

True to her pattern, Jane continued in her mocking tone. "With your pretty eyes and smooth skin, you might get a man like that to sweet talk you into being alone with him, but don't fool yourself into thinking he's in love with you. Better for you to take what you can get out of his interest while it lasts."

Star gasped and swung around to face Jane. As she did so, the plates slid from her tray and crashed to the floor. Staring in horror at the clutter, Star knew Jane had finally succeeded in her efforts. Joe appeared from the kitchen and flew into a rage at the mess.

"Clean this up and get out of here. And don't expect to be paid. The wasted food will more than make up for what I owe you this week!"

Incensed, Star drew herself up with as much dignity as she could muster under the watchful gaze of every customer in the place. "I will not clean up a bit of this mess." She glared at Jane. "You can clean it up yourself, you hateful, nasty girl." She hurried to the back, snatched up her bag and shawl, and huffed her way through the dining room.

As she stepped into the muddy street, the only satisfaction Star received was knowing that Jane would have to clean up the mess. By the time she'd walked only a few steps, her conscience seized her, and with a stomp, she spun around and headed back to Joe's.

The dining room buzzed with shocked whispers as she walked back to the mess and knelt down to help Jane clean it up. "There is no way my pa is taking you back."

"I don't expect him to, but it's not right that you should have to clean up a mess I made. Also, I'd like to apologize for calling you a hateful, nasty girl. I was wrong."

The girl gave a short laugh. "Something you learned from that Bible of yours?"

"Yes," she answered, unwilling to be goaded into an argument.

Jane studied her for a second, then scowled. "Anyone in her right mind would have walked out without a second look, especially since you and I both know this wouldn't have happened if I hadn't made you mad."

Surprised by the girl's honesty, Star nodded. "That's true, but I'm not responsible for your actions. . .just mine." She stood and deposited the tray with food and empty tin dishes on a nearby table, then glanced at Jane. "I don't know what I did to make you hate me. I wish we could have worked together. I needed the position. But more than that, I wish I could have convinced you that God loves you, Jane."

"No one can convince me of that. Thank you for coming back to help me clean up, but you'd best get out of here before Pa comes out." She turned, grabbed the tray Star had just set down, and headed back to the kitchen.

With a sigh, Star left Joe's once more, this time knowing she'd done all she could to make things right between herself and Jane.

She stood on the boardwalk and debated whether or not to go to Rosemary's next door. She wasn't ready to share her humiliating experience. Instead, she decided to go to the boardinghouse, get into some dry clothes, and practice sewing the doll dresses she'd been working on for Aimee's birthday. With her mind displaying images of frilly doll things, she stepped heedlessly into the street. She instantly regretted her lack of attention as her boot squished and water rushed in, soaking her stockings. With a groan, she tried to step over the puddle with her other foot, but she overstepped and lost her footing. The ground rose up to meet her in a flash, and she had no chance to regain her balance before plunging headlong into the mud.

Michael's heart nearly stopped as he watched Star fall. He pulled his team up and wrapped the reins around the brake, then hopped down. The sight of her trying to stand and gain her footing melted him. He slipped his way through the mud, nearly losing his own footing. By the time he reached her, she was sitting at the edge of the road looking pitifully dejected. "Let me help you, honey."

"Oh, Michael." Rather than take his proffered hand, she covered her face with her own. Seeing that she was in no state of mind to be rational, he scooped her up in his arms and carried her to his wagon.

She continued to weep as he set her carefully in the seat and walked around to his own side. He scooted close to her and wrapped her in his arms. "Shh, Star, don't cry. It's just a little mud. It'll wash off."

"M–Mrs. Barker only allows baths on S–Saturday."

Michael couldn't hold back a chuckle. He squeezed her closer for a second, then let her go. He reached inside his pocket and withdrew his handkerchief.

Star looked from the cloth to his eyes and gave a trembly smile. "Think it'll do any good?"

He laughed. "Probably not."

She took it anyway and dabbed delicately at her pert little nose.

Nearly overcome with a desire to take her into his arms and kiss the quivering from her lips, Michael reached for her. The startled look in her eyes brought him back to his senses. He drew back. "Come on," he said suddenly. "I'll take you to the boardinghouse, and you can pack a small bag."

"What do you mean?"

"Come out to the farm and take a bath and spend the night. I'll bring you back into town early enough to be at work on time."

Her eyes filled once more.

"What is it?"

"Joe fired me." She said the words with such remorse, Michael didn't have the heart to let out the whoop of glee he felt.

"Why did he do that?"

A shrug lifted her shoulders. "I dropped a whole tray of food on the floor."

"You did?"

"Yes."

The clipped answer signaled her desire not to pursue the matter, so Michael detoured the conversation. "What will you do now?"

A heavy sigh escaped her lips. "I'm not sure. Mrs. Slavens mentioned to Rosemary just a couple of days ago that she would be looking for domestic help before long. Her housemaid is getting married in a month."

Michael tried not to show his exasperation, but he couldn't understand her at all. "Why not come back home and help Ma out if you're going to do domestic work anyway?"

"Because I can't, that's all. If Miss Hannah really needed me, I'd come and attend to household duties and not ask for a penny, but we both know she doesn't. I accepted your generosity long enough. I can't go back. Something will turn up. God won't leave me helpless."

Realizing the matter was settled in her mind, Michael nodded as he pulled the horses to a stop in front of the boardinghouse. "Then how about coming to the farm anyway? Ma and Aimee have missed you something awful." He refrained from admitting his own feelings about her absence. There was no reason to lead her on when he could never marry her, though his traitorous heart wanted nothing more than to ask to court her and explore the possibility that she might be the woman for him. No matter how attracted he was to her lovely face and sweet spirit, there was no getting around the fact that she had stolen from her guardian and apparently hadn't the faintest intention of confessing. How could he overlook the dishonesty when she would be teaching and training his daughter? He walked around to her side of the wagon and reached for her.

Swallowing past a lump in his throat, he tried to still his racing heart as she slid effortlessly into his arms. "So what do you say? Will you come for a visit? I'll bring you back tomorrow." Unless Ma could somehow talk her into staying.

Star smiled through her mud-caked face and nodded. "All right. Give me ten minutes to gather my things."

He started to follow her, but she touched his arm, bringing him to a stop. "You'd best wait out here. Mrs. Barker doesn't like men callers in the house as it is and, considering my appearance, I'll have enough explaining to do."

Patting her hand, he smiled. "I'll wait in the wagon." As rain dripped from the brim of his hat, he started to have second thoughts about taking Star to the farm. As soaked through as she already was, she should probably stay inside rather than coming back out in this weather. He hated the thought of taking a chance that she might get sick and was just about to go and suggest she stay at the boardinghouse when she appeared—still in her wet gown, though she'd replaced her wet shawl with a dry one.

"Why didn't you change your dress?" he asked, as he helped her into the wagon.

A faint blush stained her cheeks. "My other dress is being laundered. I didn't want to wear the pretty ones until I get the mud off."

"Makes sense." He climbed into his seat and grabbed the reins. Cutting her a sideways glance, he snatched his hat from his head and set it on hers.

"What are you doing?"

"Protecting your head from the rain."

"I can't take your hat. You might get sick."

"I'll take the risk." He smiled at her look of worry. "Ma's going to have plenty to say to me as it is about the condition you're in."

She dropped her gaze to her fingers. The large hat covered her face, and he almost snatched it back so he could see her. "My muddy clothes aren't your fault. You rescued me."

For the first time, Michael realized Star felt the spark between them every bit as much as he did. She must wonder why he hadn't acted on it. He cleared his throat. "Listen, Star. . ."

She lifted her head, her wide, beautiful eyes waiting expectantly. "Yes?"

"I know you said before that you didn't want to discuss your past, but if there's anything you'd like to. . ." He shifted his gaze back to the horses as a frown creased her brow.

"Like to what?" she asked, her voice trembling.

"If you have something weighing heavy on your heart, I'll listen. The Bible says to confess our faults to one another."

She straightened her shoulders. "Well, how about you? If there are any faults you'd like to confess, I'd be happy to hear them."

Indignation swelled his chest. "Me?"

"Or don't you have any faults?" She was baiting him. Michael knew it and still couldn't keep from walking right into her trap.

"Of course I have faults. . . . Everybody has—"

"Then let's hear them." She folded her arms across her chest and waited.

"I'm not going to sit here and tell you all my faults."

"No?" She sniffed. "But the Bible says to confess them."

"I know what the Bible says," he growled, irritated by the twist of events.

"Then it doesn't apply to you?"

"Just drop it, all right? I'm sorry I tried to help."

Silence hung in the air, thicker than the fog rolling in, and remained between them until the house came into view.

"I don't know what you think I've done, Michael," Star said in a small voice, "but I don't want to think about the past. Your daughter was the one who taught me that our sins are thrown far away when we repent. If God doesn't remember the things I've done, why should I bring them up, and why should you worry about them?"

Her words sifted the irritation from Michael. He had his own past he'd like to forget. He nodded. "I won't bring it up again."

"Thank you."

He drew the wagon to a halt, and Star hopped down as the door flew open, effectively halting any chance he had to make an apology. Aimee ran out the door and into Star's arms before anyone could stop her.

"How come you're all dirty?" the little girl asked when she finally let Star go.

"I fell in the mud again. Can you believe that? And look—now you're all dirty, too."

Aimee shrugged. "I like it."

A giggle escaped Star's lips and reached Michael's ears like an angel's song. Contentment flooded him.

"Star!" Ma said from the doorway, her face beaming with unabashed joy. "Just look at you! Get in here so we can dry you off before you catch your death!"

Michael lifted her bag from the back of the wagon and watched as Star fell into his mother's arms.

Star was home. The only question was. . .how could he convince her to stay?

Chapter 11

Star had almost forgotten how wonderful it was to be at the Riley farm, to be fussed over by Miss Hannah. . .and admired by Aimee.

And just to be in the same room with Michael. . . Her heart had felt his absence every aching moment of each day and night during the past month. Now it soared with a joy that made her feel downright giddy.

She was grateful that the steady rain kept him hovering in the cabin, getting underfoot as she and Miss Hannah prepared dinner. The cabin echoed with the sounds of Aimee's gleeful laughter. She sat on the floor next to the fire, squeezing rags soaked with milk into the greedy mouths of five whining puppies.

According to the little girl, Mrs. Paxter from the next farm over had hot-footed it to the front door with a wiggling burlap bag in her hands. Without so much as a howdy-do, the woman had declared poor Cannonball a pa.

Michael chuckled at his daughter's telling of the story. "And Ma took every single one of them in just like she's a grammy again."

Miss Hannah rolled her eyes and shrugged at Star. "That cold-hearted Paxter woman threatened to toss the whole bag of them into the creek. Aimee let up a howl louder than an Indian war cry. What was I to do?"

Star's gaze went to Michael, and they exchanged knowing grins. They both knew Miss Hannah wouldn't have let anyone harm even one of the furry little bothers, war cry or no war cry.

Looking from one to the other, Miss Hannah let out a "harrumph" and propped her hands on her hips. "Aimee, go wash up and come to the table."

Star would have followed her into the kitchen, but Miss Hannah motioned her away. "You sit down. I'll have everything out here in a jiffy. You too, Michael. Sit and keep Star company until dinner's on the table."

Tingles raced up Star's spine as Michael's arm brushed hers when he pulled out the chair for her to sit down. He lingered just a bit longer than necessary, and Star inhaled the combined smells of soap and wood smoke. His closeness sent her heart racing. She closed her eyes as he stood behind her chair, his hand gripping her arm.

"Star. . ." His husky whisper weakened her knees, and she was glad to be sitting; otherwise she feared her legs might not have held her. He crouched down next to her. His gaze flickered over her face and settled on her lips. But just when she thought he would lean in and kiss her, he seemed to gather his wits and looked her in the eye.

Scarcely able to breath, Star waited for him to speak.

"Pa! Are they clean enough to eat?" Aimee bounded into the room and shoved her palms between Star and Michael, effectively halting conversation or anything else that might have occurred between them.

A wry grin tipped Michael's lips. He grabbed both of his daughter's dimpled hands and appeared to examine them. "Hmmm. They *do* look clean enough to eat." With that, he brought them to his lips and pretended to devour the little fingers. Aimee giggled uncontrollably and infectiously until Star was giggling right along with her.

Miss Hannah bustled through the kitchen with a pot in her hands. She sent Michael and Aimee an affectionate smile as she set dinner on the table. "All right. Stop the shenanigans, and let's eat before the food gets cold."

Michael held her hand during the blessing, as he had many times before. This time, however, he didn't let it go immediately upon saying "Amen." Star glanced up in surprise. He held her fast with his beautiful, brown-eyed gaze. His thumb caressed the back of her hand, sending physical and emotional sensations throughout her being.

After a quick glance at his mother, then at Aimee, he focused his full attention upon Star. Her throat went dry, and she couldn't have looked away if a herd of buffalo had stampeded through the room.

"Michael?"

"I need to ask you something," he began.

Star's pulse thudded in her ears.

"Can we eat?" Obviously sensing the intensity of the moment, Aimee voiced the question with a loud whisper.

"Shh," Miss Hannah scolded.

"It's all right, Ma."

Star's stomach turned in disappointment, but she could no more have been annoyed with the charming little girl than she could have denied her love for Michael.

"Aimee, can you wait just a few minutes before eating so I can ask Miss Star a question?"

Here? In front of everyone?

"I can wait, Pa."

Star's cheeks burned under Miss Hannah's watchful gaze. The woman's eyes glistened with unshed tears, and she gave a suspicious sniff. "Go on, then, and spit it out. Supper's just sitting here getting cold as December."

"All right." Michael took both of Star's hands. "I wanted Ma and Aimee here for this because they're part of my life and deserve a say-so."

Star nodded. So far, he hadn't said much of anything.

"It's no secret that I have reservations about the things you've held back—your past and all." He smiled, adding to Star's relief and confusion. "But you were right earlier when you said God doesn't hold your past against you. I believe you've given Him your entire heart. At least it seems so. I hope some day you'll trust me enough to share that part of your life with me."

"Michael. . ." Oh, how she wished she could tell him everything. What a comfort it would be to unburden herself and cry on his shoulder about Mama's death at Luke's hands. But every time she'd almost opened up over the weeks she lived at the farm, and most recently to Rosemary, she remembered Luke's biting words. "What decent man will want her when he finds out what she is?"

Michael pressed her hand. "It's all right. You don't have to share for now. I just wanted you to know that I'm here, and when you're ready, you can tell me anything or nothing. It's your choice."

Star's lips curved into a tender smile. "Thank you, Michael."

"Land sakes. Get on with the askin'!"

A scowl marred Michael's handsome face, but Star couldn't help but agree with Miss Hannah. Her palms were becoming damp in Michael's grasp, and her heart felt about to race from her chest.

He gathered a long, agonizingly slow breath and fixed her with his gaze. "I want to know if you'll. . ."

Yes, yes, yes!

". . .allow me to come courting."

A loud snort from Miss Hannah echoed Star's feelings. Star lowered her gaze in an effort to mask her disappointment with the appearance of demure consideration of his question.

"Pa wants to court Miss Star. Does that mean they're getting married?" Aimee's loud whisper, obviously meant for Miss Hannah, brought a rush of heat to Star's cheeks.

Venturing a peek at Michael, she noticed the look of stunned revelation in his eyes. His own face went red. He cleared his throat and let go of her hands to take a drink of water. "Uh—Star, it seems. . ."

Awash with sympathy for the misunderstood man, Star smiled and pressed his hand. His eyes widened with renewed hope. "I'd be pleased to accept your offer of a courtship. Thank you for asking me."

"Well, then," Miss Hannah's boisterous voice broke through before Michael could come up with an answer. "That *little* matter is settled. So how about we eat before Aimee wastes away to skin and bone."

During dinner, Star savored every single bite of the chicken and dumplings. For dessert, Miss Hannah produced a fluffy white cake, fit for a king. Indeed, Star felt like an honored guest, and more so, now that Michael was officially courting her.

In the morning, they said very little, trying to act as naturally as possible during breakfast. Conversation during the ride into town bordered on the ridiculous, and Star grew impatient as she responded to observations about the weather—which had finally cleared up—for the third time. Still, she felt she had to ask the question that had been burning in her since his question the night before. She practiced what to say in her mind for the last mile of the ride into town, missing most of Michael's not-so-fascinating tale of last year's rainy weather.

"Michael," she finally blurted, when they reached the boardinghouse and he helped her from the wagon. "What does courting mean, exactly? Wh—what do we do?"

An incredulous smile tipped the corners of his lips. "No young man's ever come calling on you before?" He released her and grabbed her bag from the back of the wagon.

She shook her head.

He offered her his arm, but she hesitated. "What about Mrs. Barker?"

"She'd better get used to me." He sent her a wink and tweaked her nose. "I'm going to see my girl safely inside every time I drop her off from now on."

Star's stomach turned over at the meaningful smile. She tucked her hand in the crook of his arm and held her head high.

"To answer your question," he said, pausing at the step, "courting means I'll escort you to services on Sunday, we'll have picnics together and go to socials and dances. You will come for dinner as often as possible. In other words, we are getting ready for the possibility of a future together."

The images his words invoked filled Star with such hope, she didn't have the heart to tell him that if she didn't find another position soon, her money would run out and she'd be forced to leave Hobbs. She pushed the grim thought from her mind and sent him her best smile. "Then I suppose you'll be escorting me to the box social next week?" The bazaar the month before had been such a success, the ladies society had organized a box social to raise money for a church bell.

He chuckled. "The gentleman's supposed to do the asking."

"After the hard time you had asking if you could come calling, I'm afraid asking anyone anything doesn't seem to be your gift." She gave him a teasing grin. "I thought I'd save us the time and trouble by bringing it up myself."

"About asking you to court instead of what Aimee said. . ." His face reddened. "I just—"

"Michael, you don't have to explain. I was—am happy that you think I'm good enough for you to come calling on me. If you decide in the future that you made a mistake. . .well, better that mistake is one you can fix."

The intensity on his face as he looked into her eyes nearly melted Star's legs into a puddle. "You humble me, Star," he said, his voice soft and filled with emotion.

The door opened suddenly, causing Star to jump. "Mrs. Barker," she said into the scowling face. "You nearly scared the life out of me."

"What are you two doing, standing out here in broad daylight?"

Michael went rigid. Star pressed his arm, hoping to thwart any comment he might feel compelled to make in their defense.

"Mr. Riley was kind enough to carry my bag to the door." Star turned to Michael, silently pleading with him not to offend her landlady.

He handed over the bag and tipped his hat. "I'll see you soon, Star. Good day, Mrs. Barker."

"Good day, Mr. Riley," the landlady returned, and Star caught a glimpse of amusement in her eyes.

"Mrs. Barker?"

The elderly lady laughed and opened the door wider to give Star room to walk through. She squeezed Star's shoulder. "He certainly is a good catch, young lady. I don't imagine I'll be able to keep him out of the parlor much longer, will I?"

A giggle burst from Star's lips. "No, ma'am."

"It's just as well you'll have a man like Michael Riley looking out for you. That Joe is here to see you."

"Joe? From the restaurant?"

With a frown, Mrs. Barker waved toward the kitchen. "Who else? He's in there. Probably intending to beg you to go back to that disgraceful place."

"Oh, I hope so," Star said quickly. "I have to work if I'm to continue to pay rent, Mrs. Barker."

An indulgent smile curved the older woman's thin lips. "I suppose you're right."

To Star's amazement, Joe did ask her to come back. Within an hour, she was back at work. She floated through the day, despite the demanding customers, Joe's grumbling, and Jane's sulking. The girl seemed to have mellowed a bit, and Star hoped she had put aside her dislike. Regardless, God had a reason for sending Star back. Her work here wasn't finished, and she prayed Jane would give her a chance to show her Christ's love.

❧

"Star will be ready in a few minutes," Mrs. Barker said regally. "She asked me to inform you that Joe held the restaurant open a little later than promised, and she is running behind. You may sit in the parlor and wait."

"Thank you." Michael groaned every time he thought about Star going back to that restaurant to work. Better that she'd taken the position as housekeeper for Mrs. Slavens. Working for the woman couldn't be any worse than working for Joe. But Star was firm in her decision, believing God had sent her back for Joe's daughter. The fact that Ma agreed with Star irked him. He had hoped to persuade her to come back to the farm for good, but even Ma balked at the idea.

"You know how folks talk." With her hands on her hips, she'd looked at him with a disgusted frown. "Now, if you had asked the *right* question the other night and made short work of the engagement, things would be a little different now, and Star wouldn't have to go back to that place."

He had no defense against Ma's argument. She was right, but Michael couldn't quite bring himself to make the commitment of marriage without more assurance that Star would be content to be a wife and mother and that she wouldn't bring trouble into his life like Sarah had. He wanted to trust Star, wanted to release the lock he'd placed upon his heart, but for now, it was better to play it safe.

With a conscious effort, he was attempting to stop comparing her with his late wife, but at times it wasn't easy. Like Sarah, Star was beautiful. Breathtakingly so, though there was a gentleness, a sweetness about Star that Sarah hadn't possessed. But what Clem had told him about her stealing from her guardian only served to strengthen the similarity between the only two women he'd ever loved.

"Michael?" At the sound of Star's breathy voice, he stood and turned toward the door. The sight of her caused a sudden lump in his throat, and he swallowed hard.

Her beautiful violet eyes stood out more than usual in the blue dress she wore. Her mahogany hair hung in curls about her shoulders and was held back with a ribbon to match her gown. "You're a vision," he said when finally able to speak.

A beguiling blush stained her cheeks. "Thank you," she whispered. "You're very handsome yourself tonight."

She'd seen him in the same Sunday suit every week since she'd known him, but the sincerity in her voice couldn't be denied. He took her hand and brought it to his lips. "Shall we go?"

Once outside, he headed for the wagon, but Star hung back and tugged at his arm. "Let's walk to the church. It's not far."

"Are you sure? The night air's a bit nippy."

Tucking her hand inside the crook of his arm, she tilted her head and dazzled him with a smile. "I'm plenty warm."

Unable to deny her something she obviously wanted to do, he covered her hand with his free one and returned her smile. "Then, let's go."

They walked in companionable silence, and Michael barely noticed the chilly air. He felt nearly uncontainable joy to know that, for the next couple of hours, he had the pleasure of her company and soon everyone would know they were courting. This pleased him on a couple of levels. For one thing, every desperate female between sixteen and thirty-five would know he was calling on Star. And two, the young men constantly vying for Star's attention would know that fact, as well. Then it occurred to him, they were going to a box social and Star had no box. How was he going to know which one was hers?

"Where's your box?"

"What? Oh, you mean for the social?"

"Yes."

"Rosemary took it to the church earlier so that you wouldn't know which one it was."

"But that's not fair. How will I know which box to bid on?"

"That's the whole fun of a box social! Isn't it wonderful? Rosemary says no one is supposed to know and you just end up eating dinner with whomever buys your box."

"You act like you've never been to a box social before."

"I haven't." She giggled. "I wonder who will buy mine."

Enchanted by her playfulness, Michael pulled her aside, into the shadow of the feed store awning. He didn't realize he intended to kiss her until suddenly she was looking up at him, her face bathed in the lamplight, eyes shining in wonder. He slid his hands up her arms and lightly rested them on her neck. Drawing a quick, shallow breath, he traced the line of her jaw with both thumbs, his fingers laced in locks of silken tresses.

"Star," he breathed, just before closing his lips over hers. She responded clumsily at first; and, delighted, Michael knew she'd never been kissed. The realization only made him desire her more, and he gathered her closer. She melted against him and wrapped her arms around his neck.

Dizzy with the feel of her in his arms, the sweetness of her surrender to his kisses, Michael almost lost all sense of reason and begged her to become his wife. He might have, if she hadn't pulled away just then, released a soft sigh, and rested her head gently against his chest. His heart pounded and he knew she must hear her name on every beat; but the trusting nature of the simple movement cooled his passion and evoked such tenderness within his breast, he laid his cheek against her hair and closed his eyes, willing his heart to return to normal.

"We better get to the social, or someone will buy your box and I won't be there to punch him in the nose."

She glanced up at him and smiled shyly. "All right."

He tucked her hand in the crook of his arm once more. "Unless of course you want to tell me what to look for. In which case, I won't have to beat anyone up and steal your box away."

"No, sir. You'll just have to be a good sport."

Raucous laughter blended with the sound of rowdy music coming from the saloon up ahead. A man stumbled outside, accompanied by a lady of the evening.

Michael scowled. "Let's cross the street."

"Why?"

"Because I don't want you that close to the trash up ahead."

Star stopped dead in her tracks and stared at him with disbelief. Her lips trembled. "God doesn't make trash."

"Maybe not, but someone does, and I'd just as soon not have you exposed to it."

"Is it me you don't want exposed to it, Michael, or you?" She stomped indignantly and walked past him.

Reaching out, he snagged her upper arm and stopped her. She wheeled around to face him, anger sparkling in her eyes. "Turn me loose this instant!"

"Lower your voice, please." Michael couldn't understand why he'd offended her, but it was obvious she would fight to have her say.

"I refuse to cross the street as though these people are somehow not as good as I. Jesus died for that poor woman's sins every bit as much as He did for mine."

"That may be," he replied through gritted teeth and righteous indignation, "but you aren't living in *that* sin. You have asked forgiveness for anything you did in the past and are living a respectable life."

"You don't know her! Maybe she has no choice. Maybe she needs help." She shook her head in disgust. "If the good, *respectable* folks of Hobbs would give women like that a chance, maybe they could change their lives, raise their daughters in a little house somewhere, and go to church without feeling like society's *trash*. Ever think of that?"

"Star. . ." She just didn't understand that women such as this one couldn't change who they were. Sarah never could.

"Don't! I'll not have you escort me to the social. You can't miss my box. I used the fabric left over from making this dress to decorate it. I wanted to surprise you and make it easy for you to figure out which was mine. But I will thank you *not* to do any bidding for my box tonight." With that she spun around and walked along the boardwalk, her heels clacking with every step. Michael bristled when she smiled at the lady of the evening as she passed. "Lovely night, isn't it? I'm so happy the rain has stopped."

The woman and man gaped after her. Then the woman turned, as though to head back inside. Michael drew in a breath at the pensive look that covered her face. But when she caught him staring at her, her eyebrows drew up and her lips curved into a sensual smile.

Disgusted, he looked away and crossed the street. *Lie down with pigs, rise up dirty and stinking of the same filth as the animals.* He'd gone that route before and had no intention of ever doing it again, nor would he allow any woman he married to voice such opinions and become fodder for speculation and gossip. If Star was to be his wife, she'd have to learn to keep to her own side of the street.

One question burned in his mind. . . . On which side did she belong?

Chapter 12

Star's heart raced when Reverend Hank, acting as auctioneer, held up her box for display.

Michael stepped forward, poised for action. Star slammed her hands on her hips. Clearly he hadn't taken her seriously when she'd told him not to bid on her box. Well, he wouldn't get away with it. She'd sooner eat with a skunk.

"Now, this is lovely," Hank called. "And if I'm not mistaken, I smell fried chicken, fresh bread." He lifted the cover ever so slightly, then looked over the room, a wide grin on his face. "Mmm. . .and apple pie. A meal fit for a king. Who wants to start the bidding?"

Michael glanced at her, and Star sent him the full force of her glare. With a scowl, he turned toward his brother. "Fifty cents."

Hank's lips twitched into a smirk, and he looked across the room. "Fifty cents? Are you young men going to let this delicious meal go for only fifty cents? Just smelling this wonderful aroma has my stomach grumbling something fierce. I'm awfully tempted to bid on it myself."

"All right. Fifty-five cents." Michael's annoyed voice filled the room, and suddenly the place roared with laughter. Star covered her mouth with her hand to suppress her own mirth.

Michael's face flooded with color at the realization that he'd just upped his own bid. He looked around with a sheepish grin and shrugged. "I'm partial to apple pie."

"Sixty cents!" Star turned to see Joe had placed a bid for her box. And then it began. From all over the room, bids of a nickel more each came in, raising the price until, at two dollars, most of the men dropped out, including Joe. Michael and Mr. Cole, a lean farmer who ate frequently at the restaurant, seemed to be warring for the box. Hank glanced at her and winked. Star's eyes widened. He knew it was hers! Did that mean Mr. Cole knew too? Or was it just a coincidence that he kept trying to outbid Michael?

"Looks like Michael is going to have some competition from now on." Star turned at the sound of Rosemary's voice.

"But how did Mr. Cole know the box was mine?"

"Besides the fact that it matches your dress?" Rosemary's teasing laugh was infectious.

Star giggled. "I didn't want to take any chances that Michael wouldn't figure out which one was mine."

"A stroke of genius!" Rosemary looped her arm through Star's and glanced toward the men. "The bid is up to three dollars. Who do you think will win?"

"From the look on Michael's face, I don't think he'll let it go, short of mortgaging the farm."

Rosemary threw back her head and laughed. "I think you may be right. But Mr. Cole looks pretty determined as well. I've noticed he spends a lot of time staring at you during services."

Dismissing Rosemary's observation with a wave, Star sniffed. "I wouldn't want a man who can't pay attention in church."

Glancing about, Star found plenty of eyes focused on her. Apparently everyone had figured out that the box was hers, and clearly they were tired of the bidding war. Everyone, it seemed, wanted to get on with the auction. Everyone, that was, except for, perhaps, the members of the ladies society who were no doubt hearing the lovely ringing of a new bell.

Stepping forward, Star released an exasperated breath. "I'm going to put a stop to this."

Rosemary grabbed her arm. "Wait. Let them drive the bidding price a little higher. They can both afford it, and bells aren't cheap." She gave a teasing grin. "Just a couple of dollars more?"

"Seven dollars!" Michael's steady, determined voice rang out. The man had lost his mind! Seven dollars for a boxed dinner that, truth be told, Rosemary had cooked while Star worked at Joe's. The only thing Star had been responsible for was the decorating. She'd done none of the cooking.

"Seven fifty!" Mr. Cole called out, his voice just as determined as Michael's.

Star managed to capture Michael's gaze. She silently pleaded with him to stop the humiliating event. The intensity of his returning stare sizzled the air between them, and Star knew he was remembering the kiss they'd shared, just as she was doing.

"Seven fifty?" Obviously, Hank could barely contain himself, so amused was he by Michael's competition. "Going once. . ."

Michael's eyes went wide, and he snapped to attention. "Hey, I'm not finished! Eight dollars."

"Eight fifty." Mr. Cole stepped next to Michael, clearly challenging him. Michael's eyes narrowed, and his jaw muscle jumped as he clenched and unclenched his teeth. "Ten dollars!" he called.

Rosemary chuckled. "Ten dollars is a big help toward the bell. Be my guest at putting a stop to this battle before everyone starves to death."

Star nodded. Stomping to the front of the room, she stood before them both. "This is ridiculous," she said, including both in her glare. "You're embarrassing me and making spectacles of yourselves."

"I'll risk the humiliation for dinner with you, Miss Star," Mr. Cole said, grinning at her.

"That's very sweet of you, Mr. Cole."

"Call me Thomas."

"No, thank you. The fact is that Michael and I are courting." She bristled at the look of triumph on Michael's face. "Although I'm mad as a wet hen at him right now, and I have no intention of eating with him even if he spends a hundred dollars on that cold chicken."

"You two are courting, for sure?" Thomas asked, looking from one to the other.

"Yes," Star replied. "So don't waste your money if you're hoping for anything more than dinner. I won't accept anyone else as a suitor."

Extending his hand to Michael, the farmer grinned. "Looks like you got yourself a ten-dollar meal, Riley. You're a lucky fellow." He turned to the room and put up his hands in surrender. "The lady has convinced me to concede. Preacher, bring out the next box, and maybe I can find another dinner companion to help mend my wounded pride."

"That's the spirit, Cole," Hank said. Through a smattering of laughter and congratulations to Michael, Hank handed over the box. He patted his brother's shoulder and grabbed the next one in line. "Mmm. . .what a surprise. This one smells like fried chicken and fresh bread, too."

Michael turned to Star. "Come on, I need to talk to you."

Folding her arms across her chest, Star jerked her chin. "I refuse to eat with you. You just wasted your hard-earned dollars."

"Ten minutes?" he asked, his lips close to her ear. He took her by the elbow, the warmth of his hand and tickle of his breath making her knees go weak.

"F—fine. Ten minutes. But that's all."

They looked around for a quiet spot, but with the bidding and laughter going on, there was none to be had. "Do you mind going outside?" Michael asked. "I know it's a little chilly."

"It's not so bad," Star replied. "Just let me grab my shawl."

Michael stepped back and allowed Star to walk outside ahead of him. "How about walking back to the boardinghouse and eating this in the kitchen?"

So much for only giving him ten minutes, but her curiosity got the better of her. "All right. I'm sure Mrs. Barker won't object as long as I clean up any mess we make. There will be plenty of chaperones in the house."

With a bit of annoyance, she noticed he led her to the opposite side of the street so they wouldn't have to walk past the saloon. She remained silent, and so did he. The last hour, she'd felt his presence as strongly as if he'd been next to her, although in truth, she'd avoided him. Hearing him call the saloon girl trash had been more than she could overlook without speaking out. Her heart ached at the thought that one day in the past, he might have been talking about her own mother—her mother, who had felt she had no choice but to stay in that life. Luke had convinced her that she couldn't raise Star without his help. But Star knew they would have been all right if they'd moved somewhere away from the mining and lumber camps. Somewhere folks wouldn't be likely to recognize them.

When the music from the saloon across the street reached them, Star ventured a peek at Michael. "There are always two sides to any story, you know."

He slipped his arm about her shoulders and drew her close as they continued to walk. "I know, honey." His gentle endearment and protective gesture sent shivers up her spine and soothed her troubled thoughts. Maybe things would be all right between them, after all.

Once they were clear of the saloon, Michael tightened his hold, and they crossed the street. "I need to explain my side of the story. I know it seems that I'm unusually harsh. But I have to be. That life is the most abominable I can imagine."

He gathered a shaky breath and stopped walking just before they climbed the boardinghouse steps. He removed his arm from around her and took her hand in one of his. "Can we sit out here for a few minutes? I'd rather not discuss this where folks might hear."

Dread clenched Star's stomach. She nodded, and they sat on the step. Michael set the boxed lunch on the landing behind them. Shifting so that they nearly faced, he drew another deep breath. "First, I'm sorry I was so abrupt with you earlier."

"I forgive you, Michael," she said softly, taken aback by the seriousness of his demeanor. She braced herself. Would he tell her he realized she wasn't the woman for him? Maybe their argument earlier had convinced him that she could never be good enough for him. Although, the fact of the matter was that he knew nothing of her life. He didn't know why Clem had been chasing her or why Luke wanted her back. It wasn't possible that he knew about her mother or that Luke wanted her to work the men at the saloon. Gathering a deep breath, she tried to calm herself. She gave him a nod of encouragement.

"I want to tell you about Aimee's mother."

So, that was it. He had realized he could never love her the way he'd loved his Sarah. She would never measure up to the woman he'd practically enshrined. The woman whose Bible he'd given to Star. The pain clouding his features bespoke his reluctance to hurt her, and she didn't have the heart to let him. She reached forward with her free hand and pressed her fingers to his lips.

"It's all right, Michael. You don't have to tell me. I don't want you to. I don't need to know about Sarah to understand why you can never love the likes of me."

A frown creased his brow, and he took her hand in his, kissed it hard, then pressed it to his chest. "That's not it. I could easily love you, but we can't take this relationship forward until you understand why I feel so strongly about things being right and proper."

There was that word. . . . Star couldn't think of any word more disconcerting than "proper." Unless it was "respectable."

"You have to understand," he went on, "why I hate places like that saloon and why I don't want my family anywhere near those people."

Those people. Star inwardly retreated. She had to tell him the truth. But if she did, she'd lose him. Her heart cried out to God. *Why did You allow me to fall in love with a man who will never love me once he finds out where I come from? Oh, Lord, help me trust You with my heart.*

"Star, my wife was one of those women before I married her."

A gasp escaped Star's lips, and she felt the blood drain from her cheeks.

"I took Sarah out of a house like that."

"Y—you used to go visit the saloon girls?"

"Wha—? Oh, of course not. Never! I was walking past the saloon one morning when I saw her. She was hurt. I found her crying and couldn't pass her by. She was so lovely and fragile. I just. . ." He glanced at Star and shrugged, shaking his head. "I fell in love with her at first sight."

A twinge of jealousy pinched at Star, but she forced it away.

"She convinced me that she wanted to leave that life. She knew all the right things to say. Her pa was a preacher. As she grew up, he'd beaten her every day, until she ran from him. When she went to work for the man who owned the saloon, she figured it couldn't be any worse than the daily beatings. By the time I met her, she'd been a saloon girl for nearly two years."

Tears burned Star's eyes. She'd heard that story—or a form of it—over and over.

"Don't you see, Michael? Not one little girl is born with a desire to grow up and become a prostitute. We all dream of marrying our handsome prince and raising babies, taking care of a home. Circumstances force many young girls into such a life. They don't want it, don't plan it, but it happens. We can't turn our backs on them. Can't treat them as though they have less worth than we do just because we were blessed to escape."

His eyes flicked quickly to hers. "Escape?"

Her impassioned pleas fell silent, and she lowered her gaze, afraid she might let slip more than she felt ready to reveal. "Anyone who grows up in a loving home and isn't forced into that life has escaped it."

"But I rescued Sarah. Or at least I tried to." He released a short, bitter laugh. "She never returned to that place. I bought her new clothes and married her before I'd known her three hours. I adored her. I thought she loved me too; but before long, I realized that I was only a means to an end for her. She'd never intended to stay with me in the first place. She only used me to escape the man who owned the saloon. He'd taken to beating her, and she'd determined to do whatever it took to get away. When she found out she was carrying Aimee, she flew into a rage. I had to practically sit on her for nine months to keep her from doing something to harm the child she carried." He drew a sharp breath. "I'm sorry, I shouldn't have told you that part."

Sickened by surfacing images long stored in the recesses of her memory, Star nodded. She knew of the dangerous measures the girls often took to lose their babies. She thanked God her own mother hadn't done that. "It's all right, go on."

"She kept telling me she was leaving as soon as the baby was born. I prayed. Oh, how I prayed she would change her mind. By that time, my illusions were over. I knew she'd never cared about me, and I certainly didn't find much to love about her. We had the baby to think of, and I couldn't bear the thought of Aimee growing up without a ma. I honestly believed motherhood might change Sarah. Or maybe I just hoped."

"She died giving birth to Aimee?" she asked softly, knowing he was emotionally drained from the discourse, but that he needed to end the tale.

He nodded.

Star pressed her hand against his cheek. "Michael, I understand why you feel as you do, but you have to understand that Sarah was only one hurting soul. There are so many hurting people in this world—people you wouldn't consider suitable company. But all of them need the love of Jesus. We can't turn our backs and treat them as though they have no value, as though association with them might stain us. That's not the way Jesus treated people while He walked the earth. We're His hands, His voice. I was reading a story in the Bible about a woman Jesus met at a well. She had been married many times and was living in sin with a man by the time she encountered Jesus. He didn't use her past against her, Michael. He forgave her. He offered her a drink from the well of life."

"What about the ones who won't accept what Jesus offers?"

"Not all will accept, but it's worth the risk of showing you care, even if you can only save one."

"I couldn't save Sarah. She died without ever seeing our daughter or accepting Christ."

"So the reason you didn't like me wearing her things wasn't because you couldn't bear to see another woman in the clothes of the woman you loved?"

"No," he answered abruptly. His gaze met hers, but he didn't speak.

Hit by realization, Star gasped. "Wearing her tight, low-cut gown made me look like her?"

"Something like that." He averted his gaze.

"You thought I looked too much like a saloon girl, and it made you think I'm like her on the inside. Oh, Michael, you've known the Lord all of your life. When will you understand that it's not what a person wears or how they look that matters to God? I may not have been a Christian as long as you have, Michael, but I've discovered that God looks on the heart. Just because I wore her clothes doesn't make me like Sarah."

"I know that now. But I have to be careful. I don't want Aimee hurt. I have to make certain the woman I invite into our lives is someone respectable, someone who won't shame us."

"Is that what you're afraid I'll do?"

The look he gave her melted her defenses. His lips curved into a hint of a smile, then he lifted her hand to his lips and pressed a kiss to her fingers. "I'm falling in love with you."

The joy Star should have felt at his revelation was sucked from her by his next words. "But I fell in love with Sarah. I believed everything she told me about wanting to change, and I married her. A woman like that! I still can't believe it. Not that I regret having Aimee, but how could I have been so foolish?"

He was afraid she was like Sarah—and she might have been, if Luke had had his way. Star shuddered. Suddenly unable to look him in the eye, she glanced down. Michael would never accept where she'd come from. She made a decision at the same moment she stood. "Michael, thank you for telling me about Sarah. It did help me to understand your reaction tonight. I—I'm sorry, but I don't think it's a good idea for us to continue courting."

"Why?" Michael stood and grasped her arm. "Star, I care about you. I don't want to lose you."

Tears stung her eyes and her chin quivered. "There is something you don't know about me. Something I don't believe you could accept."

"What?" He tightened his hold on her arms. "Tell me who you were before you came to live with us at the farm. Who is your family? You mentioned your mother passed on, but what about your pa? Brothers and sisters? Grandparents?"

Star hesitated a minute and honestly considered it. She even imagined herself pouring it all out to him. All about Mama, Samson and Lila, about Luke. But when one person knew a secret, somehow others learned of it. She knew Michael wouldn't purposely gossip, but things like that had a way of spreading. She couldn't bear the thought of people looking upon her with disdain, folks never looking her in the eye, ladies grabbing their children and crossing the street rather than being forced to share a boardwalk with her.

"Please, Michael. Just leave it alone and respect my decision. As I've said before, there are things you don't know about me. Things that would change how you feel."

"Nothing would do that."

He tried to pull her to him, but she jerked away and hurriedly opened the door. "Don't come calling. I won't see you."

"Wait," he said just before she could close the door. "I know about Luke."

Star's heart nearly stopped. "You do?" she asked in a hoarse whisper.

"Clem told me that you stole some money. I was waiting for you to confess it to me, but I understand if you can't. The important thing is that you have asked God for forgiveness. We can make things right with your guardian later."

"With my what?" Michael believed her to be a thief? Despair congealed with indignation, and she shook her head. "Michael, just forget about it. You don't know what you think you know." The last thing she saw when she shut the door was his look of utter disbelief.

She didn't blame him. She was finding it difficult to wrap her mind around tonight's turn of events as well.

Tears stung her eyes and flowed down her cheeks.

She trudged up the steps to the room she shared with Rosemary. After changing into her nightgown, she picked up her Bible, hoping to find answers or at least comfort. But the words ran together, and nothing penetrated her aching heart. Finally, she gathered a long breath and set the book on the table. Snuggling under the covers, she stared at the ceiling as though the wood slats above her might bring answers. She couldn't quite bring herself to reach beyond the ceiling in her heart, knowing she should have been honest in the beginning and trusted God with the results. In the stillness of the night, she wept in surrender to God. Tomorrow, after church, she would pull Michael aside and tell him the truth about her upbringing. He would either understand or he wouldn't, but at least she would no longer be living a lie.

Chapter 13

An icy wind whipped around Michael, and he urged his horse to a trot. He pulled his collar higher and tucked in his chin to protect himself from the blast. The ride from Oregon City didn't take as long on horseback as it did in a wagon laden with supplies, but it was still a good three-hour ride, and he hoped to be home before the snow got too deep. But before he could head back to the farm, he had to do what he came to do.

Ma had balked at his intention to travel to Oregon City on the Lord's Day, but Michael couldn't wait to settle things with Star's guardian. He didn't know for sure whom he was even looking for but decided to keep an eye out for Clem. The man was pretty unique in appearance and might be easily identified if he asked around. So far, Michael had been riding through the streets and no one he asked knew the man—or if they did, they weren't forthcoming with the information.

There are things you don't know about me. Things that would change how you feel. After Star's tearful words last night, he'd decided to pay the man the money she took so she could be out from under the burden of guilt. When he returned home, he intended to ask her to be his wife.

The streets were nearly empty, so there weren't many people to talk to. Finally, he saw a couple of men staggering out of a saloon at the edge of town. Deciding to give his search one last try, he approached the men.

"Excuse me!" he called. They stopped and waited while he dismounted and tethered his horse to the hitching post.

"Whaddaya want, mister?" one of the men asked, slurring his words.

Michael stepped onto the boardwalk. "I'm looking for a man named Clem. Big fella with a black moustache and a scar running down his cheek. Ever seen him?"

"Maybe. What's it worth to you?"

Disgusted, Michael fished a couple of coins out of his pocket and handed them over. "Now, do you know Clem or not?"

"Yeah, works for Luke."

"Where can I find him?"

The man who'd taken the money jerked his thumb toward the saloon. "At Luke's. Where else?"

Michael's stomach tightened as he lifted his head and read the sign. *Luke's Saloon.* Star's guardian owned a saloon? Without another look at the two drunks who'd sold him the information he was no longer sure he even wanted, he walked to the saloon. It went against everything inside of him to step through those swinging doors. A few men glanced up from a card game in the corner of the room, then ignored him. Cautiously, he stepped up to the counter.

"What can I get for you, mister?" the bartender asked. His burly chest stuck out; and even at Michael's height, he was forced to lift his chin in order to meet the man's gaze.

"I'm looking for a man named Luke. I think he owns this place."

"What do you want with him?"

"That's my business."

The man's arm shot out, and he grabbed a fistful of Michael's shirt before he could evade the attack. "I'm making it my business. No one bothers Luke without a good reason."

Michael swallowed hard. He couldn't very well get into a barroom brawl. Better that he just tell the man what he wanted to know. "Turn me loose, and I'll tell you."

The man let go, giving him a little shove in the process. Michael caught his footing in time to keep from crashing to the ground. He adjusted his shirt and cleared his throat. "I want to discuss a mutual acquaintance with him."

"Who's that?"

Releasing a heavy sigh, Michael leaned in. "A young woman named Star."

"Star, you say?" The bartender narrowed his gaze and studied Michael's face.

"Yes. Can you keep your voice down?"

"Stay where you are," the man commanded. "Luke's going to want to talk to you."

A minute later he returned, accompanied by a painted woman wearing a satin gown, cut high to reveal her thigh and low at the top, leaving little to the imagination. "Follow me," she purred.

Michael's face burned as she led him up the stairs. He kept his gaze fixed on the steps and nearly stumbled when they reached the top. The saloon girl wrapped her fingers around his upper arm. "Careful, cowboy. Wouldn't want you to break your handsome neck." As though he'd been burned, Michael jerked away. "I'm fine," he said abruptly. "Just take me to Luke."

"Well, ain't you just the charmer?" She let out a laugh and reached out to trace his jaw with a long, red fingernail.

"Please, lady, just leave me alone."

"Star's got you all spoken for, eh?"

"Something like that."

Thankfully, he wasn't forced to carry on any more conversation as she opened a large, ornately carved door at the end of the hall. "Here he is, Luke." She winked broadly at him and blew him a kiss.

Michael scowled and crossed the threshold. A handsome man with graying temples stood behind a large desk. He met Michael in the center of the room and extended his hand. "I understand you have some information about one of my girls."

Taking the proffered hand, Michael frowned at the reference to Star as one of Luke's "girls."

"Star Campbell. I'm here to pay off her debt to you."

The man took a cigar and silently offered one to Michael. Michael waved his refusal. "Have a seat, Mr. . . ?"

"Riley. Michael Riley." Michael accepted the wing chair across from Luke. "About Star?"

"Ahh, yes. Star. How touching she should consider me her guardian." A puff of smoke found its way to Michael's senses, nearly choking him.

"What do you mean? Clem told me you're her guardian."

Luke narrowed his gaze. "Clem?" A look of understanding crossed his dark features. "You must be the man Clem ran into the day Star disappeared." His voice was colder than the snow outside, but Michael refused to be intimidated.

"That's right. I intend to marry her, but first I want to settle what she owes you."

Luke released a hoarse laugh that never quite reached his eyes. "As much as I'd love to divest you of your money, Mr. Riley, I'm afraid Star doesn't owe me a cent."

"What do you mean?"

"What I mean is that I'm not Star's guardian. I'm her boss. In other words, she works for me. Here."

"But then why was Clem. . . ?"

"Running after her?"

"Yes."

Waving away the question, Luke took another puff of his cigar. "To tell you the truth, Star and I had a misunderstanding, and she ran out before I could explain. I sent Clem to bring her back. Your intervention thwarted his efforts, and I haven't seen Star since. I miss her, and so do the men who come in here."

Michael's heart plummeted at the inference. "What do you mean?" he asked, his voice barely audible.

Giving a nod of understanding, Luke sighed. "I suppose I can't blame Star for not wanting to admit to her—er—profession. It looks to me as though she's duped you and probably your entire town. Am I right?"

Numb with disappointment, Michael gave a nearly imperceptible nod.

"Well, if you decide not to marry her, she is welcome back here anytime. The men still ask for her quite frequently. She was a favorite around here. I'm sure I don't have to tell you why that would be." His suggestive leer sickened Michael, and he shot to his feet, knowing if he didn't leave this minute, he'd smash his fist into the suave face.

"I'm sorry I bothered you," he said abruptly. "I'll let myself out."

"Remember what I said now. Tell Star we miss her."

There are things you don't know about me. Things that would change how you feel.

Star's words took on new meaning. Feeling like an utter fool, Michael walked through the saloon in a haze. He mounted his horse and headed out of town at a full gallop. Now everything made sense. The way she'd defended the saloon girl the night before. What an utter fool he'd been! How had he fallen in love with another loose woman? He laughed at himself. The kiss must have been carefully executed on her part for her to make him believe she'd never been kissed before. Hysterical laughter rose to his throat. Never been kissed! The woman he loved—a prostitute. Laughter gave way to tears and suddenly he pulled his horse to a halt and slid from the saddle and to his knees.

"God!" he shouted at the snow-laden clouds. "Where are You in all of this? Am I a fool? Did I misunderstand when I believed I was to help Star?" He hung his head and cried until the tears would come no longer. Snow soaked into the bottom half of his trousers as he stayed on his knees. When he finally climbed to his feet, he mounted his horse with a new determination. First thing in the morning, he would confront Star, then he'd inform the folks who thought they could trust her that there was a wolf in their midst.

She'd regret playing him for a fool.

❧

Monday mornings always depressed Star. After the glory of worship services on Sunday and the restful afternoons spent visiting with Rosemary and Mrs. Barker, the thought of returning to the mundane always left her feeling a bit let down. If Joe had his way, she would work on Sundays; but at the risk of losing the job, she'd absolutely put her foot down from the first day of her employment. To her relief, he'd given in without much of a fight.

Today her heart sank even farther into depression as Joe let her into the restaurant at eight o'clock to start baking biscuits to last the day. Michael had been absent from church yesterday. After Miss Hannah had assured her that he wasn't ill, she remained tight-lipped about where he had gone.

Star was in no mood for Jane's stinging insults nor Joe's grouchy commands. Only a day and a half had passed since she'd seen Michael, and already it seemed as if a decade had gone by. With a sigh, she hung her coat on a hook and grabbed an apron.

She began pulling ingredients down from the shelf, then glanced about with a frown. "Is Jane ill today?"

Joe mumbled and pulled out his handkerchief. He blew his nose loudly and stuffed it back. "She's packin' her things."

"What do you mean?" For the first time, Star realized Joe's eyes were moist and his nose red. The man had enough heart to cry? "Joe, what's wrong?"

Fresh tears assaulted him. "My girl's leavin' me."

"Why on earth is she doing that?"

He scowled. "I told her to get out. That's why."

Mouth agape, Star blinked. "That doesn't make sense. Why would you send her away and then cry about it? What's happened?"

"I'm with child." The inflectionless response came from the kitchen door. Joe stiffened and turned away.

"Are you sure?"

The girl straightened her shoulders and nodded, her expression haughty.

"Where's the baby's father? Does he know about this?"

A short, mirthless laugh left Jane's lips. "I don't know for sure who the father is." She glanced at Joe, almost as though the words were meant as poisoned arrows.

The arrows hit their mark, and Joe slammed a ladle against the stove. He swung about to face his daughter. "How could you shame me this way? How could you shame the memory of your mother?"

"Oh, Pa." Jane sighed and dropped to a stool. "I'm leaving so you aren't shamed in this town."

"You've shamed me already." Anger burned in his eyes.

Star knelt before Jane and took her hands. "Is there anything I can do to help?"

"I don't see what you can do. I got myself into this fix. There's nothing to do but go away and have the baby and find a good home for it."

"My sweet Ella's only grandbaby given away to be raised by strangers." Joe's muttered words of pain brought hope to Star.

"Joe, it seems as though you might be willing to help Jane raise this baby. Are you sure you want her to go away?"

"Don't waste your breath, Star," Jane said. "Once my pa makes up his mind, he doesn't relent."

"Of course he does. He hired me back, didn't he?"

Jane gave her a withering glance. "That's hardly the same thing."

"You're right, it isn't. I'm not his daughter. You are, and he loves you more than anything in this world." *God, please give me the right words.*

Joe cleared his throat. "I guess you could stay on, if you want."

Jane's eyes filled with tears. "Thank you, Pa. I know how hard it is for you to even consider being the talk of the town. But what good will it do to stay here? The whole town will be against me and my baby. My child will grow up hating me for ruining his or her life. It's better if I go away and come back alone."

Tell her, daughter.

Star blinked at the words she heard impressed upon her heart. Not so much in words, but a gentle understanding, a knowing what God was asking her to do. She gathered a breath. How could she admit where she'd come from? Her hands trembled as she gently pressed Jane's hands.

"My mother raised me alone," she began.

The look of utter disdain she received from Jane nearly broke her resolve. "Raising a child alone because your husband is gone is not the same thing as raising a child alone because you got in a fix and don't even know who the baby's father is." She jerked her hand away from Star's and stood abruptly. Gathering her bag, she glanced at Joe. "I guess I best be going. I'll wait at the stage office until the stagecoach arrives."

"That won't be for hours," Joe said. "Why not stay here until it gets into town?"

"It'll just be harder to go, Pa. Good-bye."

Star watched her leave through the kitchen door.

Don't let her leave without telling her.

Following her into the dining room, Star called out to her. "Wait, Jane."

A long-suffering sigh left the girl, but she stopped and turned around. "What is it, Star? More bleeding heart acceptance? I appreciate that you haven't seemed the judgmental sort. If it means anything to you, you're the only woman I've ever felt friendly toward. But I don't need your stories. I don't need you to preach to me. I just need you to let me go." Her lip quivered, and before Star's eyes, the unimaginable happened: Some of Jane's bravado crumbled.

Encouraged, Star slipped her arm about Jane's shoulders. She held her with a firm grip and led her to the dining area and a table. "Please sit down. I would like to tell you something. You have plenty of time."

"All right. But only because if I don't, you'll follow me to the station."

Star grinned. "You're right. I probably would."

"I'm listening."

"As I said, my mother raised me alone. And it *wasn't* because my father died." She hesitated as Jane's brow arched. "The truth is that my mother was a saloon girl. I don't even know who my father was."

A look of disbelief crossed Jane's face.

"It's true. I was raised over one saloon or another until a few months ago when my mother was murdered." The familiar anger burned inside her at the memory. She pushed it aside for now. "The man who owned the saloon tried to make me take her place, but I ran away before he could force me to sell myself."

"But what about all this talk about God? You're no better than I am. Even if you never actually sold yourself to men, you're still the daughter of a prostitute. At least my ma was a respectable churchgoing woman."

Clearly, in Jane's mind, that fact raised herself to a place just above Star.

"That's just it, Jane. I know I'm no better than you are. Or anyone. Jesus sees us for who we are on the inside."

"You were really raised in a saloon? How could your mother do that?"

Star bristled a bit at the criticism of her mother, but she swallowed her quick anger, knowing God had a purpose for her conversation with Jane. "My ma never left her life because she didn't believe she could do any better. She had no one to go to, and she had me to raise."

"You didn't hate her?"

"Never!" Star replied emphatically. "I loved her more than anything in the whole world. And your child will love you, too. Children are that way."

"How can I do that to a child? Do you know how people will treat my baby?"

Star nodded. "It's possible some folks will be cruel, but you're strong, Jane. You'll have your pa to help you, too. Most women in your situation aren't so blessed."

"Listen to the girl, Jane." Star turned to find Joe standing in the kitchen doorway. He walked toward the table. "I won't let anyone say a word against my daughter or my grandchild. If they do, I'll refuse them service in my restaurant." He sat in the chair next to her and took her hands in his gnarled ones. "I don't want you to go. I've not done right by you. Haven't been a good pa. Your ma would be heartbroken if she knew how I've acted. But if you'll give me another chance, I'll do better with my grandchild."

Feeling like an intruder, Star was about to excuse herself when a knock sounded at the door. Joe gave a huff. "When are folks gonna get it through their heads that I don't open one minute before eleven o'clock?"

Star stood and placed a hand on his shoulder. "I'll see who it is." She glanced closer through the glass window, and her heart thudded in her chest. "May I have the key to open the door, Joe? It's Michael."

"All right. This time. But tell him he can't have anything to eat this early."

Star walked toward the door. She noticed that Michael's face held far from an amiable expression. His eyes blazed. She unlocked and opened the door. He stomped inside and grabbed her arm. None too gently.

"What is it, Michael? What's happened?"

A sneer twisted his lips. "What's happened? I'll tell you. I went to see Luke."

Star felt the blood drain from her cheeks. Pressing her palm flat against her stomach, she stared mutely at him.

"Didn't expect that, did you?"

Feeling dizzy, Star dropped into the nearest chair. "D–did you tell him where to find me?"

Michael placed his hands flat on the table and bent at the waist. His stormy gaze commanded hers, and Star cringed at the look of disdain. "That's it? That's all you care about? Whether or not I told him where you're at? It doesn't matter to you that I know about you?"

"I—I was going to tell you, Michael. Honestly, I planned to tell you all about Luke and the saloon yesterday, but you weren't at church. I guess now I know why."

"That's a very convenient story."

"Everything okay, Star?" Joe asked from the other end of the room.

"Y—yes. Everything's fine."

"Michael, I'm sorry my past upsets you so. I know I should have been honest from the very beginning. I just didn't have the courage."

"It's good for you that you weren't honest in the beginning, or I'd have never exposed my daughter to you. I was tempted to ruin your name, but I've changed my mind. This is between you and me. But stay away from my family or, so help me, I might change my mind again."

His boots resonated on the wooden floor as he made his way to the door.

Finding her courage, Star hurried after him. "You can be angry with me all you want, Michael, but I know I'm a child of God. Who I was before is wiped away. I'm just sorry you're so set in your ways that you can't see that."

She slammed the door behind him without giving him a chance to answer. He stood on the boardwalk, staring at her through the window while she locked the door. With a final look at him, she turned and walked to the kitchen.

Jane stood at the counter, mixing up dough for biscuits. She shook her head sadly. "You see?" she said, her voice filled with resignation. "That's what my baby has to look forward to."

Fighting back her tears, Star nodded. "Some people will turn you away, Jane. But God never will. Won't you consider giving Him a chance?"

Jane hesitated. "I'll think about it, Star. I give you my word that I will."

That was all she could ask and more than she'd hoped for.

They worked hard to open the doors at eleven, and Star barely had a chance to breathe all day. Snow fell steadily by the time she walked outside that night after twelve hours of work. She headed toward the street, trying to keep her boots from sliding on the icy surface. Just as she stepped off the boardwalk, she felt a hand on her arm. Her heart leapt.

"Michael. . . ," she breathed.

"Not quite," a familiar mocking voice said against her ear as a man clamped his hand over her mouth. "Now you be a good girl and don't scream and maybe I'll let you live until Luke decides what to do with you."

Tears filled Star's eyes as Clem led her toward two horses waiting across the street in front of the saloon.

Jesus, if You will, please help me.

Chapter 14

After two hours of staring at the ceiling, Michael finally gave up his quest for sleep. He swung his legs around and sat upright on his bed. Resting his elbows on his knees, he sought answers from God.

How could You allow me to fall in love with another prostitute? How? You knew I wanted to find a virtuous, godly woman to share my life with and to help raise my daughter. It was bad enough that I fell in love with Star when I thought she was just a thief—but a saloon girl?

The snow had finally come to an end outside and the moon had risen. Now it streamed through his window and illuminated his Bible, sitting unopened on his nightstand. He picked up the Bible and let it fall open. He wanted to read something to assure him he was right, that he hadn't been unreasonable—as Ma had said outright when he'd returned home and divulged the information he'd received in Oregon City.

She'd quoted him every scripture about God throwing sins into the sea and all the ones about His mercy and grace. Michael didn't want to hear it. If Star had truly repented, why hadn't she just told them the truth? Omission was the same as lying, so she'd been lying from the moment he'd found her asleep in the hay.

In an effort to push the memory of her lovely, sleeping face aside, he lit the lamp, stretched back out on the bed, propped against his pillows, and let his gaze fall to the Bible.

"He raiseth up the poor out of the dust, and lifteth the needy out of the dunghill; that he may set him with princes, even with the princes of his people. He maketh the barren woman. . .a joyful mother of children. Praise ye the Lord."

Star's words came rushing back to him.

Not one little girl is born with a desire to grow up and become a prostitute. We all dream of marrying our handsome prince and raising babies, taking care of a home.

Was God trying to tell him something by using the words "prince" and "joyful mother of children"? Not that Michael was a prince by any means, but Star loved him. Or she seemed to. Ma certainly felt she loved him and Aimee. He'd called women like Star "trash." Was God telling him He had raised her out of the dunghill and sent her to him so he could be her prince and make her a mother to his child?

Kneeling beside his bed, Michael cried out to God. "I love her. You know I do. What do I do with the thoughts of her being with other men?"

My love is perfect and unconditional. Let Me love her through you. Trust Me.

Time stood still as Michael surrendered his bitterness and disappointment to God. When, at last, his tears were spent, he knew he had to go and see Star. He would beg her forgiveness, and if she'd have him, he'd marry her on the spot.

A loud knock at the door interrupted his planning, and with a frown, he pulled on his trousers, grabbed the lamp, and headed down the ladder.

He opened the door.

"Oh, good—I have the right farm. It took me all night to find you."

"Miss Grafton?" Michael opened the door wider and allowed Jane entrance. "What on earth are you doing?"

"Mr. Riley, it's about Star."

Michael's heart jumped. "What about her?"

"I saw a man speaking to her after she left the restaurant tonight. At first I thought you had returned, but I realized when he seemed to be holding her against her will that it wasn't you. He took her across to the saloon and made her get on a horse, then they both rode out of town."

Grabbing Jane by the arms, he shook her. "What did the man look like? Was there a scar on his face?"

"P–please, Mr. Riley. I don't know. The street was dark. It was still snowing."

Michael turned her loose and raked his hands through his hair. If anything happened to Star, it would be all his fault. He'd led Clem right to her.

❧

Shivering and weary, Star nonetheless refused to cower before Luke's frighteningly controlled anger. "So our little Star has returned. Shame on you for worrying me so much all these months."

He stood directly in front of her, towering over her. She flinched as he reached forward and traced his finger down her cheek. "Silly girl, there's no need to worry. I wouldn't bruise this beautiful face." His gaze traveled over her frame, and Star stiffened. He made her feel undressed. When he looked at her again, she couldn't keep the defiance from her eyes.

"You don't want to rebel, Star," he said, his voice calm, but filled with warning. "You remember what happened to your mother?"

Anger raged inside Star. She'd bottled it for so long, in an effort to forgive Luke, that it came back in such a rush, it surprised her and loosened her tongue before she could stop herself. "You murdering thug. If you think you're going to get away with killing my mother, you're sadly mistaken."

"Is that so?"

"I'll go to the sheriff and tell him what I saw."

"The sheriff knows all about your mother's unfortunate demise at the hands of one of her rougher customers. A drifter. A man long gone before we even found her poor, broken body."

Fury engulfed her, and she flew at Luke, beating him with her fists. He held her off easily. "Calm down before I'm forced to tie your hands."

Chest heaving from the effort, Star glared at him. "You make me sick," she hissed.

His brow rose, and he narrowed his gaze; but true to character, Luke remained calm, as he did whenever it suited his purposes. "Now, I know you're acting this way because you're so tired. So rather than punish you for your hurtful comments, I intend to let you readjust to the saloon. You can have your old room back. But be warned: My patience won't last forever. Don't try to run away. Clem will be just outside your door. I'll give you today to rest, but tomorrow you will begin working. Oh, don't look so horrified. It won't be so bad once you get used to it. Just ask the other girls."

He cupped her cheeks and pressed a hard kiss to her forehead. "It's wonderful to see you again, my dear."

Star's stomach revolted at the feel of his wet kiss. She shuddered and stepped back.

His eyes narrowed. "Be a good girl, and you'll be rewarded. Be stubborn, and you'll suffer the consequences. Be impossible, and you'll be dead."

"I'd rather be dead than do what you're suggesting."

"We'll see." Going to the door, he motioned for Clem.

"Escort Star to her room. And fetch Lila to bring her a tray."

"Lila? She isn't dead?"

"Of course not. Where would you get such an idea?"

Star scowled at Clem. "Where indeed? Last I saw her, she was on the floor, and Clem was about to beat her down."

"She's fine."

"What about Samson?"

Luke hesitated. "I'm afraid he couldn't be saved."

Tears stung Star's eyes. At least Lila was alive. She wasn't completely alone.

❧

With his heart pounding in his ears, Michael rode his horse much faster than he should have over the snowy ground. When he stopped in front of Luke's Saloon, he barely took the time to tether the horse to the hitching post before bursting through the door.

The same bartender as before stood behind the counter. Michael didn't bother to stop this time. Instead, he headed straight for the stairs and took them three at a time.

"Hey, what do you think you're doing?"

Michael heard the gruff voice calling behind him, but he kept his focus on the door at the end of the hall. During the ride, he'd made plans in his mind, and he'd known he would have to take them by surprise and not stop to ask permission. He burst into Luke's office. A woman gasped and shot from the saloon owner's lap. She hurried past Michael and scurried out the open door.

A flicker of alarm passed over Luke's face, but he recovered so quickly it was as though he had been expecting Michael in the first place. He grabbed a cigar from his case on the desk, bit off the end, and lit the disgusting stick.

"We meet again, Mr. . .Riley, was it?"

Rough hands seized him from behind. "Sorry about that, Luke, he ran past before I could stop him."

Waving his bouncer away, Luke kept his gaze focused on Michael. "It's all right, Jack. Mr. Riley is my guest. For now, anyway. Go back to the bar and close the door on your way out."

Reluctantly, the burly bartender turned him loose. Michael could tell he'd have preferred the opportunity to give him a good pounding. He'd most likely get the chance to try before all was said and done, but Michael knew God was on his side. Somehow, he'd get to Star and take her out of this evil place.

When they were alone, Luke motioned toward the same chair Michael had occupied during their last visit. "Now, tell me why you're here."

"You know exactly what I came for."

"Star?" He gave a short laugh. "I'm afraid she's a bit tired from the trip. I gave her the night off. One of our other ladies perhaps?"

Fury burned inside Michael at the man's crude inference. "Star isn't going back to that life. We both know she was forced. I've come to take her home."

"That's where we differ, Mr. Riley." Luke leaned forward, his eyes no longer hinting at friendliness. "I say she's staying here where she belongs."

"Star belongs with me, and I intend to marry her." Wheeling about, he strode to the door. "Star!" he called as he stepped out of the room. "Where are you?"

He noticed Clem standing in front of a door at the other end of the hall. The man was poised to fight. Michael closed the distance between them in a few long strides. "She's in there?"

"You're not getting past me."

"Michael, is that you?" Star's voice came through the closed door.

"It's me, honey. I'm here to take you home."

"Oh, thank You, Lord."

"I don't think so, bub."

Michael turned just as a fist connected with his face. Everything went out of focus for an instant. Blinking, he tried to stop the spinning. The bartender took the opportunity and grabbed him by the collar. He practically carried him down the steps and tossed him out the door. Michael took a second to gather his wits, then he barreled back through the door. He made a run for the steps again, but this time the bartender had help. Four men stopped him, but instead of throwing him out the front, they carried him toward the kitchen.

"Star! I'll find a way, I promise. I love you! I'll be back!" he called.

"You don't learn so good." Those were the only words he heard before everything went black.

Everything hurt when he woke up, freezing and lying in the alley behind the saloon. His first conscious thought was that they must have mistaken him for dead—either that or they'd left him to die. He shivered and winced as pain shot through his middle. Gritting his teeth determinedly against the pain, he forced himself to his feet. He knew if he returned to the saloon they'd kill him, but better to die trying to save the woman he loved than to walk away and seal her fate.

One eye was swollen completely shut and his mouth felt puffy. He knew he had broken ribs. He also knew he had to go back inside. He stumbled to the kitchen door and opened it a crack. Through his one good eye, he perused the room. A black woman stood peeling potatoes at a table in the center of the kitchen.

Cautiously, he opened the door wide enough to gain entrance.

The woman glanced up, her eyes went wide, and she drew back in horror, confirming to Michael that he looked about as bad as he felt.

"Star." He managed to say through his swollen lips. "I. . .need. . .to. . .get. . . to. . .her. I. . .won't. . .hurt. . .you."

She chuckled. "I ain't fearin' that one bit. You cain't hurt nothin' like that. My girl say you be comin' back. I tole her you was probly dead."

"Not yet."

A tender smile touched the slave woman's face. "You be wantin' ter marry my Star?"

He nodded.

"Well, you wind up dead if you goes through there." She jerked her thumb toward the door leading to the main room. "Come on, Lila show you which room. Don' know how you plan ter get her out, though."

"Let. . .me. . .worry. . .about. . .that."

She gave him a doubtful look but took him back outside to the alleyway. They walked a few steps, then she stopped and pointed at a lighted window. "Dat be my Star's room."

"Thank you." He bent and kissed the dark, withered cheek. "Get back inside before you're missed."

He glanced around. How could he climb up there in his condition?

"Hey, cowboy!"

With a groan, Michael glanced back toward the kitchen door. The same woman who'd escorted him up the stairs during his last visit to Luke's stood, her face a mask of amusement.

"Do you really think you can climb up there in your condition?"

"I have to try."

"You'll get yourself killed."

A shrug lifted his shoulders. "She's worth it."

"Is she? Well, then lucky for you, Lila told me she brought you out here. That little old woman stayed here, sure Luke would bring Star back somehow. She wasn't about to leave Star alone with him."

"So why did she get you?"

"Lila knows I can help."

Michael looked at her, defenses alerted. "Why would you do that?"

"Well, for one thing, Star's mother was my friend. I've known Star since she was a little girl. If she has a chance at a better life, I owe it to her mother to do everything I can to help."

Michael nodded. "All right. Then how do I get up there?"

"You don't. You'll kill yourself."

"I thought you said you wanted to help."

"If you'll trust me, I can help you. My way. Is that your hat on the ground?"

He looked to where she pointed. "Yes."

"Grab it and come on. By the way, my name's Tina."

"Michael."

Still not sure what Tina was up to, Michael nevertheless knew he had no choice but to trust her. Once he was back in the kitchen, she reached up and adjusted his hat so that it nearly covered his face. "All right, Michael. Put your arm around me."

Michael drew back in alarm.

She scowled. "You're going to have to pretend you like me, cowboy. That's the only way to get you upstairs. Once we're there, don't go half-cocked and take off after Clem like you did before. It was brave, but incredibly stupid."

"What do you have in mind?"

"First, I'm going to take you into my room like you're a customer." She gave him a wry grin. "Still with me?"

He scowled as well as he could through his swollen face. "Yeah."

"I'll call for Clem, and when he comes in, I'll whack him over the head with a lamp. Then you can sneak into Star's room."

"What about the lock?"

"Luke doesn't believe in locks. That's why Clem was standing guard."

"All right. Let's go."

Michael trembled as he put his arm around the strongly perfumed woman. She laughed uproariously as though he'd said the funniest thing as they made their way through the kitchen door and toward the staircase. Michael prayed fervently that no one recognized his clothes. He'd tucked his shirt back in and brushed off his trousers to appear a bit more presentable. Playing his role, he nuzzled Tina's neck, eliciting another round of giggles from her. They nuzzled and giggled all the way up the steps. Each step burned like fire, and he nearly fainted from the pain. Michael stumbled when they reached the landing.

"Easy, cowboy," Tina said. "You've had a little too much whiskey tonight."

"You all right, Tina?"

Michael stiffened at the sound of Clem's voice, but Tina laughed and waved the thug off. "I'm fine. This cowboy's had a bit too much to drink, but I can handle him. I'll call if I need you."

She led him to a room. "All right," she said when the door was safely shut behind them. "Take a minute to catch your breath. You okay?"

Every inch of his body hurt, but Michael knew this was his one shot to rescue Star. He nodded. "I'll be fine."

"You're a real hero," she said pensively. She turned her back to him. "Unbutton me."

Michael frowned and drew back. "I don't know what you thought, but—"

"Just do it," she snapped. "When you leave, take my dress for Star to put on. Our hair is close to the same color. If you leave down the steps with her, she can keep her face turned so the bartender doesn't see her. The room's so crowded, no one will look close enough to make sure the girl in the red dress is the same one you went upstairs with." She tossed him the gown. "When you get to the main room downstairs, keep going and leave by the front door. The girls walk their customers out all the time. No one will think anything of it. Once you get outside, don't stop, and you should be safe."

"What about you? Won't you get into trouble?"

Again she waved her hand. "Clem won't know what hit him. I'm good at talking my way out of trouble."

"Thank you," he said, pressing her hands.

Her eyes misted and she quickly looked away. Grabbing a glass lamp from a nearby table, she screamed, "Clem!"

Seconds later, he burst through the door. "Tina, what's—"

Crash!

The lamp found its mark, and Clem fell unconscious to the ground.

Tina looked into the hallway. "Hurry!"

With the red satin gown slung over his arm, Michael rushed to Star's room. He flung open the door and shut it quickly after him.

"Michael!" She flew into his arms, knocking the breath from him. "Oh, my love. I thought they'd killed you." As much as he relished having her in his arms, he pushed her gently from him.

Her lips quivered. "Michael, I'm so sorry I wasn't honest with you from the very first day."

"It's all right. We have a lot to talk about, honey, but for now put this on."

Star gasped as she glanced at the gown.

"Trust me," he urged.

Hesitantly she took the dress. Michael faced the door. Listening to the rustle of the satin behind him, he inwardly cringed, hating the thought that she'd have to wear the immodest garment.

"I–I'm ready," she said a moment later, her voice trembling and barely above a whisper.

Michael gathered a sharp breath at the sight of her. The pain in his stomach extended from the physical to a very emotional pain.

She lowered her gaze, her face ashen. "I love you," she whispered. "I'm sorry to bring you into such a mess."

He went to her and drew her gently into his arms. "I love you, too. You'll never have need to be ashamed again, my love."

Pulling away, he cupped her cheeks and gently kissed her lips, despite the pain in his own.

"How touching."

Looking past Michael, Star gasped. "Luke!"

Nausea seized Star at the sight of Luke standing in the doorway, holding a gun on them. His face held no hint of its usual calm. Instead, the veins in his neck bulged. He sneered. "You look lovely, Star. Finally dressed as you should be." Turning his attention to Michael, Luke gave a mocking grin. "It appears as though you can't be taught a lesson, Mr. Riley. I believe I made it clear that Star remains with me."

Michael pulled Star into the circle of his arm. "And I told you, I'm taking her home."

"Ah, yes. You intend to make her the little wife. But don't you realize what having babies will do to her figure?"

Heat burned Star's cheeks even as she realized that he'd said Michael intended to make her his wife. Joy bubbled inside of her, pushing back the fear.

"What do you intend to do?" Michael asked.

"Well, unfortunately for me, the sheriff came in to get himself a beer. If I shoot you right now, he'll hear it, and I doubt I could make him believe another drifter killed you. It looks like we'll have to wait here until the sheriff finishes his drink."

He stepped forward. "Now, turn loose of my girl, please."

"She's not your girl," Michael said through gritted teeth.

"She'll be dead if you don't do as I said."

Unwilling to take a chance that Luke might fly into a rage and harm Michael, Star stepped away from the warmth of his arm.

Luke rewarded her with a smile. "That's a good girl. If you keep being cooperative, I won't have to punish you too much."

"You won't touch her," Michael said.

"Is that so?" Luke's free hand shot out and grabbed Star. She gasped as his fingers bit painfully into her bare arm. "Let's get one thing straight before you die. I will touch her anytime I choose and however I choose." Keeping his gun pointed at Michael's chest, he brought his mouth down hard on Star's. She fought against him; and in that wretched moment when his cold lips punished hers, she brought her hands flat against his chest and shoved as hard as she could. Then before he could get his bearings, she grabbed his hand that held the gun and knocked the weapon onto the floor. Racing forward, Star kicked it toward Michael.

"Why you. . ." Cold hatred shot from Luke's eyes. "You'll regret that." He brought his hand up.

"I wouldn't advise that." Michael's tone carried a deadly threat. Star held her breath as Luke's arm remained poised to strike. With a sneer, he gave in and dropped his arm to his side. Michael motioned him to a straight-backed wooden chair. "Get something to tie him up with, Star."

Glancing about, Star felt as helpless as a kitten until she spotted a corset hanging from a peg in the corner. She grabbed the garment and pulled out the strings. "This is all I could find."

Michael scowled. "That won't hold him for long, but it'll give us time to get out of here. Take the gun and keep it aimed at him."

Star took the weapon. Luke's lips twisted into a smirk. "Do you really think I'm going to let you go? All this is, is a little setback. Even if you do get out of here, we know where to find you. Make no mistake, Star. I'll come after you."

"Shut up, Luke," Michael said as he wound the corset strings around the meaty wrists.

Ignoring Michael's threatening tone, Luke continued to bait. "I recognized you'd be a great beauty even when you were a little girl. Why do you think I kept your mother around as long as I did? I should have kicked her out five years ago, and I would have if not for you. She barely earned enough to feed and clothe the two of you, but I knew once you were old enough, you'd more than make up for what she cost me."

Fury began to build inside Star. *Oh, God, help me.* Her finger rested on the trigger. She'd never fired a gun before, but at this range, she knew she couldn't miss.

"Shut up, Luke," she whispered. "Just stop talking."

"Come now, Star. What are you going to do? Kill me? After I raised you as though you were my own daughter? You're as ungrateful as your filthy mother was. After all I did for her, she had the nerve to threaten to take you and leave. I had to kill her, and I'd do it again."

Star's world zeroed in on one thing. . .the fact that she held the means to avenge her mother's death. All it would take was a little more pressure and Luke would be dead.

"Give me the gun, Star." Star barely heard Michael's voice through the fog of memories that roared through her mind. She heard her mother's scream. Heard Luke's taunting confession. *Lord, he deserves to die.* Tears flooded her eyes as her mind filled with the image of Jesus on the cross. She couldn't do it. No matter how much she believed he deserved to die, Jesus had died for him, too, and she had no right to take his life. She handed the gun to Michael. "Take it," she said hoarsely.

The door burst open at that moment. Tina, accompanied by the sheriff, walked into the room.

"It's a good thing you're here, Sheriff," Luke said. "These two were about to rob me. I want them arrested."

"Save it. We heard every word you said to the girl. You just talked yourself into a murder charge, Luke."

Protesting all the way, Luke was escorted out by the sheriff. Star smiled at Tina. "I don't know how we can thank you for all you've done."

The woman's face grew red. "Think nothing of it. I guess now we all gotta start thinking about another place to work." She winked at the two of them. "Unless I can find me a cowboy like yours." With a grin, she left them.

Star caught her breath and sat hard on the bed. "Oh, Michael. I almost killed him." She covered her face with her hands.

He came to her and knelt before her. "Shh," he said, taking her hands from her face and holding them firmly. "The important thing is, you didn't."

"I'm just so glad it's over, and Luke won't be able to hurt anyone else."

Michael nodded. "So am I." He captured her gaze. "I'm glad all of this is behind us and we can get on with our life together."

He stroked her hand with his thumb.

"Our life together?" she whispered, afraid to believe it.

Pressing her hands to his lips, he kissed each knuckle, then looked up to capture her gaze. "I was so wrong. I accused you of not being a decent woman, when the truth is that anything in the past is gone.

"When Luke told me what you were, I went crazy with jealousy that other men had touched you."

"Michael. . ."

"Let me finish." He kissed her hand again. "I sought the Lord long and hard about this, and I know that I have no right to hold something against you that He forgot the moment you confessed it. I don't have to be ashamed or afraid to love you and make you my wife. You're as pure as the day you were born as far as God is concerned. And as far as I'm concerned, as well."

Tears flowed down Star's cheeks. Pulling her hands gently from his, she slid from the bed to the floor and knelt beside him. "Oh, Michael. Luke told you I was one of his girls?"

"Yes, my love. But it doesn't matter. I want you to be my wife and Aimee's

124

mother." His brown eyes filled with tears. "I never want to be without you again. Tell me you'll marry me."

"Of course I will. But, Michael, you have to know something."

"What's that?"

Placing her palm against his cheek, she smiled. "Darling, I am coming to you pure."

"I know, honey. I know."

"No, you don't know." He was being so noble, she almost didn't have the heart to tell him. "Luke lied to you. I was never one of his girls. That's why I ran away in the first place—because he was going to force me to work for him. When I say I'm coming to you untouched, I mean it."

Joy lit his eyes, and he gathered her to him. Star pulled away, and for the next few minutes, she told him her story. Of Luke murdering her mother, of Lila and Sam loving her all of her life and helping her get away from Luke, of her fear that if she told him where she'd come from he might turn her out.

Michael gathered her close once more. "I might have," he admitted. "But God's changed me. I only want to make you happy."

The door flew open, and Lila's tiny frame made an imposing figure in the doorway. Her stormy gaze rested on Michael. "Turn her loose. It ain't proper, you holdin' on to Star when you's alone like dis."

Michael inclined his head. "You're right, ma'am. And since it appears you are the closest thing Star has to family, I suppose I'll be asking your permission for her hand in marriage."

Lila's face lit up like a Roman candle. "In dat case, I guess I'm gonna have ter say yes."

A lopsided grin split Michael's face. He squeezed Star's hand, then glanced back up to Lila. "Will you come and live with us?"

Quick tears misted Lila's black eyes. "You knows I will."

"Oh, Michael," Star whispered. "What a wonderful idea!"

"Yes. Ma'll be relieved. She still needs that help." He gave Star a teasing grin.

Star's heart filled with contentment as she gazed into Michael's love-filled eyes. "I guess that settles it, then," she whispered.

"I think so." His head descended, then he stopped and glanced at Lila. He grinned. "Just a quick kiss?"

Lila gave a curt nod.

Michael gave a contented sigh as his lips closed over Star's, and she knew the past was indeed gone. She looked forward to a glorious future.

Epilogue

Star smiled as Aimee bit her bottom lip in concentration just before she stepped onto the polished floor of the church aisle.

From where Star waited, she couldn't see past the doorway, but her mind created picture after picture of her little flower girl's walk down the aisle in her frilly, pink dress. *In just a few minutes, she'll be my own little girl. Will I be a good mother? Jesus, help me to be the best. . .*

The slight pressure of a hand on her shoulder interrupted her thoughts, and she glanced up to see Rosemary toss her an encouraging smile. With a flash of blue, Star's bridesmaid stepped through the door and followed Aimee down the aisle.

I'm next. Oh, Mama. Can you see me? Star knew her wedding gown was a picture of perfection and she'd made it with her own hands. Well, and a little bit of help from Miss Hannah. *Can you believe it, Mama?*

A twinge of sadness stabbed at her heart but quickly fled as music reverberated throughout the building.

This was it. The moment she had been waiting for.

Star took a deep breath and stepped into the sanctuary, hesitating for a moment just inside the doorway. Swallowing, she stepped onto the pink rose petals that trailed their way to the front of the church. A blur of faces seemed to rush by in waves on either side of her. But of course, she was the one in motion.

She straightened and lifted her chin and, as she did, her glance fell upon Michael waiting at the front of the church. An expression of total awe and joy washed over his countenance, and Star's heart leapt. *Michael. My Michael. How can it be that he loves me?*

Michael's hand reached out for hers as she reached the altar. He smiled tenderly, and Star felt her eyes misting.

"Dearly beloved. . ." Hank's voice rang out true and strong. And each word he spoke brought her closer to her dream.

Everlasting Hope

Dedication

For my brother, Rod.
Your best days are yet to come.
Only believe. . .

Chapter 1

The dusty ground rose up to meet Andy with alarming speed. He landed hard on his gut, the impact forcing the breath from him like steam from a train whistle. With a groan, he twisted around to face his assailant. George, the massive bartender, snarled down at him from the boardwalk. Andy winced as a stream of tobacco juice landed inches from his head. His beat-up hat followed.

George pointed a stubby finger at Andy and squinted hard. "Don't come back, if you know what's good for you."

The giant of a man didn't have to worry about that. All the cash Andy had carried in his pocket the night before—fifty dollars and a gold piece—was gone. Plus two hundred more that hadn't been his to spend. A split-second of fear clawed at him. Mr. Dobson was going to kill him. No way could he pay back the loan now. If only his luck had held. For once.

Andy heard the rattle of a wagon just in time to scramble out of the way as it swerved to miss him. The driver shouted a curse. "Get out of the road, drunk. I'll run you over next time!"

Andy used the edge of the boardwalk for support and pushed himself to his feet. He stepped onto the wooden platform as a woman and child passed. Holding her little girl close, the woman jerked her chin and sniffed in disdain.

He didn't care how many self-righteous biddies looked down their noses at him. He was past caring about status. What did bother him was that the little girl shrank back, her innocent blue eyes wide with fear.

The curly-headed cherub reminded him of his niece, Aimee. He'd taken Aimee a little Indian doll last time he'd seen her. Had it really been five years since he'd been back to Oregon? She was most likely becoming a young lady now. He had promised to bring her another doll. Pain squeezed Andy's heart. He blinked away quick tears. He'd never hold another Indian doll in his arms again. Alive or handmade.

His stomach lurched as his night of carousing caught up to him. Through a dizzy fog, he headed toward the alley, clutching his gut, fighting to keep from disgracing himself further in public. When the retching ended, he slid down the side of the building and sat in the filthy alley. He rested his elbows on his knees and buried his face in his hands.

Last night he'd been on top of the world. Winning at poker, the liquor making him feel in control. Beautiful saloon girls clung to each arm—oohing and ahhing over his muscles and brains. He'd found a precious few hours to numb the pain of loss. Too bad the lucky streak hadn't held up. The liquor quickly overpowered his reason, and of course, as the money stack dwindled so had his manly charms, and the girls deserted him for greener pastures.

Now, with the reality of the morning sun stabbing his eyes and heightening the pain in his head, Andy regretted not stopping when he was ahead. One thousand dollars ahead. He could have paid back Mr. Dobson and had enough left over to get a nice little start somewhere.

A groan escaped from deep inside him. Life was such a disappointment. Maybe it would be better if Dobson's thugs did find him and end his misery. As quickly as the thought slammed into his mind, a precious image eclipsed it. *Ma.* True, he hadn't seen her in a while, and he had never really done right by her, but that didn't mean he loved her any less than his brothers did. It was just that, with sons like Hank, a preacher, and Michael, an upstanding, moral man who took Ma into his home, what did she need with a no-good son like Andy? She was better off without him in her life.

The whole world would probably be better off. He'd had the thought more than once. More times than he could count, as a matter of fact, but he'd never really believed it until this moment. He'd finally reached the end of his rope. His will to live fled and, in a moment of clarity, he made a decision. He nodded to himself to cinch the deal. So that was it. There'd be no hiding from Dobson. He would face his death sentence like a man, and maybe the end would come quick. A shot to the head or heart. And then peace. *Please, God, finally peace.*

❦

Fit to be tied, Hope Parker stomped after the wagon master. She wasn't accustomed to taking no for an answer, and she didn't intend to start now. Especially from this uncouth tobacco-chewing stump of a man.

"I am willing to pay double the fare to secure a place on this wagon train for myself and my children. I can be in Independence in plenty of time to—"

The wagon master stopped and turned to her. He gathered a slow breath, obviously trying to control his exasperation. "Lady, I've already told you. It ain't a matter of money or your ability to get from Chicago to Independence. It's a matter of you being a woman alone."

"But I'm *not* alone, as I've already *told* you."

"A greenhorn boy and a maid ain't exactly what I had in mind."

"Need I remind you I will also be traveling with my driver?" She motioned toward her carriage. The aging gentleman waiting for her beside the carriage door nodded.

The wagon master snorted. "Sorry, lady."

Refraining from mentioning the eight-year-old twins who would be accompanying her as well, she squared her shoulders and matched his glare. "Perhaps I'm not making myself clear. I'm rich. I will pay anything. No matter the price."

He scowled and leaned so close, Hope had to resist the urge to retreat. But she held steady. A Parker didn't back down from anyone. And Parkers always got their way. At least when it mattered most. And this mattered. Her son's future was at stake. Perhaps his life.

"I'm telling you, lady. You could be rich as Midas and I couldn't let you on this train without a man to take care of you."

"Fine. I'll hire someone—a younger someone than my driver."

He was shaking his head before she got the words out.

In frustration, Hope stomped the ground. "Why on earth not?"

"A hired man might get sick of your bossy ways and decide the money's not worth it. Company policy. No single women are allowed space." He gave a short laugh. "If it means that much to you, go buy yourself a husband."

Hope saw red at the mockery. "I may be a plain woman, sir, but I am not that desperate. Th—there are plenty of men who want to marry me." Hated tears burned her eyes and she swallowed hard. She spun around and stomped away from the despicable man before she further embarrassed herself.

The truth was that no one wanted her. Oh, they wanted her money. She could name a half-dozen men right now who would jump at the chance to marry her bank account, but she refused to give her heart to one more gold digger. She certainly wouldn't share her bed or her life with such a man.

Francis, her driver, opened the carriage door, and she slid onto the black leather seat, hot tears of frustration making a trail down her cheeks. She stared out the window as the carriage jostled through the street. What would she do now? She simply had to get Gregory out of this city and away from his so-called friends. At only eleven years old, her son had already had several run-ins with the law. Her money would only keep him out of serious trouble for so long before the sheriff had his fill or the judge couldn't be reasoned with.

She was just about to lean her head back on the seat and close her throbbing eyes when she noticed a scuffle in the alley. A gasp escaped her throat. Three men stood over another, obviously beating him.

She knocked on the carriage roof. "Stop the carriage, Francis!" She couldn't abide bullies. Three men ganging up on one was just too much for her already agitated mind to ignore. Reaching for her reticule, she retrieved a small pistol—a gift from her deceased husband—and exited the carriage without waiting for Francis to open the door.

"You men, stop it!" She shouted a good five yards away from the alley, knowing full well that this would draw attention from passersby. Compassion was one thing, but she was not fool enough to walk alone into an alley and confront three rough-looking men.

The men turned, dismissed her with bored glances, and returned to their task—making a bloody pulp of the poor man's face. "I said stop." She fired the pistol into the air then pointed it toward the thugs. "The next round goes into one of you. I don't care which."

"Get out of here, lady," a tall, pencil-necked man shot in her direction. "We have our orders."

"I don't care about your orders. I care about that poor man. And if you don't do as I say, I'll plug you through the shoulder then I'll send for the sheriff." She nodded toward the growing crowd. "I have plenty of witnesses."

"All right." A massive bear of a man scowled past her. Hope didn't turn around, but she could hear a crowd gathering.

"You win. But when he wakes up, tell him Mr. Dobson wants his two hundred dollars by the end of the week, or next time it ain't gonna matter how many folks are watching." The three men left through the alley in the opposite direction.

"Francis?" Feeling faint with relief, Hope turned to her driver, who looked almost as ill as she felt. "Help me get him to the carriage."

"The carriage, ma'am?"

"Yes. We can't leave him to die in the alley."

Now that the show was over, the crowd had dissipated. Resentment burned in Hope at the lack of compassion. The unconscious man weighed a ton, but they managed to get him into the carriage.

Hope pulled a handkerchief from her reticule and swiped at the blood still coming from his broken nose. He reeked of sweat and vomit, and she wondered if perhaps she'd been hasty in her decision to bring him home. After all, there was a church just down the street where she was sure he'd be welcome. When a church was called The Good Samaritan, it really had no choice but to be willing to take in a wounded indigent.

A moan escaped his throat, igniting her pity once more.

"Shh," Hope soothed, gently pushing a strand of red-brown shoulder-length hair from his face. She jumped as he grabbed her wrist and buried his lips in her palm.

Hope's heart leapt in her chest. She wasn't often in the presence of such masculinity, and even stinking and wounded, this man exuded a power she found exhilarating. Disconcerted by her rapid pulse and the direction of her thoughts, she pulled her hand away.

"Yellow Bird?"

Yellow Bird? He thought she was a squaw?

"Are we in heaven, my love?"

Hope swallowed hard. A man in desperate love. Oh, why couldn't anyone love her that deeply?

"Shh," she said once more. "We'll get you taken care of. You'll be all right."

"You're not Yellow Bird."

"No."

"Yellow Bird's dead. Why? Why didn't they kill me?" The cry seemed wrenched from deep within his gut. And he passed out again.

Hope's throat tightened and she swallowed hard. What caused a man to come to the end of his rope? Was the loss of love enough to make a man give up on life? Or was there more to his story? He obviously needed something to live for.

She studied him. He was big and, given his buckskin clothing—foul though it may be—he appeared to be rustic. Just the type of man a swaggering wagon master might find suitable to "take care of her" on a westward trail.

This man was desperate. He needed to pay off that Mr. Dobson character or risk death. True, he seemed to want to die, but she highly doubted he'd want to go through another such beating.

Perhaps the wagon master had been right. If she wanted a man to accompany her west, she'd have to buy one.

Chapter 2

Every inch of his body screamed with pain. Andy tried to open his eyes but the light jabbed at him, forcing him to squeeze his lids shut.

He remembered standing up and walking toward the alleyway entrance, determined not to hide like a gopher in a hole from Dobson's men. They'd found him before he'd gone ten feet beyond the alley and had pulled him back into the narrow pathway. He'd been certain the putrid ground, flanked on either side by buildings, would be his tomb.

Years of base living had flashed through his mind at the last second, and he'd hoped to wake up in heaven, or at least not in the alternate place. Waking up on earth never entered the realm of possibilities. Why was he still alive?

He forced himself to open his eyes, moaning at the pain. His lids felt heavy and barely opened wide enough for him to see through tiny slits. Dobson's thugs had done a number on him. That was for sure. Touching his eyes, he winced. They were so puffy, it was a wonder he could see at all.

He shifted, trying to find a comfortable position for his aching body. Then he noticed the pillowy-soft, warm bed. Running his hands along the crisp, clean quilt, he felt his throat tighten.

When had he stopped feeling like a man and started to accept an animalistic existence? Lying in a bed felt foreign to him. For the past two years, he'd been passing out in alleyways, and when he could get by with it, an unsuspecting farmer's barn. Occasionally, when his luck held out, he spent a few hours in a room above the saloon. Why hadn't he realized how dirty he was before now? The contrast between him and this clean bed was startling, sobering.

Ma would be so ashamed.

He was ashamed.

Andy's ears, sharp from his years of scouting for wagon trains, picked up the sound of footsteps outside his door, coming close. They hesitated and, instinctively, he reached for his guns. Panic rose inside of him. His belt was gone from his waist. Where were his guns? His vision was limited by the swelling, but he made a quick sweep of the room. The weapons were nowhere to be seen. Unaccustomed to feeling this vulnerable, Andy sat up, poised to defend himself with his bare hands, if necessary.

The door opened, revealing the intruders. He relaxed and released a pent-up breath. Two children, a boy and a girl, stood in the doorway. They couldn't be more than seven or eight years old. Irritation shot through him as they stared at him as though he were something from a freak show.

"Who are you?" he asked, gruffly.

Apparently taking his question as an invitation, the two bopped into the room, closing the door behind them. "I'm Betsy. This is Billy. We're twins. Can you tell?"

"No." Why didn't they just go away and leave him alone? Where were their parents? Children had no manners nowadays.

"Well, we are. Only we're not identical. Except we both have brown eyes and practically brown hair. And the same birthday. We're going to be nine."

"Well, my brother Michael has hair the same color as mine. Our little brother Hank, though, has hair about as orange as a carrot."

"We are."

"Good for you." *Now, go away.*

"Woo-wee, someone busted you up good, didn't they, mister?" The little boy finally got a word in edgewise. But Andy wished he'd kept his trap shut. He didn't need a four-and-a-half-footer reminding him of why he felt like he'd been trampled by a bull.

The boy inched closer, examining Andy's wounds. "How come you got yourself thrashed? Did you steal a horse?"

Resentment burned his chest. "No. I didn't steal any horse. Only a lowdown varmint would steal from someone."

"You mean you're not a lowdown varmint?" The boy sounded disappointed. "No."

Betsy stepped closer and gave him a scrutinizing once over. "You look like a lowdown varmint to me. Don't he, Billy?"

Andy released a frustrated breath. "Where's your mother?"

The little girl shrugged. "She had to go out. Said not to disturb you."

"Then maybe you'd better obey her."

"Naw, we'll be out of here before she gets back."

"What makes you think I'm not dangerous? What if I get out of bed and scalp you like a wild Indian?"

"You won't get out of bed."

"I might."

"No, you won't. Francis took off all your clothes. Loaned you a pair of his long johns. He said they were too little for you. But he got them on you anyway."

Alarm shot through Andy. He ran his hand over his chest. The tight, scratchy long handles were definitely not his. He hadn't even noticed. And the little girl had him pegged right. He wasn't going to get out of bed without proper clothes on. "Little girls shouldn't talk about a man's state of dress. It's not very polite."

Betsy shrugged. "It's the truth."

"It's still not becoming for a pretty little girl like you to speak of such things." Andy inwardly grimaced. Now why had he gone and told her she was pretty? From the grin on her round little face, he'd won her over and would probably never get rid of her.

"You think I'm pretty?"

Determined not to encourage the newfound friendship, he grunted and closed his eyes. "Go away. My head hurts."

He heard a shuffling and sighed. Maybe they were leaving.

No such luck. He continued to listen to water being poured into a basin then little bootsteps headed back to his bedside. Lying motionless, he pretended to be asleep. A cool, wet cloth was laid gently across his forehead, followed by a gentle kiss on his cheek. "We'll leave you alone, mister." Betsy's voice sounded close to his ear. "I'm glad you're not a varmint."

Feeling his throat clog, Andy scowled but didn't open his eyes. Just like a female. Tell her she's pretty and she either wants to be your mother or your sweetheart.

Andy didn't answer the child. He listened as the twins left, closing the door softly behind them. He had to admit the kindness had done something to him. They might be precocious, but at least they had hearts.

His unnamed baby girl would have been about two years old if she'd lived. He pictured a small child with coal black hair and large brown eyes. "Daddy!" A word he'd never hear. At least not directed at him.

Tears burned his eyes. Ma would have loved Yellow Bird. They had planned to visit Oregon as soon as the baby was born and able to travel. But the baby had been stillborn and, within three hours, Yellow Bird had followed their child in death. Ma would have loved her. He should have gone home, but grief had driven him to the bottle instead.

The cool cloth on his head was soothing and soon Andy felt himself drifting to sleep, dreaming of his mother's smile and the gentle green fields of his Oregon home.

❦

Gathering a steadying breath, Hope pushed open the door to her guest's room. She stood at the threshold, debating whether or not to step inside.

His eyes were closed, perhaps swollen shut? Maybe that was for the best. If he couldn't see what she looked like, he might be more likely to agree to what she was about to propose.

"Excuse me. Are you awake?"

His eyes slowly came open. If you could call it that. She wondered how well

136

he could see. Hope's stomach dropped.

"Yeah."

There was nothing to do but go inside or look foolish. Taking care to leave the door open just in case he tried something, she took choppy steps until she stood next to his bed, just out of reach.

"How are you feeling?"

"Like I've had the feathers knocked out of me."

"That's putting it mildly, I fear." Forgetting her anxiety, she reached toward the cloth on his head.

He grabbed her wrist. "What do you think you're doing? I don't like to be touched."

"Believe me, the last thing I want to do is touch a filthy gutter rat. Take your hands off me. I was just going to rewet the cloth for you."

She thought he might have blushed, but she wasn't sure through all the bruising. Either way, he let go.

"Sorry," he muttered. "Filthy gutter rats don't always have the best of manners."

It was Hope's turn to blush. "My tongue seems to have a mind of its own at times. Especially when I get mad or scared."

"I didn't mean to scare you."

"You didn't. You made me mad."

He chuckled. "Didn't mean to do that, either."

Hope enjoyed the rich sound rumbling from his broad chest. Her gaze traveled to his shoulders. What would it be like to rest her head there? Were his shoulders wide enough to bear her burdens?

"How did I come to be here?"

Jumping, Hope felt her cheeks flood with warmth. She fervently hoped he hadn't caught the direction of her gaze.

"We found you in the alley. Three men were about to send you to Glory."

"Will your man be stopping by? I'd like to thank him for saving my life."

"You mean Francis?"

"If that's your husband's name, then I reckon that's who I mean."

Hope couldn't stifle her giggle at the thought of being married to Francis. Her driver had to be in his sixties and was shorter than she was. And, though she wasn't a large woman, he probably weighed less, as well.

"What's so funny?"

"Francis is my driver. My husband's been dead for two years."

"I see. Then who. . . ?"

"I did. I'm capable of quite a lot, actually." She set her chin a notch higher. "I do not need a man to protect me." She cringed as soon as the words left her. Wasn't she about to ask him to accompany her west for just such a purpose?

"I didn't mean to imply you did. Just trying to say thanks to whoever saved my life. Apparently that person is you." Even with puffy lips, he was obviously smirking.

Fighting to keep her temper in check, Hope took the cloth to the basin and rewet it. "The men who beat you up asked me to give you a message."

He let out a short laugh. "I can imagine what that was."

"Yes. I'm sure you can." She twisted the water from the rag and replaced it on his forehead.

"Thank you, ma'am."

"You're welcome." Settling into a chair beside the bed, she returned to the topic at hand. "The message was that if you don't pay a Mr. Dobson two hundred dollars by the end of the week, you won't get off with just a beating next time."

His chest rose and he leaned his head back against the headboard, his eyes closed as he expelled a breath. "What would you do if you only had one week to live?"

The question startled her. He was just giving up? Didn't the man have any gumption? Or was he only outwardly strong? "I don't know. I suppose I'd do everything in my power to ensure my children would be properly cared for."

He lifted his head and captured her gaze. "Speaking of your children, you ought to teach that little girl of yours not to go around kissing strange men."

The blood drained from Hope's face. "What do you mean?" she managed to croak.

"Those twins of yours came in here like I wanted their company. Made my head hurt worse."

"Bother your head, what a—about the kiss?"

"Oh, Betsy gave me a wet cloth and kissed me on the cheek." Then, he seemed to understand Hope's fear. He scowled. "I didn't ask for either. I'm not that low."

Offering no apology, Hope met his gaze evenly. "Well, a mother can't be too careful. Especially one who is raising her children alone."

He nodded. "Then maybe you shouldn't bring strange men into your house. You never know what sort folks are, and that little girl is too pretty and too sweet to be left at home when there are strangers in the house."

Sweet? "Are you sure we're talking about the same Betsy?" She couldn't resist a smirk. Obviously, this man was a pushover for a little girl's attention. Recognizing his concern for what it was, she dismissed her fear that he might be out to harm her child. He might be a drunk and a slacker, but he was no monster. Of that she was sure.

Betsy had softened a place in his heart already. He couldn't be all bad.

Perhaps he could be reasoned with to enter a mutually beneficial relationship with an uncomely woman.

"The men called you Andy. But I'm not comfortable addressing you as such. What is your last name?"

"Riley."

"Mr. Riley, what do you intend to do for a week?"

He shrugged. "I suppose I'll stay here and heal up, if you'll have me."

"Of course. I wouldn't have brought you here if I didn't intend to allow you to heal. The doctor says you have a few cracked ribs, your nose is broken, and it will probably be several days before the swelling leaves your eyes."

"Great. I should be fixed right up in time to die."

"There is no reason Dobson should have to kill you when I can offer you an alternative."

"What's that? Are you going to give me the two hundred dollars?" He sent her a mocking grin.

"I confess the thought has crossed my mind."

He shifted slightly in the bed and gave a suspicious frown. "What would I have to do?"

She drew a sharp breath. "Marry me."

Chapter 3

Andy bolted upright, catching the soggy cloth as it slid from his forehead. The woman wanted him to. . .

"What did you just say?"

Clearing her throat, she leveled her gaze at him. "Marriage would fix both of our problems."

"How do you figure that?"

Her shoulders rose and fell as she made an obvious effort to steady herself. "I'll be honest with you, Mr. Riley. I want to travel west, but the wagon master won't allow me to go unless I have a husband."

"Wagon master? Last I checked, wagon trains don't go through Chicago."

"That's true. But even mean-spirited wagon masters have families they want to see from time to time. Francis attends services with this one's sister. That's how I heard he was in town and that he's leading a train to Oregon in two months. Of course we'd have to travel by steamship to Independence."

Andy glanced around at the luxurious room, then back at her. "Why would you want to go west? Didn't your husband leave you with enough to live on?"

She gave a short, bitter laugh. "Yes, he left me plenty. My father also left me a fortune, and I have an honest family friend who looks after my affairs. But sometimes it isn't enough to be well off."

"It's a difficult journey. Perhaps too difficult for someone seeking adventure."

"This isn't about thrill-seeking, Mr. Riley." Tears pooled in her brown eyes. She clasped and unclasped her hands in her lap. "My son Gregory is falling in with the wrong crowd of boys. I'm afraid nothing I do is deterring him."

Bewilderment shot through his veins and the sentiment found its way into the tone of his voice before he could squelch it. "You want to uproot your family because of a few boyish pranks?"

Anger flushed her cheeks, adding a spark to her eyes that Andy found quite attractive. He shook away the thought, chalking it up to her proposal. A man should be attracted to a prospective wife even if he had no intention of heading to the altar. Still, the feeling must have been subconscious, because the more she spoke, the more becoming he found her.

"My son's antics are hardly simple boyish pranks, Mr. Riley. He's smoking and drinking—"

Andy grinned as wide as his fat lip would allow. "I did those things as a boy. It's natural. He'll grow out of it."

Shooting to her feet, she waved her hands in the air and brought them back to her sides with a smack. "Oh, well. If *you* did it, I'm sure he's preparing to be an upstanding member of decent society. I mean, after all, aren't you just the picture of. . ." She stopped midsentence, her eyes widening with horror. She clapped a hand to her mouth.

Humiliation burned Andy. He wanted to find the courage to tell her that he hadn't always been the man he was today. Once he'd taken pride in himself, in his accomplishments as a sought-after wagon scout. Now, he was everything he'd always despised. And he couldn't blame this woman for her assessment. Still, seeing himself through the eyes of someone like her—a woman of influence and one he admired—made him wish she'd left him in the alley.

Clearing his throat, he nodded. "I see your point. Tell me about your boy."

"Oh, Mr. Riley." She dropped back into the chair as though the strength had been stolen from her legs. "He's been in trouble so many times I've lost count. It's costing me a fortune to bribe the judge to keep the foolish boy out of jail every time he runs afoul of the law. And he's only eleven years old. What happens when he gets a little older?"

Andy's lips twitched at the thought of her stomping up to the judge's bench and slapping down a bribe.

"You think it's funny?" Her eyes sparked with anger once more, and she left the chair with a flounce. "Never mind. You're not the man I had you pegged to be."

"Simmer down. First of all, you don't know me well enough to peg me any sort of man. And if you did, I doubt you'd get it right."

She blushed, and Andy once more felt the attraction to her. Irritation bit at him, and he scowled at his foolishness.

"Well, you don't have to growl at me!" Her lip trembled.

He'd done that out loud? That beating must have rattled his brain more than he originally thought.

"I'll leave you to rest, Mr. Riley." She spun around, sniffing, apparently trying to hide her tears. "Mrs. Smythe will bring your supper in a little while."

"Now, wait just a minute."

Slowly, she turned back around, hope glimmering in her eyes.

"Marriage is serious business. Why can't we just *pretend* to be a happy couple? Then I could leave once we reach the Platte. Or sooner if you're sick of my company by then. Which you probably will be."

"I'm not a liar, Mr. Riley."

He couldn't hold back his mocking laughter. "Live by the Good Book, do you?"

"What do you mean?"

"You know, thou shalt not lie?"

"Oh, the Bible." She crossed her arms. "You're the last person I'd have thought would want to wed a churchgoing woman."

"I couldn't care less."

"Then why'd you bring it up?"

"Me? You're the one who brought it up."

"I most certainly am not!"

He released an exasperated breath. "You said you wouldn't pretend to be married because you won't lie."

"Yes. And it has nothing to do with a religious affiliation. I just don't happen to believe a liar is worth his or her salt."

"You're not a Christian woman?"

She drew herself up straight and lifted her chin. "I do not hold to any denomination. I find the whole idea to be a crutch for weak-minded individuals who refuse to take responsibility for their own actions. A person can be moral and upstanding without a book to tell her what is or isn't right."

Jaws of unease crunched at his insides. He had never had much use for religion himself, but to discount the foundation on which his ma built her life seemed wrong somehow. "My ma would disagree with you."

"And what about you? Do you also disagree?"

"I don't care if you go to church or not."

She gave a clipped nod. "Fine. Now that that's settled, would you care to hear the rest of my proposition?"

"There's more?"

"Of course. There would be terms surrounding our so-called marriage."

"So-called?"

Her look grew haughty and disdain spewed from her lips. "I have no intention of sharing my life with another man."

Andy observed her, and the more he watched her, the more intrigued he became. She was a walking contradiction. Sniffling one moment, declaring independence the next.

"If you don't intend to share your life with a man, maybe you shouldn't go around proposing marriage."

"I don't go around proposing marriage. You're the first man I've ever. . . Oh, forget it. I'm not going to justify my actions to a man who had to be rescued from an alley. Here are the terms. The marriage will be legal and binding. I have already transferred enough funds to private accounts so that no one can leave me penniless—say a man given to gambling." She gave him a pointed look.

Heat moved up Andy's neck. "A wise decision, most likely," he said dryly.

She lifted her brow in obvious surprise then went on as though he hadn't spoken. "I will fund the trip west and pay you to stay on through the first harvest."

"That'll be almost a full year after you reach Oregon."

"I'm aware of that, Mr. Riley. I will need a man to help build my home and teach us how to farm." She frowned. "D—do you know how to farm?"

"Not according to my brother Michael," he said with a self-abasing grin. "But my ma thinks I do all right."

Relief crossed her features. "That's good to know."

"So you're proposing that I essentially become a hired hand for the time it takes to get to Oregon, get settled, and bring in the first harvest?"

"Not essentially. A hired hand is exactly what you'd be. I will not share a bed with you, if that's what you're implying."

"I wasn't."

Twin spots of scarlet stained her cheeks. "Oh."

She recovered quickly and once again became all business. "I have a handbook by a Captain Randolf B. Marcy called *The Prairie Traveler*. I have studied the book in great detail and am quite familiar with the supplies we'll need to procure. Francis will accompany us west. Therefore, I will purchase three wagons. You and Gregory may share with Francis. I will share a wagon with the twins and Mrs. Smythe, though Billy may be offended at the thought of sharing with two females. No matter. He'll have to accept it. The third wagon will, of course, carry supplies."

Waiting until she stopped rambling and took a breath, Andy rushed forward with his own thoughts. "I'll sleep under the stars." What was he saying? He'd agreed to no such arrangement. Not yet, anyway.

She blew out a frustrated breath. "Mr. Riley, if you sleep under the stars, who will keep Gregory from sneaking out in the middle of the night?"

Andy's heart constricted with compassion. "If I agree to this, I give you my word your son will be by your side when you catch your first glimpse of the lush green fields of Oregon."

She regarded him for a moment then seemed satisfied. "When may I expect your answer?"

"For sure by the end of the week." He gave her a humorless grin. "Although, if Dobson can't find me, he can't kill me."

Her soft brow rose. "They followed us when we brought you here."

What little hope Andy had held on to fled with her flat statement. His head throbbed. He sank beneath the covers and closed his eyes.

"I'll let you rest. I shouldn't have stayed so long."

A thought occurred to him. "Wait."

She was already at the door when he opened his eyes.

"I don't know your name."

"Hope Parker."

"Mrs. Parker. Thank you for not leaving me to die."

Fixing him with her earnest gaze, she shrugged. "I'm not in the habit of allowing harm if I can prevent it."

She didn't wait for an answer, but stepped through the door. He heard it click shut as he closed his eyes once more.

❧

Hope closed the door behind her. All strength drained from her legs and she leaned against the wall for support. If only Mr. Riley would agree to the marriage then everything would work out.

"Ma'am?"

Francis's voice startled her, nearly sending her through the roof. She flattened her palm against her stomach. "Mercy, Francis. You scared me."

"Beg pardon. But I was here when you stepped out. If you'd turned your head you would have seen me."

Something about his grim tone raised Hope's suspicions. "How long were you standing there?"

"Long enough to hear your plans. And may I say I am disappointed in your proposition to a stranger?"

"Why, Francis!" In all of his years of service, the servant had never once hinted at insolence. Still, given his long-standing status in the house, she felt he deserved an explanation. "The wagon master will not grant us a place on the wagon train unless I'm married. Even a male servant doesn't qualify us."

He looked insulted. Hope hurried to clarify. "It isn't your age. Trust me. It's my marital status. Some hogwash about company policy not allowing single women to travel alone."

"But you'd not be alone. The children and I are accompanying you."

"Trying to reason with the wagon master was like appealing to the backside of a horse. He refused to waver."

"Then might I make an alternate suggestion?" Francis ducked his head, but not before Hope noticed his face had suddenly gone red. He twisted his hat in his gnarled hands.

Placing her hand on his arm, she smiled fondly. "What is it, Francis?"

His faded green eyes met hers. "I know I'm not nearly good enough for a woman such as yourself, but rather than giving your hand in marriage to a stranger you found in the gutter. . ." He swallowed hard. "I'd like to offer myself to you."

A gasp escaped, despite efforts to prevent it. Hope stared in disbelief at the aging servant. "What do you mean?"

"I'm asking you to marry me. Surely you see that it would be better than joining yourself to that man." He jerked his head toward the door and the lines in his face crunched together into a scowl.

"Oh, Francis." Although she knew in her heart that any marriage, to Francis or Mr. Riley, would be a farce, she needed someone who could help her build a home and get a good start on a farm. Francis hadn't lived on a farm in forty years. He would never do. But how did she tell the dear man such a thing without destroying his pride?

She lifted her gaze to his. His eyes flickered with. . .was that *anger*? Surely, she was mistaken. In his years of service, she'd never seen Francis angry. She glanced again. The careful mask of deference had returned.

"I understand, ma'am. No need for you to say anything else. I beg your pardon for forgetting my place." Giving her no chance to respond, he inclined his head and walked away.

With some regret, Hope watched the set of his shoulders. She'd wounded his pride. Thankfully, not his heart.

Releasing a weary sigh, she pressed the back of her hand to her forehead. Now what was she going to do about those twins? They'd disobeyed by going into Mr. Riley's room while she was out attending to business. She'd gone to find Mr. Dobson and pay the two hundred dollars. Otherwise, she feared the men might break in and slice Mr. Riley's throat while he slept. This was the only way to ensure he would be alive long enough to be of any service to her.

She'd long since given up on the notion of marrying for love. Her first marriage had been to a man twice her age. Her dying father's wish in order to secure her financial future—marry his best friend and business partner. A man she'd grown up calling "uncle" and his first wife "aunt" before her untimely death.

Silas had been a wonderful uncle but a not-so-wonderful husband. He was stingy and emotionally cold. She'd never fancied herself in love. But his stinginess had paid off handsomely. She now had her father's inheritance as well as her husband's, and she would never want for anything. Anything but the love of a strong, good man. Since her husband's death, she'd received gentlemen's attentions from time to time. But her bank account was the obvious draw.

Mr. Riley seemed riddled with emotional pain, and he was a drunken gambler to be sure. But, perhaps, the heart he'd shown beneath the shaggy beard and filth was as big as it seemed. If only he'd have pity on her plight and agree to the marriage. . . .

If she were a praying woman, now would be the time she'd beg for mercy. Instead, she left the prayer unsaid and simply put her hope in Mr. Riley's desire to live. If he indeed had that desire. For now, he didn't need to know he was safe from harm. He only had to realize they needed each other. She'd been used enough by men seeking her fortune. For once, she would use a man to give her what she wanted—a future for her children.

Chapter 4

The second full day Andy lay in bed, he began to shake. By the third evening, he needed a drink so badly, he clutched his bruised side and climbed out of bed in the dead of night. He tiptoed through the house barefoot in search of something to calm his nerves.

Mrs. Parker had confessed to not being a religious woman, so where was the polite drink of society? Brandy, rum, even wine? He slid his tongue across cracked lips in anticipation.

Wrapped in a blanket to cover his long johns, he shuffled through the house from room to room. After a frustrating search, he bit back a groan. Not a drop was to be found. No decanters filled with the amber-colored liquid that would make the shaking stop, the pain lessen, and the fear of death ease.

Releasing a heavy breath, he headed back to the stairs, tears of need filling his eyes. Slowly and deliberately, he climbed the steps, each foot forward sending waves of pain through his body. If only he'd found the drink, the pain would have been worth it. As it was, Andy could only keep his attention focused on the soft bed awaiting him when he reached the top of the stairs.

"Shh. You're gonna wake everyone up."

Andy's ears perked up at the whispers coming from beyond the door at the top of the steps.

"Hurry up. We ain't got all night."

Senses alerted, Andy forgot about his need for a drink. His hands stopped shaking and all of his instincts reacted to the situation.

Though he'd yet to see Mrs. Parker's troublesome son, Gregory, it didn't take a scholar to realize what was happening. The boy was sneaking out again.

In a flash, Andy twisted the knob and flung open the door.

Scrambling ensued.

"Hurry, Greg," a boy shouted and dove through the open window.

Forgetting his injuries—and his blanket, Andy hurried toward the window before Gregory could follow suit. He grabbed the boy by the collar and held him fast, despite the kicking and fighting. "Let go of me!"

"Not until you simmer down."

When Gregory landed a punch in his ribs, Andy roared in pain and dropped him to the floor. "Why, you little. . ."

EVERLASTING HOPE

Light from the full moon shone into the room, illuminating Gregory's sneer. His face twisted in the kind of look Andy's ma would have taken a switch to him for. Andy almost wished for a nearby woodshed. This child needed it badly.

"You stink, mister."

"Gregory!" Hope's horrified voice admonished from the doorway. Andy swung around, wincing, and met Hope's gaze in the dimly lit room. She stood in her robe and nightgown, a candle in her hand. Pink toes peeked from beneath her gown, and her chest rose and fell as though she'd been running.

"Oh!"

Heat crawled up Andy's neck as Hope averted her gaze and held out the blanket he'd flung off in his effort to apprehend the boy.

Taking the cover, he wrapped himself up. The pain around his middle nearly robbed him of breath and he groaned.

"Come, Mr. Riley," Hope said, her tone gentle. "Let's get you back to bed. You must be in a lot of pain." She turned to her son. "Gregory, take Mr. Riley's other side and let him lean on you if necessary."

"I ain't getting nowhere near him. He stinks like a dog." He scrunched his nose. "Worse than a dog."

Hope whipped around. "Keep your opinions to yourself and obey me immediately." Her sharp tone surprised Andy. Apparently, the terseness surprised the boy as well, for he pulled himself up off the floor and stalked to Andy's side. He glared up at him and pinched his nose.

"Don't worry, boy," Andy said wryly. "I can make it on my own."

"Good." Gregory flopped onto his bed.

Hope strode to the open window and shut it firmly. Tears glistened in her eyes.

Andy swallowed hard at the look of pain on the woman's face. The same look he'd seen on his own ma's face enough times—the look he'd caused just as Gregory was causing it now.

"You stay put," he said to Gregory. "I'm keeping an ear out for you and if I so much as hear you get up to use the privy, I'll be in here so fast it'll make your head spin."

Gregory shot from the bed. "I ain't scared of you."

Andy eyed the lad, recognizing the challenge in his stance, his tone, and the snarl marring his countenance. It wouldn't take much to put Gregory in his place. A well-aimed clap to the side of his head, a shove backward. But Andy knew humiliation would only make him more resentful.

Knowing he at least had to get his bluff in on the boy, Andy kept his tone deliberately calm and leveled a gaze at the belligerent youth glaring back at him. "I'm glad to hear that. Perhaps you'll mind your manners and obey your ma out of respect then. But just in case you're inclined to try and sneak out again, remember that just one door down is a man four times your size who will tan your hide if you try it."

"Now wait just a minute—" Hope spoke up, outrage clear in her tone.

Andy silenced her with a well-placed look and she hushed, taking a step back.

"Ma, are you going to let him—"

Holding his breath, Andy watched the conflicting emotions flash across her face. He hoped she'd trust him and back him up, because if she didn't, there was no way he could help her son.

She darted a gaze at Andy, then back to Greg. Her shoulders rose and fell with her breath, and she nodded. "Yes, I am. Now get yourself ready for bed." Her voice was stern, but Andy detected a slight tremble. "You will leave your door wide open, as will Mr. Riley. If he hears you move about, he will do as he's promised. With my blessing and thanks. Perhaps I will have one night of peaceful sleep knowing that Mr. Riley will not allow you to sneak out and roam the streets like a common hoodlum."

Gregory's jaw dropped open then he fixed a venomous gaze on Andy. "I won't try to sneak out."

"Glad to hear it. I'll say good night now." With a nod, Andy exited the room. As he shuffled down the hall, he heard Greg's voice, filled with betrayal. "Would you really let him whip me, Ma?"

"Son, I will do whatever it takes to make sure you do not ruin your life. You will be a man worthy of decent people if I have to tie you to your bed every night."

"But it ain't fair."

"Isn't fair," she gently corrected. "Fair is for children who have proven themselves trustworthy. Unfortunately, you have shown nothing but disrespect, disobedience, and you've demonstrated an utter lack of conscience in regard to the law. I have no choice but to deal harshly with you. No matter how it pains me to do so."

Andy didn't hear the reply, but before he reached his bed, he'd finally made a decision. Hope Parker was a fine woman. He had nothing to lose by agreeing to the arrangement. And, for once, maybe he could do something good for someone.

Truth be told, he missed his family in Oregon, and after witnessing Gregory's bad behavior, he felt the need to try to make it up to his ma for all the pain he'd caused her in his thirty-five years on earth. Perhaps the year spent teaching Hope and her children to farm would give him that chance. He'd marry Hope, work to make a real man of her son, and try to find a reason to live again.

✎

"Hold them steady, Greg. Those horses are going to run away with you otherwise."

"*You* hold them steady." Greg shoved the reins into Andy's hands. "Why do I have to learn to drive the wagon when I have a driver to do it?"

Andy gathered a slow breath and gave the leather straps back to Gregory. "Because, on the trail everyone has to do their share. Francis'll be driving the supply wagon, I'll be riding horseback most of the time, and your ma will be driving the other wagon. Like it or not, you're going to have to drive the third wagon. Now lace those reins between your fingers like this."

Hope watched the exchange between Gregory and her new husband with frustration. The boy simply wouldn't cooperate. And it was obvious Andy was losing patience.

They had arrived by riverboat two days ago after six weeks of whirlwind planning and packing everything they could take with them. She had left her estate in the hands of her attorney and friend, to be sold when she was settled and positive it would all work out.

They had secured a place in the wagon train, and with Andy's expert advice, Hope purchased all the supplies they would need for the trail. Now, only four days before the train pulled out, Hope's body already ached from the days of preparation and learning to handle a team of horses.

Thankfully, she'd brought Mrs. Smythe along to do the cooking. At least Hope wouldn't have to learn to cook over an open fire.

The thought of traveling two thousand miles across Indian lands and treacherous terrain filled her with a variety of emotions. Mostly fear. But a glimmer of expectancy rose when she envisioned the end of the trail, her boy growing strong and manly in a place absent the influences he so easily succumbed to in Chicago.

With only a few more days until they pulled out, it seemed as though they'd never get everything ready in time. Hope had located four seamstresses who were willing to work their fingers to the bone in order to supply them with durable clothing that would last until they reached their destination.

Hope chewed her lip at the thought of what might happen if the clothing didn't last. She had only rudimentary skills with a needle. She could fix a hem or patch a hole, but that was the extent of her talents. After all, she'd always had her clothing made for her.

Once again, she breathed a sigh of relief that Mrs. Smythe would be accompanying her on the trail.

"My hands are starting to hurt!"

The whine from Gregory brought Hope back to the situation at hand. She sighed.

"They'll callus over." Andy's stone-like face left no question in her mind that he was fed up. She knew full well most men would have clapped the boy's ears by now, but Andy hadn't raised a hand. She admired and appreciated his restraint.

But that wasn't all she admired about this man who had stood with her before a preacher only a few short weeks ago. She knew the marriage was a sham, but that knowledge alone didn't stop her heart from skipping a beat when he stood close to her.

Now that his bruises had faded and the color had returned to his face, he was more handsome than she'd dared believe possible. If she'd known what a good-looking man he was underneath the filth and swelling, she might not have had the gumption to ask him to marry her.

Even now, with his face twisted into a scowl, he cut an amazingly attractive figure as he stomped his way toward her. She couldn't help but admire him. He stood taller than any man she'd ever known, a good six-foot-three or six-foot-four, she'd guess. Being a tall woman, she was used to staring eye to eye with most men. Standing next to Andy made her feel feminine, protected almost, and she liked that feeling.

"The boy won't cooperate," he growled. "I'm wasting my time."

"I understand, Mr. Riley." And, indeed, who could blame him?

He seemed to lose his thunder before her calm response. The angry creases on his face relaxed. He rubbed his hand over his stubbly jaw. "All right. I have one more idea, but if it doesn't work, I'm through trying."

"Thank you."

Without another glance at her, he closed the distance between himself and the retreating boy in a matter of seconds. Hope strained to hear what they were saying, but it was no use; they were too far away. Her brow lifted in surprise when she saw a slow grin spread across Gregory's face. The boy hopped effortlessly into the wagon seat and grabbed the reins.

Making a mental note to ask Andy about the sudden change, she left the men to their lessons and went to find Mrs. Smythe to see what was on tonight's menu. Maybe she'd even lie down a bit before the evening meal.

She walked along the line of wagons, and her stomach twisted in excitement. So far, she hadn't thought much about what the journey might mean for her. She'd been too concerned with removing Gregory from a bad influence. But as she envisioned the lush green fields and snow-capped mountains, her excitement grew.

Perhaps the journey would be a new start for her, as well. A chance to be more than a rich young daughter, wife, or widow. Perhaps she could find something she was good at, something worthy of admiration.

Approaching her own fire, she smiled brightly at Mrs. Smythe, who unbent before the pot she'd been stirring.

"Hello, Mrs. Smythe. Supper smells delicious."

The woman met her greeting with a grim nod.

A foreboding premonition slithered through Hope, pushing her optimism into a distant memory.

"What's wrong?"

"My back's killing me, ma'am."

"Oh, Mrs. Smythe, I'm so sorry to hear that. But Mr. Riley says we'll all toughen up in a few days."

The woman shook her head. "I can't do it, Miz Parker. I hate to pull out on you like this, but I can't go to Oregon."

Swallowing hard, Hope tried to process the statement. "Wh–what do you mean? Where will I find another cook on such short notice?"

"I'm sorry, ma'am. You've been good to me over the years and I hate to let you down. But I don't want to spend my last years cutting out a new land. That's for young people, such as you and your new man. Pioneering isn't for old women like me."

"But who's going to cook for my family?" The wretched news had a stranglehold on Hope's throat and her words barely rose above a hoarse whisper.

The cook's expression softened to compassion and she patted Hope's hand.

"You're one mighty determined woman, honey. If you can pull up stakes and leave all that luxury for months on the trail when only the good Lord knows what you're going to find on the other side, you can surely learn to cook. And in the meantime, your family will just have to eat what you put in front of them until it gets better."

Tears pushed into Hope's eyes as she realized Mrs. Smythe wasn't kidding. She honestly wasn't going to travel west with her. Her gaze sought the woman, pleading for mercy.

A gentle smiled tugged at the woman's lips. "You can do it. Put your faith in God."

Hope snorted. Was God going to come down and cook her family's meals? Was He going to get blisters on His hands driving the wagon? Was He going to walk through miles and miles of harsh land? No. No more than He miraculously put a stop to her son's hooliganism.

Hope had two strong hands and a strong body to boot. She could learn to cook. She *would* learn and by the time she reached Oregon, she'd be the best cook that ever flipped flapjacks over an open fire.

Gathering her courage, she squared her shoulders and leveled her gaze at Mrs. Smythe. "Come and draw your pay. I will provide the fare for passage back to Chicago. Feel free to stay at the house until you procure other employment. I will be happy to write you a letter of recommendation, as well."

Tears glistened in the woman's eyes. Hope wrapped her arms about her.

"I feel like a traitor, leaving you like this, Miz Parker."

Hope forced a cheery tone. "Don't you think anything of it. We'll be okay."

Only a slight tremor betrayed her confidence. But Hope Parker faced what she had to face. And when things didn't work out the way she expected them to, she found another way to get what she wanted. A little snag like suddenly having to learn to cook was not going to do her in.

Chapter 5

The smell of burning meat beckoned Andy from his dreams of walking through the woods hand-in-hand with his beautiful young bride. *Yellow Bird.* Her soft, bronze skin quickened his pulse, and he pulled her against him just as a loud clanging interrupted the tender moment.

"I hate this!"

The cry of distress brought him fully awake and to the remembrance that Yellow Bird was no longer his wife. Hope was. Uneasy guilt crept through him as he dragged himself from his pallet outside the wagon opening and rubbed his eyes.

He stretched, wishing he'd been granted a few more hours of sleep. Between trying to prepare for the trek west and keeping his promise to Hope that Gregory wouldn't wander away under cover of darkness, Andy had barely slept two hours a night during the past few days. The lack of sleep was beginning to take its toll on his strength.

After taking a few moments to wake up, he joined Hope at the fire.

Smoke billowed from the skillet and Hope stood over it, waving away the thick clouds with her apron. She avoided his gaze and fanned, doing little to thin out the smoke.

"Move back," Andy instructed. Grabbing the bottom of his shirt, he used it as a glove and removed the skillet from the fire, tossing it facedown into the dirt. The smoke soon dissipated.

"I'm never going to get the hang of this cooking." Hope spewed the words rather than speaking them. She paced in front of the smoldering skillet waving her arms like a crazy woman. "We're all going to starve to death if I can't find someone to come along to cook for us."

At the catch in her throat, Andy's chest swelled with tenderness. "I don't claim to be any kind of kitchen maid, but I can rustle up bacon and eggs and some hardtack biscuits."

Hope sucked her bottom lip between her teeth and her eyes clouded with indecision. "It doesn't seem fair, with all the other things you have to do, that you should have to cook, as well."

"I don't mind." Truth be told, he'd just as soon cook the food himself and have an edible meal for a change.

Tears filled Hope's eyes and spilled over onto her cheeks. "I'm sorry, Andy. I didn't realize how difficult a job cooking could be. I just never thought about it before. Mrs. Smythe made it seem so effortless. I. . .I don't think I paid the poor woman nearly enough."

Chuckling, Andy reached out and thumbed away a tear, marveling at the softness of her skin and picking up on the fact that she'd called him by his given name for the first time in their two-month acquaintance. Hope didn't often show a vulnerable side, and Andy enjoyed it more than he would have thought possible. He was drawn to her glistening eyes, which appeared green against the backdrop of trees a few yards away. They searched his face for a moment, then clouded and looked away.

He dropped his hand. "Why don't you go and wash your face? When you come back I'll show you how to fry bacon." *Again.*

Her eyes clouded with skepticism, but to her credit, she gave a curt nod. "I'll only be a minute."

Watching her walk away, Andy's heart went out to her. He had a feeling Hope Parker wasn't accustomed to failing at something she attempted. And he had no doubt that, given time, she would master cooking as well. In the meantime, he hoped she wouldn't be too offended if he helped out. He'd cooked over an open fire on the trail more times in his adult life than he'd had a home-cooked meal.

"Oh, no. Don't tell me she burned breakfast again!"

Betsy's voice rang through the early morning air, and Andy was sure everyone in the camp heard the little girl's cry. He hurried to the second wagon and snatched her up, pulling her through the opening in the canvas before she could embarrass Hope any more.

"Hush, Bets. You want the whole camp to hear you?"

"Did she burn the bacon again?" Her tone, though decidedly softer, was just as filled with disappointment and dread. "I'm sick of burned food. I hate it."

Andy brushed a finger across her perky little nose and gave her a stern frown. "Your ma's trying her best to learn how to cook, so you show her some respect."

"Yes, sir," the little girl mumbled.

"Now take that skillet and wash it out for me. Then I'll cook us up some crispy brown bacon that will melt in your mouth."

"You're going to cook?" Betsy asked, her eyes clouded in skepticism.

"Yes, little missy, I sure am."

Emitting a long-suffering sigh, she shook her head. "I'm going to starve before we get to Oregon," she muttered, picking up the skillet and heading to the bucket of water.

Watching her go, Andy grinned and grabbed a few potatoes from the bin in the first wagon. His moving around awakened Billy. The little boy sniffed the air and gave a sleepy moan. "Ma burned breakfast again. I'm not getting up."

"Yes, you are," Andy said firmly. "And don't let me hear you saying anything to make her feel bad about it, either."

The boy sat up, his brown hair sticking out from his head like a scarecrow's arms. Andy couldn't hold back a smirk.

"What?" Billy asked, frowning.

"Make sure you take a comb to that hair before you come outside." He grinned at the boy. "Looks like you've been running in a stiff wind."

Andy walked back to the fire. Betsy had returned with the scrubbed skillet, but Hope was nowhere to be seen. Figuring she must not want much of a cooking lesson, he went ahead and started breakfast. They had a full day ahead of them—the last day before pulling out in the morning.

He sliced some bacon and, while it cooked, he peeled and cut up the potatoes. After the bacon was done, he set it on a separate dish and kept it near the fire so it wouldn't get cold. Then, he set the slices of potato into the popping bacon grease to cook. He stepped away from the fire and folded up his pallet. He set his blankets inside the wagon shared by Francis and Gregory. The old driver's bed was empty, but Gregory's snores nearly shook the wagon.

"Time to get up, son."

Receiving no response, he reached in and shook the boy. "Let's go, Greg."

The figure beneath the quilt sat up.

Andy sucked in a breath to discover Francis had been sleeping beneath Greg's covers.

"What are you doing?" he demanded of the older man.

"I would think that's painfully obvious," Francis retorted in his habitual manner of showing contempt for Andy. "I was sleeping and now I'm waking up."

Ignoring the condescending tone, Andy motioned toward the other berth. "Where's Greg?"

"How should I know where the boy is?"

"You're using his blanket."

The surprise on Francis's face couldn't have been feigned as he glanced down at his covers. "He must have laid this over me and snuck away." A chuckle rumbled the man's chest. "A bright idea."

"Yeah, the kid's a regular genius," Andy muttered, feeling like an idiot for thinking the two of them had reached a sort of understanding yesterday.

He stalked back to the fire. "Betsy, keep stirring those potatoes so they don't burn. If your mother comes back, tell her I went looking for Greg."

"That won't be necessary, Mr. Riley." Hope's accusing glare accompanied the icy tone of her voice. Greg stood beside her, disheveled, and, clearly, he'd been in a scuffle. His eyes spit rebellion; his expression dared Andy to do something about it.

Snatching Greg by his collar, Andy yanked him away from his mother and walked him back to the wagon before Hope could recover and protest. He picked him up by his shirt and belt loops and tossed him inside. "Get cleaned up and be ready for breakfast in ten minutes. We have a full day's work ahead of us."

"You can't tell me what to do!"

"Yes," he said pointedly, "I can. Francis will stay here to keep an eye on you until you're dressed." Turning to Francis, he gave the servant a look that clearly warned him not to argue.

Greg glared, all the camaraderie of the day before gone from his demeanor. Andy felt like a fool. The lad had obviously been building his confidence so he could sneak off when Andy's guard was down. And it had worked. He must have slept harder than he'd realized. And the boy had taken full advantage of it.

Stinging with wounded pride, he walked back to the fire. Betsy still stirred the potatoes, which were now a ball of mush, but at least they weren't burnt and, therefore, were edible.

He took over and spooned the potato glob onto another dish. He set Betsy and Billy to cracking the eggs into a bowl while he scraped the potato remains from the skillet. When breakfast was finally ready, the fare included cold bacon, mushy potatoes, and scrambled eggs.

Andy found himself unable to meet Hope's gaze. He knew he'd let her down, and he felt the weight of regret knot inside his gut. All she'd asked of him was that he help her get to Oregon and protect her son. He couldn't bear the thought of seeing disappointment in one more person's eyes.

Would he ever do anything right?

❧

Hope couldn't contain her tears as she scrubbed the egg-crusted skillet. Perhaps she was making a mistake after all. It wasn't too late to pull out and go home. The wagon train was due to move out first thing in the morning, but things were looking pretty bleak for Hope. Confusion twisted her stomach into knots.

The twins were beside themselves with excitement and would be crushed if she turned back. But Gregory had already found trouble. Even in a new town. Would this be his pattern forever? Did it really matter if they moved two thousand miles away from the influences of Chicago? Apparently, bad boys were drawn to each other without any rhyme or reason.

If Gregory was going to draw those sorts of influences no matter where they went, what was the point in putting herself and the twins through the hardship? This latest development with Gregory, coming on the heels of Mrs. Smythe's resignation, had crushed what little optimism Hope possessed.

The fact that she was a miserable excuse for a cook had stolen all of her confidence. Despite all evidence to substantiate the wretched truth of the matter, she had trouble wrapping her mind around the fact that her cooking was inedible. Hope Parker did *not* fail. She did whatever it took to succeed. So this lack of culinary ability bit her to the core. No matter how hard she tried, she just couldn't seem to get the hang of it. She wiped the skillet dry and hung it on a peg on the outside of the wagon. At least she could wash a dish. That was something, anyway. Though she had to admit she didn't much care for the chore.

Wiping her palms along the sides of her skirt, she glanced about the camp. White tents sat alongside wagons and small fires smoldered as the campers prepared for their final day before they officially became emigrants. In the wagon directly next to theirs, a young bride blushed at something her gangly husband whispered in her ear from behind. She shooed him away, feigning offense. The young man grabbed her wrist and pulled her toward him. The bride gave up all pretenses and melted against him.

Hope bit back a smile and averted her gaze to give them privacy. Young love such as theirs had eluded her. And now, she was in the second loveless marriage of her own choosing. Pushing down the melancholy, she steeled her heart against an onslaught of emotions. She had entangled herself legally in a marriage of convenience for Gregory's sake. What sort of fool was she to think that the boy would make a miraculous turnabout just because she'd sacrificed?

Climbing into her wagon, she sat at the edge of her berth and looked around the cramped quarters—her home for the next five months. She buried her face in her palms and tried to focus her raging, conflicting thoughts into something concrete. A plan of action. That's what she needed. And it had to be fast.

She had two choices. Sell the wagons and supplies she'd purchased and go back to Chicago on the next steamer up the river. Or forge ahead with her plans and hope for the best where Gregory was concerned. The choices made her head spin.

She still couldn't believe the boy had slipped through Andy's fingers last night. She knew it wasn't her husband's fault. The poor man had barely slept in weeks in order to keep Greg from sneaking out and running away as he'd threatened when he discovered Hope's plans.

She had to admit, Andy had more than paid back the measly two hundred dollars she'd paid to get Mr. Dobson to call off his thugs.

With a rise and fall of her shoulders, she considered her actions over the past weeks. What sort of a fool married a stranger and paid him to stay married to her? Especially when it appeared Gregory would be no better off, despite the two thousand miles separating him and the bad influences awaiting him back in Chicago.

Perhaps she should allow Andy an annulment and take the children and head back to Chicago. Standing, she tied the makeshift cot to the wall and started to climb down. A warm hand on her back startled her, and she let out a screech.

"Take it easy," Andy's voice broke through her panic. "I was just going to help you down."

Heat suffused her cheeks. "Wh—where's Greg?"

"Working the team with Francis."

"I'm glad you came back, Mr. Riley. . ."

"Are we back to that?"

Frowning, Hope tipped her chin and met his gaze. "What do you mean?"

The soft brown eyes twinkled as they stared down at her. "You called me Andy earlier. I thought maybe we were dispensing with formalities."

"Oh. I. . .I suppose that would be all right. Except that. . ."

He cocked an eyebrow. "Except what?

"I was actually just about to come and find you."

A valley formed between his eyes as he scrutinized her. "Come here." His hand wrapped hers easily in its warmth, and he led her to the bench he'd crafted the first day in camp. They sat. Keeping her hand firmly in his grasp, he demanded answers with his gaze.

"I think I made a mistake coming here." Unable to bear the intensity of his questioning gaze, she stared at their clasped hands and cleared her throat. "I. . . um. . .I just think that we might all be better off if I just go back home."

His eyes narrowed. "What are you getting at?"

"Just what it sounds like. I've decided to take my children home. You're welcome to the wagons and supplies. It's the least I can do after all your help."

"What about the bad influences you were so concerned about?"

Hope chilled to his mocking tone. Her defenses rose. "Apparently Greg will find trouble no matter where he goes."

"Maybe. Maybe not." He dropped her hand. "I don't guess I can blame you. I didn't keep my end of the bargain."

Self-condemnation burned in his eyes. Hope touched his arm. "I didn't mean that. You've done remarkably well these past weeks. Sometimes you just can't run away and expect things to be any different than they were in the first place."

"I didn't figure you were running away so much as breaking a path for your children to have a better life." He captured her gaze. "I admired you for it."

And now he doesn't.

"Thank you, Mr. Riley. I'm sorry to destroy your admiration, but I see no point in uprooting the twins for a child who will most likely not change despite my efforts."

He stood and nodded. "I can see your mind's made up so I won't try to hold you. But I think you're making a big mistake. A lot can happen to change a boy in five months. I think it'll do Greg a world of good. But you're his mother. I'll start packing the gear and I'll let the wagon master know we won't be traveling with the train in the morning."

Watching him stride away, Hope pushed aside a sudden rush of doubt. Depression settled over her as she began rifling through her belongings, separating the items to keep and those they would resell.

It was for the best.

Chapter 6

Andy tethered his horse to a hitching post a full block from the saloon entrance. His throat thickened as he fought an inward battle. A battle he'd thought was over weeks ago. Now it raged with a ferocity that left his gut quivering, his hands trembling as he clenched and unclenched his fists.

For the past two hours, he'd wandered through streets, on horseback, trying to find a reason to turn around and ride back to the wagon train without giving in to the temptation.

He wiped his parched lips with the back of his hand, anticipating the warm feeling of liquid amnesia. He hadn't touched the stuff since Hope had pulled him out of the alley. Once the shaking stopped and the cravings dulled, he'd had the fortitude to vow never to touch another drop. But that was when he had another purpose in life. Now that Hope and the children were leaving for Chicago, what reason did he have to keep walking the straight and narrow?

Back at the campsite, he knew the pioneers were making last-minute preparations. Excited children were being put to bed by equally excited parents. All but one family who, instead of preparing for tomorrow's adventure, was spending one more night in the wagon train and would board a steamer in the morning to head back up the Missouri River. The thought sent daggers of regret through him.

Disappointment propelled him, once more, toward the sound of the out-of-tune piano music accompanied by raucous laughter. The kind of laughter born, not of humor, but of the desperate need to laugh rather than cry. Because once the crying started, there was no stopping it.

He hesitated and stared again at the swinging doors. His emotions and desires played a tug-of-war with reason and good sense.

The last few weeks had changed him. He could admit that. When Yellow Bird died three years ago, life lost all meaning. Hope and her children had redefined that meaning. For a little while.

This morning, stark reality came flashing back to him. Reality that nauseated him. Made him want to slam his fist into a wall to let out some of his frustration. Failure seemed to chase him like a wolf after a rabbit.

Perhaps he could turn his luck around once he arrived in Oregon. Back home where, hopefully, his ma and brothers hadn't forgotten about him. Tomorrow he would begin the trek west.

At Hope's insistence, he'd accepted the wagons and supplies as payment for his help over the past few weeks. Payment. Andy's bitter laugh raised a curious glance from a passing cowpoke who was headed into the saloon—no doubt to spend every penny of his hard-earned salary.

Andy hadn't needed payment. Hope had saved him, married him, and for a while had given him a glimpse of a new life. If either of them deserved some kind of payment, she did. Now, because he'd failed to keep his promise to protect her son, she was leaving him. He'd never see Billy and little Betsy again. Even Gregory, as much as he frustrated Andy, had found a spot to call his own in Andy's life.

Tentacles of pain once again clutched Andy's heart, tearing away the last of his resolve. With purpose, he stepped toward the doors.

"Pa!"

He jerked around just as someone slammed into him. Scrawny arms gripped him around the waist and held him tightly.

"Greg?"

"Help me, Pa! Don't let them take me."

Andy glanced up to see the sheriff striding toward him, lines of anger etched in his face. Dread burned inside of him. What had the boy done now? "Why aren't you at the wagon train looking after your ma?" Carefully, he set Greg away from him.

"Why aren't you?" Greg shot back.

Heat burned Andy's neck, but he had no time to set the lad straight. "What seems to be the problem, Sheriff?"

"This your son?" The sheriff gave them both a dubious once-over. Andy could only imagine what a contrast they made in appearance. With his dark blond hair and hazel eyes, Greg didn't even come close to resembling Andy.

"By marriage," he replied truthfully.

The man nodded. "Well, I'm afraid he'll have to come with me."

"What are the charges?"

"Stealing. And I caught him red-handed so there's no point in telling me I've got the wrong boy. The other two got away, but this one was right there with them."

"Don't let him take me, Pa. It ain't true."

"Be quiet, Greg!" Thankful that he wasn't trying to think through a whiskey-induced fog, Andy searched his mind for a solution to this predicament. He grasped Greg's upper arms and forced the boy to look him in the eye. "First thing we're going to do is go with the sheriff so I can get to the bottom of this."

Fear flashed across Greg's face. "My ma ain't going to like that."

"Well, your ma ain't here," Andy retorted. "I am. And I'd rather go to the sheriff's office than stand out here on the street and tell the whole town about your thieving. I think your ma would be a sight more ashamed of that. Lead the way, Sheriff."

Once they reached the jail, the sheriff opened the door and stepped aside so Greg and Andy could precede him into the building. "I'm going to have to lock him up." He grabbed a large metal key and Andy heard the sound of metal clanging upon metal then the barred door opened.

"No! You can't put me in jail!" Greg latched onto Andy. "Don't let him put me in there. Please. I'll do anything you say."

Andy's throat grew thick from concern and disgust. The boy was acting like a papoose. Worse than a papoose. Most Indian babies were disciplined early on. Greg desperately needed to be taught a lesson. Disentangling himself from Greg's grasp, he nodded to the sheriff.

"Let's go, boy."

Greg backed away, his eyes wild with fright. Andy's heart went out to him, but he knew there was nothing he could do. The boy had to learn about consequences. Reaching around, he gripped Greg's arm. "Take it like a man," he said quietly.

Angling his head so that he looked up into Andy's eyes, Greg fixed him with a rage-filled glare. Raw hatred that clearly blamed Andy for the mess he was in. He jerked his arm free and sauntered into the cell. "My ma'll get me out by tomorrow anyway, then we're headed back home."

"Don't count on it, son." The sheriff banged the cell shut.

"Care if I have a word with you outside, Sheriff?" Andy motioned his head toward the door.

The sheriff nodded. Once on the boardwalk, Andy studied the lawman. "What did the boy do, exactly?"

A heavy sigh passed through the sheriff's lips. "I caught three of them sneaking out of Gray's General Store."

Relief sifted through Andy. Anything the boys had stolen from a store could be returned to the owner. "I'd be happy to see the boy returns anything he took."

"I wish it were that easy." Shaking his head, the man leaned against the building. "Somehow those boys found out that Mr. Gray keeps a locked box of cash in a secret space under the counter. Mr. Gray claims there was over a hundred dollars in the box."

"What about the other boys?"

"I didn't catch a good look at them. I got ahold of your son in there, but the others took off lickety-split. They took the box."

Andy's heart sank. "What'll happen to the boy?"

"The judge should be through in the next couple of weeks, and he'll most likely sentence him to a juvenile reformatory somewhere."

"A reformatory?" Andy had heard about boys who went to the so-called "houses of refuge." Generally, children came out worse than when they entered such a facility.

"Be glad he has that option. Otherwise he'd go to prison along with grown men."

"There's no way you can drop the charges?"

He scratched at the stubble on his chin. "Mr. Gray is madder than a wet hen. Unless he drops the charges himself, my hands are tied." He nodded across the street to the sign indicating the store. "You're free to try to reason with him, seeing as how young your boy is and all. Wouldn't hurt to give it a shot. Just knock on the front. He lives in the storeroom."

"Thanks. I believe I'll do just that." Andy shook the sheriff's hand and said good-bye. A scowl crunched his face as he walked across the street. If the boy had to rob a store, couldn't he have used good sense and picked one that wasn't across from the sheriff's office?

He knocked on the door. No one answered, so he knocked again. With more force.

"Who is it?" The gruff voice came from within, but Andy couldn't see into the darkened store.

"Name's Andy Riley."

"Store's closed. Come back in the morning."

"Actually, I came to talk to you about one of the boys who robbed you tonight."

Silence ensued until the key slid into the door, and a bell dinged as the man opened up. "Did the sheriff find my money?"

White tufts of hair stood out from the middle of the man's head where his hairline receded. The wrinkles on his face pinched together in a scowl that Andy couldn't quite begrudge him. After all, when a man had been robbed, he had a perfect right to be angry. But Andy hoped reason might prevail over anger.

"The only boy he caught didn't have it on him."

"Well, at least one of those hooligans will spend a good long time locked up for stealing in the first place. Maybe that'll be a warning to the rest of his friends." He swiped his gnarly hand over his hair. "Not that that does me much good."

"Mr. Gray." Hoping to appeal to the man's sense of reason, Andy latched on to his last statement. "That's exactly the point I'd like to make. My boy isn't the only one involved and he doesn't have any of your money. His mother is leaving for Chicago in the morning and would be heartbroken if forced to leave her boy behind."

"Just what are you getting at?" Deep creases formed between the man's eyes. "You want me to drop the charges?"

"I'd be obliged. We can assure you that Greg won't be around town to do you any more harm."

"But that still don't get me my money back." He shook his head. "No. The boy's got to learn a lesson."

"What if restitution were made?" Andy swallowed hard. How would he come up with a hundred dollars? His mind shot to the saloon. A few good hands might do the trick. But could he really risk it when he only had ten dollars to his name?

"Well, now. I might be inclined to talk to the sheriff if I had my money back in my hands by morning."

Despite the hopelessness of the situation, Andy found himself promising to repay the full amount by the time the store opened the following day. He shot a glance toward the jailhouse then headed that way, determination guiding his steps. Before he came up with a plan to get that money, he and Greg were going to come to an understanding.

$\sim$

A gray dawn followed a sleepless night for Hope. She'd watched Andy ride away from camp at sundown, but hadn't seen him return. Her heart sank to her toes as she surmised where his destination most likely had been.

After seeing Gregory safely tucked into bed with Francis's promise not to let the boy out of his sight, she had retired, as well. Her mind swam with possible futures. What if she did return to Chicago and Gregory was worse than ever? What if he straightened up and decided he'd caused her enough grief? What if she went on to Oregon? Would he be a changed boy by the time they arrived? Or would he be worse than ever?

An even worse scenario presented its horrifying image sometime near dawn. What if they were attacked by Indians and the whole wagon train was murdered and scalped. What sort of mother took her children across two thousand miles of rough terrain and hostile lands? On the other hand, what sort of mother took her troublesome son back to Chicago where he most certainly would reconnect with his bad friends?

"If You could give me some sort of sign about what I should do, maybe I'd believe in You," she whispered into the darkness of her canvas home.

A knock outside the wagon startled her, and she felt like she'd been caught stealing. She shook her head at her foolishness. She'd actually said a prayer.

"Just a moment," she called, reaching for her wrapper. When she was decent, she opened the flap. Her heart reacted to Andy's presence standing tall and handsome outside of her wagon. Gregory stood next to him. "What are you two doing together?"

"The boy has something he'd like to say to you."

"What is it, Greg?"

His face reddened considerably and he swallowed hard. Andy nudged him. "Go on."

"I. . .I just wanted to say I'm sorry for all the. . ." He paused and leaned toward Andy. Andy turned his head away and whispered. Greg nodded. ". . .grief I've caused you in my young, miserable life."

He paused again. Andy whispered again. Hope felt a giggle coming on and fought hard to suppress it.

Greg cleared his throat. "I appreciate the sacrifices you've made to make me straighten up." Pause. Whisper. Nudge. "And I think I would become a much better citizen if we go to Oregon like we planned."

Fighting hard to keep her laughter at bay, Hope regarded her son evenly. "Are you sure this is what you want, Greg?"

The boy scowled. Andy cleared his throat. Loudly. "Yes, Ma."

"It's not too late?" She turned the question to Andy.

"All the supplies are still here. The only thing is that I'm going to help drive the wagons instead of riding horseback."

"What will you do with your mount?"

Greg and Andy both stared at the ground. Now it was Andy's turn to pause. He scrubbed at the perpetual stubble along his jaw. "I. . .uh. . ."

"He sold it, Ma."

A gasp escaped Hope's throat and she looked from Greg to Andy. "But why?"

"I can't share my reason, Hope. You'll just have to trust me that I didn't get into trouble. I didn't lose it in a game or sell it for the same purpose."

He gazed at her with such earnestness that Hope couldn't question him. She decided to trust her husband. Whatever he'd done to convince Greg to straighten up had been brilliant. The boy looked more subdued than she could remember in a very long time.

She smiled at her son, and then Andy. "Well, I'd better get dressed. We have a long day ahead of us. I suppose you'd better give me that cooking lesson after all."

"My pleasure." His smile reached his eyes, making Hope's pulse race.

Flustered, she averted her gaze. "F—fine. I'll be out in a few minutes."

Without waiting for a response, she dropped the flap. A smile curved her lips as she hurriedly donned one of her new, serviceable gowns. "Wake up, sleepy-heads," she called to the twins. "We're going to Oregon today!"

Billy raised his head and gave her a sleepy look. "Did you forget? We're going back to Chicago."

Ruffling his head, Hope laughed out loud. "No, I didn't forget. Our plans have changed back. We're going west. So get up so we can start the day."

Billy whooped and jumped up. "Betsy! It worked! We're going to Oregon.

It really worked!" His exuberance overwhelmed him and he flung himself into Hope's arms. She laughed.

"What worked?" she asked.

"The reverend said if we prayed and it was God's will for us to go to Oregon that God would talk to your heart and make you think it was your own idea."

"Oh, the reverend did, eh?" Indignation rolled over Hope, smothering her sudden joy. "Well, just remember it's okay for people to have their own beliefs."

"Yes, ma'am. And I believe God is sending us to Oregon just like we prayed!"

"And Ma thinks it's all her idea, just like the reverend said she would." Betsy hopped up and joined her brother's antics, jumping around the tiny space. "It's a sign!"

A sign? Hope suddenly felt cold and hot all at the same time. What had she prayed only a few minutes earlier? *If You could give me some sort of sign about what I should do, maybe I'd believe in You.*

Jerking her chin, she pulled at her hair, setting it into a firm knot at the top of her head. "And maybe I will."

"What?"

She glanced at her bewildered twins. "Never mind. Get dressed and meet me outside." She crawled toward the flap then turned back and grinned. "Today we go to Oregon!"

Chapter 7

The excitement of pioneering wore off before the first exhausting week on the trail came to an end. Now, several weeks later, the thought of spending every day for the next four months staring at the backside of a horse seemed intolerable. Cruel, in fact.

Furthermore, despite Andy's assurance that she would grow accustomed to the rigors of the trail, her screaming muscles contradicted the promise with every movement. She woke each morning with knots of pain in her legs and arms.

But she would have gladly endured whatever hardships were demanded of her if only she didn't have to cook. Not only was she a complete failure at the task, she hated every second of it. There wasn't one thing she could fix that her family deemed tasty. Indeed, her efforts were met with dread and disgust. But who could blame them?

More often than not, it was Andy who—under the guise of giving a cooking lesson—prepared the meals. This was the bane of her existence. As if the layers of dust weren't bad enough. At the end of the day, she had the humiliating experience of the entire camp witnessing her failure.

But today, she was determined not to focus on the negative issues like trail grime and bad cooking. The wagon master had presented the pioneers with an unaccustomed reprieve from the monotony of life on the trail, and she had every intention of enjoying a few hours of relaxation.

Last evening, the wagon train veered off the beaten path, camping only two miles from a small town. Though the wagon master usually stayed clear of settlements, he announced his opinion that the little band of emigrants needed a change of pace. The travelers heartily agreed and began preparing for a day to explore the countryside or roam the town.

To Hope, neither roaming nor exploring held any appeal. She'd decided to spend the day resting. She allowed Andy and the children to gallivant while she stretched out on her berth and rewarded her aching muscles with some much-needed relaxation.

The stillness of the camp was broken only by the occasional lowing of cattle or the sound of industrious men making repairs to their wagons or reinforcing axles. In the distance, she heard the strumming of a guitar accompanied by soft singing. The gentle strains lulled her to a semi-conscious state. And soon she submerged under a veil of dreamy darkness.

Tap tap tap.

Hope woke with a start and sat up quickly. Sleep-induced confusion caused her to blink and glance around the wagon, wondering why on earth she was sleeping in the heat of the day.

Then it came back to her. She stretched and smiled in guilty pleasure. The last time she'd slept in the middle of the day, she'd been ill with a raging fever.

Tap, tap, tap.

Now fully awake, Hope glanced toward the flap. "Yes?"

A woman's voice penetrated the veil between them. "Mrs. Riley?"

The name never failed to give her pause. Could she really claim the title of Mrs. *anyone* when the marriage was a sham?

"Just a moment," she called. She pulled on her boots and smoothed her hair then tied up her berth and opened the flap.

"Oh." The sight of a much-too-thin, middle-aged woman with haunting blue eyes met hers. "Can I help you?"

"Are you Mrs. Riley?"

"Yes, but I'd prefer to be called Hope."

The woman smiled, revealing the absence of several teeth. "Hope's a nice name. I'm Lucille."

Hope took the woman's proffered hand, finding herself relaxing and returning the woman's smile. "I've never seen you around before. Are you traveling with the wagon train?"

"No, ma'am." She ducked her head. "But I'd like to. That's what I've come to see you about."

"Let me climb down from here and maybe you will start from the beginning."

Lucille moved aside while Hope exited the wagon. Hope smoothed her skirt and smiled at the woman. She motioned toward the bench next to the wagon. Once they were settled, she turned to Lucille. "Now, what makes you think I can help you?"

Twisting her hands together, Lucille took a few deep gulps of air. Finally, it appeared she had gathered enough courage, for she met Hope's gaze, entreaty clear in her eyes. "My husband has been gone now for about three months, may he find peace for his wretched soul. I'm having a terrible time making ends meet in that one-horse town."

"I'm so sorry for your loss," Hope said, covering Lucille's hands with her own.

"Don't be sorry. I knew it was only a matter of time before he cheated the wrong man. If you want to know the truth, I'm surprised he lasted this long."

Taken aback by the woman's icy stare and equally cold tone, Hope raised her eyebrows and stared back. "What is it you think I can help you with, Lucille?"

The question seemed to bring the woman back to the present. Her words burst from her, and she squeezed Hope's hand so tightly, Hope was afraid a couple of fingers might pop right off.

A sob escaped Lucille's throat and tears glistened in her eyes. "Oh. I have to get out of this town. Start a new life somewhere. When the wagon train stopped only a couple of miles from town, I thought perhaps the good Lord had finally heard my prayer. But the wagon master won't let me come along. I have plenty of cash for supplies."

Hope nodded. "Let me guess, he told you no women are allowed to join the wagon train unless they're married."

"Yes. And marriage is obviously out of the question."

"I understand exactly how you feel, Lucille. But I still don't see what I can do."

Lucille gathered a slow breath and fixed Hope with a frank stare. "The wagon master said I might ask you for employment in exchange for a place to sleep in your supply wagon. I can provide my own supplies, but not a wagon."

"What sort of employment are you seeking?" Humiliation began deep inside Hope and released in the tone of her voice. She knew exactly what sort of employment the wagon master was referring to.

The woman's scarlet face attested to the fact. "I'm handy in a kitchen." She smiled. "Or over an open fire."

Fighting between two emotions—indignation that the wagon master had dared bring attention to it and relief that help might have arrived—Hope scrutinized Lucille momentarily, then nodded. "Tell me about yourself."

～

Andy frowned as he stood a little ways off from the creek and watched the children squealing and splashing about the water—all the children except the Parker children, that is. Gregory had no interest in cooling off in the creek with the rest of the children, so he'd left the boy repacking the supply wagon, putting new supplies in the back, and bringing the older goods forward.

The twins sat glumly on the bank, legs crossed, chins resting on fists as they observed the merriment. Finally, unable to endure the curiosity a moment longer, he slipped from his clandestine position and strode to the bank.

"Why aren't you two swimming with the others?"

Billy angled his head and looked upward at Andy, his eyes squinting in the brightness of the late afternoon sun. "We can't."

"What do you mean? Did your ma tell you to stay out of the water?" If so, Andy would go and have a talk with her. One thing he admired about Hope was her ability to be reasonable.

"That's not it." Betsy scowled up at him, as though he were a dolt for not knowing exactly what Billy meant.

"What then?" Squatting down next to them so that they didn't have to crane their necks to see him, he tugged one of her braids.

"We can't swim."

"What do you mean you can't swim?" He and his brothers had learned to swim about as early as they learned to walk. He couldn't fathom a circumstance whereby a child wouldn't know such a basic skill.

"We never went swimming."

"Well, it's time you learned, then." Andy hopped to his feet. "Let's go."

Unabashed joy shone in both sets of eyes. "You mean it?" Betsy squealed, jumping from the ground.

"I sure do."

Billy's eyes clouded. "Ah, we can't let you teach us to swim in front of all the other children. They'll laugh at us."

Andy saw their dilemma. "It's all right. We'll go down from camp a ways."

Betsy gasped. "Captain Jack said we're not to walk away from camp because of redskins."

A grin threatened Andy's lips. "Tell you what. I'll protect you if we see any Indians, okay?"

Truth be told, he had seen signs they were being followed for the past week, but felt certain it was more out of curiosity than a threat. If they'd wanted to harm the wagon train, the Indians would have more than likely attacked days ago.

But doubt persisted in Betsy's eyes.

"We won't go far," he promised. "We'll stay where we can see the others, but far enough away where they won't know I'm teaching you to swim. How's that sound?"

A slow grin split her face. "Okay."

Both children were quick studies and before long had the basics down enough for Andy to retire to the bank to dry off while he kept an eye on them. Affection stirred inside his chest as he watched them splashing and listened to their giggles.

"There you are."

Andy turned at the sound of Hope's breathless voice. The circles that had darkened the skin beneath her eyes had faded a great deal, and he returned her relaxed smile.

"You seem to be feeling better."

"I took a long nap, I'm ashamed to say."

"Nonsense. Today was for doing whatever you wanted to do. I'd venture to say the sleep did you a world of good."

She nodded. "I think so."

"Hi, Ma!" Billy called from the water. "Watch me swim!"

A gasp escaped Hope's throat. "They're swimming?"

Andy's lips twitched. "What did you suppose they were doing out there?"

"Wading." She tossed the one-word answer without taking her gaze from the children in the water. "Bravo, Billy. That's wonderful."

"Watch me!" Betsy piped in, never one to be outdone.

"My, you both are quite the wonders, aren't you?" She clutched the neck of her dress and lowered her voice. "Are you sure they know how to swim well enough to be out that deep?"

Hearing the nervous tremor while she tried so hard to be brave for the children, Andy placed his hand on her shoulder. "Do you think I'd endanger their lives?"

She turned to him. "No. I suppose not."

"I'm fond of those youngsters of yours. You can trust me to do my level best to see nothing bad happens to them."

Almost as though she did it without thought, Hope reached up and covered his hand with hers. "Thank you, Andy. I do trust you with them. Greg's been doing so well and the twins love you as though you were their real. . ." Her words faltered and she snatched her hand away. "I'm sorry."

"For what?"

"Forgetting the true nature of our marriage for a moment. It's better if the children don't love you, isn't it? Considering the circumstances."

For an instant, Andy wasn't so sure. Family life was beginning to grow on him, but he wasn't sure if the settled-down sort of existence his brother Michael lived was something he could take day in and day out. He glanced at his bride. As much as he admired her spirit, he knew that was as far as it went. Every time he thought of her in terms of a wife, he remembered his beautiful Indian bride, and Hope paled in comparison. As unfair as it was to compare one woman's appearance with another's, he couldn't help himself.

She met his gaze and her cheeks flushed. Andy's stomach dropped as he realized from the flash of hurt in her eyes that she had a pretty good idea where his thoughts had been. She cleared her throat and abruptly focused her attention upon the children in the water.

"Billy. Betsy. Come on out of the water now and get dried off. Supper's about ready."

"Supper?" Andy couldn't help the surprise in his tone. "You didn't need my help tonight?"

She looked stung as she turned back to him. "No. I've hired a cook. A widow from town. She's all alone and needed a means to join the wagon train. I felt it a good solution. And I know the rest of you will agree. Apparently, my plain looks aren't the only thing that make me undesirable as a wife. But at least you and the children won't have to endure my ineptness any longer."

"Hope, I'm sorry I hurt your feelings."

Turning her full body to face him, she met his gaze, her face expressionless except for her eyes. After years of associating with thugs, gamblers, drunkards, and thieves, Andy wasn't accustomed to such unabashed honesty, and her frank stares never failed to unnerve him.

"I am well aware of my shortcomings, Andy. I know that I am not beautiful, or even pleasant to look at. I know that I am a failure at learning to produce an edible meal. But I am not a fool nor am I a silly schoolgirl, so you needn't worry about hurting my feelings. I'm not in love with you, and I'm perfectly content with our arrangement."

At a loss for words, Andy watched her whip around and stomp back toward the campsite. He grinned in spite of himself. He surely had that tongue-lashing coming.

But she was wrong about one thing. . .he found her pleasant to look at. She wasn't beautiful in the obvious sense, but she was attractive in her own right. Especially when her eyes flashed in anger such as they had a moment ago, or in merriment, which was more common. Her figure wasn't bad to watch, soft looking in all the right places. She could stir a man's blood. As he followed her with his eyes, he suddenly wondered why she didn't know that.

What sort of man had married her and led her to believe she wasn't desirable? He knew he had no right to wonder such a thing. But the thought stayed with him through the children's lively chatter as they walked back to the campsite.

The sound of her laughter reached him before he saw her, and he inwardly mocked himself for worrying about her. Apparently, she wasn't wasting time pining away over whether or not he thought her desirable.

"Who's that?" Betsy asked. Andy's gaze followed hers to a woman standing over their fire.

"Your ma hired her to do the cooking." Feeling disloyal to Hope, he clarified. "She needed a place to stay on the wagon train, so your ma decided to offer her a position in exchange for a place to sleep in the supply wagon."

Betsy and Billy exchanged looks of wonder.

"What?" Andy asked, curiosity aroused by their subdued attitude.

"It's another miracle," Betsy breathed out in a barely audible tone.

"Yeah," Billy replied, his tone echoing his sister's.

"What sort of miracle?" Andy couldn't resist a chuckle. The twins had made no pretense of their desire for more palatable meals.

"We prayed for someone to do the cooking."

Gooseflesh rose on Andy's arms and the hair on the back of his neck lifted. A chill crept up his spine and he shivered. "You mean you prayed your ma would learn to cook?"

Billy shook his head. "No, sir. We figured it'd be easier on God if He just sent a whole different person to cook like Mrs. Smythe used to do."

"What made you think to pray about something like this?"

Betsy grinned, her eyes bright with infectious excitement. "We figured God worked it out fine for us to come west. So we hoped maybe it was His will for someone to come and cook for us."

"So you prayed for God to let us come west, then you prayed He would send a cook?"

"Yep," Betsy said, her braids bouncing around her shoulders as she gave a vigorous nod. "And would you just smell that? What is it, Billy?"

"I can't tell. But it sure smells like something good."

"Let's go find out how long before we eat."

Without so much as a good-bye, the twins ran off, leaving Andy to ponder whether the newest member of their company was a pleasant coincidence or the result of children's faith.

Chapter 8

Hope stood in the creek ankle deep, scooped up water, and rubbed it over her face and neck, enjoying the coolness after an unseasonably warm day for May.

What a relief it had been not to have to bear the indignity of her disastrous attempts to produce something edible. The children were certainly grateful. Betsy had even insisted upon saying grace. Apparently, the twins had decided that this would be a new occurrence at mealtimes.

Hope grinned into the night. She could indulge them that much. Whether Lucille's presence was a result of divine intervention or merely a welcome coincidence, Hope couldn't have been happier to have the burden lifted from her shoulders.

Lifting her skirt to her knees, she waded another step into the water.

"You scared me to death, woman!"

Hope screeched as Andy's angry voice and the sound of boots splashing into the water broke her solitude. He grabbed hold of her arm and walked her from the water, none too gently.

"Let me go! How dare you?" She jerked away, scowling at him in the pale moonlight.

He matched her, glare for angry glare. "Didn't you hear the captain's orders not to leave the campsite?"

"If I'm not mistaken," she pointed out, "I am precisely at the location where you brought my children today for a swimming lesson."

"That was different."

Jerking her chin, Hope dropped to the ground and grabbed her stockings, her anger outweighing modesty at the moment. "I fail to see how."

Andy sat next to her, drawing a heavy breath. "For one thing, it was daytime and we were within sight of the camp. For another, I was with the children to protect them in case Indians showed up."

She pulled her boot on and reached for her other stocking. "Well, you needn't be concerned about me. I can protect myself."

"Oh, really?" He leaned in dangerously close. "And how would you do that? I don't see a gun."

Hope's heart picked up at his uncomfortable nearness. Her hands shook as she slipped on her second boot. Suddenly conscious of her hiked-up skirt, she stood, letting it drop to the tips of her boots. She cleared her throat, aware that he was still waiting for an answer.

"Well, I don't know exactly what I'd do until I'm faced with the situation. But don't worry, I think quick on my feet."

Andy stared up at her from his spot on the ground. "Do you?" In one swift movement, he reached and snagged her behind the knees. Hope's arms flailed wildly as her legs shot out from beneath her. She gasped, landing hard on his lap. Strong arms encircled her.

Andy's warm breath tickled her face. She gulped, unable to move. Not sure she even wanted to.

"How would you protect yourself in this situation?" he asked, his voice husky, sending tingles down her spine.

"I. . .I don't know. I have to be on my feet t–to think quick." The absurdity of her own statement combined with the nerve-wracking closeness pulled a giggle from her throat.

He chuckled then grew serious as his gaze swept her face, resting on her lips. And almost before she knew what was happening, his head swooped downward. Warmth flooded her as his mouth took hers, all at once gentle and demanding.

New sensations coursed through Hope. She'd been kissed before, of course. But never like this. Conflicting emotions warred within her until finally she melted against him, matching him kiss for kiss. When his hands moved up her back, she suddenly came to her senses and dragged her mouth from his.

"Stop," she whispered.

"We're married, remember?" His impassioned tone was nearly her undoing. "We've both been married before." He moved forward to reclaim her lips.

Hope flattened her palms against his chest. "I said stop."

To her relief, he didn't try to hold her. She stood quickly. Turning toward the water, she drew in deep gulps of air in an effort to compose herself. Her lips still tingled, and she swiped at them with the back of her hand.

Andy gave a short laugh. "That bad, huh?"

She turned back to him. "I don't know what you mean."

"Wiping away my kiss?"

More likely wiping away the unsettling effects of his kiss.

He climbed to his feet and stood close. Her insides quivered with his nearness.

His warm hand covered her shoulder and she closed her eyes, pushing back the impulse to lean her cheek against it. "I'm sorry I forgot myself for a few minutes. I guess I just wanted you to know that I find you to be a desirable woman."

"Oh, I see. So you only kissed me to make me feel better?"

He narrowed his gaze. "First you get upset with me for kissing you, and now you're upset because I apologized? Make up your mind, do you want my kisses or not?"

"I don't need a man to kiss me because he feels sorry for me."

"That's not why—"

Giving him no chance to finish, Hope went on as though he hadn't spoken. "Our marriage is one of convenience only. I paid your debtor and you made it possible for me to go west and make a new life for Gregory and the twins. There is nothing more to it than that."

Indeed, she couldn't allow her heart to become any more invested than it already was.

A sardonic grin twisted his lips, and he made a lazy sweep of her figure with his eyes. "It seems to me that you're getting a lot more out of this bargain than I am. A marriage, a man's help on the trail, and a full year's worth of work once we get to Oregon. That's an awful lot for two hundred dollars."

Her face flamed and she was glad for the cover of darkness. "The deal seemed fair enough when your neck was on the line. Now you want to go back on your word?"

His lips twitched. He reached forward and stroked her jaw line with his index finger. "Not go back on, maybe just renegotiate our terms a bit."

Realizing he was teasing her, Hope jerked her chin, temper flaring. "Fine. When we get to Oregon, I'll give you an increase in salary."

He chuckled and dropped his hand. "Not exactly the kind of reward I was hoping for."

"Too bad. That's the only kind you're getting."

A twig snapped close by and Hope froze. Andy put his finger to his lips, his other hand going to his holster.

Her mind spun with the fearsome images of marauding Indians. Though the Indians were peaceful for the most part, it didn't take much to set them off. A misunderstanding. An unintentional insult.

The biggest threat seemed to be in the manner of petty inconveniences. Running the horses off during the night, stealing livestock, begging for food. These things could be easily dealt with. But who knew what a group of warlike Indians might do to a couple of pioneers caught alone in the night?

Another twig snapped and Hope's mouth went dry. Andy slipped his gun from the belt. Hope heard it cock.

"Don't shoot," a nearly panicked voice called from the bushes.

Relief washed over Hope. "Gregory, what are you doing?"

He stepped out from behind the bush. "Is it true?" By his accusing tone, Hope realized he had heard the entire conversation.

"Did you only marry her for money?" He spat the words at Andy.

"I guess you heard something you shouldn't have heard, son." Andy's tone remained calm as he studied Greg, obviously expecting the worst.

His expectations were justified as Greg sneered, leaning toward Andy, challenging him. "I'm not your son."

"Greg. Watch your tone. Whether Mr. Riley is your pa or not, he's still your elder."

He turned on her, his eyes flashing anger in the moonlit night. "You paid him to marry you?"

Standing beneath her son's disgusted gaze, Hope felt small and ashamed. And even more so when he continued his discourse. "You're no better than those women. . ."

Andy stepped forward in a flash and snatched Greg's arm. "Watch yourself, boy. I won't be held responsible for what I do to you if you finish that sentence."

Watching the exchange between the two, Hope felt like weeping. Greg and Andy had come such a long way in the past weeks. She had witnessed Greg slowly change from a bitter, rude boy to a hard-working, swarthy young man with a daily sense of purpose. Had one unguarded moment ruined all of his progress? Her heart sank to her toes at the very real possibility.

As Greg and Andy stared at each other, Hope knew that neither would back down.

"Gregory, I will not stand for you speaking to me in such a disrespectful tone. I know you're angry and shocked by what you've learned. But I want you to know, I had my reasons for doing this."

A sneer marred his face. "Because you couldn't—"

Andy stepped in once more. "Boy, you don't learn very fast, do you?"

In a nightmarish second, Greg took the initiative and stomped down hard on Andy's moccasined toe.

Andy roared in pain and grappled to regain his hold on the boy. But being adept at getting himself away from the authorities, Greg darted out of reach and ran toward the campsite.

"I'll go after him," Hope said, unable to meet his gaze.

She started to sweep past him, but he reached out and took hold of her arm. "Hope."

Suddenly weary, she released a heavy sigh. "Yes, Andy?"

"He's just a boy. He doesn't know what he's saying or understand our kind of arrangement."

"I know. Thank you for championing me. But I don't need protection from my own son. Furthermore, I am capable of meting out my own discipline."

Despite his look of astonishment, she forged ahead. "As we've reestablished this evening, our marriage isn't real. Therefore your claim to my children is not that of a father, but more like a hired hand. It isn't your place to manhandle them when they are disobedient."

His jaw tightened and he released her arm, his eyes hard as glass. "Whatever you say, boss." He tipped his hat and walked away in the opposite direction, his jerky gait evidence of his anger.

Hope straightened her shoulders. She could only go after one of them and Greg was her boy. There was no question. A twig snapped in front of her. She smiled and turned toward the sound. "Greg, I'm so glad you came back."

But the figure that stepped from the shadows wasn't Greg. She took one look at the long black hair and high chiseled cheekbones and felt the scream at the back of her throat. His hand shot out and covered her mouth before she could make a sound.

It took Andy a full hour to cool off from Hope's admonishment. He supposed it was the only logical approach to the issue of discipline, given the fact that he would be leaving after a year. It wouldn't do for the children to grow accustomed to him only to watch him leave and never return.

As much as he hated to admit it, Hope was right. He owed her an apology as much as Gregory did. He hadn't treated her with any more respect than he would have treated one of the women Greg had likened her to.

He strode back into camp long after all but the sentry fires had been doused. Making his way first to Gregory and Francis's wagon, he peeked in and nodded in satisfaction as two distinct tones of snoring were heard. At least the boy had learned enough not to run off alone on the prairie. He reached inside and grabbed his bedroll, then let the canvas lower once more.

He glanced at Hope's wagon, thought to check on her and the children, but decided against it. Let her get a good night's sleep. He'd apologize in the morning.

Memories of holding Hope in his arms assailed him as he tried to drift to sleep. Many women had come and gone for a brief hour or two above one saloon or another since Yellow Bird's death, but none had taken her from his mind. Not for one second.

His eyes popped open as he realized the woman he'd been kissing had actually been Hope. Not some figment of his tortured imagination. He wasn't sure what that meant. But there was no time for him to ponder the ramifications as Betsy's voice called to him.

He sat up and looked to the wagon she shared with her mother and Billy.

Placing his finger to his mouth, he stood and strode to the wagon. "What's wrong, sweetheart?"

"Where's Ma?"

"What do you mean? Isn't she sleeping?"

"She never came to bed."

"Are you sure? Maybe she just had to take a trip to the woods."

The little girl was shaking her head before he finished his thought.

"Her berth is still tied up. That's how I know."

Unease gnawed Andy's gut. But he patted the little girl's head, trying not to show his worry.

"Go back to sleep. I'll find her."

After Betsy was settled back into bed, Andy turned around, trying to decide his course of action. Self-condemnation screamed at him. If only he hadn't walked away from her before seeing her safely back to camp.

His mind moved toward two possible conclusions. One, she'd lost her bearings and wandered in the wrong direction. Two, the Indians he'd witnessed following the wagon train from time to time over the past days had recognized an easy target.

He'd get her back. But at what cost?

Suddenly he felt alone. Responsible. The fate of this woman—his wife—was in his hands. If he didn't bring her back, three children would be left alone in the world with a man who was to blame for their mother's fate. The weight bore down upon him, and he suddenly lifted his face skyward, remembering a long-forgotten friend.

"God in heaven," he prayed, knowing there was no time for excuses. "I don't deserve anything from You. But there are a couple of youngsters here who believe You can do miracles. If that's true, and I'm not saying whether I think it is or not, but if it is, I'm asking You to do a miracle now. Because that's the only way I'm going to be able to bring Hope back to her children."

Chapter 9

Hope's head felt like it might burst any second if she wasn't allowed to sit up soon. She'd been slung facedown across the back of a horse for what seemed like hours. Fear, combined with the trail dust, made her throat and mouth so dry, she had no saliva with which to wet her lips or tongue.

Dawn was beginning to break when they finally halted. Hope could only imagine the number of miles the group had put between themselves and the wagon train. Had they discovered she was missing yet? Would anyone come after her, or would they believe her to be dead?

Just when she thought the Indians planned to leave her on the horse while they rested, Hope felt a rough hand on her back, dragging her across the saddle. She landed hard on her feet, stumbled back, and hit the ground with her backside. The fierce-looking band of warriors laughed uproariously.

Too miserable to be humiliated, Hope scowled as her gaze took in the five bronze-skinned men. "Go ahead and laugh," she barked. "If you'd been flung across a horse all night like a dead animal, you'd have a hard time standing up, too." She swallowed hard. "I need some water. Or do you plan to let me die of thirst?"

The warrior who had kidnapped her came forward and shoved an army canteen toward her. "White woman not die."

Hope accepted it gratefully and tipped it up in her hands that were still bound together at the wrist. Her throat closed up and she choked, spewing water out at her captor. He snatched the canteen from her hands. She gasped and sputtered, trying to apologize through her coughing so the Indian wouldn't take a tomahawk to her skull.

When she regained her composure, she ventured a glance at the man. He scowled and offered her the canteen once more. Deciding to leave well enough alone, Hope shook her head.

He tossed her a slice of dried meat. Her stomach lurched at the thought of eating, but she knew from the lectures the captain had given that Indians took a dim view of spurned gifts. So she nodded and yanked off a chunk with her teeth.

Emboldened by her captor's kindness thus far, Hope found her voice to ask the question screaming in her mind. "What do you intend to do with me?"

"White woman mine."

She gulped hard, swallowing the rest of the bite. "What do you mean?"

"Need squaw."

Outraged, Hope struggled until she stood. "A squaw!" Her temper flared at the man's audacity. "You intend to make me a squaw?"

The warrior thumped his chest. "My squaw."

"Never!" She stomped her foot, eliciting a round of laughter from the other braves.

He stood, barely meeting her eye to eye. For the first time ever, Hope was grateful for her uncommon height. "You my squaw!" He clapped his hand firmly on her shoulder and shoved her back to the ground.

She glared back at him, too angry to care about using good sense. "I'm no man's squaw. I am, however, another man's wife. And I have three children who need their mother."

He thumped his chest again. "Five sons. No mother. You be new mother. Have new children."

Tears pricked her eyes as she saw her new future looming before her. "Please. I already have a husband. Surely a man as—as handsome as you can find a nice Indian woman among your own people who would be pleased to marry you and be a mother to your sons."

A scowl twisted his face. "You."

"I—I will never surrender."

"Then I beat until you do."

She set her shoulders and fixed him with her gaze. "Then you will beat me every hour of every day until you succeed in beating me to death."

Fierce anger flashed in his black eyes and a vein enlarged at his temple. Just when she thought he might strike her, commotion from the other side of the camp arrested his attention. Hope followed the sound with her gaze. Her stomach flip-flopped at the sight of Andy, flanked on either side by two warriors. He stood tall and proud, and only his tight jaw betrayed his tension.

"I've come to reclaim my squaw," he announced. Hope's heart leapt. Funny how angry she'd been when the Indian had called her his squaw. But when Andy did it, she kind of liked it. And despite their precarious position, Hope felt butterflies swarm in her stomach at the thought of truly belonging to her handsome rescuer.

Her captor, the one who had claimed her, stepped close to Andy. "I take woman."

Andy sized the little man up. "And I'm taking her back."

"Your squaw?" he asked, jerking his thumb toward Hope.

"Yes."

"Then why you sleep on ground?"

Hope gasped. They'd been spying long enough that they knew of her sleeping arrangements?

"I like sleeping under the stars. My wife prefers a comfortable bed in the wagon."

The brave shook his head. "I think squaw too much argue. You sleep outside so no have to listen."

A slow grin spread across Andy's mouth. "I see she's already given you the sharp edge of her tongue."

The Indian looked back at Hope, then folded his arms across a burly chest and faced Andy. "I trade her."

"I have one horse to trade. That's all."

"No, one horse not enough."

The brave reached toward one of the men holding Andy's arms. The Indian handed him a knife that Hope recognized as Andy's. Andy had been quite proud of the ivory-handled knife.

"Horse and knife for squaw."

Without hesitation, Andy nodded.

The Indian turned and stalked toward her. He jerked her to her feet and slashed the leather bindings from her wrists. He gave her a shove and she landed hard against Andy, who immediately encased her in the circle of his arm.

"Are you all right?" he whispered against her hair.

She nodded. "Are they going to kill us?"

"No. But we best get moving anyway. Indians have been known to change their minds."

While the Indians admired the knife and horse, Andy and Hope slipped quietly away on foot.

⁓

Weary and dirty, Hope and Andy walked into camp by suppertime the following night. A cheer rose up from among their fellow travelers, and the three Parker children raced to their mother's side. "I knew you'd be okay, Ma!" Betsy proclaimed.

A tired smile curved Hope's lips. "You did? Let me guess. You prayed."

"That's right."

"I have to admit, I was doing a bit of that myself."

"But you don't believe in praying."

"Some events in a person's life lend themselves to hoping there is a source of power greater than oneself."

Greg jerked his head toward Andy. "He found Ma," the boy said to the twins. "Not some God."

Andy stepped forward. "I admit that I said a prayer of my own. There's not much of a chance that I could have tracked five Indians in the dead of night and found them by morning."

Andy smiled down at Betsy and Billy. "You two keep on praying for your miracles. Seems like whatever you're doing, you have the Almighty's ear."

Captain Jack came forward and stuck out his hand. "Good to have you back. I did as you asked and didn't send out a search party. But we would have by daybreak if you hadn't shown up."

"I'm obliged to you. I wasn't sure how many, if any, were watching the wagon train, just waiting for the majority of the men to ride off looking for Hope. They might have attacked and taken a lot more than just one woman."

"Well, I'm glad everything worked out the way it did." The captain looked up. "Everyone try to get plenty of rest tonight. We've lost an extra day and will push harder the rest of the week to make up the lost time."

Andy followed Hope and the three children back to their campfire.

Lucille stood beside the fire, a relieved smile widening her mouth. "I'm pleased to see you made it back with your scalp, Mrs. Riley."

"Please, Lucille," Hope said, dropping wearily onto the bench. "I've asked you to call me Hope."

"Yes, ma'am. Now, you sit yourself down and relax. Supper is just finishing up and I'm going to pour you a nice hot cup of coffee."

"Thank you."

Andy watched Hope in concern. She appeared to be on the verge of tears. He debated whether to step forward and pull her into his arms, but before he could make a move, the twins sat on either side of her.

"So how'd Andy get them to let you go, Ma?" Greg asked.

"Gregory," Andy admonished. Did the boy have any sensitivity at all? "I don't think your ma really wants to talk about it."

"It's all right. Andy traded me for a horse and a knife." Her flat statement narrowed Andy's gaze.

"You mean the ivory-handled knife?" Greg asked, turning accusing eyes on Andy.

"Yes, that's the one. And considering that it was your fault your ma got captured in the first place, I figured you'd be more than happy for me to trade it."

"Sure," Gregory muttered. "I guess this means the deal is off."

Hope glanced from one to the other, her brow furrowed. "What do you mean? What deal?"

"Andy was supposed to give me that knife if I behave myself on the trail and do my chores and don't try to run away."

"I see." Hope's cold gaze studied her son. "I'm sorry to disappoint you."

Gregory's face grew red. "I didn't mean—"

Her expression softened and she reached up and took his hand. "I know you didn't. But just the same, when we arrive in Oregon, I'll order you a knife as close to that one as we can get."

Gregory shook his head. "It's okay, Ma. I don't need one." He slid his hand from hers and backed away. "I got chores to do."

Andy watched the exchange and his optimism grew concerning Gregory. Perhaps the boy had the makings of a man after all. And he liked to think he might have had something to do with that change over the past weeks.

He sought Hope's gaze to see if she recognized the boy's step forward in maturity. The eyes that looked back at him were far from warm. They were downright frosty, in fact.

Taken aback by her hostile attitude, Andy excused himself and headed for the creek to clean up before supper. Who knew the mind of a woman? Save her from a band of Indians, lose your best knife and one of Captain Jack's horses doing so, and she gave you the kind of look that clearly said you did something wrong.

❧

Hope waited until later, when she was safely tucked away inside the wagon, before she allowed the tears to fall. Andy had flat out told Captain Jack not to form a search party for her? That she wasn't important enough to risk the wagon train for?

Her heart had nearly broken at his words and even now, the memory squeezed her heart.

They might have attacked and taken a lot more than just one woman. Just one woman.

Is that all I am to you, Andy Riley? Just one woman?

From the moment he'd so bravely strode into camp and demanded her release, Hope had known she was hopelessly in love. All day, she'd wanted to tell him so, to ask him if he might consider making their arrangement permanent. After all, even if he wasn't in love with her, his kisses the night before had proven that he did care for her—at least that's what she'd thought.

Oh, how glad she was that she hadn't made the offer. . .hadn't begged him to be her real husband. What a fool she'd been to think that just because a man held her close and kissed her like he meant it, that he wanted more than a simple night in her bed.

Hope swiped at the tears flowing down her cheeks and made a firm decision. Never again would she forget the arrangement. She alone was to blame for the kisses the night before.

Andy must have been picking up on little lovesick signals for days or even weeks. It was only natural he'd respond to them. But no more. From now on, she would treat him like Francis or Lucille. Just another hired hand.

Just one woman. She was just one woman in a crowd to him.

Swallowing another sob, she turned over and buried her face in her pillow.

She would never make a fool of herself again. When the time came for him to leave, she'd let him go. That was the bargain, and she'd never forget it again.

Chapter 10

Hope and Andy settled into a silent agreement. There were no kisses, no talk of their marriage or disciplining the children. Day after day, life became about moving forward. One step and then the next and the next, with the promise that, one day, they'd step forward and their feet would land in Oregon.

The rest of the spring passed with little incident, but by mid-July, mishaps began to befall the weary band of pioneers. Wagon wheels broke, axles wore out, and almost daily, the wagon train was forced to halt for a couple of hours while repairs were made.

Stock died from the rigors of the trail or lack of water. Some were run off by Indians. Not one family among them had been unaffected by some calamity.

Water had to be rationed, and many times, a full day would pass without a drop of water to moisten parched throats. During such times, doubts assailed Hope. Had she brought her children to the wilderness to die?

The days were endless, and Hope slept restlessly at night, always fearing lest a band of marauding Indians attack while they slept. Her clothing hung from her, until she looked like a child playing dress-up in her mother's gowns. She'd become so thin, even Andy had expressed his concern.

Toward the end of July, Captain Jack announced that they were finally past the halfway point. But before their cheers had died down, the first case of cholera broke out, bringing with it swift death and constant fear.

Quickly, the disease spread, and the wagon train was halted daily for burials. In the first week, two children, one father, and the elderly reverend and his wife succumbed. Still, the wagon train buried the dead and continued on, leaving the bereft with little time to grieve. There was no time to wait out the illness. They had to reach Oregon before winter, or they might not arrive at all.

Hope bargained with God. *Keep my children safe, and I'll believe in You.* It had worked once before. The first time, she'd asked for a sign and somehow she'd found herself on the trail. And if the truth be told, she wanted to believe. She needed something to believe in. Needed to know there was a benevolent God who loved her children more than she did. A God with the power to keep them safe. Alive.

She knew she hadn't lived a righteous life—not like most of the women in the group—so she figured she'd need to resort to negotiating. She was good at negotiating. She'd gotten her trip to Oregon by bargaining with Andy. And her bargain with God had solidified it. She hoped against hope that this one would pay off for her, as well.

But it wasn't to be. Gregory failed to show up to breakfast one morning and, with dread, Hope made her way to his wagon. She climbed inside, fearing what she might find.

He trembled beneath the quilt. "I have it, Ma." His voice was so quiet, Hope had to lean close to hear, but she knew it was no use asking him to speak up. He had no strength even to speak.

"I guess you do, Greg." She tucked his blanket closer about his shoulders. "But you'll be okay."

Shaking his head, he turned soulful eyes on her. Pleading eyes. Defeated eyes. "I'm going to die for all the bad things I done, Ma."

Tears burned Hope's eyes. She smoothed back his hair. Against convention, he'd been following Andy's example and was growing it out. His blond tresses now fell almost to his shoulders.

"Gracious, son," she said, forcing a cheerful tone, "your hair is about as long as Andy's."

A weak smile tugged at his lips. He nodded. "I wish I'd been nice to him. Andy's a good man."

"Yes, he is."

"I'm glad you married him."

A sob caught in her throat and she forced it back. If she hadn't married Andy, Gregory wouldn't be lying here, possibly dying.

"He taught me a lot, Ma."

She wished he'd stop talking like it was over. As a matter of fact, she was going to put a stop to it this instant. She hadn't brought her son across hundreds and hundreds of miles to save him from thugs, only to see him die of cholera. She wouldn't stand for it.

"Now, listen to me, young man. You are going to fight this sickness. Any boy who can sneak out in the middle of the night, carouse all night, and run from police has the gumption to lick this disease. Do you hear me?"

His eyes were closed. He hadn't heard. Hope's stomach lurched and her heart nearly stopped at how deathly pale he looked. She placed her hand on his chest and breathed a relieved sigh when it rose and fell.

But how many times would it do that before the ragged rise and fall ceased altogether?

"Is Greg sick, Mama?"

Panic shot through Hope at the sound of Betsy's voice. She turned on the child. "Get out of here. Do you want to get sick?" Her sharp tone sent a wave of shock across Betsy's face, and the little girl retreated quickly.

Hope sat back onto the wagon floor, hands in her lap, and wept. She prayed through great gulping sobs, pleading with God for her son's life.

The wagon lurched forward, and the new day began. Resentment burned inside of Hope. How dare they move on when Greg was sick? When *her* child walked a fine line between death and life.

Greg spent the day in and out of sleep. Hope left the wagon only to empty the waste bucket along the trail. The heat inside the cramped space was stifling and by the time the wagon stopped at noon, sweat dripped from her chin and stained her armpits and chest.

She glanced up dully when the canvas flap opened.

"Hope." Andy's voice was firm, but gentle. "Come out of that sickly air. I'll sit with him for a while."

She shook her head. "He needs me."

"So do Betsy and Billy."

Fear clutched at her. "Are they sick, too?"

"No. But *you* will be if you don't take better care of yourself." He reached for her. "Come on. At least eat a bite of lunch and have a cup of coffee."

Hope nodded. "Just until we start moving again."

Andy held her hand and steadied her as she climbed from the wagon. Rather than take time for a full meal, Captain Jack had instructed the travelers to keep lunch simple and eat what didn't have to be cooked. Hope gnawed on a leftover biscuit and stared vacantly into the fire, her mind focused on her son.

"Ma?" Betsy sat next to her on the bench. Absently, Hope slipped her arm about the child's shoulders and pulled her close.

Betsy snuggled closer. "I'm sorry for making you mad earlier."

"Oh, honey. I'm sorry for hollering at you. I just don't want you catching your brother's sickness."

Betsy laid her cheek on Hope's shoulder. "You don't have to be afraid. Greg's not going to die."

"I hope you're right, Bets." She stroked the girl's braids. "All we can do is hope for the best."

"I dreamed he was real sick, but that he didn't die."

"When?" Hope pulled Betsy around to face her.

With wide, innocent eyes, the girl regarded her. "Right before I woke up."

"Today?" Hope's pulse picked up. If that were the case, Betsy would have had the dream before anyone knew Greg was ill.

"Yes. That's what I wanted to tell you. In my dream, you kept giving Greg lots and lots of water to drink. And after awhile he got better."

A shiver began at the base of Hope's spine and traveled quickly up her back. She shuddered and kissed Betsy hard on the head. "Thank you, sweetie!"

Hope shot to her feet and hurried to the wagon.

It seemed reasonable that if Greg was losing fluid from his body he would need to replenish it. Thankfully, they'd camped near a creek for their noon stop. They could fill extra pots with water before they headed out. It might not stay cool, but it would replace the fluids he was losing. Was this another miracle brought about through the twins' faith? She hoped so, more than she'd ever hoped for anything in her life. When she reached the wagon, she threw open the flap.

"Andy, I know what we have to do."

When Gregory emerged from the wagon weak, shaky, and pale, but alive nonetheless, the entire wagon train exploded in applause. Of all those who had come down ill, he alone survived.

In all, ten adults and fourteen children, including one newborn, had succumbed. Now, a week after Gregory's recovery, no new cases had been reported and cholera had finally run its course and moved on.

The pioneers breathed a collective sigh of relief. And for nearly a month, it appeared the face of God smiled on them.

The distant mountains loomed before them as a promise, calling to the weary travelers, "Don't give up. Keep coming. It's been hard, but you've made it this far. Once you make the final climb, you'll enter your valley, your fields, your rivers and streams. Your promised land."

By early September, the breathtakingly beautiful mountains suddenly were no longer a distant goal, but a very real danger. As they ascended, jagged edges, slippery, snow-covered slopes, and near blizzard conditions made for slow going. Some days they traveled no more than a mile or two. But they pressed on, the air charged with determination. They hadn't come this far, lost stock, keepsakes, and for some, loved ones, only to fail. The trail down the mountain was even harder. Oxen and horses were walked down while wagons were lowered down by ropes.

Along with the change in scenery, Andy noticed a change in Hope. Serenity, reminiscent of his mother, radiated from her. When the children bowed their heads to say grace, she folded her hands and prayed along with them, not by way of humoring the twins, but in sincere thanks.

Gregory, too, seemed to have found comfort in faith since his close call. There was no denying the boy had changed. He worked willingly and swiftly. His face lit with an almost constant smile, as though he had a secret pleasure. Andy almost missed the incorrigible Gregory, the one who had made Andy feel as though Hope needed him. Now the boy was downright docile. Obedient. Good. And determined to become a preacher some day.

All this change made Andy uncomfortable. He hadn't counted on his new little family getting a dose of religion en route to their new home. Religious women made Andy nervous. Would Hope still be willing to keep to the bargain?

Now that home was only a couple of weeks away, Andy was having second thoughts about introducing Hope and the children to Ma.

Ma would take them into her heart before he finished the introductions. How could she help it? How could anyone not love the Parkers? *No, not the Parkers,* he reminded himself. They were his family. They were Rileys now.

"I was getting worried."

Hope's gentle voice broke through Andy's thoughts. He smiled. "Our worries are over now," he answered.

"Are they?"

Her tone held a serious note that he wasn't sure he could address just yet. There were too many questions floating through his own mind. Questions only he could answer. So he gave her a grin and pretended she meant physical worries. "Sure they are! We're safely over the mountains and in a few days, you and the children and I will veer away from the wagon train and head toward Hobbs, where my family lives."

"How long do you think it will take to file a claim and get our home built?"

"To tell you the truth, I have my own land already. I thought we'd build there."

"Oh, Andy, no. I can't take your land. You might want to build a. . .a home of your own, someday."

Her indomitable spirit gripped him. Andy observed her face, red from the sun and wind and cold. Now that they were on the other side of the mountains the weather was mild once more, but the harsh conditions had taken their toll on Hope. "If anyone deserves that land, it's you. I'd be pleased to give it to you and the children. I was never cut out to settle on a farm."

She lowered her gaze, but not before Andy noticed the disappointment flash across her face.

"Hope. . ."

Looking him full in the eye once more, she nodded. "It's all right. We had a bargain. And you have kept yours so far. I won't try to hold you past winter."

"But what about spring planting and harvest?" Andy's brow furrowed.

"You were right, Andy. I asked much more of you than you received payment for." She smiled and shame filled Andy as he remembered the night he'd tried to share her bed. She didn't dwell on that subject, but moved on. "Between Greg and me and perhaps a hired hand or two, we should be fine." She gave him a self-mocking smile. "If worse comes to worst, we wouldn't absolutely have to farm. I have plenty of money to last us. And my investments in Chicago are more than secure."

"Then why even bother? It's a rigorous life."

A shrug lifted her shoulders. "The Bible says hard work builds character. Or something like that."

"You have more character than anyone I know." The compliment flew from Andy's lips before he knew it was coming.

"Thank you, Andy. That means so much to me to hear you say that." She smiled and touched his arm. "But I am thinking more of my children. In the city, Greg got into trouble because he didn't have enough to occupy him. Coming to Oregon won't do anyone any good if I repeat the same mistakes I made in the first place."

"Greg's not the same boy he was when you left Chicago."

"Thanks be to God."

"Yeah," Andy muttered.

"And thanks to you, too. You taught him so much."

And it had been his pleasure. The boy was his one accomplishment, except now Hope was giving God the credit for the lad's change in behavior.

"Well, Lucille says supper is going to be ready in just a few minutes. That's the main reason I came looking for you." She turned to walk back to the circle of wagons then swung back to face him. "And Andy. If you meant it about the land, I'd be proud to build my home on your land. I just need to know. . ."

Andy tensed, afraid the question might be whether or not he intended to share in their life from time to time. The question frightened him, because where he'd once known for certain that he had no intention of returning once he left, now he wasn't so sure. "What do you need to know?"

"I just. . . Well, do you want me to pay you for the land?"

Outrage filled Andy's chest and he scowled deeply. "Of course not. You're my family!"

A gasp escaped her lips before he realized what he'd implied.

"A–all right, Andy. Thank you, then. We accept your kindness."

She spun around and hurried away, leaving Andy to wonder why on earth he'd blurted such a fool thing. How had this gone from a business arrangement to the desire to provide for this family? His family.

He kicked a rock across the ground and headed in the direction Hope had taken. For the first time, he began to see the seriousness of bringing home a family to meet Ma and his brothers. They wouldn't understand the bargain. They wouldn't understand when he rode away.

Andy clenched his fist. They would be disappointed. But they didn't know the loss he'd endured. A loss so devastating, there was no way he could risk that again.

He had to keep his heart in check. To love as deeply as he'd loved Yellow Bird and his tiny daughter had nearly destroyed him. Never again. He pushed aside the longing and gathered a long, full breath in order to strengthen his resolve. Never, ever again.

Chapter 11

The children's excitement was palpable as the town of Hobbs came into view. Hope's anticipation matched theirs, but anxiety slowly replaced her eagerness as she observed the neatly put-together townswomen walking along the boardwalks.

For the first time in months, Hope wondered about her appearance. Her mirror had long since broken, but she could only guess what a spectacle she made. How on earth could she possibly meet Andy's family in this condition?

"What's wrong?" Andy placed his hand on her arm.

"Oh, nothing."

It never failed to amaze Hope how intuitive Andy could be at times. A wave of sadness washed over her. He had the potential to be a wonderful husband. But she'd resigned herself to the situation.

Andy took both reins in one hand and slipped his other arm around her. "Something's wrong. If it's about my family, you have no reason to worry."

He released a shaky laugh, and Hope realized for the first time that he was nervous about seeing them again. "Believe me, they'll love you and the children. I'm the one who's likely to get a thrashing from one or both of my brothers and a sharp tongue-lashing from my ma, and possibly my niece, since I didn't bring her another Indian doll."

"Well, you deserve it for not coming home in five whole years."

With a chuckle, Andy gave her an affectionate, one-armed hug and returned the reins to both hands.

Hope released a heavy sigh. "I just feel so. . ." Loath to whine about something as trivial as the need for a bath and a new dress, Hope left the sentence open and averted her gaze to the dusty street.

"I understand."

In a few moments, the wagon pulled in front of a large two-story home. Andy hopped down and reached for Hope.

"I thought your family lived on a farm."

"They do. It won't hurt us to take an extra day to bathe and sleep in real beds before we go out to the farm."

Tears of relief stung Hope's eyes. "Do you think there are enough rooms available?"

193

"Only one way to find out." He winked and strode up to the front door. A few moments later, the dowager who came to the door had agreed to rent them two rooms for the night. Baths and supper cost extra. But Hope gladly paid for them all.

Francis had chosen to hook up with a small train headed to California and was no longer with the little family, so Gregory and Billy shared a room; Hope, Lucille, and Betsy occupied the other. Andy declined the invitation to share the boys' room.

"Where will you sleep?" Hope asked after he'd carried in her necessities for the night.

"I figure I'll look up my brother Hank and bed down at his place. Unless you think the parsonage might cave in if such a sinner slept in one of its rooms."

"Don't be silly." She smiled fondly at him. "Thank you for being so thoughtful, Andy. I'm looking forward to being clean."

He nodded. "Will you be all right for the rest of the day and evening? Or should I come back and take you to supper? There's a restaurant down the street."

Hope wished he had come out and said he'd be back to take her to supper. She would have loved the opportunity to share their supper together in Andy's hometown. But he apparently had other things on his mind.

"We'll be fine. I imagine we will take our supper here at the boardinghouse."

The process of bathing was a slow one. Water had to be heated and tossed out after each bath because the grime was so thick.

Mrs. Barker, the woman who owned the boardinghouse, obviously begrudged them every single bucketful, though she did seem pleased with their ability to pay for each bath.

By midafternoon, they were all clean and infinitely more comfortable than they'd been in months. When a knock sounded on the door, Hope assumed it was Mrs. Barker announcing supper, but a lovely woman stood there. She smiled, her green eyes twinkling in merriment. Several garments were slung over her arms.

"Hello. You must be Hope."

"Why, y—yes, I am." Clearly the woman had been sent. "What can I do for you?"

"My name's Rosemary. I'm a friend of Andy Riley's brother Hank. Andy mentioned you might be needing some gowns. I just happen to own a dress shop. Isn't that a happy coincidence?" She gave a merry laugh.

Hope smiled. "It's wonderful."

The woman's friendly smile widened. "May I come in?"

"Please do." Hope opened the door further.

"Thank you." She walked to the bed and dumped the entire armload.

"I'm afraid I don't have anything for a child," she said, giving Betsy a worried frown.

Betsy's face drooped. "That's okay, ma'am," she murmured.

Hope smiled. "May I procure your services, Miss Rosemary? We all need new clothes."

"Yes, you may. It just so happens that I am fresh out of orders for now."

"Ma..."

At the sound of Billy's dread-filled voice, Hope smiled.

"Run along and find your brother." Relief washed his features.

Hope and Rosemary exchanged grins. It didn't take much to figure out the boy had dreaded the thought of being forced to stay in the room.

After he disappeared through the door, closing it behind him with a loud bang, Hope turned to Rosemary. "Maybe you can take Betsy's measurements while you're here and make her the first dress. Let's see, we'll need at least two serviceable gowns for Lucille and myself. And a couple of Sunday dresses each. W—will that be enough, do you think?"

The woman flashed a dimple, and Hope had a momentary spark of longing. Why couldn't she be beautiful like other women? Would Andy think Rosemary was lovely?

If he did, who could blame him?

The woman gave her an innocent, wide-eyed look and such a genuine smile, Hope felt foolish for her jealousy.

"I think five each will be plenty. Would you like to take a look at the gowns on the bed? You might find something to your liking among them." Rosemary rummaged through the gowns on the bed until she found the one she'd apparently been looking for, as evidenced by her smile of satisfaction. She gathered it by the shoulder fabric and held it up. "Oh, yes. Dark blue is going to look lovely on you."

Hope gave the gown a dubious look and sighed. Nothing was going to look "lovely" on her. The most she could hope for was passable.

"You don't like it?" Rosemary's disappointed tone captured Hope's attention from her maudlin thoughts. Hope nodded. "Of course. I'm sorry. It's a beautiful gown. Do you think it's going to be long enough for me? I am rarely able to buy ready-made dresses without alterations."

Rosemary sized her up. "Hmmm, you're rather tall, aren't you? But that shouldn't be a problem if you leave off a hoop."

Hope laughed. "I haven't worn a hoop in five months. I'm not sure I even remember how to sit in one."

"You'll find the women around here are typically very practical. They dress in a proper manner, but practicality is much more important than fashion. It just so happens, this gown was ordered by a young bride-to-be whose engagement was called off at the last minute." The young woman held out the blue gown. "How about if you try this on while I start measuring Miss Betsy here?" She winked at the little girl, eliciting a bright grin.

Hope took the gown and moved behind a privacy screen situated in the corner of the room.

"Do you and Andy plan to farm close to Michael and Star?" Rosemary asked, as she pulled out a tape measure and began taking measurements.

Hope felt her cheeks warm. She'd been anticipating the first questions about their plans, but thought she'd have another day at least. Neither she nor Andy had brought up the subject of how they would explain their arrangement. "We, uh, Andy mentioned building on land he has already. I assume it's close to his brother. I am looking forward to learning how to farm."

That seemed to satisfy the seamstress. She smiled. "Let's start with this one. I may have to take it up a bit."

For the next hour, the women concentrated on tacking the gowns where they were a bit big on both Lucille and Hope.

Each of the weary women came away with two dresses, despite Lucille's protest that Hope should keep all four. But Hope wouldn't dream of it. Lucille had been worth her weight in gold. Hope planned to put her up in the boardinghouse until Andy finished building their home, then Lucille would come to cook for them.

After the fittings and Rosemary's expert sewing skills took care of the mildly ill-fitting gowns, they ate a delicious meal of roasted chicken, potatoes, and carrots. Fresh bread topped the list of foods they'd done without for months. But best of all, Mrs. Barker had baked a fresh apple pie.

No one wanted the meal to end. When every morsel was cleaned from the table, Mrs. Barker finally proclaimed her kitchen officially closed. She seemed gruff, but Hope could tell the woman relished the compliments and declarations of pure joy at the fare she'd set before her flavor-starved boarders.

By the time Hope settled into bed that night, Betsy beside her and Lucille on a cot, her mind whirled with the events of the day. Rolling into Hobbs with Andy at her side, a real bath, new clothes, a wonderful supper, and now a soft bed. She smiled into the darkness. She wasn't sure she'd want to get out of bed in the morning. But she knew she'd have to. Andy was anxious to see his ma.

Tension suddenly clutched her stomach as she remembered that tomorrow she'd be meeting her mother-in-law for the first time. What would the woman think when she learned the nature of her relationship with her son?

Squeezing her eyes tightly, she tried in vain to force herself to drift to sleep, but despite the feather bed, she couldn't still her mind. So much had changed since they'd set out on their journey last spring. So much. She'd changed. For one thing, she believed in God now.

How could she not after all the miracles He'd performed during the journey? And not just for her and her children. She'd seen the pioneers beat the odds over and over and, more often than not, the results could only be attributed to something greater than human effort.

Andy's unwitting prophecy concerning Gregory had come to pass. The boy had changed so much that Hope barely recognized the same child. Not only had he grown physically, he had truly changed. Where it counted the most. In his heart.

Grateful tears slipped from her eyes and wet the hair at her temples. Every hardship had been worth it for this end result.

She tried not to think about what would happen once winter ended and Andy left. Sometimes she could kick herself for giving him that early out. Why hadn't she hung on for the full year? Every moment with him was that much longer that he might, just might, fall in love with her and decide to stay with them forever.

Flopping over onto her stomach, she breathed out a frustrated sigh. If she didn't stop thinking foolish thoughts that would never, ever come true and get some sleep, she'd meet Andy's family with bags under her eyes and look even more hideous than ever.

Listening to Betsy's even breathing lulled Hope to a state of relaxation, and the last thing she wondered before she drifted to sleep was whether or not Andy was ashamed to introduce her as his bride. Was that why he'd left her at a boarding-house while he went to his brother's home?

⁓

Andy could feel Hope's apprehension, and it was starting to make him nervous. Hank had sent word to Ma and Michael and Star last night that Andy was home and would be bringing his new family out today. He hadn't had the heart to tell Hank the truth of the matter—that Hope had essentially hired him to be her husband and would set him free, if not legally, then certainly morally.

Andy already knew that his mother would be mortified, Hank disapproving, and Michael downright disgusted at the arrangement. For the first time, he wondered if perhaps they shouldn't tell the family. Hope was going to have enough adjusting to do without bearing the brunt of family speculation.

"Hope. I have an idea."

"Oh?" Hope turned to him, her silky eyebrows lifted. Her blue eyes were twice as vibrant as usual. Andy had to admit she looked quite attractive in her new blue gown and bonnet.

Forcing his mind back to the topic at hand, he leaned in a little closer so the children who sat in the back wouldn't overhear them. The day before he had removed the canvas and had replaced the nearly dead oxen with a pair of fresh horses. He figured they made quite a domestic picture. Ma, Pa, and youngsters all going to Grandma's house. The picture excited him and disturbed him all at once.

"What is it, Andy?"

"Look. I don't want my family asking a lot of questions. I. . .what do you think of just keeping our arrangement between the two of us?"

"They're going to find out sooner or later anyway."

He scowled. "Better later than sooner as far as I'm concerned."

"I won't lie to keep you from being uncomfortable. But as long as no one asks me, I won't volunteer the information."

A smile tipped his lips. He reached out and covered her hand. "Thank you."

Andy's heart leapt at the first sight of Ma standing outside the log cabin home. Andy appraised the cabin. It appeared Michael had added a room since Andy had been here last. He wondered what reception he'd get from his sister-in-law, Star. He'd insulted her when he'd last visited home. As a matter of fact, his words had caused a scuffle with Michael. Andy had left the next day. According to Hank, Michael and Star had married that winter. The following year, Star had borne Michael a son. She now carried their second child.

The news had caused Andy a restless night, dreaming about Yellow Bird and their child. Would he ever be free?

Feeling Hope tense beside him, he came back to the present. And to his ma's beaming face. He stepped down and before he knew it, Ma was in his arms, weeping for what Andy hoped was joy.

"It's so good to see you, son." Her words were muffled against his shoulder and he could feel her plump body shudder with sobs.

She pulled away. Andy produced a handkerchief and pressed it into her hand. She wiped at her eyes and nose then grasped each of his upper arms. "Let me look at you." Andy squirmed a bit under her scrutiny. Her brow furrowed in worry.

There were more lines in her face than he remembered, and he couldn't help but wonder with more than a little guilt if he was the cause.

"Are you going to introduce me to your new family?"

"Huh? Oh! Of course." Heat seared Andy's ears. He turned to the wagon where Hope still sat. Shame slithered through him. He should have helped her down before he even embraced his ma.

"I'm sorry," he whispered, pulling her a little closer than necessary. Her eyes lit with surprise as she looked up at him.

"It's all right, Andy. I didn't mind."

He took her hand and led her to his mother. "Ma, this is Hope, my. . .uh. . . wife."

Tears sprang once more into Ma's eyes. She stood between Andy and Hope and looked between them. "I just knew when you found the right woman you'd finally come home." Hope seemed stunned to find herself suddenly cradled in Ma's embrace. Her eyes grew wide as she looked at Andy over Ma's shoulder.

Andy grinned. That was his ma. A mother to all.

"Can we get down now, Ma?"

Billy's impatient voice broke the emotional moment, and Ma pulled away with a laugh. "Yes, you may come over here and meet your new Grammy."

Predictably, the children and Ma formed an instant bond. Andy's chest swelled and he suddenly felt as though he truly had come home.

Chapter 12

I'm sorry? You want us to. . . ?" Hope nearly choked on a bite of venison roast as she stared across the table at her mother-in-law.

"Stay here while your house is built, of course." The lady looked back at her with brows furrowed. "Where else did you intend to stay?"

"I thought, well, I hadn't really thought about it. The boardinghouse, I suppose."

"And subject the children to Mrs. Barker's ridiculous rules? The woman allows bathing only on Saturdays. She won't abide talking loud enough for her to hear past seven o'clock because she retires early. Can your children whisper all evening? And if you are ten minutes late for breakfast, she refuses to serve you. Isn't that right, Star?"

Star Riley, Michael's wife, nodded, her beautiful violet-colored eyes sparkling in amusement. "That isn't the half of it. Believe me, you're better off staying here."

"Oh, but we couldn't put you out, could we, Andy?"

He'd been so busy shoveling food into his mouth, Hope doubted he'd heard a word his mother had said. If he had, he certainly didn't seem too concerned. Hope gave him a sound kick under the table.

By his pained expression, she realized she might have applied more force than necessary.

"What were you saying?" he asked, but Hope could tell by his too-innocent expression that he knew exactly what they were saying. Her temper flared at his cowardice. He just thought he'd weasel his way out of having to confront it like a man. Why did even the manliest of men turn into a sniveling child when it meant standing up to his ma?

"Your mother invited us to stay here while the house is being built."

"Yes," Mrs. Riley said in a definitive tone. "It's much more convenient. Besides the practical matter of saving money on the boardinghouse, you will only be a couple of miles from the building site. It's not reasonable to go back and forth to town each day."

Andy caught Hope's attention, clearly won over by his mother's logic. Glowering, Hope gave him another kick.

He grimaced. "Really, we couldn't put you folks out. We don't mind staying at the boardinghouse for a couple of weeks."

"Nonsense," Michael spoke up. "With the new room we added last spring, we're floating in extra space. It would be an insult for you to pay for a place to sleep when you can stay here. Betsy can bunk with Aimee, the two boys can have the loft, and you and Hope can share our old room. It's just sitting empty now waiting for the new baby."

Hope inwardly groaned at the word "insult." Given Miss Hannah's logic and Michael's use of the guilt-inducing word, there was no way they could justify not accepting the offered hospitality.

She gave a helpless shrug and Andy smiled—a mildly triumphant smile. "I suppose we'll have to accept. Thank you for your kind offer."

"Thank goodness, that's settled." Miss Hannah bit into a slice of bread, capturing Hope's gaze. She stared for just a flash too long. Before she looked away, Hope saw concern in the older woman's eyes. Alarm seized Hope. If Andy's mother were that astute, there would be no keeping their secret, not if they were living under the same roof.

⬙

A heavy knot formed in Hope's stomach as she changed into her nightgown in the darkness. True, Andy wasn't in the room, but that didn't mean he couldn't walk in any second. After she'd excused herself for the night, she'd heard him ask Michael to show him a colt that had been born during the spring.

Hope had a fleeting suspicion that he might have done so in order to give her a little privacy. But she gave a short laugh at the notion. If Andy were truly noble, he would have just come right out with the truth, no matter what the consequences.

But that wasn't really fair either, because she wasn't crazy about the idea of the family knowing the truth herself. They knew what was most important for them to know, that she was married to Andy in a legal and binding manner. There would be no annulment. But Andy would walk away when he was ready and that would be that. She would be left to explain it to his family and the twins.

Her temper flared at the thought. How dare he just leave her to do the dirty work! To pick up the pieces of her children's broken hearts.

By the time she heard Andy's footsteps walk down the hall and stop at their door, Hope had worked herself into a full-blown mad. She turned her back and pretended to be asleep just as he stepped inside.

The other side of the mattress sank beneath his weight as he sat and started to remove his boots. Her pulse pounded in her ears. When he stretched out, she couldn't take it another second. In one swift movement, she flopped over to face him.

"What do you think you are doing?" she demanded.

Andy let out a yowl and shot from the bed, clad in his long handles. "Woman, you scared me half to death!"

Averting her gaze, although it wasn't necessary in the darkened room, Hope hissed, "Keep your voice down, you imbecile. Or do you want your whole family to come running?"

"Why were you pretending to be asleep?"

"Because I didn't want to talk to you."

"What changed your mind?"

"I realized you thought you'd actually sleep in the bed with me."

"Where else?" Andy sat on the bed once more.

"On the floor, of course. We brought plenty of quilts so that you can make it nice and comfy. You are not sleeping in this bed with me."

"I'm not sleeping on the floor after five months on the ground. You have my word that I won't come near you."

"That's not good enough." Hope sat up, covers to her chin. "I insist that you sleep on the floor."

Andy gave her a stubborn scowl and leaned in so close Hope could feel his breath on her cheek. "If my word isn't good enough, then I guess you'll have to sleep on the floor yourself."

He stretched out and closed his eyes.

A gasp escaped Hope's throat at his utter lack of chivalry. She jumped out of bed. "Fine, Andy Riley, I'll make a pallet and sleep on it myself."

She made herself a thick pallet and stretched out. Andy sat up on his elbow and watched her. "Why won't you just sleep up here? My promise is good."

"Your promise has nothing to do with it. I believe you. It's my promise to myself that I care about."

"What sort of promise?"

"That I wouldn't share my bed with another man who doesn't love me."

Andy remained silent for a moment, then he swung his legs over the side of the bed and rested his elbows on his knees. "You win. I'll take the floor."

"Never mind. I'm down here now. I might as well stay."

"Get in the bed, Hope."

"No."

A low growl emanated from his throat. Before she knew what was happening, Hope felt herself being lifted from the floor.

She kicked her feet in protest, but it did no good. He stomped to the bed and gave her a toss.

"When I say I'm sleeping on the floor, that's exactly what I mean." His chest heaved and he glowered at her. The sight of him leaning over her sent Hope's heart into a tizzy.

"Hope. . ."

Some day she'd learn not to be so transparent. "Forget it, Andy. Business arrangement only."

"Fine by me." His hard tone gave a hint at his wounded pride, and Hope wished things could be different. But she had to protect her heart. At most, she had six months with Andy. It was going to be difficult enough to let him go without falling into a real relationship with him. She gave a deep sigh. From the pallet, she heard Andy do the same.

                                                   §

"Whoa, take it easy, Andy." Hank gave him a good-natured clap on the shoulder. "You're going to clean out these woods in one day at the pace you're going. I can't keep up."

Andy straightened up and sank the ax head into the stump of a tree he'd just felled. He accepted the proffered canteen and gratefully took in several gulps of water.

"Thanks."

"So do you want to tell me what's bothering you?"

Andy gave a short laugh. "Don't start pulling that preacher stuff on me."

A flash of hurt appeared in Hank's eyes, and Andy immediately regretted his rash comment.

"Hey, I was teasing. Nothing's wrong. I just want to get Hope's house built as soon as possible. The sooner she's settled in her own home, the better."

"Is there a problem at Michael's?"

Other than the fact that I'm sleeping on the floor every night, gritting my teeth to keep from climbing into bed with my wife and taking her into my arms?

Of course he kept the thought to himself. He shrugged. "You know a woman wants her own kitchen."

"I thought Hope hired a cook."

"Well, yeah. Hope doesn't want her own kitchen." Andy scowled, knowing he'd been caught in his fib. "That's just a figure of speech anyway."

"I see." Hank straddled the newly downed tree and regarded Andy with eyes that seemed to capture the essence of his soul. Shifting uncomfortably, Andy averted his gaze.

"Is everything all right with your marriage, Andy?" Hank's voice sang with genuine caring, and as much as Andy would have liked to suggest his brother mind his own business, he couldn't. So he lied instead.

"Everything's fine." He forced a grin. "Hope's quite a woman. Just the kind of spitfire an old grizzly bear like me needs to keep me on the straight and narrow."

"Are you on the straight and narrow, Andy?"

Andy gave himself a swift inward kick. Why had he used such idiotic words when talking to a preacher?

"Now, Hank. I told you not to start that preacher stuff with me."

"Whether I was a preacher or not, I'd still be concerned for your soul."

"Don't be."

"So you're telling me you're doing fine with God? Or are you telling me to butt out of your affairs?"

"Little brother, God forgot about me a long time ago." He felt a twinge of unease. He couldn't deny God's help in retrieving Hope from the Indians.

" 'Whither shall I go from thy spirit? or whither shall I flee from thy presence?' "

The hair on the back of Andy's neck rose at the sound of Hank's voice.

" 'If I ascend up into heaven, thou art there: if I make my bed in hell, behold, thou art there. If I take the wings of the morning, and dwell in the uttermost parts of the sea; even there shall thy hand lead me, and thy right hand shall hold me. If I say, Surely the darkness shall cover me; even the night shall be light about me. Yea, the darkness hideth not from thee; but the night shineth as the day: the darkness and the light are both alike to thee.' "

Silence saturated the air between them, like a fat cloud about to burst with rain.

"You don't know where I've been for five years, Hank. If you knew, you wouldn't be so all-fired sure that God of yours was looking out for me."

"Tell me where you've been."

Heaving a troubled sigh, Andy shook his head. "Some things are better left alone."

"Anything hidden will eventually be brought into the light, Andy. One way or another."

"I suppose you pulled that from the Bible, too?"

"Yes."

Andy nodded. "Well, I guess break time is about over. Those logs aren't going to pull themselves to the building site."

"Looks like we're in for a storm."

Andy followed his gaze to the sky, suddenly dark with storm clouds.

Hank tossed the canteen into the back of the wagon. "Maybe we'd best head on back to the house. It's about supper time anyway and you know what Ma said."

A grin tipped Andy's lips. "We'd best not be late or we'll be eating with the pigs."

"Ma's a character." Hank chuckled as they began loading the axes and saws into the wagon. "You know, she's beside herself that all her sons are settled down close to her."

"I reckon she is." Andy swallowed hard and climbed into the wagon. He took up the reins and waited until Hank was seated before nudging the horses toward home.

"She's taken quite a liking to Hope and the children."

"Yep." Why couldn't he just be quiet about it? Andy's stomach churned. Hank's fresh optimism had always been a source of irritation for Andy and no less now.

"The boy, Gregory, seems to be a good lad." Something in Hank's tone raised Andy's suspicion. He cut a glance toward Hank.

"He is."

"He came to me a couple of days ago and told me he'd like to become a preacher. Asked me for some advice. What do you think of that?"

Andy shrugged. "The boy has a right to do whatever he wants. I guess you didn't turn out too bad. Any advice you give him couldn't hurt." He sent his brother a sardonic grin. "What help would I be to a boy hankering to be a preacher?"

"There's more, actually, that I should probably just come right out and tell you."

Swallowing past the sudden lump in his throat, Andy stared straight ahead. Focused on Hank's forthcoming revelation, he didn't flinch when a flash of lightning streaked across the sky.

Hank cleared his throat. "The truth is, Gregory's concerned about your relationship with his ma."

Andy scowled. This was the last conversation he wanted to have. Irritation shot through him at the boy, but he supposed he couldn't really blame Gregory, not after what he'd seen and overheard that night by the creek. But did the boy have to go telling all their secrets? True, they'd never actually told him not to go blabbing their relationship to people, but some things should be a simple matter of common sense.

"Do you have anything to say to what I just told you?" Hank's voice seemed a little irritated, and Andy's defenses rose.

Unsure what Gregory had revealed, he decided to keep his comments nonspecific rather than give Hank more information than he needed.

"Well, I guess it's natural for a boy to worry about his ma's new man. But don't concern yourself, we'll work it out."

Hank slapped his thigh in a rare show of frustration. "Listen to what I'm telling you, man. Your new son told me about your arrangement with Hope. I know you two don't have a real marriage, I know she's paying you to build her house, and I know you plan on leaving after a year."

The truth on Hank's lips made the whole thing suddenly seem like a bad idea. Andy could feel everything unraveling. He hated the thought of what his ma would think once she discovered what a cad he was. Andy glared at his brother. "All right. So now that you know, what do you plan to do about it?"

Chapter 13

Hope had sensed Andy's foul mood all evening. His stormy expression matched the storm outside. She only hoped he didn't start thundering.

The tension inside the cabin was so thick, Betsy and Aimee had excused themselves to their room. The two girls were close enough in age, with Aimee being only three years older, that they'd formed a fast bond. It did Hope's heart good to see her daughter with her first true girlfriend ever. But she couldn't help but feel a little sorry for Billy. He hadn't been prepared for his sister's defection, and he had been moping for days. Next week she intended to send the children to town school, so she prayed Billy would find a friend.

Miss Hannah sat in her wooden chair and rocked before the fire, her knitting needles clacking against each other, moving so fast it made Hope dizzy to watch her. Star, too, sat with knitting in hand. Thanks to these two women's efforts, Star's baby would be well outfitted.

Michael sat at the table going over the accounts of the farm and looking mighty pleased with himself, from what Hope could tell.

Only Andy seemed out of sorts. He paced, sat, paced, sat, and paced some more until Hope could stand it no longer. She jumped up, announced bedtime to Billy and Gregory, and bade everyone good night.

Inside her bedroom, she quickly donned her nightgown, spread Andy's pallet for him—figuring that was the least she could do—and slid beneath the covers. She'd barely closed her eyes when she heard Andy's heavy boots.

Without making his usual attempt at courtesy by trying to be quiet, he got ready for bed. Alarm seized her when she felt him lift the covers and slide in beside her.

With a gasp, she sat up pulling the covers to her chin. "What do you think you're doing?"

He gave a snort. "So, you're not really asleep. I don't know why you always pretend to be asleep when I come into the room. I told you I wouldn't bother you."

"Whether I'm asleep or not is none of your business," she snapped. "What are you doing in the bed? I. . .I fixed your pallet for you."

"How sweet."

His sarcasm was beginning to grate on her good nature. But she bit back a hostile comment, afraid it might make him more determined to be stubborn.

"Andy," she said through her gritted teeth. "We had an arrangement."

Her heart nearly stopped as he sat up. The starless night allowed for no light to shine in the room; still, she could see the hard lines of his face, determined. He slid his hand behind her neck, lacing his fingers through her hair. In a swift movement, he brought her face close. "Maybe I'm tired of the arrangement."

"Y—you can't just get tired of it." Barely able to emit a sound through her closed throat, Hope wasn't sure he'd heard her. He pressed kisses over her cheeks, eyelids, and forehead.

"Andy, please." She despised the trembling in her voice.

Oh, how she wished she could share her life and her love with this man. But how could she give him the most precious gift she had to offer when he would be leaving in a matter of months?

"You promised," she whispered.

"Promises are made to be broken," he said, his voice filled with husky emotion.

Hope steeled her heart, knowing if she didn't put a stop to this immediately, his lips would find hers and she would be lost.

In a beat, she maneuvered away. His face came down on her shoulder.

"Hey," he growled.

"W—we had an agreement." Gathering the blanket close, she swallowed back tears. "I thought you were an honorable man."

He gave a short laugh and flung himself back on the bed. "I don't know what ever gave you that idea. When you met me I was about to be killed for gambling away another man's money. Not much honor in that, is there?"

Unable to bear his mocking tone, she took his self-deprecation as a personal affront. "Don't you dare belittle yourself, Andy Riley. I don't know what drove you to drinking and gambling, I can only guess you were in love and lost her."

He drew in a swift breath of air. "Why do you say that?"

"You called me Yellow Bird that first day when you were so badly injured."

All the fight seemed to leave him. "She was my wife."

Hope's outrage melted away, and Hope lay on her side, her ear pressing into her palm as she rose on her elbow. "Do you want to talk about it?"

"She was the most beautiful thing I'd ever seen. I fell in love with her from the first moment I laid my eyes on her."

Hope's stomach sank at the longing in his tone, and she wished she hadn't opened the door for him to confide his grief. He seemed to have forgotten she was there anyway as he spoke into the darkness.

"Yellow Bird was the first woman I ever loved. I spent my youth scouting for wagon trains, carousing when I could, and generally spending time with women who weren't looking for a man to settle down and make honest women of them."

Uninterested in hearing about his association with those kinds of women, Hope swallowed and pressed, "And how did you meet Yellow Bird?"

"I was hunting away from the wagon train one day, and something spooked my horse. I'm not sure what it was. Yellow Bird always believed it was The Great Spirit who did what was necessary so we could meet." He gave an affectionate laugh.

Jealousy twisted Hope's gut. This unknown woman still had Andy's heart. Her husband's heart. The pain of it nearly took her breath. But she pushed it aside. "Go on."

"I was thrown from my horse and knocked unconscious. My first memory when I woke up in a Sioux village was Yellow Bird's face leaning over me, her black hair loose and brushing against my face. It took me minutes to realize she wasn't a dream."

His voice faded as he became lost in thought. Hope waited in the silence until he remembered she was there and continued.

"I stayed longer than I needed to. And soon I decided not to leave at all. The Sioux often adopt captives into the tribe, and even though I wasn't technically a prisoner, I became one of the tribe. Those were the happiest days of my life. In a few months, I had enough ponies to offer Yellow Bird's father an extravagant bride price. He accepted, and Yellow Bird became my wife. She was with child very soon." His voice choked.

Sensing that this was the first time he'd ever opened up about this, Hope pushed aside her own hurt that she was competing with a dead woman for his affection. She wasn't sure she'd ever win his heart, but for certain, Andy would never love her until he was free of Yellow Bird's memory.

She reached out and placed her hand on his arm. He grabbed it as though taking hold of a life preserver. She winced as he clung to her.

"Yellow Bird was so happy to be carrying our child. She knew in her heart that she carried a girl. We haggled over names. I teased her by calling the baby Becky and Mary and Elizabeth. But she insisted there was no meaning in such common white names. And that we would decide what to call her after we knew her."

He gathered a ragged breath and gripped Hope's hand tighter. "But we never got to know her. A few months into the pregnancy, Yellow Bird started to bleed. It happened so fast. One minute she was grinning and sitting on my lap, tickling my chin. The next she was doubled over and three hours later she was dead. And so was our tiny baby girl. Sh—she was barely the size of my hand."

Tears thickened Hope's throat. She swallowed hard. "Oh, Andy. I'm so sorry."

"Her family wanted me to stay in the village. But I couldn't. Everything reminded me of her. The only way I could get relief was from a bottle. And that's what I did. I gambled and drank. I'd borrow money to gamble, and then made back more than I borrowed. Until my luck ran out a couple of years ago.

"The way you found me in the alley—that's the way I'd been living for two years. I've been beat up more times than I can count for owing money. I thought this time my luck had finally run out for good. I was ready to be put out of my misery. I wanted to join my wife and daughter, wherever they were. But you saved me and here we are."

Hope wasn't sure how to respond. She recalled his misery when he'd discovered he wasn't dead. Ridiculously, she almost felt as though she should apologize for saving him. But of course she didn't. "Thank you for sharing that with me, Andy. I'm honored you trusted me with it."

"Thank you for listening." He slid his thumb over the back of her hand. "I'm sorry I tried to take liberties. I'll get down on the floor."

"Wait a little while, Andy. It makes a lot more sense for you to lie up here while we talk. I. . .I was hoping you'd tell me about the plans for the house. How are things coming along?"

Her eyes had adjusted to the dark room and she made out his smile.

"We cut down several trees today. Hank and Michael think we can start building next week. We hope to get a couple of main rooms up and a roof before the first real winter storm hits."

They discussed the building plans until long into the night. Finally, during a lull in the conversation, Andy's snoring alerted her to the fact that he'd fallen asleep. Hope was about to ease out of bed when the door opened. Betsy slipped inside. "Are you awake, Ma?"

Alarm shot through Hope. What would the little girl think of seeing Andy in her bed? Heat seared her cheeks. But there was nothing she could do about it now.

"I'm over here, Bets. What's wrong?"

"I have to tell you something."

"Okay. Keep your voice down so you don't wake Andy."

The child nodded but didn't seem to notice one way or another where Andy was sleeping. Hope marveled. Things were so simple for children. Married people shared a bed and that was that. They didn't think beyond the obvious.

Betsy knelt beside Hope's bed. Hope turned onto her side, much as she had when listening to Andy, and once again rested her head on her palm. "Tell me what's bothering you."

"Do you know about Jesus, Ma?"

"You mean in the Bible?"

Betsy nodded.

"I suppose I do, honey. You know I've been believing in God ever since he made Gregory all well."

The little girl shook her head impatiently, almost frantically. "It's not enough just to believe in God. You have to believe that Jesus is His Son."

"Where did you hear that, honey?"

Hope had a rudimentary knowledge of religious beliefs from her association with the wagon train folks. But throughout her growing-up years, her father had seen to it that her primary playmates were children of intellectuals who, at best, believed only in the existence of a powerful being. Religion was scoffed at, Jesus considered a myth. Hope intended to procure a copy of the Bible at the earliest opportunity so that she might study it for herself.

"Are you listening, Ma?"

Betsy's voice snapped her back to the present. "I'm sorry, baby. Yes, I'm here."

"Aimee told me tonight all about Jesus." Tears quivered in Betsy's voice. "Ma, He *died* because I'm a sinner."

Taking Betsy's hand, Hope looked the girl square in the eye. "Sweetheart, you are not a sinner. You're a sweet little girl." Anger flared at Aimee, though the child was obviously twisting something she'd been taught. Parents should be more careful what they said in front of their children.

"Ma, we are *all* sinners. That's why Jesus had to die."

"Sweetie, I know Aimee believes that, but sinners are people that steal or kill people. Not folks like us and certainly not little girls like you." She smiled and smoothed Betsy's hair away from her face. "Does that make you feel better?"

The little girl flung Hope's hand away and stood. "Ma!"

"Shh, Betsy, come back here and keep your voice down. Do you want to wake Andy?"

Betsy obeyed. "Ma, you have to listen to me. The Bible says we are *all* sinners. Only the blood of Jesus can wash us clean."

"Oh, Betsy, really, blood? What have you two girls been talking about?"

"Mama, please." Tears flowed in earnest now, and Betsy took Hope's hand in both of her little ones. "Please listen to me."

"All right, sweetheart." Hope made a mental note to clear this whole thing up with Miss Hannah in the morning.

Betsy drew a shaky breath. "Aimee said only accepting what Jesus did on the cross could make us acceptable to go to heaven. Even if you're a good person, unless you understand the sacrifice God's only Son made then you aren't saved."

"I've never heard of such a thing, Bets."

"I know, but Ma, when she was talking, my heart started beating really fast. Like now. And I just couldn't stop crying, thinking about the nails hammered in Jesus' hands and feet."

"Oh, baby, don't think about it, if it makes you cry. It's just a story."

"No! Ma, it's the truth. You know how you can always tell when Billy and me is lying?"

"Yes. But that's—"

"I just knew that Aimee was telling me the truth. And then she read to me out of her Bible. All about how He healed people and I thought about Gregory. Jesus healed him, Mama. Jesus did it, and we didn't even know He died for us. He just healed Greg because we asked Him to."

The conviction in Betsy's voice couldn't be denied. The child was a believer through and through. But what if it was all a myth like Father had always maintained? What if Greg had simply beaten the illness on his own? The very thought felt disloyal.

She thought of her studies. What of Pascal's wager? The philosopher had argued against his opponents that believed there was no God. Pascal responded that it was better to go ahead and believe in God. Because if there was no God and you believed anyway, at the end of your life, there would be no repercussions for your belief. If, on the other hand, you didn't believe and discovered after you died that indeed there was a God all along, then you were damned for your disbelief.

Hope had taken that wager to heart as a young girl and had allowed herself a rudimentary faith in God. Though the strength of her belief had varied over the years. Now she was faced with something different. This wasn't a vague belief in a distant God, this was a gut-wrenching, life-altering conviction. Something she'd always sworn never to adhere to or allow in her children.

"Betsy. Don't you remember the reverend on the wagon train?"

"Yes."

"If this were true, don't you think he would have told you about Jesus?"

"I think he thought we knew. He used to mention Jesus and the cross, but I never understood what he meant. And I didn't want to make him feel bad by telling him I didn't know what he was talking about."

Releasing a heavy sigh, Hope felt compassion well up for her daughter. How young to be so conflicted. She was so glad her father had kept her away from religion until she was old enough to make up her own mind.

"Honey, I don't want you to listen to Aimee about this anymore, all right? Tomorrow we'll discuss it with Miss Hannah."

"I can't wait until tomorrow. I have to do it now."

Hope frowned. "Do what?"

"Pray to ask Jesus in my heart."

"Ask Jesus into your heart? What on earth does that mean?"

"Aimee said it means that you tell Him you believe who Jesus is and you tell Him you're sorry for all of your sins. And then you ask Him to wash you clean and you get to start all over with no sin."

Hope gave her daughter an indulgent smile. "That sounds a little like magic."

"Not magic, Mama. A miracle."

The hair on the back of Hope's neck stood up at the awe in her daughter's voice.

"I can't wait another minute to pray. But I had to come tell you about it, too. Will you pray with me?"

"Oh, Bets. I don't know what you want me to say."

"Just say you will."

Hope could not deny her daughter, but neither could she pretend to embrace this new idea of asking Jesus into one's heart. It sounded a little strange.

"Tell you what. I will bow my head just like I do before we eat, okay? And you pray whatever you want to pray."

"Oh, I wanted you to ask Jesus to come into your heart, too."

"I can't do that. This idea is too new to me. But I promise I will purchase a Bible soon, and I'll keep an open mind while I read it. Fair enough?"

Betsy gave a hesitant nod. "Promise you'll get one tomorrow?"

"I'll try. Are you ready to pray your prayer now?"

"Yes."

Betsy bowed her head. "Dear God. Aimee says I'm a sinner. And I know she's telling the truth because I felt it in my stomach when she said it. But she said you sent Jesus and He died on the cross so that I don't have to go to the place where bad people go." She dropped her voice to a whisper. "I'm not allowed to say the name of the place bad people go, and I didn't think You'd want me starting off by disobeying Ma."

Hope smiled through tears. She couldn't help herself. Betsy's simple, wholesome belief in what she was saying filled her with a sense of awe.

"I know I done a lot of bad things. There are so many I can't remember them, but Aimee said I don't have to list them, just have to ask You to forgive them. So that's what I'm doing. Please make me good. Jesus, I never knew until tonight that You died for me." Her voice cracked. "B—but now that I do, I. . .I have to thank You. I wish You were down here in person so I could hug You to show You how much I love You. But I know You feel it. Just like I do right now. I. . .I didn't ask You yet, but I think You live in my heart now because I feel different. Oh, thank You, Jesus. Amen."

Hope opened her eyes and stared at her daughter.

"Can you tell I'm different, Ma?"

"I. . .well, Bets, not really."

"You will."

"How do you know you're different? What if it didn't take?"

"Aimee says we have to accept these things by faith. And that if we believe we're truly different, we'll start acting different."

"I think you're pretty sweet just the way you are, so don't act too differently, okay?"

Betsy giggled. "I have to go wake up Aimee and tell her."

"Don't you think you should wait until morning?"

"I can't."

The little girl jumped to her feet and tippy-toe ran to the door.

" 'Night, Ma."

" 'Night."

Hope lay back down, bewildered by what had just transpired.

Closing her eyes, she thought fleetingly that she should perhaps retire to the pallet, but her weary body refused to move.

She listened to the sound of distant thunder as the storm finally moved away. A gentle rain still tapped the window, and the wind sifted through the branches outside.

As she sank into the first phase of sleep, she was almost certain she heard the wind whispering, *"Only believe."*

She wanted to open her eyes, to see if someone had spoken to her or if the wind outside had caused her ears to play tricks on her. But her eyes were too heavy. Finally, she surrendered to sleep.

Only believe.

Chapter 14

Andy stood inside the door of the home he'd built for Hope. His gaze took in the wooden rocker he'd crafted with his own hands, the table with two benches for the children and two chairs, one at each end. He'd worked on the furniture as a surprise. He'd built a bed frame for her, and with Ma's help, he'd stuffed a mattress.

Betsy, too, had a bed. The boys would sleep on pallets in the loft until he could build the other bed frames. Taking the time to make furniture had extended their stay at Michael's for two extra weeks, but Andy resisted the idea of bringing Hope to an empty house.

Lately, he could sense that she was getting antsy, and he had begun running out of excuses as to why she couldn't come see the cabin. And, though he still worked hard and took some satisfaction in knowing Hope would have her own home, the joy and anticipation he'd expected to feel were glaringly absent. And he knew why. It had all started a month ago. When Betsy had tiptoed into their bedroom and proclaimed herself a sinner.

The Bible says we are all sinners. Only the blood of Jesus can wash us clean.

For weeks, those words had haunted Andy. They pounded into his brain with every swing of the ax, every bang of the hammer. Every waking moment.

In his dreams, Jesus, His eyes filled with love and compassion, beckoned with nail-scarred hands. Andy's dreamlike self tried to reach Him, but always stopped short of touching the hands. If he could only reach Jesus, Andy knew his restlessness would be over.

But he always awoke, drenched in sweat and tears and feeling emptier than he'd ever felt in his life. More than empty, he felt lost.

He wished he'd never eavesdropped on the conversation between Hope and Betsy that night. Had Hope known he was awake, she would have taken Betsy in the other room so as not to disturb him. But he'd been mesmerized by the wonder of the girl's discovery of things Andy had known from childhood. He'd allowed his heart to cry out for peace and with the acknowledgment of that longing, his faith had resurfaced.

But believing in God again opened another door—the feeling that he didn't—nor could he ever—measure up. To deny the existence of a Holy God was to excuse his behavior, no matter how despicable. There was simply nothing to aspire to. As a youngster, he'd learned that was the easier road. The narrow road Ma had always talked about seemed too hard. Andy never could quite get it right.

Because of that failure, he had always felt like the outsider in his family. Michael was the responsible one. Hank, the holy one. Andy had found his place as the black sheep, the troublemaker, the one who broke his mother's heart.

"I think that about does it." The sound of Michael's voice pulled Andy from his brooding.

"I guess so."

"I reckon Hope will be glad to have her own home."

Andy gave him a sharp glance. "You mean you're ready for us to move on?"

A frown creased Michael's brow. "No, that's not what I said. I just imagine your wife is ready to set up housekeeping for herself. You know how women are."

Knowing he owed his brother an apology didn't sit well with Andy. He scowled. "You don't know Hope. She's not like most women. She's been a real trooper—on the trail and since we've been staying with you."

Michael gave a curt nod and gathered a breath. Andy could tell he was trying to keep his temper in check, but he didn't care. He was in no mood to get along.

"Anyway, we'll be out of your hair tomorrow."

"You're not in my hair," Michael replied through gritted teeth. "And you're welcome to stay all winter if you want."

"I'm not such a freeloader that I'd take advantage of your hospitality any longer than necessary. So just get off your high horse."

Taking up his hammer and saw, Michael stared at Andy for a moment. "I can see you're spoiling for a fight, and I'm not about to go along with that."

Andy gave a short laugh. "Probably just as well if you know what's good for you."

Emitting a frustrated growl, Michael dropped the tools. "What's bothering you, Andy? I thought you'd be happy now that the house is ready and the furniture is finished. You wanted to surprise Hope. And just when you're about to, you're acting like someone did you wrong."

"Nothing's wrong. Nothing you or anyone can fix, that is." He swiped at the sweat on his brow. And dropped onto the porch.

Michael joined him on the step. "I'd like to try and help."

"What could someone like you do?"

"Someone like me?" He gave a wary lift of his brow.

Andy drew a breath and as he expelled it, he knew he wasn't going to hold back. "You have everything a man could want. A beautiful wife and daughter, a son, and another child about to arrive any day. Ma worships the ground you walk on. You've made the farm a rousing success, even better than Pa ever did." He gave a mocking laugh. "What could you do to help me? You can't even understand me.

Everything you touch turns to gold. Everything I touch is ruined."

Silence hung between them for a moment. Then Michael's chest rose and fell with a heavy breath. "I do have a wonderful family. And I thank God for them. And Ma's happy in our home. She was a big help to me after Sarah died and Aimee was a baby. But she gives me what-for on a regular basis. And as for me having everything a man could want, it seems to me you do, too."

Andy started to rebut the statement, but stopped himself short of doing just that. How could he tell Michael that his marriage was a sham, that his step-children weren't his to raise, that his so-called wife slept as far away from him as she possibly could, although they'd finally agreed to share the bed—for sleeping only.

"You don't think you have a good life, Andy? Are you so ungrateful that you can't thank God for blessing you with a wonderful family?"

Disgust laced Michael's voice. But Andy was used to that. Used to disappointing his brother. Everyone, in fact. His entire life had been a disappointment. Until Yellow Bird came into it, then everything changed. Her love had made him a success. She loved him for the man he was and never once did he see that disappointment in her eyes. "You don't know everything, Michael."

"I guess not. But I know a man in love when I see one. I can also see that something's not right between you and Hope. But I don't suppose that's anyone's business but yours."

Andy stared. A man in love? He gave an inward laugh. A gleeful laugh at how wrong Michael was. Hope was a good woman, but he wasn't in love with her by any means. A frown puckered his brow as he thought for a second. "What do you mean you know a man in love? What am I doing?"

Michael chuckled. "You don't know?"

Andy glared. "Would I have asked?"

"A man doesn't work to build a home with such detail unless he loves the woman he's building it for. He doesn't work night and day to build nice furniture as a surprise."

"Any man would."

"You wouldn't."

Andy's ears warmed at the candid response. He couldn't blame his brother, really. The man Michael knew five years ago had never known the love of a woman. Had never held his dead baby in his hands. Hadn't lain in the gutter waiting to die. The Andy he'd known didn't exist anymore.

"I suppose you're right."

Michael grinned. "That was a little too easy."

Andy shrugged. He wouldn't deny loving Hope. Why intentionally shame a good woman? They'd all figure it out soon enough. After the spring thaw when he left. He'd decided to join up with another wagon train and offer his services as scout.

He was just about ready to suggest heading back to Michael's cabin when the sound of horse's hooves thundered toward them.

"It's Greg," Andy said, more to himself than Michael. "Something's wrong."

The boy reached them before they could speculate. He reined in the bay mare and took two gulping breaths.

"Take it easy, son," Andy said, grabbing the bridle. "What's wrong?"

"Miss Star."

Michael stepped forward. "Is she. . . ?"

Greg nodded and Michael ran to his horse. He untethered the black gelding and rode off at breakneck speed.

"Miss Star's having her baby, huh?"

"Yes, sir."

"You want to see the cabin?"

"Shouldn't we get back?"

Andy chuckled. "I don't think they need us there. As a matter of fact, I can almost guarantee you that they'll run us out of there as soon as we get there."

Gregory gave a sheepish grin.

Andy clapped him on the shoulder. "Come on. I'll show you, but you have to keep quiet about it. It's a surprise for your ma."

"Sure, Pa. . ."

Andy stopped dead in his tracks. He turned and stared at Greg.

The boy's face glowed red. "I'm sorry. It just came out, naturally. I didn't mean to."

Swallowing past a sudden lump in his throat, Andy fought the pleasure he'd received at hearing the unfamiliar title. He liked it. Too much.

Leveling a gaze at the boy, he could see the dread in Greg's face. Still, it had to be said. "You know how things are between your mother and me."

"Yeah," the boy muttered. "I just thought maybe things were different since we got to Oregon."

Instinctively, Andy knew he meant since he was sharing a room with Hope, but he didn't pursue the topic. Some things weren't suitable for a boy Greg's age.

"I think highly of her. And a finer woman I've never met."

"She's pretty, too." Greg glared at him, daring him to deny it. Andy almost chuckled to see a hint of the old Greg. He supposed he could bring out the worst in anyone.

"This isn't about how pretty she is. This is about our arrangement."

"You haven't told your family the truth."

"They'll know soon enough."

"When you leave, you mean?"

"Yes."

"Will your ma want us to stop calling her Grammy?"

"My leaving won't change anything for you, Greg. I married your ma legally. Nothing is going to change that either. Grammy is still your Grammy. Michael and Hank are still going to be your uncles."

"But you won't be our pa." The bitter edge in the boy's tone cut into Andy's conscience.

"Believe me, having those two as uncles is a lot better than having me as a pa."

"No one's a better pa than you."

The blade twisted inside Andy. He reached out and ruffled Greg's hair, which he now had to cut to keep shoulder length like Andy's. "If things were different, I'd be proud for a son like you."

"What things have to be different? Why can't you just stay? I know ma wishes you would."

Andy eyed the boy sharply. "Did she tell you that?"

"No. But I can tell she's taken a shine to you." His face grew red and Andy elbowed him.

"Ah, what do you know about women?"

Greg shrugged. "I know my ma."

"Maybe you do. But in this instance I think you're seeing what you want to see rather than what's actually there. Now, come on and let me show you the cabin."

Greg's nod was anything but enthusiastic.

Between Greg and Michael and God, Andy knew he was in for a long winter.

❧

Hope paced in front of the fire and tried to keep Michael calm. Two days and still no baby.

Andy had finally admitted that the cabin was ready and had taken all the children there to wait out the labor. But before he left, he'd wandered about the cabin white-faced, and Hope knew he was reliving Yellow Bird's death delivering their baby.

Miss Hannah sat with Star. Hope stayed in the front room, trying to keep Michael occupied.

Michael dropped his head into his hands. "Why didn't I insist on finding a doctor by now?"

Hope went to him and knelt on the floor by his chair. Should she put her hand on his arm? The thought of touching a man who didn't belong to her in such an intimate manner made her stomach churn. When he started to cry, she pushed aside her modesty and placed an arm about his shoulders. "Shh. Michael, it'll be all right."

"She needs a doctor."

"Sometimes babies take awhile. Having a doctor here probably wouldn't make a difference at this point."

The door opened, bringing a gust of wind. Hope's pulse sped up at the sight of Andy. "I came to do chores," he said.

"Thanks." Michael's voice was muffled by his hands.

Andy beckoned her with the swoop of his hand. Hope accompanied him to the porch. "How is she?"

Tears sprang to Hope's eyes. "Getting weak. It's been too long."

"It's just like Yellow Bird."

"No, it isn't."

Tears shimmered in his eyes as he looked at her. "It feels like I'm living it all over again."

"Well, you're not, Andy." Hope's voice was sharper than she'd intended, but frustration and weariness dulled her sensitivity and bluntness took charge of her tongue. "This isn't about your wife and baby. This is about your brother and the fact that his wife may very well die if the baby doesn't come soon."

Tears slipped down Andy's cheek and soaked into his three-day-old beard.

Compassion replaced irritation, and Hope took him into her arms. He pressed his face into the curve of her neck and sobbed. Hope stroked his hair, running her fingers through the tresses.

"Shh, Andy. We have to pray. Remember when Greg took cholera? God did a miracle. We just have to pray for a miracle. That's all."

Grabbing her tighter, as though afraid she might try to pull away, Andy spoke into her ear. "But will He listen to someone like me?"

"You said only God could have led you to where the Indians had me that day. He heard your prayer then. Let's both pray."

Andy nodded against her shoulder. "God, please make the baby come." He barely uttered the words when sobs overtook him once more.

Tingles traveled up Hope's spine like butterfly wings against her skin.

"God," she whispered, suddenly shy. "The twins asked for miracles, and You gave several during the trail. And then when Greg was sick, You made him well when all the others died." Andy shuddered against her, and Hope caressed his hair like a child's. "We need to ask You to do a miracle for Star this time. Her baby is taking a long time to get here and I'm afraid her strength is almost gone. Andy and I are just asking for You to please do us another miracle. Make the baby come. Michael's a good man, but he needs his wife, and those two children of theirs need their mother. So we hope You'd like to do another miracle."

She pulled back and looked at Andy's tearstained face. "Do you feel better?"

He scowled.

"What?"

"You forgot to say amen."

Before she could reply, the door flew open and Michael stood wild-eyed. "Hope, Ma says come quick. The baby's coming."

Chapter 15

Hope's first sight of her new home stole her breath away. The log home stood beneath a harvest moon, the porch railings on her little cabin as regal to her as the most beautiful pillars on the most elegant mansion in Chicago—or anywhere for that matter.

"Oh, Andy. I love it."

He set the wagon brake and hopped down. Her heart skipped a beat when he held up his arms for her. Willingly, she slid into his embrace, her gaze never leaving his.

"Thank you," she whispered.

He kept her close and returned her stare. "I need to thank you for tonight."

"I didn't do anything, Andy."

"Yes, you did. You pulled me out of my past. When we started praying for Star, I finally let Yellow Bird and our baby go. I know I'll always have a place in my heart for them, but the grieving days are over."

Tears welled up in Hope's eyes. "Are you sure?"

"Yes." He held her tighter and dipped his head. "If you'll have me, I'd like to stay on here. To be a real husband to you and a pa to Gregory and Billy and Betsy."

Laughter bubbled to Hope's lips at the reality of the words she'd only dreamed of for months. "Oh, Andy. Are you sure?"

In answer, he swooped her into his arms and carried her up the steps and inside the cabin. "Your new home, Mrs. Riley."

Still reeling from being carried over the threshold like a new bride, Hope stared at the beautiful room. Her eyes widened. "I can't believe it!"

She'd expected to come home to bare rooms, needing to be filled. A fire in a lovely stone fireplace provided sufficient light to reveal a beautiful hand-carved rocking chair. "Put me down, Andy," she said, barely able to force the words through her tight throat.

When he complied, she walked across to the rocking chair and stroked the arms, the back, marveling at the softness of the wood.

"Wh–where did this come from?" She looked at Andy, then made a sweep of the room with her hand. "All of this?"

"I—" He cleared his throat.

221

Hope's jaw dropped as she realized the source of his embarrassment. "Are you saying you made these things?"

"I guess so."

She hurried to him and threw her arms around his neck. "Andy," she said over his shoulder. "This is wonderful. You have such talent. I had no idea you could do something like this."

He shrugged. "Just a hobby."

"A hobby?" She pulled away and held him at arm's length. "Do you realize how much people would pay in the city for handcrafted furniture? The quality is magnificent."

"I never really thought about it." He grinned. "You really think I could make a living at it?"

"Are you serious? Andy, look at this beautiful home. I'll be the envy of every woman for a hundred miles." She walked across to the table, in awe of the craftsmanship. Then her eyes found the corner and she gasped. A beautiful armoire occupied the space. "Oh, Andy." She walked toward the cabinet and opened the doors, revealing shelves and drawers. Though she'd had enough money to buy whatever kind of furniture she'd wanted to fill her home, nothing had ever compared to the magnificence of Oregon maple crafted into pieces of beauty.

"It has to be a divine gift."

Andy fairly beamed under her praise, and Hope realized just how fragile her husband truly was. For some reason he didn't believe he had much worth.

She made a decision that she would work for the rest of her life to let him know what a treasure she considered him to be.

"Do you want to see the rest of the house?"

The low tone of his voice sent her heart racing, and she forgot about the rocking chair and the table and even the armoire. "Where are the children?"

"Asleep, I imagine. Hank's in the loft with the boys. Want to check on the girls?"

Keeping her gaze locked on his, she slowly shook her head.

"Are you sure?" She knew he wasn't asking about the children.

"I'm sure," she whispered, her love for him eclipsing her embarrassment at being so bold.

He closed the distance between them swiftly and took her in his arms. His lips closed over hers. She clung to him and returned his kiss with equal ardor. For the second time tonight, he swept her into his arms and carried her across a threshold.

❧

"Where's Ma?"

Andy looked up from his coffee at the sound of Betsy's voice. "She's still sleeping. It was late when we got home from Uncle Michael's house."

Betsy grinned broadly, showing a missing eyetooth. "Did Aunt Star's baby come?"

"Sure did." He tweaked her nose. "A pretty little girl, but not quite as pretty as you."

Clapping happily, Betsy slid onto the bench. "We knew it would be a girl. Aimee wanted a baby sister so bad."

Andy chuckled and got up to pour himself another cup of coffee. One by one, the household began to stir. Aimee and her three-year-old little brother emerged from Betsy's bedroom. She squealed when Betsy told her the news about her baby sister.

Hank climbed down the loft ladder right ahead of Billy and Gregory.

When Hope finally appeared, Andy was tongue-tied. "Good morning, everyone." She smiled at the children, but didn't meet his eye. Tenderness turned in Andy's heart at her modesty. He'd never had much use for such things in women, but he found that he loved and admired it about Hope.

"Would you like a cup of coffee?" Andy asked.

"Thank you." She ducked her head, refusing to look at him while he poured.

"Would you like me to help with breakfast, Aunt Hope?" Aimee asked.

Silence hung like a blade over a chopping block. The twins exchanged glances, and Andy could see the ax was about to fall. If he didn't step in quick, Hope would be humiliated.

Andy cleared his throat. "Well, let me see. Since this is our first official family breakfast in our new home, I vote we let your Aunt Hope off the hook and I'll cook this morning."

"N—no, Andy. I'll cook."

"I don't mind."

She stood. "I can manage. Everyone go get dressed and make your beds, and I'll whip us up something in no time." She turned to Andy. "I guess I should ask if you were as competent at filling our food stores as you were about filling our home with furniture."

Andy felt his chest swell under her admiration and he was relieved Michael had suggested just that thing.

"I still need to fill the smokehouse with meat, but that'll come after freeze up. I thought we'd buy a couple of hogs to slaughter. Until then, I can shoot whatever we need daily. I have some bacon that Michael gave us to see us through until we can replenish. Ma gave us a couple of her laying hens. I've already gathered eggs." He motioned to a bowl of eggs on the counter. "And Ma sent over a couple of loaves of bread."

She swallowed hard. "Sounds good. I'm sure you have chores to do, so don't let me be keeping you."

"I'll just bring in that bacon first."

She gave him a distracted nod, and Andy knew she was concentrating on her upcoming task.

Hank rose, draining his cup. He swallowed and grinned. "Nothing I like better than bacon and eggs for breakfast. I'll just help Andy with those chores. That'll work up a hearty appetite, so be sure and cook plenty." He gave her an affectionate brotherly peck on the cheek.

Andy chuckled. She seemed determined to fix breakfast herself, so maybe Ma had taught her a thing or two in the weeks they'd been at Michael's. He cast one last glance at her before he went outside. He hoped so, anyway.

An hour later, he stared at black bacon and runny eggs and realized that of all the wonderful qualities his wife possessed, cooking wasn't one of them.

Silence reigned supreme over the table, no one daring to make a peep. Andy ventured a glance at Hope. As though feeling his attention, she looked up, burst into tears, and ran for the bedroom.

Andy stood. He strode across the room and muscled Hope's rocking chair in his arms. Then he walked toward the door. "I have to go to town. You girls clean the dishes while I'm gone. I should be back before lunchtime."

Hank stood. "I'll saddle up and ride with you. What are you doing with the chair?"

"My business."

"Fair enough."

Once they got outside, Hank turned to him. "Hope going to be okay?"

"She'll be all right."

"I don't think I've ever met a woman who couldn't cook."

Andy frowned. "Well, now you have. Nothing wrong with that. I'm not much of a farmer like most men."

"You'll have to learn to be a farmer now, won't you?" Hank chuckled. "Unless you want to take up another line of work, say preaching."

"I'm willing to become the best farmer in Oregon for Hope's sake."

"Whew, you really have changed."

"Just wait, little brother. When you meet up with the right woman, you'd be willing to give up just about anything to make her happy."

Hank's face reddened.

Andy laughed. "Who is she, Reverend?"

"What do you mean?" he asked a little too innocently.

"My guess is you've already taken a shine to some lady."

"All right. I have. But I don't think she feels the same way."

"Have you asked her?"

"Of course not. I would never put her in the position of having to reject me.

That might hamper our friendship. And I don't want to risk it."

"The woman in question wouldn't happen to be a certain seamstress, would it?"

Though Andy didn't think it was possible, Hank's face grew redder, making his freckles pop out. But he didn't deny it. "Rosemary."

"Don't wait too long to talk to her, Hank. Time is too precious to waste."

Inwardly, Andy chuckled that he was giving anyone advice on love. He supposed once a man finally stopped struggling against it and found the woman who was meant just for him, he just wanted everyone to be as happy as he was.

He hooked up the team while Hank saddled his horse.

Though he hated to drive the wagon, the task he had in mind required that he do so. Despite his preference for riding on horseback, he had to remember he was doing this for Hope, the woman he loved. A wide grin spread across his lips as he imagined the look on her face when she saw her surprise.

~

When Hope finally got up the gumption to leave her bedroom, she was happy to find the kitchen clean and the children playing quietly in the living room. Gregory had even kept a fire going to ward off the autumn chill.

"Where's your pa?" she asked.

Gregory sent her a sharp glance. "Town."

"Did he say when he was coming home?"

"Before lunch."

"Aunt Hope. When may I go home and see my little sister?" Aimee asked.

"I don't know, sweetheart. I suppose your pa will come after you sometime today."

"What did Mama name her?"

So much had happened since Hope had given the baby girl her first bath, she had to stop and think hard for a moment. Then it came back to her. "Oh, yes. Hannah." She laughed. "How could I forget that? They named her after your grammy."

The girls giggled. "Grammy has such a pretty name, don't you think, Betsy?"

"My favorite name ever!"

"Hannah Riley." Aimee dimpled. "My favorite name, too."

Hope filled the coffeepot with water from the bucket on the counter. Andy would be home soon and she at least wanted to present him with hot coffee to warm him after a chilly ride to town and back.

Listening to the girls chatter about the new baby, Hope smiled to herself. Perhaps this time next year, she'd be holding a new baby of her own. She felt a sudden shiver of glee at the thought of giving Andy his own child. She found herself praying another prayer. *Please, let me give him a baby.*

Chapter 16

I can't tell you how happy I am to see you, Mr. Riley. That Mrs. Barker is a regular sea captain. Hollering about this and that. I don't know how she stays in business."

Andy grinned at Lucille's attempt to keep her voice down, but from the doorway, he heard Mrs. Barker's loud harrumph.

Lucille shrugged. "How is Mrs. Riley?"

"Fine. But she's ready for you to come to the house. We only have half the loft for you to sleep in for now. But we'll build you a room of your own come spring."

"Believe me, half a loft will seem like a palace compared to living in this prison."

Lucille's exaggeration elicited a chuckle from Andy.

"How long until you can be ready to go?"

"I best give the room a good going over before I leave. I'd hate for that woman to besmirch my name after I'm gone and tell people I didn't keep a tidy room."

"An hour?"

"That'll be fine."

"All right. I'll be back then."

Andy's next stop was the general store. The smell of leather oil and pipe tobacco greeted him when he stepped through the door. Andy walked up to the counter where a black-haired customer leaned easily against the counter, dressed in a black suit of clothes that spoke of privilege.

The proprietor placed his hands flat on the counter. "What can I do for you?"

"I...um..." Andy cleared his throat. His palms were damp and his heart beat a rapid rhythm within his chest. Trying to procure honest work was going to be harder than he'd thought it would be.

"Well?"

The owner's prodding brought Andy back to his senses.

"I make furniture."

"I have a good supply of nails over on that table."

"No. I didn't want to buy nails. Well, actually, I could probably use some. Just finished building my wife's cabin."

"Congratulations," he replied, without much enthusiasm. "As I mentioned, nails are over there."

Stalling, Andy grabbed two bags of nails. He paid for them and stuffed them inside his coat pocket. The little man behind the counter gave him a questioning look. "Well? Anything else I can do for you?"

Embarrassment crept up Andy's neck. "To be honest, I'd like to sell some of the furniture I build, and I thought you might be interested in placing it in your store for a percentage. I have a sample in the wagon just outside, if you'd like to take a look."

The other man at the counter followed Andy's pointing finger. Andy scowled at him. Obviously taking the hint, the man gave a curt nod and headed for the door.

Turning back to the proprietor, Andy waited while he seemed to be considering the proposition. Andy held his breath.

The little man finally nodded. "Can't hurt to take a look. I'm not making any promises, though."

"I understand."

Andy's heart thundered in his ears while the man examined Hope's rocking chair.

"This is better than average work." The man stroked his chin. "How much you asking for it?"

"This one belongs to my wife, so it isn't for sale, but I can make another one, and if you'll display it, I'll give you a percentage."

"I might be interested. What else do you make?"

Andy went down a list.

"Well, come inside, and I'll write up an agreement for us both to sign."

Excitement nearly exploded in Andy's chest as he followed the man inside. Hope had been right. Perhaps he could make a living doing what he loved to do.

After the man wrote up a rough contract of sorts, he pushed it across the counter. They haggled a moment about percentage until they came to a satisfactory compromise. Andy signed and pushed the paper back.

The proprietor started to sign then looked up, his expression suddenly hard, his eyes firing anger. "You Andy Riley?"

"That's right."

"The name Johnny Harper ring a bell?"

"I haven't heard it in quite a few years, but yeah, I used to know Johnny." Andy had met Johnny the first year in Oregon. He'd just been about Gregory's age at the time. The young man had taught Andy how to smoke and drink whiskey.

Johnny had tried to talk Andy into robbing the bank with him, but Andy's conscience wouldn't allow such a bold act. Johnny had gotten caught. He tried to pin it on Andy, but thankfully, Andy had been home with his parents at the time, attending a picnic with neighbors.

"How do you know Johnny?" Andy finally replied.

"You don't recognize me, eh? He was my boy." The man's eyes grew misty.

"Was?"

"He was sent to prison for the robbery. After he got out, he was more of an outlaw than when he went in. He was finally hanged."

"I'm so sorry, Mr. Harper. I didn't know."

"How could you have known?" The man's bitter tone caused Andy's heart to sink. He didn't even recognize the man, he'd grown so old in the last eighteen years. But clearly, he still believed Johnny's original claim—that Andy was the real thief.

"I am sorry about Johnny, Mr. Harper. I didn't know him for very long."

"Just long enough to turn him down the wrong path." The man's bitter response cut into Andy's sense of hope. "Get out of my store before I put a bullet in you."

Andy walked in bewildered silence into the cold November air. He shivered as a blast of wind slipped under his collar. But the chilly air didn't even come close to the icy chill invading his heart.

He climbed into the wagon. Hope had been wrong. He'd tried to do right by her. Had wanted to come home with the news that he would be building and selling furniture, as she'd been so sure he should. But how could she have known that a man couldn't escape who he was?

Loud music and shrill laughter reached his ears from the saloon down the street. Andy's mouth suddenly went dry. His heart rate increased. He hadn't been tempted to drink in months. But now he could almost feel the burning sensation of whisky in his throat. Could almost sense the welcome, numbing fog that would soon follow. Abruptly, he maneuvered the horses in front of the saloon. He didn't allow second thoughts. This was the only life he'd ever know. What was the point in trying to be anything more?

He hesitated only a second as Hope's face shot through his mind. The sweetness with which she'd given herself to him the night before. Rather than dissuade him, the image spurred him forward in frustration. He would never be good enough for a woman like Hope. Should never have thought to try to be a family man like Michael.

He reached for the door.

"Andy?"

A growl escaped Andy's throat at being detained from his mission. He turned to face Hank.

Hank narrowed his gaze, his eyes stormy. "What are you doing?"

"You're a smart man, figure it out."

Hank quickly closed the distance between them and stood between Andy and the saloon entrance.

"Get out of my way, Hank."

"I can't let you do it."

"You don't have any choice."

Hank folded his arms across his chest. He stood several inches shorter than Andy and was more wiry than muscular. Andy knew he could take him if he needed to, but he wouldn't. How could he blame Hank for looking out for his best interests? He knew his brother would stay planted in front of that door until he knocked him out of the way or gave in. How badly did he really want to go into that saloon? He studied the determination in his brother's face, the sincerity in his eyes, and Andy's fight left him.

He clapped Hank on the shoulder. "You win, little brother."

Relief washed Hank's face. "Do you want to talk about it?"

"Naw, I'll be all right. Listen, Hank, I need a favor."

"What's that?"

"Take the wagon and go get Lucille from the boardinghouse."

"The woman Hope brought west with her?"

Andy nodded. "She's ready to come to the cabin, and I told her I'd pick her up in an hour. I have some things to do first."

Suspicion clouded Hank's eyes. "Like what?"

"Don't worry. I'm not going into the saloon."

With a look that clearly said he wasn't so sure Andy was telling the truth, Hank gave a hesitant nod. "All right. Use my horse."

Hank climbed into the wagon.

Andy extended his arm. "Thanks, Hank."

Nodding, Hank clasped the hand. He held on. "Are you sure you're okay, Andy? Do you want to go over to the church and talk about it?"

"No. I need time alone." He hesitated a minute, then decided to come clean. "I'm going up to Pike's cabin. Do you still want me to take the horse?"

"Go ahead. I'll get one from Michael. But you shouldn't go up there now. Before long the pass will be too dangerous for you to go through until after the spring thaw."

Andy nodded. "That's what I'm counting on. Do you need your saddlebag?"

Hank scowled and shook his head impatiently. "There's only one thing in there and you need it more than I do. What about Hope and the children?"

"They have enough wood cut to last the winter, enough food except for meat and Gregory's pretty near as good a shot as I am. They won't go hungry."

"Maybe it's not so much about hunger as needing a man in the house. You know how winters can be. Do you really want your wife and children to be alone?"

Like an arrow, his words struck their mark, but Andy's mind was already made up. He would never be the man Hope believed he could be. Today's fiasco had proven that. "Will you give Hope a message for me?"

"If you're determined to do this thing, then I suppose I have no choice."

"Tell her I meant everything from the bottom of my heart. And I'm sorry."

"Andy, don't do something you'll regret."

"Good-bye."

Andy watched the wagon until it rolled out of sight, then, without another glance at the saloon, he mounted Hank's horse and rode out of town, in the opposite direction that his heart wanted to go.

⌇

For three days straight, Hope lay in bed, nursing her grief. She felt like a fool for believing a word he'd said. Her face burned at the memory of their night together. How eager she'd been. Wherever he was, he must be laughing at her for being an idiot. And she couldn't blame him.

A knock at the door interrupted her self-deprecating thoughts. Irritation bit her. In no mood to be bothered, she ignored the knock.

A moment later, the door swung open. "What do you think you're doing in bed?"

Hope sat up, smoothing her hair, although after three days without a brush there wasn't much point. "Miss Hannah!"

Miss Hannah looked down at her and the outrage on her plump face turned to pity. "Oh, honey." The mattress sank beneath her weight as she sat. She took Hope into her comforting arms. Without a word, Hope let loose a flood of tears. Great, wrenching sobs shook her. When finally her tears were spent, she snatched her hanky from the bedside table.

"I can't believe he left."

"Wasn't that the plan all along?"

A gasp escaped her lips. "You knew?"

Miss Hannah nodded. "Greg spilled it."

"I'm seriously regretting ever teaching that child to speak!"

A chuckle left Miss Hannah's throat. "That's good. You still have a sense of humor."

"Anyway, Andy wasn't supposed to leave until spring at least. And after the other night, I thought. . .I mean, he said—"

Hope twisted the hanky between her fingers, face flushing hot at what she'd almost revealed.

"I see. . ."

"Oh, Miss Hannah. I miss him. I never thought I'd fall in love. But it hit me so fast. Almost from the moment I met Andy. Even when he was stinking and barely recognizable from the beating he took."

Miss Hannah's face blanched. "Maybe you should tell me everything from the beginning."

Slowly, Hope started from the time she found Andy in the alley. She told about Gregory's trouble, and the miracles that occurred. The older woman's eyes misted, and she grabbed her own hanky from her wristband when Hope told her about Yellow Bird and the little grandbaby Miss Hannah would never hold in her comforting arms. And finally, she told of Andy asking her to take him as a real husband.

"Oh, I'm so stupid for believing him!" She smacked the bed in frustration.

"Andy's been running for a long, long time. I've plumb wore out my knees praying for him."

"Do you think if I pray for another miracle, God might send him home?"

"Maybe, but Hope, you know God isn't just up there doling out miracles to suit us. As much as He wants to bless us, the most important thing is the miracle of new life."

"You mean, you think I could be carrying Andy's child?"

Miss Hannah chuckled. "Well, you'd know more about that than I would. I'm not talking about human life. I'm talking about a new spiritual life."

"Like asking Jesus into your heart?"

"Exactly like that."

"I've been studying the Bible, Miss Hannah. For over a month, I've been listening to Hank at church and reading the Bible. I'm just not sure it's all true. D—do you think that's why God sent Andy away? Because I didn't pray the prayer with Betsy?"

"No, I don't. But the very fact that you asked me the question proves that you do believe and are just resisting."

Hope couldn't deny that her heart stirred every time she read the Bible.

"So if I surrender and ask Jesus in my heart, do you think God will do another miracle for me and send Andy home?"

"What would you do if He didn't? Would you still believe in Him, or would you decide there's nothing to Christianity after all?"

Hope considered the question. "I don't really know."

"You see, Jesus wants a relationship with you. How would you feel if your children only came to you when they needed something?"

Knowing Miss Hannah didn't expect an answer, Hope kept silent and pondered her words.

"God sent His Son to die so that humanity could be reconciled back to fellowship with Him."

"I thought it was so we didn't go to hell."

"That's the end result of knowing Jesus. Heaven. But most of us have a lot of living to do between now and then. God wants to be involved with our daily lives, our struggles, and our joys." She brought the hanky up for a quick swipe across her nose. "Yes, he wants to perform miracles for us. But sometimes we have to struggle. Those are the times when we really learn to trust God. To have faith that even if things don't turn out the way we expect or hope they will, we still have a God who loves us and who wants to hold us while the hurting lasts."

"So you're saying that Andy might not come back, even if I pray?"

"Honey, I've been praying for my son all of his life. He's been gone for the better part of fifteen years."

Dread clenched Hope's heart at the thought of Andy leaving and staying gone forever.

As if sensing her need to be alone, Miss Hannah rose quietly. "I'll be here when you're ready to come out and face the world."

"Thank you, Miss Hannah. Please tell Lucille you'll be staying to supper."

"Who do you think sent for me?"

Hope smiled. "Lucille's a real gem."

"So are you, Hope. And I hope Andy figures that out and comes back."

Tears filled Hope's eyes once more, and her throat clogged as Miss Hannah shut the door behind her.

Left alone, Hope felt the solitude through and through. Was Jesus really able to fill that emptiness for her? Would He even want to? Somehow, she found herself on her knees beside the bed. She closed her eyes and said the only thing that came to mind. "Jesus."

Suddenly, a sob began deep within and shot from her lips almost of its own volition. But once the sobbing began, it continued. Deep and painful wails that cried of her shame, her sins, her deep desire to know Jesus the way Miss Hannah knew Him, and Gregory and Betsy, and even Billy.

As the weeping gave way to gentle tears of surrender, Hope understood Betsy's joy. She understood why Miss Hannah could still believe in Jesus when her prayers for her son seemed to go unanswered year after year. She understood that Jesus loved Andy even more than she did, and that He, too, wept over His lost love.

Chapter 17

Andy rode for a full day to reach the cabin. Snow made the ride slow going as the horse slipped and slid up the mountain. Andy knew that, in another week or two, Hank's prediction would come true and the pass would be too dangerous to ride through.

With mounds of snow flanking the narrow trail that allowed for passage through the mountains, one slip of a horse's hooves or a sneeze could start an avalanche. More than one man had been buried alive for his folly.

On Andy's first day of solitude, he used the ax found inside the cabin and chopped enough wood to last several weeks. The cabin had once been used by trappers, but now stood pretty much for anyone who needed a place to hole up.

The second day, he brought down a deer with one shot. Days three, four, and five, he stared at the fire and thought about his wife and children. A lonely ache began in the pit of his stomach and combined with his boredom to create a healthy dose of frustration.

On day six, a very real feeling that he was going mad led him to Hank's Bible. He was willing to do anything to occupy his mind. He flipped through the pages until he found something familiar. He read about Noah and the ark. Next, he started reading about David and read all the way from the shepherd boy's time in the fields tending his flock to the king's death. Andy read and read and reread for two weeks, avoiding the four gospels at all costs.

After a month, his beard had grown out fully.

Three days of blizzard-like conditions had kept him inside and he felt restless. Grabbing his rifle, he followed deer tracks in the snow until he spied a massive buck standing in the distance. He took a step forward and heard a *snnnnaaaap*. Pain cut into his leg like no pain he'd ever experienced.

Sinking to the ground, he screamed out as the snow stained crimson.

Andy had always heard when a man faced sudden death, he repented for all of his wickedness. For Andy, this proved to be true. Blood flowed quickly, and the pain soon became more than he could bear. Waves of dizziness overcame him. He surrendered to unconsciousness breathing one name, "Jesus."

❧

Andy woke to the soft hum of voices. For the second time in less than a year, he'd passed out expecting that he'd never wake up. He could smell the wood smoke and knew he had been rescued.

This is the second time You've spared my life, God. Is it even possible that You have a purpose for me?

He craned his neck to locate his rescuer but was unable to see who had saved him. Pain shot through his leg as he rolled to get a better view. He groaned.

"Do not move." The soft voice was urgent.

A trace of shock slithered through him. "Yellow Bird?" Perhaps he had gone to heaven, after all.

She stood over him, her silky black hair brushing his arm. "You must lie still or your leg will reopen."

Tears filled Andy's eyes. "You're not Yellow Bird."

The young Indian woman gave him a sympathetic smile. "No, I am not. I am Little Moon."

A bearded buckskin-clad man came to stand behind the young woman, towering above her like a grizzly standing next to an average-sized man. The man's gentle voice belied his massive size. "Someone was looking out for you, little brother."

"What happened?"

"I'm ashamed to say the snow covered my trap."

"And my leg found it?"

"Yes. My wife and I found you just in time. It's been a fight with all the blood you lost."

"How long have I been here?"

The young woman held up three fingers. "Now I will bring you soup to make you strong."

The thought of food curled Andy's stomach, but the Indian woman waved away his protest. "You must eat."

The determination in her tone left no room for argument. "Yes, ma'am."

"You called my wife Yellow Bird."

"I'm sorry. For a second, she. . .uh. . .reminded me of someone I once knew."

"And loved?"

"Yes. For a very short time."

"My name's Hal Fulton. Little Moon has been my wife for a little over five years. Don't ask me what she sees in an old mountain man like me, but I thank God daily for sending her to me."

The young Indian woman returned with a bowl. She gave her husband an indulgent smile. "I see his beautiful heart. And I know this is the man God has made for me."

Taken aback by the easy way she spoke about God, Andy couldn't help but question her. "How do you know about the white man's God?"

She narrowed her gaze and straightened her shoulders. "God so loved *all* of the world that He gave His Son. He does not belong to white men only."

Andy felt his neck warm. "I didn't mean to insult you. I know God wants to be a God to all mankind. But my experience with Indians has taught me that most tribes serve their own gods and don't believe in Jesus."

She nodded soberly. "This is true. But my mother was a white woman captured by my father. She taught my father the ways of the true God." She smiled, her eyes alight with joy. "He became a Christian and offered to take her home to her people, but she loved him and chose to live in the village."

Andy couldn't help but respond to her warmth.

"Now, no more talking. You must eat and then rest. And eat again, and rest again. And soon you will be strong."

Andy had been gone two months when Hope knew for sure. She was carrying his child. Excitement and dread combined with her already heightened emotions, and she often found herself reduced to tears. They spent Christmas with Andy's family at Michael's home.

Miss Hannah's eyes misted when Hope revealed her condition, but made her promise not to tell anyone else for now, until she'd had a chance to share it with the children. Miss Hannah had promised. But she squeezed Hope's hand and whispered, "Maybe now God will bring Andy home."

Hope smiled tenderly at her mother-in-law. "But even if He doesn't, God will take care of us."

That had been two months ago. Now, four months pregnant, headaches, nausea, fatigue, and constant snowstorms confined her inside. Depression set in, driving her to her bed most days, wondering what kind of fool she was to travel more than halfway across the country only to be left alone in this forsaken place. Today happened to be one of those days. She hadn't left her bed all day.

A knock at her door drew her from the monotony of staring at the log walls wondering what she'd ever seen in Andy Riley. "Yes?"

Gregory entered, carrying a tray. "I brought you some supper, Ma."

One look at her handsome son and she remembered exactly why she'd come here. And she'd do it all over again. A smile formed from deep inside her and found its way to her lips.

"Thank you, son. But I think I'll eat with the rest of you tonight. I have a wonderful announcement to make."

She brushed her hair, changed her clothes, and sat at the head of the table.

Glancing about at the expectant faces, she gathered a breath for courage and forged ahead. "I'm going to have a baby."

Unabashed joy lit Betsy's face. "You mean it?" She jumped up from her seat and flung her arms around Hope's neck.

Hope laughed. "Yes, I mean it."

"When?"

"August."

Billy gave her a shy grin. "Is it a boy or a girl?"

"We'll know in about five months, won't we?"

"I hope it's a boy."

Hope turned her attention to Gregory. "You're awfully quiet. What do you think?"

The look of utter betrayal on his face hit Hope with a force and her heart nearly broke.

His questioning gaze sought hers. "How could he just leave?"

"He didn't know, Greg."

"But h—he lied to me. He told me it was just a business arrangement."

Hope's cheeks blazed. "That's between Andy and me."

"Yes, Ma," he muttered and stared down at his plate.

"Will Andy come back now, Ma?" Billy asked.

"I don't know, son. But if not, we'll be okay."

"I miss him," Betsy broke in.

They hadn't spoken of him in so long, Hope had begun to wonder if they even really remembered him, though she knew that couldn't be the case.

"I miss him, too, Bets. We just need to pray that wherever he is, God is taking care of him."

Greg hopped up. "I have to go do chores."

Her heart nearly breaking, Hope watched him go. *Father, please watch over Greg. And don't let Andy stay gone so long that he does irreparable damage to his relationship with Greg. If he comes back at all.*

How she wanted to get word to him somehow that he had a child coming. But even though Hank knew where he was, the pass would be closed for another two months at least, Hank assured her. So there would be no getting word to him, anyway. And he might be long gone before anyone could find him.

Besides, Hope wanted him to come home because his heart was sending him, not because of guilt or duty. If he didn't love her and want to be her husband, then she didn't want him to come back.

She'd lived through one loveless marriage. The only thing different had been that she didn't love her husband either, though she'd had respect for him as a man and for his position. But she was desperately, wholeheartedly in love with Andy. And she knew she couldn't settle for part of him. She'd have his heart. Or nothing.

Chapter 18

Andy mended slowly, but thanks to Little Moon applying poultices and dried herbs, infection was minimal and he recovered with full use of his leg. Rather than helping him back to his cabin, Hal and Little Moon insisted he wait out the winter with them.

Remembering the mind-numbing boredom of that first month in the mountains, he quickly agreed.

He moved to a thick bed of buffalo hides, and Little Moon hung a blanket to enclose the corner sleeping area she shared with her husband.

Once he was able to join Hal, they spent their days looking after Hal's traps, evenings reading scripture or discussing something they'd read.

"The pass will be opening up in another month or two, little brother," Hal observed one evening over supper.

"Yeah, I guess so." Andy liked the way Hal always called him little brother. He quickly understood that Hal saw him as a brother in Christ. As their relationship had deepened into friendship, so had Andy's relationship with God.

He couldn't very well deny God anymore. Not after God had twice saved him from certain death. Andy spent many hours reading the Bible, taking questions to Hal, and learning to pray. He knew that he was a different man inside than the man who had been caught in that trap weeks ago.

"So, when the pass opens, will you be headed for home?"

Andy couldn't help but grin over his friend's attempt to gather information. So far, Andy hadn't felt like he could open up. It wasn't that he didn't want to. As a matter of fact, he'd come to appreciate Hal's wisdom on many subjects. Perhaps that was the reason he didn't want to admit to all his past doings. And for leaving Hope and the children the way he had. Could he take the chance at reading disappointment in Hal's eyes?

He shrugged. "Maybe."

"Little Moon thinks you're still pining away for Yellow Bird."

"Yellow Bird?"

"You talked about her the first night."

He remembered. And for a few nights after that, her memory had invaded his mind, most likely because of Little Moon's ministrations. He hadn't spent any time with an Indian woman since leaving the Sioux village.

But soon the memory faded again, to be replaced by Hope's image. If he was pining for anyone, it was for his wife.

Hal's chuckle brought him back to the present. "I think Little Moon is right. She suggested we take you along with us when we go back to the Indian village. Perhaps one of the young women will take a liking to you, too. If a grizzly bear like me can be blessed enough to find a woman like my Little Moon, I'm sure a handsome fella like yourself can catch someone's eye."

Taken aback by the suggestion, Andy couldn't speak. When the silence became uncomfortable, Little Moon cleared her throat softly. "Perhaps Andy does not wish to find another Indian woman."

"Oh, it isn't that." He had no desire to insult the woman who had taken such good care of him and nursed him back to health. "It's just. . .well, to tell you the truth, Yellow Bird has been dead for several years. I have a new wife now. Her name is Hope."

Hal's laughter fairly shook the cabin. "Well, why didn't you just say so? You must be awful lonesome for her."

Andy nodded. "I am."

Little Moon frowned. She put her hand on her husband's arm. "Something is not right between you and your wife, Andy?"

How did women always know these things?

Andy shrugged.

Hal leaned forward. "Maybe you'd better tell us what the problem is. I've been told I'm a pretty good listener. And I can vouch for Little Moon, too."

Knowing the time had come to share his story didn't make it any easier. He pushed back his bowl and gathered a slow breath. "I'll start when Yellow Bird died. She was my wife and was carrying our only child. . . ."

Andy felt the irony that a story six years in the making only took moments to tell. He capped off the story by telling about the incident with Mr. Harper in the general store. And, finally, of his flight to the mountains to escape his inability to be a man Hope could be proud of.

Little Moon wiped her eyes. "You must return to Hope. She will love you for the man you are."

A glimmer of hope rose and fell almost simultaneously. "I've made so many mistakes."

"Well, she knew that when she decided to be your wife." Hal's gentle voice held a note of compassion.

"What does your heart tell you, Andy?"

"I know God has forgiven me of all my past mistakes. But what if I can't be the kind of man Hope deserves?"

Little Moon reached across the table and took his hand. "This woman loves you. She knew the man you are when she shared your bed. You've broken her heart by leaving her. That is what you will have to work to mend before anything else. Trust God to make you worthy of her."

"My wife is a smart woman, little brother. If you have any sense, you'll listen to her." Hal beamed with love for Little Moon. She sent him a tender smile.

Watching the interaction of this couple who loved each other so madly, he suddenly knew he would go home and make things right. No matter how long it took or what he had to do or where he had to sleep, he was determined to win Hope's love once more.

One thing he knew. The next few weeks until the pass opened were going to be the longest of his life.

Hope took not-so-secret joy in tending her very first garden. Michael had plowed a spot off to the side of her house, and Star had come to teach her to plant. She couldn't believe how many details there were to attend to. Learning the difference between weeds and shoots. It was enough to keep her mind occupied.

Now she sat on the ground, pulling weeds—at least she hoped they were weeds.

"Company's coming, Ma," Greg called from where he stood over the pig trough dumping food for the hogs.

She followed the direction of Greg's gaze and her heart nearly stopped. Even at a distance, she'd recognize that posture. "Andy," she whispered.

Apparently, the idea occurred to Greg, as well, for he took off at a run toward Andy. Hope had no idea what to expect. Her heart sank when the boy started yelling. "You can't come back! We don't need you."

Andy dismounted and clapped his hand on Greg's shoulder. "I know I did you wrong, son."

"I ain't your son. You didn't want me to call you Pa, remember?" He threw off Andy's hand and continued to glare.

Giving a solemn nod, Andy continued to regard the boy with patience. "I've spent all winter thinking about you. And about things I said and did. I came to ask your ma and you children to forgive me. If you'll take me back, I promise I'll never leave again."

Hope could see the struggle in Greg's face. She understood, for she felt the same struggle. The boy hesitated and she thought he might not forgive Andy. But in a split-second, he flung his arms about him.

"I'd be honored if you'd call me Pa," Andy said, still holding the boy.

Hope stepped forward as Gregory stepped out of Andy's arms. Andy's eyes grew wide as his gaze took in her figure. She felt the blush rise to her face. "Greg, will you please go inside and keep the twins occupied while your pa and I have a talk?"

Apprehension covered Andy's features at her words. When Greg was in the house with the door shut, Hope regarded Andy frankly. "What made you decide to come back?"

"A lot of things." He motioned to her stomach. "Are we having a baby?"

"Yes. Why did you run away the day after?"

"Let's get you off your feet and I'll tell you everything, all right?" Warmth enveloped her arm as he took her elbow and led her to the porch.

She settled in, enjoying the experience of being taken care of.

For the next several minutes, Andy opened up about all the events that happened after he left the cabin that morning.

She gasped when he told of his accident. But she thanked God when he told of being rescued. When he got to his renewed relationship with the Lord, she wept.

"Your mother will be so blessed to know her prayers have finally been answered. And Andy, you needn't have left. A man came around the day after and asked for you. Apparently, he'd coerced Mr. Harper into giving him your name and pointing him to your ma, who pointed him up here. He said he saw your work and wanted to hire you to make the furniture for a new hotel he's building. He only wanted the best, but handmade furniture would be a good advertising tool for the hotel."

"Ah well, it's probably too late."

"That's the beauty of it, Andy. It's not. He was traveling back to Boston and said he'd be back this spring sometime when they actually start building the hotel. He hoped you'd be available to discuss terms when he returned."

A grin tipped Andy's lips. "And will I be?"

She looked out over their fields, freshly planted by hired help. "Just look at that beautiful land." She glanced at him and grinned. "And get used to looking at it, because you're going to be here for a very, very long time, Andy Riley."

His eyes filled with tears and he took her face in his hands. "I know I don't deserve this second chance. But I'll make sure you don't regret it."

Leaning in, he took her lips with his and for Hope it was as though she herself had come home again. Just as Andy deepened his kiss and moved closer to her, the baby kicked hard. He jumped back. "What was that?"

"What do you think?"

Awe covered his features. He started to reach toward her stomach, then drew his hand back and met her gaze. "May I?"

"Of course."

The baby rewarded him with several kicks. Overcome with emotion, Andy gathered Hope in an embrace that nearly took her breath away.

He leaned back and held her at arm's length. "It's like I've been given a second chance with my entire life. God, you, the baby, the furniture business. I'm almost worried it won't last."

Hope laughed and pressed her palm to his perpetually scratchy cheek. "Don't worry about anything, Andy. God has chosen to give you a second chance for a reason."

Andy covered her hand with his and gazed at her with such an intensity of emotion, he almost stole Hope's breath away. "I love you, Hope Riley. I missed you while I was gone, but I'm glad God sent me to the mountains so He could reach me." He turned her palm over and kissed it. "I could never have been a good husband, no matter how much I loved you, until I gave my life fully to God and left the past behind."

Tears sprang into Hope's eyes. "Oh, Andy."

He kissed her once more, and she yielded easily. She sent a hasty prayer of thanks heavenward. She looked to the future with anticipation and hope. When they broke the kiss, they were both breathless.

Andy smiled at her and kissed her nose. He turned to look across the field, and Hope saw the spark of pride in his eyes.

"Beautiful, aren't they?"

"They are. Fresh and green and full of promise."

"I don't pretend to know what God has planned for our lives, but one thing I do know. . .our best days are still to come."

Slipping his arm about her, Andy pulled Hope close to his side and looked down at her. "Our best days are still to come."

He brought his face close to hers once more. And when he kissed her, Hope knew that for them both, the past was gone and the only thing that mattered was the future God had set before them.

When Andy let her go, she sighed and snuggled into his embrace. As they watched the beautiful sunset, Hope thanked God for the joy of today and the hope for tomorrow.

Epilogue

Weddings always made her cry. Hope sniffled, tears stinging her eyes as she watched Gregory smile tenderly at the bride. Her heart nearly burst with love and motherly pride. He'd come such a long way from the troubled boy he'd once been. Only God could have brought about such a magnificent change.

He had even finally cut his hair. Another sign of maturity as he didn't wish to offend anyone. Especially the members of his new little flock.

No one had thought it would ever happen, but after twenty years of secretly loving each other, Rosemary and Hank were finally tying the knot. And Gregory was performing his first act as pastor of the church in Hobbs—officiating the nuptials. Andy sniffled beside her. She gave her husband a tender smile and pressed her handkerchief into his hand.

"Sawdust from these new benches," he said gruffly, denying his tears.

Hope nodded and squeezed his hand. She understood her husband's emotion, his pride in the son he'd raised. Gregory stood so handsome and tall, a man of God, wholly committed to the calling he felt so strongly.

Fifteen-year-old Eva squirmed on Hope's other side. "When's it going to be over, Ma?"

Hope silenced the girl with a stern frown. Eva was her father's child through and through. She'd inherited his reddish-brown hair and brown eyes. Lashes that brushed her cheeks when she closed her eyes. And a dimple next to her lip that crinkled every time she laughed. Oh, the girl was a charmer.

Hope worried over her free spirit, though. She moved with the same recklessness that had once controlled Andy. Hope only prayed that God would get hold of the girl before she grew to be a woman. She prayed that Eva would be spared the heartaches her pa had been forced to endure because of his unwillingness to allow God to temper his wild spirit.

For now, Hope kept her close. She had a few more years to try to temper her. Beyond that, she knew she could trust God to do what was best for Eva. One thing Hope had learned for certain over the past fifteen years was that God loved her children more than she ever could. She had to have faith in His unfailing love. Trust Him to do what was best.

She caught her breath at the look of utter joy shining in Rosemary's face as she lifted her chin and accepted her new husband's kiss.

Hank had turned over the church to Gregory, and he and Rosemary were starting an orphanage in Oregon City. So many children reached the end of the Oregon Trail motherless and fatherless. Too often, the children ended up on the streets to fend for themselves. Hank and Rosemary were determined to make a difference.

Hope's gaze shifted to Miss Hannah, who occupied the seat in front of Andy. She could understand her mother-in-law's pride in Hank. There was something special about a child whom God had called to preach the gospel.

Next to her, Aimee made a lovely figure in a gown of rose-colored silk. The sweet-spirited, twenty-six-year-old young woman would have made the perfect preacher's wife. And from the look of adoration on her face when she looked at Gregory, Hope knew Aimee agreed.

Hope's heart went out to the girl. To Gregory, she was a beloved childhood playmate, a cousin by marriage, someone to protect, tease, love as much as one could love a family member, but he would never, ever fall in love with Aimee.

Hope knew some day Aimee would understand that. She only hoped the girl didn't allow true love to slip through her fingers while she dreamed of the impossible. Next to her, Betsy cradled her newborn son whom she'd named after her pa, Andy. James, her proud husband, slipped his arm about her shoulders and smiled down at his sleeping son.

Hope breathed a contented sigh. She cast a quick glance toward the door. With a gold star pinned to his leather vest, Billy sat, ever watching to make sure law was preserved. He wouldn't have missed the wedding for anything but had made it clear he'd have to sit close to the door in case he was needed. He considered his love of the law to be every bit the calling Gregory's preaching was, and Hope didn't doubt it for a moment. Everyone agreed he was a fine sheriff. And she couldn't have been more proud.

"Can I go outside now, Ma?" Eva's tug at her sleeve brought Hope to her senses. She realized the wedding was over and the bride and groom were being presented as Mr. and Mrs. Hank Riley.

Hope stood with the rest of the congregation. She glanced around, and her heart filled with a sense of contentment. These people represented everything God had brought into her life at a time when she thought life held nothing but heartache for her. He'd brought her the love of a godly man, children who knew and served the Lord. She didn't know what the coming years would bring for her loved ones, but she believed with all of her heart that God had good things planned for the Rileys. Her heart nearly burst with thankfulness.

As if sensing her mood, Andy turned away from the bride and groom and looked at her. She gave him a weepy smile. He took her hand and pressed it close to his heart. Hope rested her head on his shoulder.

The past fifteen years had brought her more happiness than she'd ever dreamed possible. But as she stood in the midst of her family, hope, stronger than ever, sprang in her heart, and she knew the best years of her life were yet to come.

Beside Still Waters

Dedication

To Tracie Peterson.
Thank you for everything.

Chapter 1

Spring 1880

Eva's chest swelled with exhilaration as Patches raced across the open field, his hooves throwing chunks of earth in his wake. Clinging to her beloved pinto's neck, Eva tossed a delighted laugh into the dewy air. She'd been in such a hurry to greet the day that she hadn't bothered to saddle or bridle her faithful friend. But she knew he didn't mind. Patches looked forward to their morning runs as much as she did.

The eastern sky exploded with orange, pink, and blue. Eva wished it were possible to ride straight into the horizon and lose herself in such beauty. A pity the earth was round. How wonderful might it be to ride clear to the edge of the world and stop just short of falling off?

At eighteen years of age, Eva knew everyone expected her to stop her wild ways, find a nice young man, settle down, and raise a gaggle of babies. Hadn't she received that sentiment from just about every dowager in town? The consensus of the Ladies' Auxiliary of Hobbs, Oregon, seemed to be that time was passing her by.

Eva wanted to settle down. Eventually. But so far, every time she thought she might be in love, her hopes had been dashed by some foolish act on the part of the young man who had looked so promising. She'd come close to the altar three times—and each time backed out just before making a dreadful, permanent mistake.

Even Ma agreed with the townsfolk. If Eva didn't accept one of her many proposals and actually go through with a marriage soon, she might as well take a teaching position somewhere and resign herself to spinsterhood. She shuddered at the thought. Not the spinster part, the teacher part. She'd tried teaching. Had lasted one week. How on earth could a person stay locked up inside all day, every day, when there was such a marvelous world outside just waiting to be admired and enjoyed?

Ma didn't understand, Eva's sisters didn't understand, none of the females she knew understood, except possibly Cousin Aimee, who had waited until she was twenty-seven years old before she married. Her wedding had taken place two years ago, and she was happier than any bride Eva had ever seen. So Eva saw no reason to rush. And with Pa on her side, she had at least two allies.

By the time horse and rider reached the river, Eva's heart was nearly bursting from her chest and Patches was slobbering like a rabid dog. The pony didn't bother to stop at the water's edge. Instead he walked right into the shallow water and dipped his neck.

Eva laughed and gave him a pat. Her hand came away slick with his sweat. "I'm a bit parched myself, old boy. I suppose I could do with a handful of the river." She swung her leg around, preparing to slide from the horse's back, just as a massive, hairy dog darted into the water, nipping at Patches's legs. The horse reared up, sending Eva splashing into the river.

Patches landed and began running along the embankment. Eva sputtered in the two-foot-deep water, sitting back on her hands, her knees up, feet planted on the riverbed. "Wha—"

The tail-wagging beast chased Patches a few yards upriver, then halted as a shrill whistle split the air.

"Lord Byron," a man's voice commanded. "Get yourself back here."

Eva glanced up. Her heart picked up speed as long, muscled legs waded through the water. Eva looked up as the handsome stranger bent and extended a hand. Eva scooted away from him. How many times had Pa warned her not to be friendly with strange men? The dog reached them just then and gave her a wet lick up the entire length of her cheek.

"Disgusting." Eva wiped her face with the back of her hand and pushed at the dog with the other. His massive paw caught the gold locket around her neck and yanked it off. It landed in the water, and the river swept it downstream.

"No!" Dread paralyzed her, and she remained where she sat. With a groan, she stared after her most precious possession.

"Hold on, I'll get it." The stranger splashed through the water. "There it is." He dove in and came up holding out a closed fist. "Got it!"

Relief flooded her as she took the locket and held it close. "Thank you, sir. This was a gift from my pa the day I was baptized. I've had it since I was twelve."

He wrung out his shirt and swiped dark locks of hair back from his forehead. "My pleasure. And the least I could do since my dog is the one who caused the locket to come loose in the first place. Not to mention your current position in the river *and* scaring your horse away."

As if trying to make amends, the dog gave her another lick. "Oh, for pity's sake."

"Get back, Lord Byron," the stranger commanded. "I'm sorry about that crazy dog. Here, let me help you up."

"No thanks, I can do it myself. You just keep that beast of yours from knocking me down again."

He extended his hand anyway.

"I mean it. I don't accept aid from strange men. And if you come any closer, I'll scream loud enough to make your ears bleed."

His eyebrows rose. "Ah, a spirited young miss," he said in an English accent—obviously put on, since he'd spoken with a perfectly normal accent only seconds before. Something about his tone and the amusement sparkling in his deep blue eyes gave her the unsettling feeling that this man was making fun of her.

As much as she wished to simply toss her head and refuse to speak to him, her curiosity got the better of her. "Where are you from?"

"Texas." His white-toothed smile dazzled in the morning sun.

Eva sniffed. "Then why were you trying to sound like a foreigner?"

"I was teasing. Sorry." He rubbed his palm against his thigh, then reached down again. "Come on, let me help you up," he said in a decidedly Texas drawl. Then he added, in that strange English accent, "I promise I'm not going to try anything, lest your scream cause my ears to run red with blood."

Was this man daft?

Once more she spurned his help. She struggled to her feet, her face burning as she realized how awkward she must look trying to stand up in the water while maintaining her modesty.

"Suit yourself," he said. He saluted her, and she noticed that he held a book in his other hand. "Just trying to be mannerly, considering my beast is the one responsible for your precarious position."

There he went with that highfalutin talk again. It was enough to make her head spin. Still, as she stood in the shin-deep water, she took a moment to look him over. Broad chest, square jaw, and deep blue eyes that made her legs weak didn't quite match up with a man given to books. Only weak men liked to read, in her experience. This fellow looked like a romantic hero described in the dime-store novels her best friend, Lily, liked to snatch from the shelves of her pa's general store.

He cleared his throat, and she realized she'd been staring. Heat spread across her cheeks.

"I've never seen you around here before," she said, wading past him toward the bank.

He followed. "My family just settled here from Texas last month. Bought a few acres just to the south."

Eva's stomach dropped. What did he mean by "family"? Was he married with half a dozen children? Though she was dying to ask, she couldn't drum up the courage. Instead she simply smiled. "The old Winston place. I'd heard they were selling, but I didn't know anyone had bought it. They never were much to attend town functions or church."

She stepped up onto the bank. A beautiful chestnut mare, tied to a nearby tree, blinked at her. Eva turned and caught the stranger's eye. "I haven't seen you. . .or your, uh, wife at services."

"Haven't left the house much. Still settling in. And I'm not married." He winked, making Eva's cheeks burn. "I suppose Ma'll talk Pa into attending soon. She's getting lonesome for Christian company."

"But not you?"

He captured her gaze, as though he knew she thought him about the most magnificent-looking man she'd ever seen. Interest flickered in his eyes, or perhaps curiosity. But definitely something that went beyond mere politeness.

Eva hurried to clarify. "I mean, for your soul's sake, of course. You don't want to stay out of church very long. Believe me, I know how easy it is to fall into sinful ways."

"I'm sure your sins were many and of the most sordid kind." He made no effort to hide a grin.

Why, he wasn't a gentleman at all! Eva didn't care how handsome he was. It was obvious this man had not been properly raised. "There are sins of the heart and mind just as there are actual hands-on sins. Didn't you know that?"

There. Turn the tables on him. Make him feel as though she thought him a complete idiot.

Only he didn't appear a bit shamed by her chastisement. His eyes crinkled with silent laughter. And then he winked.

Oh my! Eva's eyes widened, and a crushing retort danced on the tip of her tongue, but the stranger spoke up first.

"And pray tell, what were these inward sins that blackened your heart against the goodness of God?" He pressed his hands to his chest in what Eva could only consider to be mockery.

Anger, for instance, and mean thoughts. Not unlike those tainting her heart at this moment. But she had no intention of revealing such things to this man.

"That is between myself and my Lord," she fumed.

"I can respect that." His eyes sobered. "A person has a right to private thoughts." He looked deep into her eyes, as though sharing a soul-changing moment.

Confusion clouded Eva's mind, along with the sudden, unsettling realization that she didn't really know what he was talking about.

She rarely took much time out for inner reflection beyond her time with God. She was who she was. She served God with the same gusto she did everything else. Her personal Bible times in the old gazebo Uncle Michael had built for Aunt Star deepened her love and faith. And at times, her soul flew away on the wings of praise.

But she hated attending church. The confinement indoors, the drawn-out prayers and lengthy sermons that left her squirming on her seat until Ma's scowling expression told her to be still.

She never could quite understand why people felt they needed to erect a building to put God into anyway. As far as she was concerned, they should hold services outdoors, in the nature God had created, instead of in a stuffy building that was cold in the winter and stifling in the summer.

Still, she felt it her duty as a Christian to inquire as to why this man hadn't included himself when he said his ma and pa would most likely come to church.

"I hope we see you at the service today," she said softly. Which, judging from the placement of the sun in the sky, was set to begin in just a couple of hours.

"Do you?" He smiled. Eva had to admit he could be charming when there was no mockery in his eyes.

Still, his bold assumption that there was anything personal in the statement sent her defenses rising. "Of course I do. I'm concerned for anyone who doesn't attend services on the Lord's Day."

"Are you sure that's all?" His lips twisted, and all the charm left his smile.

Oh, he was baiting her. She recognized a teasing challenge. Didn't she have two older brothers? She knew the best course of action would be to ignore his implication, yet she couldn't help but allow her rising defenses a voice.

Eva sniffed. "If you're trying to imply that I have personal motives, then you're sadly mistaken, Mr. . . ." Eva searched her mind. She didn't even know his name. Only an ill-bred man would allow this much time to pass without so much as offering his name and requesting hers.

Perhaps he didn't care to know her name. The thought grated.

"Jones," he supplied. "Benjamin Jones. But my friends call me Jonesy."

Eva felt his challenge. If she called him Jonesy, he would laugh at her assumption that he wanted to be her friend. "Well, Mr. Jones, there is nothing personal in my query. It was simply a Christian invitation for you to join our fellowship."

"Very well, Miss.   " His brow rose, and his boyish grin melted Eva's irritation.

She smiled and held out her hand. "Riley. Eva Riley."

Instead of a polite shake, Jonesy lifted her hand and pressed warm lips to her fingers. She caught her breath and jerked back. "As I said, Mr. Jones, my query was not of a personal nature."

"Very well, Miss Riley. Although I must admit my pride is wounded." His eyes continued to sparkle in amusement. "I suppose it's just as well you hold no personal interest," he said boldly. "I'm only staying in Oregon long enough to help Pa get the farm producing. Then I'm going back to Texas to start my own ranch."

Eva ignored the sudden disappointment pinching her insides because he wouldn't be around long enough for her to really get to know him. Honestly, men and their land. What difference did it make? All she needed was a wide-open space to run Patches.

Patches! At the thought of her companion, she looked about, searching for any sign that he'd come back. That wretch of a horse had run off and left her at the mercy of a strange man and his overgrown beast. Home was a good five miles away. And she didn't relish the walk. Ma would skin her alive for being late to breakfast. Especially on the Lord's Day.

Patches would certainly not be receiving a sugar treat today. The coward.

"I suppose I should be going home," she announced. "I'm sure my horse will arrive there soon and everyone will worry." She pushed damp curls from her cheeks and nodded to the handsome stranger.

She could only imagine what she must look like. She hadn't even taken time to braid her hair this morning but had merely tied it back with a ribbon—which now floated down the river. "Good day, Mr. Jones. It was. . .interesting meeting you."

Jonesy. She liked how it sounded in her mind. The name suited his rugged looks. Scratchy stubble lined his jaw. Some men might have appeared unkempt without a full beard or a clean-shaven face, but not this one. His deep blue eyes and thick dark hair caused Eva to swallow hard. Wait until she told Lily.

"It was lovely meeting you, Miss Riley. I'm sorry about my dog. I'm afraid Lord Byron is rather short on manners."

"Why do you call your dog Lord Byron?"

A chuckle rumbled in his chest as he dropped to the ground and removed his boots. "Simple. He likes to sit and listen to me read the poetry of Lord Byron." He turned his boot upside down. Water poured out.

Poetry? Eva couldn't abide poetry. Mooning men and women extolling their true loves. It made her positively ill. She'd rather read a dime-store novel. At least those were entertaining.

Eva's soaked skirt was cooling off with the early morning breeze, and she shivered. "Well, good day."

"How far are you from home?"

She waved her hand in front of her. "Only about five miles. I can walk it in no time."

"It would be my honor to escort you home on Lady Anne." He cocked his head. "I named her after Lord Byron's wife."

Eva smirked. "Does she also enjoy poetry?"

"Naturally. She thinks I'm reading about her beauty." He pressed his index finger lightly to his lips. "Don't speak too loud; she might overhear. I don't want to insult her. She's quite vain."

"You have my word; she will never hear from my lips that she isn't the subject of the poems."

Jonesy pressed his hand to his heart and gave an exaggerated bow. "Thank you, kind lady. I am forever in your debt. Therefore, you must allow me to give you a ride home on the back of my horse."

The thought of riding so close to him sent a wave of heat to her stomach. Ma wouldn't approve.

She shook her head. "No. I can't accept, though it was kind of you to offer."

"I understand. It might not be proper." He frowned in thought. "Then you must take my horse."

A gasp escaped her throat. "Why, I can't do that. How will you get home?"

"The same way you planned to. The two strong legs God bestowed upon me."

"So you do believe in God."

"Never said I didn't."

He made her positively dizzy. "Regardless, I can't take your horse."

"I live less than a mile from here. It only makes sense."

Eva narrowed her gaze. "Not to me, it doesn't. It's your horse. Mine ran off. You've no obligation to see me home. I can take care of myself."

"I'm walking home. If you don't take Lady Anne, she will feel abandoned and may never recover from the tragedy."

"Why should that matter to me? She's your horse." Eva shrugged and turned to go, but her conscience got the better of her. "I wouldn't leave her alone if I were you. There's been some horse thieving going on in these parts lately. Your lovely mare probably wouldn't be here when you got back."

His brow went up, and Eva noted a flicker of uncertainty in his eyes. It left as quickly as it had come. He shrugged. "I suppose that's a chance I'll have to take."

He was bluffing. Eva knew he must be. "Suit yourself." Her shoulders squared, she turned and began walking toward home, sufficiently confident that she'd won the battle.

"Farewell, my sweet lady. . . ." Jonesy's voice, in that fake English accent, caused her to falter a step. She turned back and scowled. He wasn't speaking to her but to the horse.

"You've been a grand companion," he said, stroking her mane, "and I shall miss you terribly. But I would never be able to live with myself knowing I'd sent a young woman off to trudge her way home across the harsh land while I rode comfortably on your strong back."

Eva rolled her eyes. He must be joking. Surely he wouldn't leave Lady Anne behind after she'd told him about the horse thieves.

Then again, this man seemed daft enough to do it, just to prove a point. "All right, you win."

He looked at her and grinned, not even trying to be gracious in victory. "Excellent. I'll meet you and your family at service this morning and retrieve my beautiful mare."

Eva suddenly realized that accepting his offer would give her a chance to see him again. Smiling to herself, she accepted the reins from his strong, calloused hands.

Eva tried not to read too much into the brush of his fingers against hers. Her mind whirled with the events of the past few minutes as she mounted Lady Anne and nudged the mare into a trot.

Finally she'd met a man who might hold her interest, and he had no plans to stay in Oregon! Eva took a deep breath and made a firm decision. She would return Lady Anne to him and never again think about his deep blue eyes or full lips. As far as she was concerned, all thoughts of Jonesy as a suitable companion or possible mate were strictly forbidden.

Chapter 2

Joncsy faced in the direction of his house, opened his book of poetry, and tried to lose himself in the words as he walked home. In an uncommon lack of focus, he stared at the print on the page, but the capacity to form sentences from the disjointed words seemed to escape him. Instead his mind conjured up the image of Miss Riley.

"Eva." The name tasted sweet on his lips, and he felt an unsettling stirring in his breast. Tucking the book under his arm, he replayed every word of their conversation. Her bedraggled appearance after taking that toss in the river had been plenty enchanting in an outdoorsy sort of way.

He chuckled to himself, remembering her dire warning about the temptations of sin. Though he highly doubted she had anything to worry about, she did have a point. Even with daily Bible reading and prayer with his family after supper each night, he was more than ready for a service with fellow believers.

By the time he reached home, the sun had burned the dew from the grass and the delicious smells of bacon and freshly baked biscuits wafted from the house. The door was open to allow in the morning breeze. Jonesy stepped across the threshold.

The sight of his parents locked in an embrace in front of the stove brought a rush of heat to his cheeks. His mother gently pushed out of her husband's arms when she noticed Jonesy standing in the room. She reached up and patted her hair, giving her son an embarrassed smile.

"I was beginning to wonder if you'd been swept away to some magical kingdom again by one of those books of yours." Her tone rang with amused scolding. "Good thing your pa stood up for you. I was just about to feed your breakfast to Sally Mae and her piglets."

Jonesy tossed a quick glance at his father. Elijah Obadiah Jones stood six feet two, a full head taller than Jonesy's mother, and the difference was never quite as noticeable as when she stood in the crook of his arm, looking up at him with adoration.

Her slender, work-hardened fingers rested on Elijah's chest, and her eyes squinted with fondness. "Of course, your pa's an old softy. He insisted we give you a few more minutes."

Jonesy smiled. "Thanks, Pa."

Elijah tightened his grip on his wife's shoulders and drew her closer. "I wasn't about to let her feed my son's breakfast to an old sow."

Contentment swelled Jonesy's chest. His parents shared a deep love. Either would have moved heaven and earth to make the other happy. He knew love was the only reason Ma had agreed to leave a prosperous ranch and move the three younger children all the way to Oregon so Pa could fulfill his sudden desire to give up ranching and try his hand at farming.

Jonesy stopped by the washbasin and splashed water on his face. "Sorry I'm late, Ma."

"I declare, son." She eyed him up and down and shook her head, giving an exasperated huff. "What happened to you?"

"Lord Byron scared a young lady's horse, and she ended up in the river. I waded in and tried to help her."

"Tried?" Pulling away from her husband's arm, she grabbed a plate and began dishing up breakfast. "What's that supposed to mean?"

He felt a dumb grin spread across his face. "She's feisty. Threatened to scream loud enough to make my ears bleed if I so much as laid a finger on her."

"How ungrateful!" His mother's brow furrowed with indignation, but a chuckle left his pa's throat.

Moving behind his wife, Pa kissed her cheek. "Sounds like your ma in her younger days. She was a feisty little thing herself. Watch out for this one, son. She might just snag you into marriage. Like your ma here did me."

Ma turned with plate in hand and rolled her eyes as she moved past him toward the table. A harrumph escaped her throat. "Your pa chased me until I finally let him escort me to the Christmas dance, just to make him stop asking."

"Yep, and that's all it took. We were married three months later."

Ma set the plate on the table. "Come eat your breakfast, son, so we're not late to services."

"Yes, ma'am." Jonesy sat down and took a whiff of the bacon, eggs, and biscuits with great appreciation. "And you don't need to worry about any woman snagging me. I'll be back in Texas long before the Christmas dance."

His comment brought an end to the lighthearted atmosphere. Ma gathered a deep breath. Pa cleared his throat. "Well, I suppose I'd best go put on my Sunday meetin' clothes."

Regret seared Jonesy as he watched his father leave the room. "Sorry, Ma."

"Oh, son, there's no need to apologize. We're just thankful you came to help out for as long as we can keep you here." She patted his shoulder. "I suppose I'll get myself ready, too. Rinse your plate when you finish, please."

Jonesy nodded. He hated to disappoint his parents. But he had to live his own life. And with his brothers Terrance and Frank, both almost grown, Pa would have plenty of help with the farm. Besides, what did Jonesy know about farming? He'd been raised on a ranch. Just because Pa had decided he'd had enough of ranching and wanted to try his hand at farming, that didn't mean Jonesy had to do the same.

An hour and a half later, the family approached the little white church building in the town of Hobbs. Jonesy had visited town several times to pick up supplies from the general store, and he'd eaten a few meals at Joe's Restaurant. Not bad. But certainly couldn't hold a candle to Ma's cooking.

He rode next to his ma on the seat while Terrance and Frank rode on horseback. Twelve-year-old Dawn sat demurely in the back of the wagon, being the perfect little girl she'd always been. A real young lady. Nothing like the spirited woman he'd met this morning.

Jonesy's heart picked up a beat at the memory of those soft brown eyes rimmed with bristly dark lashes. Her skin had a bronze hue. Most of the young women he knew tried desperately to keep their skin shaded from the darkening effects of the sun. Quite a feat in Texas. But this woman didn't even seem aware of those sorts of things. Or if she was, she didn't bother herself with matters such as darkened or freckled skin, or wild hair that curled when it got wet.

He scanned the churchyard, which was full of wagons and horses. It seemed the church would be quite full this morning.

A low whistle from Terrance arrested his attention. "Now I understand why you'd loan out the Lady."

"Woo-wee," Frank expounded.

"Boys," Ma admonished.

Jonesy's stomach did a flip-flop at the sight of Eva Riley standing next to Lady Anne. She smiled as she held the mare's reins and waved.

"Eyes full of life and fire," Elijah mused.

Jonesy dragged his gaze from Eva and stared at his pa. "What'd you say?"

"Snappy eyes. Just like your ma." The amusement in his voice, followed by his brothers' laughter, brought heat to Jonesy's cheeks.

"You all hush up and stop teasing Ben." Jonesy's ma had never taken to calling him by the nickname he'd been given by his two older brothers, who had families of their own now and had remained in Texas. The name had stuck with his pa and everyone else. But Ma wasn't to be swayed from the name she and Elijah had bestowed upon their son.

He didn't have a chance to respond to his family's teasing. Eva had drawn close with Lady Anne.

Elijah reined in the team, and the wagon rolled to a halt. Terrance dismounted, his grin telltale. Jonesy stepped between him and Eva before the young man could embarrass her with his teasing brand of humor.

"So I see you are honorable." He swept his Stetson from his head and smiled, keeping his voice even.

"Honorable?"

"You brought the Lady back to me safe and sound like you said you would."

"Oh." She handed over the reins, her smile tentative. "Yes. Thank you." Her subdued manner took him aback. Was this the same girl who had snapped at him and verbally sparred with him earlier? He allowed his gaze to sweep over her. Chestnut hair, which earlier had been loose and clinging to her face, now swept upward, every strand demurely in place. She wore a modest gown of light blue and moved with grace. "I. . .um. . .appreciate your kindness."

A loud, obvious throat clearing came from next to the wagon, where his parents stood waiting to be introduced. "Oh, Miss Riley, I'd like you to meet my parents, Elijah and Caroline Jones."

Eva smiled with warmth and extended her hand first to his mother, then to his father. "It's a pleasure to meet you both. I'm so glad you've made it to our little fellowship."

His mother, who had been cautiously inspecting Eva, relaxed immediately, and a smile spread across her plump cheeks. "I've been longing for Christian fellowship."

Eva tucked her hand through the older woman's arm. "Come, let me introduce you to my ma. But I warn you, she'll recruit you to make clothing for the children in my uncle's orphanage."

"Oh, how wonderful. I'd be delighted."

Eva whisked his mother away as though she'd known her forever. Jonesy stood back and watched, slack-jawed.

"Those two look about as thick as a couple of newborn pups." Pa clapped him on the shoulder before following the women.

Ma looked over her shoulder. "Coming, son?" By the look in her eye, Jonesy knew she thought she'd found her ticket to keeping him firmly planted in Oregon.

≈

Eva's mother, Hope Riley, wasn't one to pass up an opportunity to invite a new family in the area to Sunday dinner. So an hour and a half after her brother Gregory finally dismissed the service, Eva found herself sitting across from the most intriguing yet strangest man she'd met in her whole life.

She glanced up and caught Jonesy's gaze. He grinned, and her throat constricted as she tried to swallow a bite of venison roast.

The bite lodged, cutting off her air. Still eye to eye with Jonesy, she pointed at her throat. He frowned, then his eyes widened. He pushed his chair back from the table and shot to his feet as Eva fought for air.

"Son, what on earth are you doing?"

Eva's head began to spin. He pounded her on the back, and she started to cough. Finally she felt the bite begin to move, and her airway cleared.

"Here, drink this," Jonesy said softly. He handed her a glass of water.

She took it gratefully and let the cool liquid soothe her burning throat. "Thank you," she croaked.

"Are you okay?" Hope asked.

Eva nodded. "Fine."

"Thanks to quick thinking from Jonesy here," Eva's pa said, approval ringing in his voice.

Now that she knew she wasn't going to die, Eva couldn't help the embarrassed warmth that spread across her cheeks. "May I be excused, Ma?" she asked, unable to look anyone in the eye. "I'm not very hungry anymore."

"Of course."

Eva rose and came face-to-face with Jonesy, who stood close enough to take her in his arms if he chose to do so. Which, of course, he didn't. And why would she even think such a thing? "Thank you, Mr. Jones. Excuse me, please."

She maneuvered around him and fled outside. Once on the steps, that familiar sense of longing, for what she didn't know, reached into her heart and squeezed until she found herself heading instinctively to the barn. She needed to burn off some energy. And the only way to do that was to saddle up Patches and ride across the open fields. Ma would disapprove of her leaving when they had company. But Pa would understand and would come to her defense.

The pungent odor of hay and horse manure filled her nose as she stepped inside the barn. "All right, Patches, old boy. You don't deserve this ride after the way you left me to the mercy of a perfect stranger this morning, but I need it, so there's no choice." In no time, she saddled the horse and led him through the barn doors.

She stopped short when she came face-to-face with Jonesy.

"Going somewhere?" he asked, raking his gaze over Patches and then back to Eva.

"For a ride."

"Mind if I come along?"

Eva shrugged. "Suit yourself."

"You never know when you might need rescuing."

His teasing tone raised her ire. "I never need to be rescued. I can take care of myself."

Brow lifted, he grinned. "Really? And yet I've been forced to come to your aid not once but twice today."

"Wh–what?" Eva sputtered. She couldn't even try to deny he'd saved her from choking. But twice? "I was having a perfectly nice ride with Patches this morning before your rude dog scared my horse half out of his wits. So if I needed 'rescuing,' as you put it, that was only because your dog can't mind his manners." *Much like his master.*

"I see you've been thinking about it quite a lot. Dare I hope you've been remembering me with affection?" His self-assured grin might have irritated her beyond words, and normally she would have put him in his place with a few well-spoken words and a glare of disdain. However, her traitorous sense of humor bubbled up, and laughter sprang from her like a gusher. "Tell me, Mr. Jones, are you always so sure of yourself?"

"Almost always. Aren't you?"

Eva mounted Patches, trying to decide how to answer. He squinted against the late-afternoon sun as he stared up at her. Eva returned his gaze evenly. "There are two kinds of people, Mr. Jones. Those who know who they are and act accordingly. And those who *act* as though they know who they are."

"And which are you, Miss Riley?"

Eva gave a short laugh. "You have to ask?" She left him to draw his own conclusion and nudged Patches forward.

It took all of her inner strength not to turn around to see if Jonesy was following. Patches strained at the bit, wanting to open up into a full gallop, but Eva kept the reins tight. What if Lady Anne were too much of a lady to catch up to the pony?

In moments, the sound of a horse's hooves confirmed that Jonesy had indeed saddled the Lady and had every intention of catching up. Eva's competitive nature rose to the surface, and she gave Patches what he'd been craving. She loosened her grip on the reins, and both horses raced across the field toward the river.

Two horses, two riders. Eva laughed out loud from the pure joy of warm wind in her face and the feel of Patches's straining muscles against her legs. Her hair fell from its modest trappings and whipped out behind her like a flag blowing in the breeze.

Her laughter stopped, however, when Lady Anne drew close, then came alongside, and finally pulled ahead. The sound of Jonesy's laughter echoed across the field.

Anger burned in Eva, and she urged Patches harder. "Come on, boy. Are you going to let a girl beat you?"

Apparently sensing the challenge, Patches increased his speed. But by the time Patches and Eva reached the river, Lady Anne had already halted and was taking a long drink.

Humiliated, Eva glared at Jonesy's smug face. "We weren't ready."

Laughter exploded from him. "Then I apologize for taking unfair advantage of you and your paint pony."

Was he insulting Patches? Her beloved pinto had been a gift from Pa's trapper friend and his Indian wife. "My horse could win against that mongrel of yours anytime."

"That 'mongrel' comes from a thoroughbred mother and a very respectable wild stallion. The two met after Lady Anne's mother snuck out of her stall one night and ran to meet up with a wild herd."

Though still smarting from the defeat, Eva couldn't help but see the quality in the lovely brown mare. "She's beautiful." She sent him a half grin. "Sorry for the slight to Her Majesty."

"Don't worry about it. She's not really as arrogant as I made her out to be this morning."

"Unlike you, huh?"

"Me?" He pressed his Stetson over his heart. "I'm truly hurt by that remark."

Behind the words, Eva could see the amusement she'd come to expect from him. Was the man ever serious about anything?

Dismounting, she turned loose of Patches's reins and let him drift into the water for his own drink.

Jonesy led Lady Anne to a nearby bush and wrapped the reins around a branch. He eyed Patches, who had drifted a few yards downstream. "Do you think you'd better go get him?"

Eva followed his gaze. "He'll be fine. He's just wading."

"You're going to let your horse roam after the way he ran off this morning?"

"Lord Byron scared him half to death, or he never would have left me like that."

"Are you ever going to forgive my poor beast?"

"Maybe. . .if you teach him some manners."

"Then I'm afraid he's doomed to be forever in your ill favor."

"There's no hope for him?" Why was it that she tended to fall into playacting so easily with this man?

Jonesy gave a heavy, dramatic sigh. "He's a lost cause. I've resigned myself to a life of apologizing for him."

Eva threw back her head and exploded into throaty laugher. "You're funny, Jonesy Jones."

A flush of pleasure crawled across his face, and he smiled. "I'm sure I'll have all my animals in stitches when I start my own herd."

Instantly sobering at the thought, Eva nodded and turned away. "Patches, come here, boy." She gave a shrill whistle, and the horse trotted back. She took his reins. "We'd best be getting back, Mr. Jones."

"Eva, wait." Jonesy stepped forward and held on to Patches's bridle. He towered over her, and Eva had to cock her head to meet his gaze. "I just want you to know. . ."

He swallowed hard, and so did Eva. "You want me to know what?"

He shrugged. "I don't even know what to say. I've never met anyone like you."

Eva's heart pounded in her ears. "I've never met anyone like you, either."

The depth of his gaze left little doubt in Eva's mind that he was being sincere. Usually when a man shared his feelings like this, it meant a proposal was forthcoming. But she knew that wasn't going to be the case with Jonesy. Bracing herself, she nodded her encouragement.

Clearing his throat, he looked away and fingered Patches's bridle. "The thing is, Eva, I'm not staying in Oregon. I can't get tangled up with a woman and take a chance you could talk me out of my dream."

Eva gasped at his assumption that she had any desire to talk him out of leaving. "For your information, Mr. Jones, I have no intention of entangling myself with you. So don't flatter yourself."

"Maybe I'm the only one thinking along the lines of what might be between us, then?"

Drawing a long, slow breath, Eva took a chance. "No. You're not the only one. I just don't see the point of bringing it up when you've made your position so crystal clear."

"I enjoy your company. I'd like us to be friends."

"Without any chance of romantic notions, is that right?"

He nodded. "Is that too presumptuous of me?"

"We can be friends." She squared her shoulders and tamped down the disappointment. After all, she barely knew him. But so far, he was the only man whose company she truly enjoyed.

Perhaps friendship was all she was cut out for. Maybe she would be an old spinster after all. Just as the town gossips predicted. There were worse things in life. Better to enjoy a friendship with a man who made you laugh than to spend your life married to a man who made you cry.

"Friends, then." He grinned and pressed her shoulder with his palm. He went to retrieve Lady Anne while Eva mounted Patches.

"We'll race you back." She grinned down at him, then nudged Patches into a full gallop.

"Hey, that's cheating," Jonesy called after her.

Eva laughed into the air and gave the horse his head. This time she was determined not to lose.

Chapter 3

The summer flew by in a variety of fun-filled days, and Eva soon wondered how she ever endured life without Jonesy's friendship. Now that the summer heat had cooled to a lukewarm autumn, she tried to push from her mind the fact that Jonesy would soon be leaving.

Harvest was a busy time, and she'd barely seen him in the past couple of weeks. Desperate for some companionship, Eva jumped at the chance to ride to town for a bag of flour for Pa's birthday cake. At least she could spend a few minutes catching up on town gossip with her best friend, Lily.

She let Patches have his head, and they raced down the road, throwing up dirt and pebbles from the path.

All at once, Patches stumbled. The ground rose up to meet Eva with alarming speed. She landed hard and lay on the road for a moment, trying to get her bearings. Pain jabbed her left hip. She groaned. The blue sky above her came back into focus, and she sat up slowly. In six years, Patches had never once thrown her.

The horse stood at the side of the road, favoring his right front leg. Ignoring the pain in her hip, Eva struggled to her feet and limped to Patches. She patted his neck and slowly moved around to the leg. After a quick inspection, it was clear why Patches had sent her sailing from his back. He'd thrown a shoe.

"I'm sorry, boy. You must have hit a rock and bruised your hoof. We'll get you fixed up in no time."

Blowing out a breath, Eva glanced down the road, then back toward the direction in which she'd come, debating whether to walk the rest of the way to town or go back home. The distance would be about the same. But in town she'd be able to get the flour Ma needed for Pa's birthday cake. And she could visit the livery stable and have Patches reshoed. She could rent another horse for the ride home and leave Patches there while he healed up from the bruise.

Her mind made up, she took hold of Patches's reins and led him toward town. The September day brought a mild breeze. As Eva walked along the road, she lifted her face to the wind, enjoying its soothing caress.

Normally autumn was her favorite time of year, but dread had been her constant companion all summer. The closer harvesttime came, the more aware she was that Jonesy's time in Oregon was almost over. She tried not to think about it, tried to just enjoy their time together. Taking long rides along the river's edge, sitting in the gazebo while Jonesy read poetry to her. She was even learning to tolerate some of the wounded-heart cries from scorned loves.

Jonesy had made a valiant attempt to read one of her dime-store novels, but he'd declared it to be the downfall of cultured literature.

Eva smiled at the memory. She'd tried not to show how much she was beginning to love him. Of all the men who had courted her, professed love for her, sought to marry her, Jonesy was the one who had finally caused her to surrender to love. And her heart belonged to a man who loved his dream of owning a ranch in Texas more.

Familiar daydreams began to filter through her mind. . . . Her wearing a wedding gown. Jonesy reading poetry aloud at the end of a long day of working in the fields. But he had his own dream. And that dream didn't include marrying a girl who would tie him down to a land he didn't love.

What Jonesy apparently didn't realize was that Eva would follow him anywhere. To Texas or the ends of the earth. Besides, there was something exciting in the possibility of scratching a living in a new land. Building from the ground up. Starting with nothing and ending up prosperous, the way her parents had.

Of course, her ma had been wealthy when she'd met Pa, but they still had to work together. Pa was a craftsman, not a farmer. His furniture sold widely, and now they were one of the most prosperous families in the state. He'd done that on his own, Ma's money notwithstanding. And though Eva's older half brother, Greg, and twin half brother and sister, Billy and Betsy, all had large inheritances from their own pa's estate back in Chicago, Eva's inheritance would be just as great. Her pa had seen to that.

Caught up in her thoughts and the enjoyment of being outdoors in the cool fall day, Eva didn't notice the sound of horses' hooves until it was too late to duck into the woods and hide herself. She stopped and waited as three men approached.

Please, Lord, let them go on past.

"Well, look at this, boys. What do we have here?"

Eva's stomach churned at the man's gruff voice. He spat a stream of tobacco juice and narrowly missed the hem of her skirt. Her knees grew weak under the lecherous scrutiny of the three men.

Still, if there was one thing Pa had taught her about dealing with precarious situations like this, it was to never show fear.

"You fellas lost?" Her voice trembled only slightly. She prayed they hadn't noticed.

The second speaker, a younger, thinner man with a scraggly red beard and a mouthful of black or broken teeth, leaned forward in his saddle. "Well, now, what makes you ask a question like that? Don't we look like we belong in these parts?"

"I've lived here all my life and have never seen you. That's all I meant."

Eva felt the third man's dark gaze raking over her. "If we was lost, would you help us get unlost?"

The innuendo in his tone sent warning bells ringing through Eva's mind. She'd heard whispered rumors of what could happen to a woman caught alone on an abandoned road. Her pride had kept her from thinking anything harmful could happen to her. She'd always figured Patches would get her safely wherever she needed to go. He'd only been outrun by one other horse ever: Lady Anne. But there was nothing either of them could do now to avoid what was possibly to come.

Eva tried to form a plan of escape. With Patches injured, running would be futile. If only she carried a pistol! Pa had given her one, but she hadn't bothered to carry it with her. She prayed her arrogance wouldn't get her killed. Or worse.

"Whatsamatter with your horse, little lady?" the first man asked, nodding to Patches.

Eva shrugged, attempting nonchalance. "He threw a shoe. I think he must have a stone bruise, because he keeps limping."

The hulking man dismounted. Eva caught her breath at his sheer size up close. He loomed over her, taller by more than a foot, she was sure. Her stomach dropped. There was no way she could fight off this man. Not in her own strength.

A silent prayer formed in her mind. *Lord, I'm not ready to die. Please send help.*

His meaty hands slid over Patches. "Yes siree, this is one fine horse. I bet he'd bring a good price."

"My horse is not for sale," Eva said, summoning enough courage to give the man a cold tone.

The man turned steely eyes on her. "He ain't, huh?" He gave Patches a pat on the neck. In a flash, a knife appeared in his hand.

Eva gasped and backed up. If she ran down the road, they'd catch her easily on horseback. In the woods, there'd be no chance of anyone finding her and coming to her rescue.

Oh, Lord, what do I do?

He reached his fat hand to her locket and yanked it from her neck.

"Hey! My pa gave me that."

"That was real nice of him. But you won't need it where you're goin'."

"I—I won't?"

"Now, you be a good little girl and be still, and this won't hurt a bit."

"Wh–what won't hurt?"

He gave a wicked laugh. "Don't worry, honey. I only want the horse."

Somehow, knowing she wasn't about to be violated gave her a sense of dignity. She lifted her chin. If there was to be no escape, she would at least die well.

Like the Indians Pa so loved and admired. Closing her eyes, she waited for the end to come.

❧

Jonesy took his ma's list of supplies and his pa's instructions to pick up the new wagon wheel from the blacksmith's shop and flapped the reins at the team of horses. The wagon jerked forward and rattled down the road. Jonesy noted the cool air, and his mind began to wander.

Harvest was approaching rapidly. Before long, all the crops would be in. He'd be ready to head home to Texas soon. His brother Theodore was keeping an eye on the one hundred acres of land Pa had given to him—part as inheritance, part in payment for coming to Oregon and helping get the farm started. His end of the arrangement was almost fulfilled.

Jonesy's stomach churned with excitement as it always did at the thought of his own ranch. He'd saved every dime he'd earned as a cowhand on Pa's farm, working since he was sixteen years old. He now had enough to start with a small herd of his own.

The sound of an approaching rider captured his attention. He glanced over his shoulder and waved as he recognized Nathan Compton, a newly married young man with a small ranch a few miles south. He pulled his horse to a stop. Heavy breathing and a wild look in the man's eyes caused Jonesy to tense with anticipation. "What's wrong?"

"My father's ranch. . ." He gulped in a mouthful of air.

"Take it easy," Jonesy interjected. "Slow down and tell me what happened."

"Thieves." Nathan swiped the back of his hand across his forehead. "Two of Pa's hands were murdered. One got away."

"Did he say how many there were?"

"Said he counted seven."

Seven men shouldn't be too hard to find, provided they stayed together. "How many of your horses did they make off with?"

"No more than five, near as we can figure."

"Five shouldn't be too hard to track."

"These fellas are wily. They've stolen from at least a half-dozen families over the past year, and no one has been able to catch them."

"Then it's time someone did. You headed to the sheriff's office?"

Nathan nodded. "Times like this, I think the farmers have the right idea."

"Why's that?"

"Nothing to steal. Unless you're a bird."

"I'd rather take my chances on a ranch any day." Jonesy flapped the reins, and the horses moved forward. Nathan's mare kept pace.

"Me, too. But seeing Shem and Booker dead like that shook me up a mite."

"No one could blame you."

Nathan frowned as he glanced at the road ahead. He jerked his chin. "What's going on up there?"

Jonesy's heart nearly stopped when he noticed Patches standing at the side of the road. Three men, two on horseback. A third one standing over Eva, brandishing a knife, poised to. . . *Oh, Lord, help me.*

"You packing a rifle?" he asked Nathan.

"Yeah, and a pistol, too."

"When I give the signal, fire into the air. Once. Just to get their attention."

Jonesy pulled his pistol from his holster and urged the wagon forward. "Now, Nate."

Gunfire blasted the air. Eva's would-be attackers swung around.

"Throw down your weapons," Jonesy warned the men. He aimed his pistol at the man on the ground next to Eva. "Step away from the lady and drop that knife before I send a bullet into your skull."

"Take it easy now, mister," the man said, tossing his knife into the dirt near his feet. "We didn't mean the girl no harm."

"You filthy, stinking liar!" Eva's outrage shot through the air. "Don't believe him, Jonesy. He was just about to slice my throat."

The man glared at Eva. "You ain't got no proof of that."

"What I saw was proof enough," Jonesy said. "Eva, kick that knife far from his reach, and then come to the wagon."

She did as he instructed. Relief spread through him when she came close enough for him to confirm that she was unharmed. He hopped down and helped her to the seat. He handed her his pistol. Then he pulled some rope from the back of the wagon. "Cover me." He walked halfway to where the three men were—two still on horseback, the other standing in the road.

He looked first at the scraggly-bearded redhead on the black-and-white paint. "All right, Red, slowly dismount and make your way over here. And don't try anything. Nate wouldn't hesitate to shoot."

"Neither would I," Eva called.

Jonesy's lips twitched.

The burly man dismounted, and Jonesy tied his hands behind his back. Jonesy eyed him carefully. "Slowly walk to the wagon."

With a snarl, the bound man shuffled toward the wagon.

"Nate, once he's in there, tie his feet."

"I'll do it," Eva piped up. "Nate needs to cover you."

"No, Eva. Stay away from him." When Jonesy turned to reiterate his words, the other horseman kicked his horse's flanks and took off at a gallop, nearly knocking the third man to the ground.

"Stop!" Nate fired into the air, but the rider didn't slow. "Want me to go after him, Jonesy?"

"No. I'm going to need your help getting these two to the sheriff." He grabbed the knife off the ground, stuffed it into his waistband, then tied up its owner with the remaining rope.

"You're making a big mistake, fella," the man said, squirming. "You ain't got no proof that I did anythin' wrong."

"I saw you standing over this young lady with a knife in your hand."

"He's a horse thief, too." Eva's voice was filled with anger. "I can testify to that."

"Your word against mine, little girl."

"Who do you think my brother, the sheriff, is going to believe?" Eva shot back.

That silenced him.

"And another thing," Eva said, glaring. "Give me back my locket."

Jonesy turned to the thief. "Where is it?"

"In his shirt pocket."

Jonesy reached inside the pocket and retrieved Eva's prized possession.

"It's worthless junk anyway," the man said, spitting on the ground.

Eva gave a sniff. "Then you're a stupid thief."

Jonesy smiled with satisfaction. Eva was one spunky girl. Once, he'd thought he preferred the kind of soft-spoken, demure woman depicted in his beloved poetry. But that was before he met Eva.

The thought of this man threatening her sent anger shooting through him. He finished tying his hands, a little tighter than necessary, then gave him a shove toward the wagon. "We'll get these two situated in a cell, where they belong. Then we can go after the other one. Unless I miss my guess, the one that got away will most likely lead us straight to the rest of the horse thieves."

"You don't know what you're talking about, mister," the redheaded man said. "The rest of the gang's long gone by now."

"Shut up, you idiot," the apparent leader growled.

"That's real interesting information," Nate said with a nod. "I'm sure the sheriff's going to be grateful. He's been trying to catch you rattlesnakes for some time."

❧

Eva still trembled by the time her brother Billy, known as Sheriff Bill Riley to folks in the area, finished questioning her. Fortunately, he determined there was enough evidence to detain the two thieves until the circuit judge rode through.

Her brother wrapped her in a strong hug, then held her out at arm's length. "You sure you're okay? Do you need to go talk to Gregory? He could pray with you."

"There's no need to bother Greg. It's all over now." Eva smiled with great affection at her brother. "Besides, I have to pick up a bag of flour over at the general store. Ma's making Pa a cake tomorrow. Be sure to come out for some."

A flush spread across her brother's face. "You, uh, going to see Lily?" Though nearly ten years her senior, Billy had never made time to find a wife. Now he seemed enamored of Eva's closest friend, Lily. The storekeeper's pretty little daughter had been waiting so long for him to notice her that she'd almost despaired of finding a husband.

"Yes. Do you have a message for her?"

Jonesy chuckled.

Billy frowned and cleared his throat. "No. Not at all. Why would I? She's your friend, not mine."

"Fine," Eva retorted. "But I wouldn't wait around too much longer if I were you. She's getting awfully tired of holding out for you." Without giving him a chance to answer, Eva looked up at Jonesy. "You ready?"

After a quick farewell to Billy, they stepped out onto the boardwalk. "I'll drop you off at the general store," Jonesy said, "then take Patches to the livery. Would you mind giving Lily my ma's supply list? I could pick up the order when I come to get you, after I get Patches settled in and go see about a wagon wheel at the smithy."

Eva nodded. "I wouldn't mind at all."

Jonesy stopped when they reached the wagon and placed a hand on her arm before she climbed in. "Are you sure you don't want to go talk to the preacher?"

"I'm sure. It's just all so. . .overwhelming." Unbidden tears filled her eyes. Traitorous tears.

"Honey, come here." Jonesy's tender voice washed over her like a warm summer rain, and she willingly went into his arms, despite the curious onlookers. "I praise God that Nathan and I came along when we did."

He stroked her hair, and she was almost sure she felt him press a kiss to the top of her head. Eva snuggled into the embrace, her cheek resting on his solid chest. She closed her eyes as tears squeezed out and ran down her cheeks. For the first time in as long as she could remember, she was afraid to be alone.

"People are beginning to stare. I guess we should get going." Jonesy pushed her slightly from him and reached into his pocket. "Here, take my handkerchief." He assisted her into the wagon.

Shame filled Eva. She felt more helpless than she'd ever felt in her life.

They rode in silence until they reached the general store. "Are you sure you're going to be all right?"

His eyes held such compassion that Eva almost started crying again. She blinked back the tears and nodded. "I'll be fine. I'll just wait for you inside until you return."

Reaching forward, he trailed his thumb along her jawline. His eyes roved over her face. "I'll hurry. And don't worry, Eva. I'm not going to let anything happen to you. Come on, I'll walk you inside."

Eva took his arm, and they stepped into the general store together. He nodded to Lily, who peered at them with curiosity and large eyes that spoke volumes.

"I'll be back later, okay?" His eyes were filled with such concern that Eva couldn't help but smile.

"Don't worry. I won't be afraid while I'm with Lily."

The bell above the door dinged as he departed.

Eva gathered a deep breath and pivoted on her heel to face her wide-eyed friend. She walked toward the counter. "Lovely day, isn't it?"

Lily gave a huff and, ignoring Eva's attempt at diversionary conversation, got straight to the point. "I vow, you two have the strangest relationship. Is Jonesy courting you, or isn't he?"

Eva smiled.

Her friend sighed with exasperation. "Come on, Eva. I'm your best friend in the world. Can't you tell me what's going on?"

Eva shrugged. "I've told you over and over. Jonesy is my friend, and that's where it ends. He only plans to see his pa through the harvest, then he intends to go back to Texas before the winter weather sets in." She bit her trembling lip. Her emotions were so raw that anything might cause her to burst into tears, and she didn't want to do that.

"And he's never tried to hold your hand or steal a kiss?"

"Nope. Not even once."

Lily's blond ringlets bounced as she shook her head. "After all these months, he hasn't changed his mind? I don't know whether to believe that or not. You two looked awfully chummy driving up together. And why did he lead your horse away tied to the back of his wagon?"

Eva couldn't share her experience on the road with her friend. Even as dear as Lily was, the thought of reliving it with words sent a cold trickle of sweat sliding down her spine.

"Patches threw a shoe while I was on my way to town. Jonesy saw me walking with my horse. Since he needed to pick up a wagon wheel that was being repaired, he kindly agreed to take Patches to the livery."

"I see. So he'll be back to collect you after he's done his manly errands." She wrinkled her nose in amusement. "Sounds very much like a married thing to do."

"Trust me. It's nothing like that."

The look of suspicion on Lily's face expressed her skepticism. "What's that in your hand? Is it a list for me?"

Heat spread across Eva's cheeks. "Jonesy asked me to gather a few supplies for his ma while I'm here."

A delighted smile split Lily's pretty round face. "Oh, Eva. You really are acting like a married couple."

Eva's jaw went slack. "Don't be ridiculous."

Rolling her eyes, Lily held out her hand. "Fine, have it your way. Give me the list."

"Ma needs a five-pound bag of flour, too."

"That all?"

"Yes. She'll come into town for more supplies in a few days, but she wants to do some extra baking for Pa's birthday tomorrow. A mouse got into the pantry."

Lily shuddered. She grabbed the bag from the shelf behind her and dumped it on the counter. "There you go. Now what about Jonesy's list?"

Avoiding eye contact, Eva handed it over. "Any new books?"

"Oh yes, a new shipment arrived a few days ago."

Eva left Lily to fill the order and walked to the display shelf. She glanced over the new selections. Her eye focused on a book of poetry. She couldn't resist picking it up. It didn't mean anything, she tried to convince herself. Not only had Jonesy saved her life, but he would be leaving soon. A going-away present was perfectly acceptable between friends.

Jonesy returned to the general store just as Lily finished filling the order. Eva waved good-bye to Lily, then headed out of town with Jonesy.

The noon sun shone down with much more warmth than earlier in the day. They chatted about everything, it seemed, except what was weighing the heaviest on Eva's mind.

When they approached the spot in the road where she'd nearly been killed earlier, she started trembling. Jonesy took her arm and pulled her to him. "Come here." He slipped his arm around her shoulder. "You're safe with me, honey."

Eva relaxed as the wagon rolled past the fearsome spot in the road. She felt safe with Jonesy.

But what about in another month, when he was gone? Would she ever feel safe again?

~

From the woods, he watched for a sign that the girl might be riding back alone. When he'd seen her earlier that day, he'd known she was for him. Beautiful dark eyes and dark hair. Long eyelashes. Skin that begged to be stroked. He shuddered as he waited for her.

He never would have let Randy kill her. He'd been just about to step in when those two men had shown up. Fury burned in him at their interference. But at least they'd supplied him with her name. *Eva.* That's what they'd called her.

The sound of a wagon rattling on the road arrested his attention. His heart nearly clogged his throat at the sight of his Eva. He narrowed his gaze as anger scorched out the love he'd felt mere seconds before. She was no better than his mother. No better than all the other women he'd loved.

He watched her lay her head on the man's shoulder. Her betrayal sent shards through his stomach. She would pay for this disloyalty.

Chapter 4

On the night of the harvest dance, as he dressed for the party, a wretched bit of truth hit Jonesy hard. He'd worked so much the past couple of weeks that he'd forgotten to invite Eva to the last dance he would be attending in Hobbs, Oregon. He couldn't believe he'd never caught the hints. Now he understood why she'd brought it up last Sunday after the church service.

He groaned as he slicked back his hair. It was curling slightly at the ends. Another reason to kick himself. He needed a haircut. But Ma was already dressed for the dance, so he couldn't very well ask her to cut it for him. He raked his fingers through the thick strands and shrugged. It would have to do.

He snatched his Stetson from the hook on his door and headed down the hallway to the kitchen. Since Eva's run-in with the horse thieves, the sheriff had advised folks to travel in groups as much as possible. Jonesy would ride Lady Anne but stay near the wagon with Pa and Ma, as would Terrance and Frank.

"It's about time you got yourself prettied up." Terrance's teasing laughter met Jonesy as he stepped into the front room.

Ma gave him a scrutinizing frown. "Gracious, son, your hair needs a pair of shears, doesn't it?"

"It can wait."

"No, it can't. Now you sit down and let me trim it up. I won't have it said that my sons aren't respectable."

"I'd hate to make you late for the dance."

"Nonsense. Terrance and Frank can go on ahead."

"Ma," Frank said, "we agreed that you wouldn't go anywhere without all of us escorting you. It's safer that way."

Ma waved away his protest. "It's been two weeks since Mr. Compton's horses were stolen, and no one has seen hide nor hair of the rest of those thieves. They're probably long gone by now. I'll be plenty safe with Ben and your pa." She raised up on her dainty toes and pressed a kiss to Frank's cheek. "You're a good son, but I'll be fine."

Frank and Terrance looked at Jonesy for support. In answer to their silent appeal, he smiled at his mother. "Really, Ma. I think I can go out in public one more time without a haircut."

The door opened, and Pa stepped inside. "What's the holdup? The team's all hitched and ready. Are we going to this thing, or ain't we?"

Apparently not the least bit intimidated by her husband's crotchety attitude, Ma waved him to a chair. "Coffee's still warm. Pour yourself a cup while I cut Ben's hair."

"Isn't it a bit late for that?"

"It'll only take a minute if we can get started," she said pointedly.

Pa blew out a breath. "All right. There's no changin' her mind when she's got it set on somethin'." He poured his cup of coffee and glanced at the two teenaged boys. "You two best go along to the dance before Elizabeth McDougal gives up on the both of you and picks some other fellow to dance with."

Jonesy laughed out loud as the competitive young men bounded for the door. The house shook as they slammed the door behind them. Jonesy pulled a wooden chair away from the family table while Ma brought her shears from the kitchen shelf.

"Look at this," she scolded. "I can't believe you were going to take Eva to a dance looking like this."

"I'm not taking her."

"What do you mean?" A frown creased her brow. "Eva's going with some other young man?"

Heat spread across his face. "I don't know. I forgot about it and never asked her."

She gave a huff of indignation. "Do you mean to tell me after all these months of beauing her around, you forgot to ask her to the biggest dance of the year? It'll serve you right if she did take up with someone else."

Mindless of the sharp shears next to his ear, Jonesy turned to look at his mother. "Beauing her around? Eva and I are only friends. She knows what my plans are."

Pa gave a snort from his seat at the table. He swallowed a sip of coffee and spoke evenly. "What a woman knows in her mind and what her heart tells her are two different things."

"What does that mean?"

"He means Eva Riley is in love with you, son. It's as plain as the nose on her face every time she looks at you." Ma's voice gentled. "And unless I miss my guess, you're in love with her, as well."

"Maybe."

A slow smile crept across her mouth. "You're not going to deny it?"

"Nope." Jonesy gave her a grin. Finally admitting his love for Eva made him feel freer than he'd felt in a long time. "I knew for sure that day on the road. I'd never felt so protective of anyone as I did Eva."

"So what are you going to do about it?"

"I don't know. I have to get back to my land, but Eva's whole life is here. I don't know if I can ask her to leave."

"Maybe you should let her make that decision." She scrubbed his neck with the towel and brushed at his back. "All done. Let's go."

Jonesy kept his thoughts to himself as he rode alongside the wagon on Lady Anne. Some things were just too private to share. Things like whether he could ask Eva to go to Texas with him. In addition to big considerations like leaving her family, it would also mean a quick wedding. That thought sat well with him, but he couldn't be sure how Eva would respond. After all, neither of them had spoken of any feelings beyond friendship. And though he suspected Eva returned his affection, a proposal would still come as a surprise.

Wagons and horses littered the street between Joe Grafton's restaurant at one end of town and the livery stable at the other. The empty lot next to the livery had been transformed into a dance floor, as there was nowhere large enough to hold everyone who would be attending from the town of Hobbs and the surrounding area.

Long poles had been erected at the four corners of the floor and rope strung between them. Hanging lanterns lit up the entire area, including the tables and benches set along the sides of the dance floor. Caleb Owens and Victor Mansfield made up the band: Caleb on the banjo, Victor playing the accordion.

Jonesy tied up Lady Anne to the nearest hitching post and walked the rest of the way to the dance. He scanned the area for any sign of Eva.

He saw the sheriff leaning against a post, sipping punch and watching the dancers. Jonesy came up beside him. "Evenin', Sheriff."

Billy acknowledged him with a nod. "You made it."

"Any reason to think I wouldn't?"

A side grin split his lips. "According to my little sister, you'd better not show up if you know what's good for you." He clapped Jonesy on the shoulder. "You have about as much to learn about women as I do. Only don't wait so long as I did, or you might just end up all alone."

"Yeah, thanks. I'll remember that." He continued his perusal, but the dance floor was so crowded, it was hard to see faces unless they were right in front of him. "Where's Eva?"

"I saw her dancing with Pa a minute or two ago."

"Help me look, will you?" He saw her just as she saw him. Her eyes widened, then narrowed. Her lips pressed together, and she lifted her chin, turning away from him.

So she was going to be stubborn. He'd show her right good and well. He grabbed Billy's arm and strode across the dance floor. The sheriff yanked his arm away. "If you think I'm dancing with you, you're crazy."

"I need you to dance with Eva so I can talk to your pa."

"Pa? Oh, boy. I hope you know what you're doing, because this is going to make Eva right hot under the collar."

"For a little while maybe. But we both know she can't stay mad longer than it takes to saddle a horse."

He chuckled. "From the look on her face, I'm thinking this might be the first time she holds a grudge."

"Don't let him cut in, Pa." Eva's low tone reached Jonesy's ears as her gaze cut through him like a hunting knife.

Andy Riley filled out his buckskin jacket as though he were still a young man, and Jonesy wouldn't have wanted to tangle with him for any reason.

Ignoring Eva's outburst, Jonesy glanced at her pa. "Sir, may I have a word with you?"

Eva sputtered. "You came out here to get my pa to leave me on the dance floor? Why, you. . .you. . .baboon."

Billy took her by the arm. "Take it easy, sis. He brought me along to take Pa's place."

"I don't need you to find me a dance partner, Benjamin Jones. I can find one on my own." Jerking away from Billy, she stomped up to the nearest man, Lily's pa, the owner of the general store. "Dance with me, Mr. Brewster?" She turned to Lily. "You don't mind dancing with Billy, do you?"

Lily flushed, then gave a shy wink of her dimples. "I—if the sheriff doesn't mind, I don't suppose I do."

Billy turned red. "It'd be my pleasure, Miss Lily."

Eva turned to Mr. Brewster. "Well then. Now that that's settled, how about you and me?"

The old-timer scowled. "That was sort of embarrassing for my daughter, Miss Eva."

"Embarrassing?" She took the first step and placed her hand on his shoulder, then waited expectantly for him to do his part. "Mr. Brewster, Lily is my dearest friend. Don't you know I have her best interests at heart? Besides, if you'll dance with me, I'll tell you a secret."

He placed his hand on her waist and took her upraised hand. "What sort of secret?"

Jonesy watched as she charmed the old buzzard.

"My brother Billy has been moon-eyed over your daughter for as long as I can remember. And why do you think she won't look at another young man? She's mooning over him, too. So I did them both a favor."

A smile spread across the wrinkled face. "I see. Then the least I can do is give you this dance." He swung her around and swept her away.

Jonesy and Mr. Riley stood in the middle of the dance floor while dancers whirled past. Some frowned at the two men, others grinned in amusement, all looked curious.

Andy Riley eyed him evenly. "I hope you have a good reason for making a spectacle of my daughter, not to mention the rest of us."

"I tried to make less of a spectacle by bringing Billy along to take over for you."

It would have gone smoothly, too, if Eva weren't so mule-headed. But there was no sense in antagonizing Mr. Riley by being critical of his daughter. Especially now. Even if it was a fact, not to mention common knowledge for anyone who knew her.

"I guess you have a point there," Mr. Riley acknowledged. "Let's get out of everyone's way before they tar and feather us."

When the two men had made it safely through the maze of dancers and found a quiet spot next to a wagon, Mr. Riley faced Jonesy. "Now what do you want that couldn't wait until I was finished dancing with my daughter? Dancing with her for the fourth time, I might add, because it appears all the eligible young men who might have asked her to dance believe you are courting her, and they don't want to move in on another man's girl." Andy folded his arms across his barrel chest. "Suppose you start by telling me why you allowed my daughter to come to a dance alone for the first time since she was thirteen."

Jonesy rubbed his jaw and cleared his throat. "That was purely an oversight, sir. I would have asked her, but I didn't think about it. I just figured we'd show up with our parents like we do for church and then spend the rest of the dance together." He raked his fingers through his newly shorn hair. "I guess I am a baboon, like Eva said."

Laughter rumbled through Andy's chest. "Well, at least the two of you agree on that point. But that's not why you interrupted our dance."

"No, sir." Jonesy shifted from one foot to the other. This was ridiculous. He had no reason to be nervous. He was a grown man, not a boy. Eva was a grown woman and pretty well past the age when most women married anyway. "I intend to ask for Eva's hand in marriage," he blurted out.

Mr. Riley stared and said. . .absolutely nothing.

Jonesy swallowed hard and went on with nervous energy. "I want you to know that I love her and I'll do right by her, if she agrees to marry me."

"Are you saying you plan to stay on and farm after all? Or will you try to build a ranch around here?"

"Well, neither. . . I. . ."

"I see." Mr. Riley's voice dropped. "You want to take my daughter away."

"If she'll have me, then yes, sir. I already own a hundred acres in Texas and have money saved to start my herd. Even have a cabin and a barn, and a small bunkhouse for the cowhands I'll need to hire. I can't up and leave it for good. Any more than I could leave Eva without at least asking her to come with me as my wife."

The hulking man's shoulders slumped. "I see you have your mind made up. I can't say I blame you. As a matter of fact, it shows right good sense and stability on your part." He drew a short breath and nodded. "If my daughter will have a baboon like you, then you have my blessing."

Joy leaped into Jonesy's heart, and he felt like shouting. He grabbed Mr. Riley's hand and pumped it. "Thank you, sir. Thank you very much."

Mr. Riley chuckled. "No need to thank me. Eva will make up her own mind. But I warn you, she's come close to the altar more than once and hasn't gone through with the 'I do' yet."

Jonesy grinned at Mr. Riley. "She will with me."

"We'll see. Now if you don't mind, I'm going to go ask my wife to dance. She's starting to look like a wallflower, and if I don't do something about that, I won't get a decent meal for a week."

Jonesy watched him walk away. Hope Riley, Eva's ma, turned as though sensing her husband was coming. Her face, illuminated by the lantern light, brightened even further at the sight of him.

What would Eva be like in twenty-five years? Loving him. Growing old with him. She was aggravated with him at the moment, but by the end of the evening, she would be his bride-to-be.

❧

Eva stiffened as Jonesy approached her at the refreshment table. It was his fault she was forced to get her own drink in the first place. She sipped her punch and deliberately turned her back to him.

"Eva," he said, in that scolding tone he used when she was being "stubborn," as he called it.

"I'm not speaking to you, Mr. Jones."

He gave an exasperated huff. "Yes, you are." Taking her by the arm, he led her away from the table.

"How dare you manhandle me?" Eva demanded, but she didn't pull away from him. It was rather thrilling for him to be acting this way. Like more than just a friend. "I've half a mind to tell my pa and just see what he does to you."

"Tell him. He's dancing with your ma."

"Well, what do you want? I don't want to leave the dance, although no one is dancing with me but my family."

"Listen, Eva." He stopped short and spun her around to face him. "I'm sorry I didn't ask you to the dance. I just didn't think about it."

Eva sniffed. "You and all your romantic poetry. Hasn't it taught you anything?"

Heat crawled across her cheeks. She hid her embarrassment behind what she hoped was a nonchalant shrug. "So why did you drag me out here? To apologize? Well, apology accepted. Now can we go back to the dance? You can make it up to me by letting the other men know they're safe to ask me to dance."

As she stepped away, he caught hold of her arm. Drawing her back, he looked down at her with a deep level of some emotion. What was it?

"Jonesy? What's wrong?"

Was he leaving sooner than he'd planned? She'd been counting on two more weeks with him.

He took her hands in his. Eva shivered.

"I've been thinking, Eva. We've been trying to be friends. But it just isn't working out."

Tears sprang to Eva's eyes. "I thought it was. I'm sorry if you don't want to be my friend."

"Eva." He let out a short laugh. "The reason it isn't working out is because I've fallen in love with you."

He pulled her closer and touched his forehead to hers. "I'm so in love with you I can't stand the thought of leaving you."

Giddy relief filled Eva. "Oh, Jonesy. Finally."

"Finally?" he whispered.

"I've loved you since the moment I met you. I thought you were going to go away and I'd never see you again."

Jonesy straightened up and lifted her hands to his lips, pressing a kiss on one and then the other. "Will you marry me?"

A smile spread across Eva's lips. "With all my heart, Jonesy."

Then he did what Eva had dreamed of since the day they'd met. He gently released her hands and gathered her around the waist. His fingers spanned her back as he pulled her closer. His head lowered.

At the first touch of his warm lips on hers, Eva's eyes closed, and she sank against him, accepting his tender kiss and responding with all the love she had to offer him. Her knees weakened as he deepened the kiss.

Disappointment flooded her when he pulled away. "Let's go back and tell our folks." His voice was husky and a bit breathless.

Eva nodded and grabbed his hand. "Ma is going to be so happy that I'm finally settling down. Only I can't imagine what all the old dowagers in town will have to talk about now. But just think. I can join their little Ladies Aid Society." She pinched her nose and spoke in a high tone, mimicking Mrs. Barker, the prim and proper owner of the town boardinghouse: "Because don't you know, only married women are allowed because they often discuss childbirth and other subjects unsuitable for delicate, unmarried women." Eva squeezed his hand. "But now they'll have to let me in."

She'd expected him to laugh, but he didn't. As a matter of fact, when she studied his face in the light of the bright moon, his expression appeared downright sickened. "I don't have to join the ladies' society. But I'll have to come up with a good reason to give Ma; otherwise she'll insist, and I'll give in."

"Eva, honey, stop talking for a second."

Heat rose to her cheeks. "I'm sorry, Jonesy. I thought you were just as happy and excited as I am."

"Excited? I'm ecstatic. My joy has no bounds at the thought that you love me and want to become my wife."

"Then..."

He gathered a shaky breath. "Eva, I still plan to move back to Texas in two weeks."

Eva's ire rose, sudden and hot. She jerked her hand from his. "Then what was all this, Jonesy? A game?"

"Of course not."

"Well, what sort of marriage do you suppose we could have if you're all the way in Texas and I'm—" She halted in midsentence as clarity struck her hard, like a tall tree crashing on top of her. "Do you mean to tell me you want me to come with you?"

"Yes."

"Oh." All of her strength sifted from her. It hadn't been that long ago that she'd believed if only he'd ask her, she would follow Jonesy anywhere. But faced with the wretched reality of leaving her family, how could she possibly make such a choice? "I—I don't know, Jonesy. How can I leave? My grammy and grandpa came west in the early days when wagon trains first brought settlers to Oregon. My pa is the only one who has ever left, and he came back. All my cousins and aunts and uncles live no farther than Oregon City, which is just a day's ride from here."

"Don't you see? This is your chance to build a life with me. You'll love Texas, Eva. There's no place on earth like it. Wild, open country."

"Apaches," Eva said flatly.

Jonesy smiled. "Not where we'd live."

"Oh, Jonesy," Eva moaned. "Isn't there any chance you might stay in Oregon? We could build a nice life here. Ranch if you want to. Or we could grow an apple orchard or even farm the way your pa does. I've heard you made a good crop. Do you know how unusual it is to bring in a good harvest the first year? You must have a knack for it."

"The land was already primed and ready for us when we got here. Mr. Winston was preparing to spend another planting and harvest season just in case the place didn't sell."

"Still. . .won't you consider it? I mean, really, what is the difference between me leaving Oregon and you deciding to stay here? Either you sacrifice or I do. Why does it have to be me?" Eva knew she sounded like a petulant child, but disappointment brought out the puerile attitude. She wanted to marry Jonesy, but she didn't want to move away.

Jonesy held her hand and pressed it against his chest. Eva could feel the beat of his heart against the back of her hand. He spoke softly. "I've dreamed of building my own ranch since I was old enough to pull on my first pair of boots. Ranching is in my blood. Texas is in my blood. I know how to make a good living for a family there. Our family, honey. Ever since I arrived here to help Pa and Ma settle, I've counted every day, every hour almost, waiting for harvest to be over so I can go home. The only thing that has kept me from going stir-crazy has been my relationship with you. I love you, Eva. Come build a life with me in Texas. I promise you'll never regret it."

"How can you promise something like that, Jonesy?"

He stared into her eyes. "Because I'll spend every day for the rest of our lives seeing to it." He drew her close and held her.

Eva could feel his tension. "Let's go back to the dance. I need time to think."

He nodded. "I won't say anything to our parents just yet."

When they reached the edge of the crowd around the dance floor, Eva hung back. "I'm not ready to face people. W—would you mind getting me a cup of punch? I must have left mine back at the refreshment table."

A sad smile lifted the corners of his lips. "I'll be back."

Eva's insides churned as nervous energy danced through every vessel in her body. She needed to think, to pace, to move. She glanced up and saw the line of horses next to the water troughs and hitching posts. Patches stood near the end of the row, pawing the dirt as if eager to be on the move.

She'd missed her morning runs with him. Pa had forbidden them since the incident with the thieves on the road. But right now, that's just what she needed. Determination and a need to dust off some energy overrode her desire to obey her pa.

Besides, she'd be safe. The man who had almost killed her was in jail along with one of the others. They were awaiting trial, which wouldn't happen until the circuit judge came through in three months. The third man had most likely joined the rest of the horse thieves. They were probably all halfway to Mexico by now.

She was tired of being afraid. Tired of staying close to home. She and Patches needed to run. In a flash of decision, she hurried to her beloved pony and mounted him. She whipped around and left the dance.

She waited until she was out of town before she gave Patches his head. Joyous laughter exploded from her as the wind caught her hair.

By the light of the moon, there was no mistaking horse and rider. He had almost given up. But there she was. This must be a sign that she belonged to him after all. He took careful aim with his pistol.

Chapter 5

When Jonesy returned to the tree where he'd left Eva, she was nowhere in sight. Assuming she'd simply gone to take care of nature's call, he stood there sipping a glass of punch, holding another glass for Eva. But after fifteen minutes, his glass was empty, and he was growing concerned.

He enlisted Mrs. Riley's help, then came back to the spot beside the pine and waited for a report.

Mrs. Riley returned moments later, shaking her head. "No one's seen her." Her troubled gaze scanned the yard and the street, where the wagons and horses had thinned out quite a bit as people left for home. She touched his arm. "Jonesy! Patches is gone."

"Eva rode to the dance?"

Hope nodded. "Alongside the wagon. She was so upset about having to go alone, I didn't have the heart to forbid it. Didn't you say the two of you worked all that out?"

"Yes, ma'am. But I upset her in another way."

A smile touched her lips. "By asking her to marry you?"

"Mr. Riley told you?"

"Of course. We tell each other everything. Did she accept your proposal?"

"She was very excited, chattering on the way she does. We were headed back to the dance to tell you and Mr. Riley and my folks when we realized we didn't have the same location in mind to build our life together."

"She assumed you'd stay in Oregon."

He nodded. "And I figured she'd know I wanted her to come with me to Texas."

"Eva loves you." She said it so softly, he had to lean forward to hear it. When she spoke again, Jonesy recognized the pain in her voice. "She'll go with you. A woman in love will follow her man to the ends of the earth."

Faith that Eva might actually say yes surged through him. "Well, she might be all the way at the ends of the earth by now the way she rides that horse of hers. Let me walk you back to the party, then I'll go after her."

Mrs. Riley took his proffered arm, and they hurried back to the dance floor. "I wish she wouldn't go off alone on that wild horse of hers. But that's her pa's blood in her."

He chuckled. "Maybe I ought to put her to work around the ranch. I bet she could run down and rope a steer better than most cowhands."

"You just let her cook your meals and wash your shirts. Leave the rough riding to your men."

Jonesy grinned and tipped his hat. "Yes, ma'am."

"And when you catch up to Eva, will you take her home? Andy and I will be leaving in the next few minutes, so there's no need to bring her back here."

"Yes, ma'am."

It hadn't occurred to him that Eva might have come to the dance on Patches. Why hadn't he noticed the pony hitched up somewhere? His stomach churned as he mounted Lady Anne.

He dug his heels into the mare's flanks and urged her faster as he followed the road out of town. If he knew Eva, she'd take the road as far as her uncle Michael's property, which extended for several miles, then she'd cut across the field where she could really run Patches.

He'd definitely have to have a discussion with her about her taking off like that. Running a horse at night, even a good horse like Patches, was dangerous. She should know better.

After trotting for a few miles, Lady Anne suddenly pulled back and whinnied. A shadowy form in the road blocked their path.

Bitter panic threatened to choke Jonesy. "Eva?" he called. As he drew closer, he realized the form was too large to be a human. It looked more like. . .a horse.

Oh, Lord, is it Patches? He pulled Lady Anne to a halt and drew his pistol, then moved cautiously toward the horse.

As he came close, the light from the moon confirmed his fear. He knelt beside the pony. Patches lifted his neck, then lowered it back to the ground.

Jonesy scanned the area. Eva was nowhere to be seen. She never would have left Patches alone. She knew folks would be coming this way after the dance. If the horse had stumbled and fallen in the dark, she would have waited for someone to happen by.

Acidic fear burned in his stomach. "Eva!" He looked closely around the horse for any sign of which way Eva had gone. A smear in the dust around Patches made him bend for a closer look. Eva hadn't walked away. Someone—or something—had dragged her into the woods.

Operating on instinct, he gripped his pistol and entered the woods in the direction of the drag marks on the road. Even during the daylight hours, the woods could be dark and foreboding. Able to hide anything that didn't want to be found. How on earth was he going to find a woman who was most likely hurt and had been dragged away against her will?

Lord, he prayed, *I know You have Your eyes on Eva right now. Please lead me to her.*

"Eva!" he called out. "Eva, it's Jonesy. Where are you?" He pushed a branch away from his face. "Eva! Make some noise so I can find you, honey."

Branches and leaves crashed in front of him. In the dark woods, he could just make out a human form running in the opposite direction. He knew it couldn't be Eva. She'd never run away from him. Perhaps it was her attacker.

"Eva!" Panic rose higher. He moved through the woods with no sense of direction, just putting one foot in front of the other.

"Eva!"

Please, Lord. Please.

"Eva!"

Oh, Lord. Please. Please. Please.

He tripped with the next step, and even before he hit the ground, he realized what his foot had caught on. A human body.

Jonesy pulled himself up to his knees. When he recognized the still form, fear gripped him with an unrelenting fist. "Eva, sweetheart. Oh, please, God. Can you hear me?"

She moaned, and he thought his heart would stop.

"It'll be all right, honey." He smoothed back her hair, and his hand came away slick with blood. The thought of anyone harming his Eva made him nearly insane with anger. But more urgent was the need to get Eva to the doctor.

He lifted her in his arms. She moaned again as he stood. His heart clenched. There was no time to see if she had any broken bones. No time to worry about whether or not movement would cause her more pain.

He buried his face in the curve of her neck. As he carried her back through the woods, tears flowed down his face.

He couldn't risk riding with her on horseback. Instead he cradled her against his chest and walked toward town, not caring if his horse became the next in a line of horse thefts. He moved with swift footfalls. His sobs were the only sound on the lonely road.

❧

Wails of agony awakened Eva from deep, nightmarish unconsciousness. When the pain hit her full force, she realized the wails were coming from her own throat. She forced herself to be silent and tried to make sense of the pain. The darkness. Searing pain stabbed her sides, her head, her leg.

A moan escaped her lips.

A door creaked open.

"Wh–who is it?" Darkness engulfed her as if she were entering a cave without a candle.

Ma's soft voice reached into the darkness. "Darling, it's all right. You're safe." Gentle hands took hers between them.

"Ma?"

"Yes, Eva, it's me."

"Why can't I see anything?"

"Your eyes are swollen shut. But Doc Smith says you'll be able to open them soon." Her voice caught in her throat, and Eva could tell she was fighting to keep from breaking down. "I'm so glad you're finally awake. I'm going to send Pa to town. Doc said to let him know the second you woke up."

Panic gripped her. Eva made a grab for Ma's hands before she could take away their warmth. "No, wait, Ma. P–please don't leave me."

"All right, darling. We'll wait until Pa comes in from his shop. Then he can go get the doc."

Relief that she wasn't to be left alone in the dark flooded her. "What happened to me?"

"You don't remember?"

Eva shook her head. "Not entirely." She'd been riding Patches at a run when all of a sudden a shot rang out. Patches fell, and she hit her head. She gasped. "Patches. Is he all right? I remember hearing a gunshot. Did someone shoot Patches?"

"Yes, darling, but it's only a little wound in one of his hind legs. His running-wild days might be over, but he'll live. He's in the barn getting fat on oats."

Eva nearly wept with relief, but the swelling of her eyes kept tears at bay. "I don't understand, Ma. Who would want to shoot Patches?"

Feeling a thick wall of hesitation, Eva squeezed her mother's hand. "It's all right. I need to know."

Ma's breath came in shaky bursts. "Eva. A man dragged you into the woods. He beat you and. . ."

Eva's throat went dry. Horror slashed through her mind as more clarity returned. She remembered being dragged through the woods. She remembered. . . . *Oh, dear God.* She remembered it all.

"Ma!" Her own shrill voice sounded foreign. She pressed her hands against her ears.

"I'm sorry, my darling. I'm so sorry." Ma's arms surrounded Eva. But no comfort came this time. In fact, Eva felt nothing as she rested her head against her mother's shoulder.

"What all is wrong with me?" she asked in a flat tone.

Ma pulled back. "Several broken ribs. Your leg is sprained. The doctor thinks that happened when Patches fell. You've been unconscious for four days, so Doc Smith wasn't sure about the extent of your head injury. But praise the Lord, it appears you'll be fine. No memory loss or brain damage that would have kept you unconscious forever, which is what he'd feared."

Hearing her ma use the term "praise the Lord" brought an anger to Eva that she had no idea was possible to feel. Praise the Lord that she'd been beaten but not killed? How much better if she'd never been found. She surely would have died.

"Jonesy found me, didn't he?"

"Yes. As soon as he realized you'd left the dance. He walked three miles carrying you back to town before your pa and I happened upon him. That man loves you with every ounce of his being. He'll be so relieved to know you've come to. He's been here every day. As a matter of fact, I expect him anytime."

"Ma, no."

"No what?"

"I don't want to see him."

"Oh, Eva. Jonesy doesn't blame you for what that man did to you."

Deep, soul-crushing pain nearly pushed the breath from her body, leaving her an empty, nonbreathing shell. Dead. That's what she should be. She'd known she was going to die that night. Had wanted to die. And then she'd heard Jonesy's voice calling to her. Her eyes burned with tears that had no way to escape.

"I don't ever want to see him again."

"Eva, give yourself a few days to adjust. You'll feel differently."

"What good will a few days do? Will my eyesight erase the fact that I am not fit to be a wife for a good man like Jonesy?"

Eva heard a soft gasp escape her mother's lips. "Eva. That is not true. Of course you're fit to be a wife. No one thinks any of this was your fault."

"But it was. I knew better than to ride off like that. But I did it anyway. I might as well have offered myself to that man."

"Don't talk like that." Ma's tone was harsh with shock and distress. "You are as pure in the eyes of the Lord as you were before this wicked, horrible thing happened to you, darling. Jonesy knows that."

"Oh, Mother, please." Eva turned toward the window. She knew light must be shining through. If Pa was still working, nightfall hadn't arrived. Still, darkness surrounded her. Deep, all-consuming darkness that invaded her soul.

Ma's hand rubbed along her leg. Eva's skin crawled, and she had to fight the urge not to shake her off. Even that small touch caused her pain. Not physical, but another kind of pain, one she couldn't identify. But she knew something was different inside her.

It was fear. She'd never been afraid.

"Eva, believe me. Jonesy loves you."

Eva gave a short, bitter laugh. "He would never take back his proposal. But you can be sure he's been praying every night that I won't wake up or, if I do, that

I'll let him out of it by refusing him."

"Eva Riley. You know Jonesy better than that."

Ignoring her ma's interruption, Eva continued her thought as though she'd never spoken. "Since I've obviously awakened, I'm going to have to give him the second option. I'll just have to refuse to marry him and send him on to Texas without me."

"Don't make rash decisions after the ordeal you've been through. Take some time to think about it."

"My mind is made up. I don't want to see him. If you love me, please respect my wishes. I don't want to see Jonesy." She winced as pain stabbed her head.

"We won't talk about this for now. You're in too much pain to think clearly. Dr. Smith left some laudanum for you, but I'm not sure you should have any until he examines you."

"Please, Ma. The pain is unbearable."

"All right. I'll give you less than he suggested. That should still help some."

Ma left and returned a moment later. She spooned the bitter liquid between Eva's swollen lips. "There you go, darling. You get some rest now."

"Stay with me until I fall asleep?"

Ma patted Eva's hand. "I'll be right next to your bed in that chair."

Almost immediately Eva grew drowsy. Despite her inability to see past her swollen eyes, in her mind she couldn't escape the vivid images of her brutal attack. She welcomed the approaching sleep.

Perhaps this time she wouldn't wake up.

Chapter 6

Whaat do you mean, she won't see me?" Hurt slashed at Jonesy as he stood on the Rileys' porch, staring into Andy's brown eyes. Eyes so like Eva's.

"Give her some time, son. She's been through quite an ordeal."

"With all due respect, sir, I know what she's been through." Jonesy released a frustrated breath. "I want to be there for her. To help her get well. Why doesn't she want to see me?"

"Shame, most likely. You don't understand what something like this does to a woman."

"I want to understand, Mr. Riley. I want Eva to lean on me. I want to take her away from the memories. I'll postpone my trip until spring to give her time to heal. Will you tell her that for me? I can't bear the thought of living the rest of my life without her."

He'd been so close to marrying her. They should be celebrating. Making plans to travel to Texas. Oh, sure, she hadn't agreed to marry him yet. Well, he supposed she had accepted his proposal, but he was fully aware she'd only done so assuming they'd remain in Oregon. Regardless, he felt sure she would have eventually come around to his way of thinking. "On second thought, I should be the one to tell her I still want to marry her. If she hears my voice, she'll know I'm being honest."

"You're a decent man, Jonesy. And I know you love my daughter as deeply as I love her mother."

"Then please," Jonesy pleaded, "let me see her."

Andy shook his head. "I'm sorry. But I can't go against her wishes in this."

Dejected, Jonesy turned away and mounted Lady Anne. The most frustrating thing in the world to him was that his Eva lay in that bed day after day, hurting physically and emotionally, and he could do nothing to ease her pain. He wanted to hold her, to reassure her. To let his gentle touch soothe away the memories of violence and pain.

As he rode away, helpless fury overtook him. He turned the mare in the direction of town. His throat clogged when he reached the spot on the road where Eva had been accosted, dragged into the woods, violated. Tears burned his eyes.

With single-minded purpose, he guided Lady Anne forward toward town, his mind repeatedly replaying the sight of his beloved Eva when he'd found her.

He halted the horse in front of the sheriff's office and dismounted.

Billy stood up when he entered. "I expected you a few days ago."

Surprise lifted Jonesy's brow. "You did?"

"Yep. I figured you'd be looking for some answers from those two vermin." He jerked his thumb toward the back room, which was divided into four jail cells.

"Have you questioned them?"

He nodded. "Even tried to cut a deal with them."

"What kind of a deal?"

"Let one of them go for information on where the others went."

"How will that help us find the man who hurt Eva?"

"I figure he was the fellow who got away. He's most likely fled the area. And unless I miss my guess, he's headed straight to the camp where the others are hiding out with Mr. Compton's horses."

Jonesy nodded. "That makes sense."

"The big guy in there says the man who got away has done the same thing to other women. None of the others lived."

This was all his fault. He should have paid closer attention. If only he could go back and change things.

"So you offered to let one of them go in exchange for information on the rest of the gang's whereabouts?"

Billy nodded. "I didn't figure they'd go for the deal. I mean, what good would it do to lead me to the hideout? I'd still arrest them for horse thieving."

"Can I talk to them?"

"I suppose I can give you a few minutes alone with them. Leave your gun on my desk."

An idea formed in Jonesy's mind as he walked from Billy's office to the room that housed the cells.

The only occupants were the two horse thieves. The older man was stretched out on a bench, one enormous arm flung across his forehead, covering his eyes.

The younger one gave him a shove when he saw Jonesy. "Hey, Randy," he whispered. "Wake up. We got company."

"What?" Randy snorted and sat up. He smoothed back his unruly gray hair. A sneer twisted his nasty, half-toothless mouth. "What do you want?"

Jonesy grabbed the wooden chair sitting against the wall opposite the cells. He carried it forward about three feet from the bars and straddled the seat, resting his forearms on the back of the chair, facing the outlaws. "I'm here to offer you a deal."

Randy let out a humorless chuckle. "Save it. Your sheriff already tried to make a deal. Problem is, he gets unfair advantage, and we'd just get caught again."

Jonesy inclined his head. "I agree that was a bad deal for you. You're too smart to be fooled by some lawman who wants to make a name for himself in this part of the country."

Randy's eyes narrowed. "What could you offer that's any different? You ain't even a deputy."

Jonesy leaned closer. "Keep your voice down. I don't want the sheriff to hear this."

"What is it?" The younger fellow had *stupid* written all over his face. His mouth hung half open, and his eyes were round with curiosity.

"Hush up, Timothy. I'm askin' the questions." Randy took a swipe at him with the palm of his hand. Timothy ducked out of his way. Maybe he wasn't quite as dumb as he looked.

Jonesy spoke in low tones. "I'll get you both out of here if you'll take me to the man who hurt Eva."

A scowl creased Randy's wide face. "That's the same thing the sheriff offered. I said no to him, and I'm sayin' no to you."

Jonesy returned his frown. He was in no mood to be turned down by a couple of thugs with no other options but hanging. "What I'm offering isn't the same deal."

"Oh yeah? How's yours different?"

Jonesy shrugged and kept a steady eye on the criminal in order to gauge his reaction. "I'm not talking about releasing you legally. I could break you out."

Young Timothy laughed and nudged Randy. "That does sound different, don't it, boss?"

"It's a trick, you idiot."

"If you don't take me up on my offer, then you're the idiot." Jonesy glanced cautiously toward the door, then back to the outlaws.

"So what's in it for us?"

"Freedom, pure and simple. The punishment for horse thieving is hanging. You have one chance to get out of this cell, and that's by agreeing to my plan."

"How do we know you won't lead the sheriff straight to us?"

"After he figures out that I've let you escape and that I'm with you, I'm going to be a wanted man, as well."

"He's got a point there," Timothy said.

Randy nodded thoughtfully, ignoring his companion's enthusiastic response. "Then why would you take the chance?"

"As long as I get the man who hurt Eva," Jonesy said with fervor, "I'll sit in jail for however long I have to."

"Let's say I agree to this." He raised his eyebrow. "And I ain't sayin' I am. But just supposin'. . ."

Jonesy's heart increased in rhythm, and he fought to keep the eagerness from his voice. "All right. Supposing."

"How do you plan on breaking us out?"

"Easy. Billy is escorting a certain young lady to a town musicale tonight. He'll be gone for two hours, and most of the town will be at the meeting hall."

"The sheriff'll most likely take the keys with him," Randy pointed out, stroking his stubbled jaw.

"I know where the spare set is. We've been friends for months. And his sister is my bride-to-be."

"You mean the one that Pete—"

"Yes," Jonesy broke in. "So do we have a deal?"

"You're just going to walk in and let us out?"

Jonesy regarded him with a grim smile. "You'll have to keep your wrists tied. I don't intend to have my throat slit."

"What's to stop you from slicing mine?"

"I'm not after you. I'm after your friend. You lead me to him, and I don't care what you do. Until then, you'll have to stay tied up."

"All right. We'll do it your way. It's less than a day's ride, unless they got tired of waiting and left without us."

Timothy's eyes grew wide. "You don't think they did, do you? Sam owes me four dollars for that last ranch we—"

"Shut up, Timothy."

Jonesy smirked. "I don't care about all that. I only care about getting the man who hurt the woman I plan to marry."

❧

Eva stared toward the light. It had been two days since she'd awakened, and she was just beginning to see images and light through the slits in her eyes. The swelling had receded enough to allow little slices of vision. For that, she was grateful.

Fear had taken hold of almost every waking minute as her imagination took her to the dark, shadowed corners of her mind. Horrific memories came back with such startling detail that often she shook in her bed. The man had wanted her dead. Had said angry things that made no sense, as though he were her husband and she had been unfaithful.

She jumped when the door opened. "Who is it?"

"It's only me, darling." Ma's presence afforded Eva small moments of peace. They only lasted as long as she was in the room and only if she didn't speak of that night or of Jonesy.

"I've brought you some leftover chicken pie from last night's supper."

"Thank you, Ma. I am a little hungry."

The painful process of sitting up left Eva breathless. Ma set the plate in her hands and handed her a napkin. "You can see a little better today?"

Eva nodded. "A little."

Ma sat on the chair next to the bed, rustling pages. She read the Bible to her four times a day. At breakfast, lunch, supper, and bedtime. Eva had tried to dissuade her, but this was not something on which Hope Riley was willing to compromise. Resolve flowed over Eva. No sense in fighting it.

"Today we read from Psalm 118. 'O give thanks unto the LORD; for he is good: because his mercy endureth for ever. Let Israel now say, that his mercy endureth for ever. Let the house of Aaron now say, that his mercy endureth for ever. Let them now that fear the LORD say, that his mercy endureth for ever. I called upon the LORD in distress: the Lord answered me, and set me in a large place. The LORD is on my side; I will not fear: what can man do unto me?'"

Eva gave a short laugh. "What indeed?"

Ma's silence filled the room.

"Well?" Eva asked, hearing the anger in her own voice. "Don't you see my point?"

"Yes, darling. But sometimes bad things happen to good people due to the wickedness of mankind. That has nothing to do with the goodness of God."

"Then why does God promise protection? Why does He say angels will guard us? Why even pretend to be God if He can't keep us safe? Or if He can, why didn't He?"

The shaking of Eva's faith over the past few days had left her feeling emptier than she'd felt in her entire life. Since childhood, she'd known that God was almighty, sovereign, omnipotent. She'd felt securely tucked in the cocoon of her sheltered life and her large, protective family. She hadn't needed to question her faith, because she'd never faced any real ordeals. Until now. And now she knew that God wasn't who He claimed to be.

Bitterness seeped around purity until her innocence was all but gone. Smothered by hatred.

"What if I ask Greg to come and speak with you? You might find comfort in confiding in a parson."

"No, thank you, Ma. I'm not interested."

"Oh, honey. Don't turn your heart away from Jesus. He's the only One who can get you through this time of sorrow and pain."

"I didn't turn away from Him, Ma. He turned away from me."

Chapter 7

Rain beat down without mercy on Jonesy and the two men as they set out at dusk. Getting the two out of the jail unnoticed couldn't have been easier. Between the musicale and the drenching rain, not many people ventured out. And those who did weren't interested in three men riding away from town. Jonesy had brought two extra horses from home. He'd unlocked the cell and walked them out the front door without a lick of trouble.

"Look here, mister," Randy whined. "You're gonna have to untie us, or we ain't gonna be able to make it through this mud. My horse is about to toss me off."

Jonesy glanced at Timothy, who appeared to be having no trouble at all with his mount. Randy was obviously faking it.

Jonesy knew better than to untie the men. If he was going to meet up with the man who had violated Eva and make sure he got what he deserved, he had to keep the upper hand with these two—especially Randy. "If you fall off the horse, you'll walk."

"You ain't got no heart, do ya?" But he sat up straighter in the saddle and stopped struggling, just as Jonesy had suspected he would.

By the time they'd ridden for two hours, the rain had stopped, the clouds had rolled back, and a bright moon lit their path. Jonesy allowed no stops. For any reason. The men rode in silence, listening to the occasional sounds of wolves howling in the distance, the hooting of owls, the horses' hooves pounding the trail.

When the morning sun broke through ahead of them, Jonesy remembered the morning he'd met Eva. Her indignation at falling in the river. Her smile that lit the morning like the dawn.

Then the memory of her battered body ripped through him.

"How much farther?" Jonesy's tone was gruff, leaving no room for foolishness.

"A couple hours," Randy replied. He gave a short, humorless laugh. "You know, my gang ain't gonna let you just walk outta there with one of our own."

"I don't need them to let me do anything," Jonesy growled. "If I'm holding a gun to their leader's head, they'll hand him over."

"Why are you doin' this, anyway? It's just a woman. Plenty more where she came from."

Timothy snorted. "Yeah, plenty more."

Repulsed, Jonesy kept his thoughts to himself. Why was he going to all this

294

trouble to find the man who had hurt Eva? *Simple.* The only way she would ever be free was if she knew the man would not be coming back.

Besides, that horrible creature had to be punished for what he had done.

And according to Mr. and Mrs. Riley, Eva was ashamed. Tears of mercy threatened to spill over. How could she believe she was to blame for anything that had happened to her?

Randy's grating voice cut through his musings. "Cat got your tongue?"

"Shut up. My reasons are my own. Besides, someone like you would never understand."

"What do you mean by that? I ain't good enough?"

"No, you're not."

Randy didn't respond.

Jonesy's conscience pricked him. He knew every hair on Randy's head was numbered by the God of love and grace. Despite the contempt Jonesy felt for the man, he knew God loved him.

"Maybe you just never had a chance to be the kind of person you were meant to be, Randy. I don't know." The offering cost him. He had no desire to be anything but brutal to this man. Even if he wasn't the one who did the ultimate damage to Eva, Randy had been about to slice her throat and steal her horse the day he'd come upon them on the road. He was no better than the rapist. "Any man who could hurt Eva doesn't know the kind of love I have for her."

"I loved a woman once," Randy replied in his defense.

Jonesy doubted it. Still, they had a long ride ahead of them, so why not play along to pass the time? Timothy seemed to be far away somewhere in his mind. "If you really loved someone, tell me about her."

"I ain't telling you nothin' about nobody."

"Have it your way."

Randy turned in his saddle and stared at Jonesy. The man's frown cut deep grooves between his eyes. "She was nice to me."

"And that made you fall in love with her?"

"Yep."

"What was her name?"

"Cynthia. Her pa was the town preacher."

"Really?" Jonesy hadn't meant to say the word out loud, but he'd expected Randy to say the woman was a saloon girl who had to be nice to him as part of her job.

Apparently offended by Jonesy's surprised tone, Randy snorted. "You don't think I can fall for a good girl?"

"I guess you could. But what good girl would return your feelings?"

"If you're goin' to insult me, just forget the whole thing."

With a shrug, Jonesy let it go. After a minute or two, Randy resumed the conversation as though he'd never been offended.

"It was my first time in jail. I was young and not so fat. The ladies seemed to have a thing for me." He grinned.

Jonesy was hard pressed not to spit. "I'm sure they did." In Randy's mind, maybe. "So how did an outlaw meet a pretty preacher's daughter?"

"Her ma fixed supper for the prisoners, even though she had a big family of her own to feed. Cynthia was the oldest of ten young'uns. One day when her mama was laid up having a baby, she came in to give us our food. The sheriff was busy, so she had to bring us our basket herself." He drew a sharp breath as though reliving the memory. "She didn't shy away from me like most other respectable women."

"I can understand why you took a shine to her."

"You don't know the half of it. She was the most beautiful thing I'd ever seen. Her hair was like corn silk. When she handed me a plate, she looked right into my eyes and smiled."

"So maybe she wasn't such a good girl after all?"

A growl crawled from Randy's throat. "I don't like your tone."

"Well, I don't like that you almost killed Eva."

Randy's eyes took on a reflective stare. Jonesy's statement had apparently hit home.

"What happened with Cynthia?"

A breath lifted Randy's shoulders. "Her ma was laid up for quite a spell, so Cynthia brought the food every day."

"The sheriff allowed a young woman to bring dinner to a bunch of thieves?"

"More than that. He let her stay and talk to me. She brought her Bible and read out of the Good Book."

"Ah, so the jail was Cynthia's mission field."

"I guess. But it was more than that between her and me."

Apparently Randy really had cared for someone.

"Since I was just the lookout and didn't hurt anyone or steal anything, I got out before the rest of them."

"So then you started courting Cynthia, I guess?" Jonesy said it flippantly, sarcastically. No respectable family would allow an outlaw to court the town sweetheart and preacher's daughter.

But the sarcasm seemed lost on Randy. "Her pa offered me the barn loft to sleep in, for good honest labor. I didn't care too much for farmwork, but I'd have done anything to be near Cynthia."

Jonesy understood that feeling.

"I went to church regular-like with her family and finally understood about Jesus."

The holy name coming from this outlaw's mouth shot through Jonesy like an arrow piercing his heart. How could a man like Randy know Jesus?

His face softened. "Shortly after that, I married her."

"Married?" Jonesy hadn't expected that. "What happened?"

"She died just three months later. Snakebite." He sniffed, then cleared his throat. "She had just told me we were going to have a baby."

"I'm truly sorry, Randy."

"She wanted to name him Luke, after my pa."

"Maybe you do know how I feel about Eva, then. Think about Cynthia next time you or one of your pals is about to rape a woman."

Anger flashed in the black eyes. "I ain't never done anything of the sort. And I wouldn't have let Pete do it if I hadn't been locked up in here. So it's your own fault that happened to your girl. If I hadn't been in jail, he wouldn't have done it."

Anger boiled Jonesy's blood. This man had the nerve to blame him? "If I hadn't stopped you that day, Eva would be dead. So don't pretend you're any better than Pete." The name of Eva's attacker tasted foul in Jonesy's mouth. He spat on the ground.

A loud snort from Timothy diverted their attention. He jerked his head up. "Are we almost there?"

"Boy," Randy said with disgust, "were you sleeping?"

"I guess so." He gave a sheepish grin. "Ma always says I kin sleep just about anywheres."

Jonesy shook his head and retreated to his own thoughts. He didn't want to hear about these outlaws' mothers. It was bad enough that he now saw Randy as more than a thug. The man obviously suffered from deep inner wounds. If Cynthia hadn't died, Randy would probably be a respectable farmer with a wife and a crop of children by now.

Bitterness, anger, and unforgiveness could blacken any man's soul. That's why Jonesy had to bring Eva's attacker to justice. Give her a chance to heal. Then the forgiveness could begin.

He looked at Randy, a big, brawny man with blood on his hands and the end of a rope facing him someday. A man who had loved so deeply he couldn't bear the loss. As Jonesy watched Randy's slumped shoulders, he thanked God for grace.

❧

When Eva opened her eyes, the first thing she noticed was that she could actually see the morning sun shining through the bedroom window. She squinted against the brightness she'd been unable to see for the past few days.

Having her sight restored raised her spirits considerably. She'd ask Ma to have Lily pick out some new dime novels so she would have something to help pass the time. Maybe she'd even ask for a book of poetry. Jonesy had forced her to listen to it so much, she'd actually grown fond of Lord Byron.

Jonesy. Eva's heart picked up a few beats as his image flickered in her mind. She would have been planning a wedding right now if. . .

If only. . .

❦

"There."

Jonesy jerked his head up at the sound of Randy's voice. The first words between them for two hours.

"In that cliff. There's a cave."

"You have horses in a cave?"

"That's where we brand them. Every couple of days, one of us takes two horses and heads to Oregon City to sell them."

"I'm supposed to believe you're going to give me that information just like that?"

"Don't matter none anyway. You ain't gonna make it out of this alive."

"I will."

"We'll see."

Jonesy cautiously rode a couple of miles more until they reached the bottom of the cliff. Then he dismounted and lifted his pistol from his holster. He grabbed his extra rope and nodded at Timothy. "Get down."

Timothy unlooped his bound wrists from the pommel of his saddle and dismounted.

"Over there," Jonesy said, pointing the barrel of his pistol to a tree. "Sit down."

"What are you gonna do?"

"I only need one prisoner. And I have a feeling your friend is more important to the rest of your gang than you are."

Timothy sat still while Jonesy tied him to the tree, then took the boy's handkerchief from his pocket and tied it through his mouth. "Sorry, but I can't have you calling out a warning."

Jonesy looked up warily at Randy. Standing a safe distance from the horse, he nodded to the outlaw. "Your turn. Get down."

Randy dismounted awkwardly. Jonesy regretted that he couldn't gag Randy, too, but he didn't want to holster his pistol with the man's powerful legs still free.

"All right," Jonesy said. "Let's go. Slow. And don't try anything. As soon as I have Pete, I won't try to hold you."

He glanced down at Timothy. "You'll be all right. They'll come and untie you as soon as I'm gone."

Timothy's eyes widened, but his focus went over Jonesy's shoulder.

"Drop the gun."

Dread clenched Jonesy's gut at the unfamiliar voice. He turned slowly. Two men stood holding guns on him. One, who looked identical to Timothy, was wearing a pair of buckskin chaps and a ripped calico shirt.

Jonesy knew better than to try anything stupid. He tossed his pistol forward.

"Good to see you, Al," Randy said, a chuckle rumbling in his barrel chest. "This fool thought he'd walk outta here with Pete."

"Pete?" The redhead kept his rifle on Jonesy but turned to Randy. "We thought he was with you."

"What do you mean?" asked Jonesy.

Al sneered and backhanded him hard across the jaw. "Shut up." He nodded to the redhead. "Untie Randy and your dim-witted brother."

"This feller's girl got attacked," Randy said while Timothy's brother dismounted. "We figured Pete did it and ran off to find you."

"Pete got another one?" Anger marred Al's brow. "You know what I told him after the last one."

Randy nodded. "Guess that's why he didn't come lookin' for you. We probably ain't gonna see him again."

Panic seized Jonesy. "You mean to tell me Pete's not here?"

Al glared. "I told you to shut yer mouth."

Jonesy glared at Randy. "We had a deal."

"I kept my part of the bargain. I brung you to the gang, didn't I?"

"You knew Pete wouldn't be here. I'm a day away from Eva, and that monster could still be around Hobbs. How am I going to protect her?"

"That ain't our problem, mister," Al broke in.

Jonesy kept his focus on Randy. "Wouldn't you have given anything to keep Cynthia safe?"

Randy's face reddened, and his eyes flashed in anger. "Shut up about her."

"What if someone like Pete had snuck around watching her for two weeks and then violated her? Almost killed her?"

"Shut up!" Randy stepped forward until they were nose to nose, his rancid breath nearly choking Jonesy.

"Enough of this," Al barked. "We're pulling out with the last two horses tonight. And we ain't takin' an extra man, so move outta the way."

His words sliced through Jonesy like an ax head, but he refused to be deterred. "Think about it, Randy."

"Cynthia died a long time ago." He nodded toward Al and the twins. "This is all the family I got left. If I turn against them, I'm alone."

"Turn against us?" Al frowned. "You thinking about being a turncoat?"

"No."

"Then let's get it done." Al handed him a knife. "Use this. We don't want to make any noise."

Jonesy saw hesitation mar Randy's expression. He jumped on it. "Randy, what would Cynthia want you to do?"

The second the words left his lips, Randy's face darkened. He approached with utter hatred flashing in his eyes. "I told you not to talk about her anymore. I'm done remembering."

Randy raised the knife to Jonesy's throat.

He returned the man's murderous gaze with unflinching dignity, though everything in him screamed to beg for his life.

A blast of gunfire sounded. The twins dove for cover.

Randy landed with a thud on the ground. He clapped his hand to a bleeding shoulder and looked up at Jonesy with accusing eyes. "You double-crossed me."

Jonesy glanced at the sheriff, who had been following them since they left Hobbs, then turned back to Randy. "Now we're even."

Al dropped with the next blast from Billy's gun.

Jonesy dove for his pistol, which the outlaws hadn't bothered to retrieve from where he'd dropped it.

When his fingers were inches away from the gun, Jonesy felt a sharp pain slice through his leg. Crying out, he looked down. Randy pulled the knife out and raised it again. In a split second, Jonesy kicked with his other leg and knocked the knife from Randy's hand. Randy rolled to his feet and ran for the nearest horse.

Despite another round of fire, Randy rode away amid a cloud of dust. Jonesy crawled to cover and snatched his handkerchief from his pocket. His leg throbbed, and blood poured from the knife wound in his calf.

"Jonesy," Billy called. "You okay?"

"I'll live."

"How many more are there?"

"Just two, and neither of them seem that smart. We won't have any trouble bringing them in. It's dead or alive, right?"

"That's right. And I brought along plenty of bullets, so I'll outlast them."

"Wait!"

Jonesy recognized Timothy's voice.

"Don't shoot. We're coming out."

"Do it, then," Billy said. "Slowly, with both hands in the air. Any sudden moves, and I'll open fire."

Within moments, Billy had both of the red-haired men tied up. He glanced at Jonesy. "You going to make it back home?"

"I'll have to."

Billy nodded. "Which one is Pete?"

"Neither." Jonesy flinched against the pain in his leg as he limped to his horse. "Apparently this isn't the first time he's done something like this. Even these vermin didn't care for it. They had told him not to do it again. That's why he didn't come back to them."

Billy's face blanched. "You mean he could still be in town?"

Jonesy gave a grim nod. "Or close by."

They slung Al's lifeless body over one of the horses. Once the others were mounted, they headed toward Hobbs.

Chapter 8

Though she had awakened this morning with optimism, now, mere hours later, depression clouded over Eva as she scooted beneath the blue coverlet, ready for sleep. Darkness had fallen, and Jonesy hadn't come by today. Even though she had no intention of seeing him, the fact that he had given up disappointed her.

It had only been a few days. But she supposed he had to start making his plans to go back to Texas. After all, his land meant more to him than anything.

She had told him to leave, she reasoned, so it wasn't fair to be angry with him for giving up. Still, he hadn't tried for long.

A heavy cloud hung over her, and she thrashed about as sleep eluded her. Only the darkness, and fear of what might be there if she left the safety of her bed, prevented her from throwing off the covers and pacing away the nervous energy buzzing in her stomach.

Where was Jonesy now? Was he still at home? Had he finally taken her hint yesterday and left for Texas?

In a fit of frustration, Eva labored to sit up. She glanced about the dark room, lighted only faintly by the moon shining through the window.

Her heart was racing by the time her back rested against the feather pillows propped against the headboard. A scratching noise by the window caught her attention. She tensed, fear gripping her tighter than a corset. Paralyzed, she watched as a shadow passed by, stopped, and came back. She wanted to scream, to cry out, but her throat tightened.

Then she remembered the words her attacker had whispered that awful night: *This ain't over.*

The screams found their voice. Eva couldn't stop even when Pa and Ma burst through the door.

"What is it, little papoose?" Pa took Eva into his arms, and the screams gave way to silent sobs.

"He came back for me, Pa. Just like he said he would."

"What do you mean?"

"I saw him outside the window."

"Oh, honey, you must have been dreaming," Ma said. "That evil man is gone. As a matter of fact, Jonesy and Billy tricked those other two outlaws into leading

302

them right to the hideout for the whole gang of thieves and cutthroats. So you don't have anything to worry about."

"Hope," Pa said, his voice ringing with frustration, "Billy told me that in confidence. Eva wasn't supposed to know about this until it was all over."

"Jonesy went after the outlaws?" Eva asked.

Pa patted her leg and stood. "I'll go have a look around outside."

"No!" Palpable fear slithered up from Eva's gut until she felt it in her chest and in her throat. "You can't go outside. What if he's still out there?"

"I've survived a lot of things in my day. I'll be careful." He leaned over and kissed her forehead. "Don't worry. I'll be right back."

With foreboding, Eva watched him leave.

Ma took Pa's seat on the bed next to her. "It'll be all right, Eva. I'm sure you were only dreaming."

"No, I wasn't, Ma." Eva pulled away. "I know what I saw."

Ma's eyes flashed hurt, and guilt pricked Eva. But she had to be heard.

"I couldn't sleep, so I sat up. And when I looked over to the window, I saw him walking back and forth. Then he tried to get inside." Ma still didn't look convinced. Eva sat up slightly and patted her pillows. "Mama, look! Why would my pillows be propped up if I had been sleeping?"

For the first time, a worried frown creased her mother's brow. A light glowed outside the window where Pa held the lantern.

"Eva, darling. What did you mean when you said that he came back for you like he promised?"

Swallowing hard, Eva fought the image. "I was barely conscious, Ma. But when Jonesy started calling my name, that scared him. Before he ran away, he said he'd be back. He kept saying I had betrayed him. But the only time I've ever seen him was that day on the road. He must have mistaken me for someone else. I kept thinking he'd realize I wasn't the woman he thought I was and he'd stop. But he didn't."

"Oh, Eva. You've been through so much." Hope put her arms around her daughter. But Eva stayed limp, unmoving. Surprisingly, for the first time since thinking or talking about that night, there were no tears. She was just so tired.

"Jesus, heal her."

Ma's prayer was cut short when Pa came back into the room carrying several boards and a hammer. Eva searched his eyes, and terror cut a line through her heart. "I was right, wasn't I?"

He gave a grim nod. "Someone was out there, all right. I looked around and couldn't find any signs that he might still be here. But I'm not taking any chances that he might come back."

Pa made an imposing figure when he was determined. Eva had always been a little in awe of him. Spending his young adult years as a wagon scout, meeting Indians. He'd even married an Indian girl who had died before he met Eva's ma. His wild spirit had always reached out to Eva. Had always inspired her. How her cowardice must disappoint him.

He glanced at Ma over his shoulder. "Hope, will you come hold the other end of the board?"

Ma stood immediately and went to him.

Eva watched her parents close her in, nailing boards over her window as though she were a princess in a tower. Keeping her locked away and safe from the dangers of the big, bad world.

Though part of her enjoyed the safety those boards afforded, another part of her deeply resented the confinement. Now there was nothing for her to see but the inside of this room. No light shining through, no birds flying by.

"That ought to do it." He walked across the room. "If you hear one sound, you be sure to call out. We're going to leave your bedroom door open."

Eva's heart picked up speed.

Pa studied her face. "I'll spend the night in the chair. Don't worry, honey."

"I'm sorry, Pa."

Setting his hammer on the table next to the bed, he sat beside her. "For what?"

"For being so afraid."

"No need to be sorry. It's a pa's job to keep his little girl safe."

"But I'm not a little girl anymore."

"You're my little girl. And I'll sit next to your bed as long as it takes for you to feel safe again. Until then, just know that your family loves you."

"Thank you, Pa."

He started to say something else but hesitated.

Eva smiled. "I know. You want to tell me that Jonesy loves me."

Pa gave a soft chuckle. "You know your pa pretty well, don't you?"

"Yes. We're alike in so many ways."

Ma moved softly across the room toward the bed. "I'll leave the two of you alone." She bent forward, and Eva caught the scent of apple blossoms that always seemed to cling to Ma.

She pressed a soft kiss to Eva's forehead. "Good night, darling."

"Good night, Ma."

Eva had grown increasingly short-tempered with her ma over the past few days. Not that she'd be openly disrespectful, but inside, she wanted to tell her to stop trying so hard to make her feel better. Stop feeding her cookies and cake and chicken pie, even though it was her favorite meal. Stop asking her to get out of bed and take a bath. Didn't Ma realize that no matter how many baths she took, she'd never feel clean again?

After Ma left the room, Pa picked up the Bible on the nightstand.

Eva groaned. "Oh, Pa. Do we have to read tonight? Can't we just talk?"

She received a stern glance in response. "You got something against the Bible all of a sudden, Eva?"

"No. But we haven't just talked together since. . ." Eva dropped her gaze to her fingers, twisting the covers until her knuckles grew white.

"Eva." Pa leaned forward and covered her hands with one massive paw. "No amount of talking about the weather, or how the furniture making is going, will help your soul break free from the pain."

"Oh, Pa. I'm the one who has to live with the memories. Can't I just try to live with them my own way?"

"By staying in bed? Not bathing? Turning your back on God? Honey, He's the only One who knows how you feel."

"All right, Pa." Eva closed her eyes. "Go ahead and read."

Pages rattled, then Pa's baritone voice began to read. " 'The LORD is my shepherd; I shall not want.' "

Eva felt a strange comfort in the psalm. Peace drifted over her, and the image of a gently flowing stream filled her mind as Pa read. "He leadeth me beside the still waters. He restoreth my soul." In that place between awake and asleep, Eva was aware of Pa finishing the psalm, then moving carefully to the chair next to her bed.

She drifted to sleep, feeling safe for the first time in days.

≈

Jonesy limped up the steps to the Riley home, determined that this time they weren't going to keep him from seeing Eva. It had been a full week since he'd gotten home from his useless trip to the outlaw hideout, and he had been forced to sit in bed half of that time due to the knife wound in his leg. Dr. Smith had told him he must have an angel watching over him, because if the knife had hit an inch higher, it would have tapped an artery behind his knee and he would have bled to death in a matter of minutes.

Jonesy had come out yesterday. But Mr. Riley had met him at the door. The day before, Mrs. Riley had met him. Each had the same message from Eva: "Go to Texas and forget about me."

Today he'd been smart. He'd gone to town and asked Lily to come out with him. Eva would see Lily, and he would wait on the porch, hoping her friend could convince her. If she still didn't let him in, he'd try something else tomorrow.

"I still don't think this is going to work, Jonesy," the pretty, petite blonde said, nervously patting her hair and smoothing her gown. "Even if they let me in, that doesn't mean Eva's going to see you."

"I know." He knocked on the front door.

Soon Mrs. Riley appeared. She gave him an indulgent smile. "I'll say one thing for you, Jonesy. You're persistent."

"I don't intend to give up, ma'am."

She patted his arm. "I hope you never do."

Her comment raised his hopes. "May I see her?"

"I'm afraid she still refuses." She turned a pleasant smile to Lily. "She will, however, see you."

Lily gave him a look of sympathy. "I'll try to talk to her," she whispered as she moved around him and hurried through the door.

"You know where her room is, Lily," Mrs. Riley said. "Just go on back there."

"Thank you, ma'am."

Jonesy fought the envy rising inside him as he watched Lily disappear from view, while he wasn't even allowed past the front porch.

"Come on in, Jonesy. My daughter might not want to see you, but that doesn't mean I can't enjoy your company while you wait for Lily to come out."

"Thank you, ma'am." Jonesy stepped inside. "I appreciate the offer."

Chapter 9

*A*bsolutely not. She would not see Jonesy no matter how many people he sent to speak for him.

"He's not going to stop," Lily said matter-of-factly.

"He will. Eventually."

Lily shook her head. "Trust me. I've never seen a man so determined. Why won't you see him? It's becoming ridiculous. Poor Jonesy. At least tell him to his face that you have no intention of marrying him."

"If I do, do you think he'll go away and leave me in peace?"

"If he truly believes that you aren't going to marry him, I think he'll give up. But he won't until he hears it from you."

Eva's legs trembled under the covers. "What if I write him a letter and you could give it to him?"

Lily's face screwed up into a scowl. "Don't be a coward."

"Coward? You think fear is what's keeping me from Jonesy?"

Lily's nod infuriated Eva. She was afraid of a lot of things nowadays, but telling Jonesy to go to Texas without her wasn't one of them. "All right. I'll see him." As soon as she said the words, she regretted them. "Wait."

But a smiling Lily was already across the room and had the door open.

Eva's mind whirled. Why had she given in to Lily's baiting so easily?

The sight of Jonesy filling the doorway made her stomach jump. "I must look awful."

A smile touched his lips, and he moved forward. "You're a sight for sore eyes."

False laughter gurgled in her throat. She dropped her gaze before his look of pity. "Always a romantic—even when you're telling a lie."

"I would never lie to you."

Silence pervaded the room, and suddenly Eva sensed his presence too deeply. She clutched the covers up to her throat.

Jonesy's eyes flickered over her. "It's so good to see you, Eva. How are you doing?"

The last thing she wanted to discuss with Jonesy was her ordeal. "I'm fine."

"Are you in a lot of pain?"

The truth was that only twinges and light bruising remained. But Eva was ashamed to admit it to him and try to explain why she was still in bed, unable to leave her room.

"Not a *lot* of pain anymore."

Admiration flickered in his eyes, making Eva feel even worse.

"Really, Jonesy, I'm almost all healed."

"How long before you can get a wedding planned?" The intensity of his gaze thrilled her and terrified her at the same time.

"Jonesy, please try to understand. I'm just not ready to leave my family."

"Then I'll wait."

"That's not going to do any good. I don't ever want to move to Texas." Eva fingered the flowers on her comforter. "I'd like for you to go away and stop asking me. I'm not going to change my mind. Ever."

"Yes, you are." He said it with such finality that Eva almost said yes right then and there. But her common sense prevailed. "There are reasons." Her face burned, and she knew she must be flushed.

Jonesy remained silent for a long moment, until Eva ventured a glance into his face. His eyes were closed. "Jonesy?"

He opened his eyes and regarded her with sadness. "I don't know how to say this delicately. But I don't hold you responsible for what that man did to you." Stepping forward, he knelt beside the bed. Tears glistened in his eyes. "My love for you reaches so far beyond the physical that nothing matters except sharing my life with you."

The raw honesty shining from his eyes sifted all embarrassment from the conversation. Eva gave him the candid answer she had held in her heart for the past weeks. "I don't know if I could ever be a proper wife to you. I could cook and clean. I could keep you company and read poetry with you, but I don't know that I could ever sleep in your bed and bear your children."

The blood drained from his face as though he hadn't even considered that she might not want to share his bed. As though he'd only been thinking of his own reaction to the fact that she'd be coming to him tainted, unclean, impure, used goods.

Anger boiled inside her at his vanity. "I see that does matter to you. You don't mind that I've been used by another man as long as I let you use me, too." She turned away. "Get out, Jonesy. Go to Texas. Build your ranch and find a woman who wants to be your wife. Once and for all, will you please leave me in peace?"

Bitter pain twisted like a knife inside Eva's heart as Jonesy stood and left the room. She tightened her jaw and refused to give in to the sobs threatening just below the surface of her restraint. Tears would do no good.

Lily appeared a second later. "What happened? Jonesy looks positively ill."

Eva gave a short laugh. "I told him the truth. That I won't share his bed. I think that convinced him I'm not the woman for him."

A gasp escaped Lily's throat. "I don't know what to say."

Lily's face turned three shades of pink. Eva shook her head. What did delicacies matter anyway? Did they prepare a girl for the truth about relations between a man and a woman? Humiliation, fear, pain. She'd never give a man that kind of power over her again.

"Jonesy would never hurt you." Lily's voice had a troubled hesitance. As though she was trying to convince herself.

"Oh, Lily. You know nothing about it."

"Billy wants me to marry him." She said the statement flatly. Eva grimaced. A month ago they would have squealed and giggled and started to make plans for the big day.

Instead Eva shrugged, her numbed emotions unable to muster even cursory excitement for her childhood friend. "I hope you'll be very happy. I know Billy has always cared for you."

"Y—you don't think I should say yes?"

Eva looked at her evenly. "I would never encourage any woman to put herself through the things a woman must endure to be a wife to any man. Even a good one."

Lily's voice trembled, but Eva felt no remorse. She'd simply told the truth. What sort of friend would she be if she allowed Lily to enter into marriage with the same naive beliefs with which every other woman entered the institution?

A soft tap on the door preceded Ma's entrance. "Lily, Jonesy said he needs to take you home so he can help his pa with chores."

"Yes, ma'am."

Ma looked from Eva to Lily. Her brow wrinkled. "What's wrong?"

"Nothing, Mrs. Riley." Lily turned to Eva. "Good-bye, Eva. I'll come see you again soon." But as she left, Eva had the sinking sensation that she wouldn't be back.

Hope turned her questioning gaze to Eva. "Did you two have a disagreement?"

"No."

"Then why is Lily as white as a sheet and about to cry?"

"Well, if you must know, Lily told me Billy asked her to marry him."

Joy spread a wide smile across Ma's face. "It's about time that brother of yours got around to marrying that girl. I was afraid she'd find someone else. You don't look a bit happy. Isn't this what you've always hoped for? Lily and you will truly be sisters now."

Eva shrugged. "We're not children anymore. Besides, I know about what happens in a marriage. And now Lily does, too."

Ma's eyes widened in horror. "What did you tell her?"

"The truth."

"Oh, Eva. It's not that way between a husband and wife who love each other. What happened to you was a violent act of evil. Love is gentle and kind and patient."

"Ma, please. I'd rather not discuss this."

Ma moved to the door, a heavy sigh pushing from her lungs. "All right. I'll leave you alone. But I'm having your pa fix a tub for you later."

"No! I don't want to."

"Eva Star Riley. The whole house is beginning to smell bad. You are going to take a bath, and I'm going to wash your bedding. And that's final. Furthermore, you will take your meals with the rest of us from now on. And, honey, no more slop jar. You'll have to begin walking to the outhouse again."

"How can you treat me this way after what I've been through?" Tears of fury burned her eyes. "I cannot endure more mistreatment."

"Eva Riley, you're my darling daughter, and my heart aches for what you've been through. If I could take away the memories and the pain and fear, I would. But I can't. We have all tried to help you through the healing. But you must start living again, darling. You can't stay hidden away in your bedroom for the rest of your life."

She left the room, closing the door firmly behind her. Eva pounded the bed with her fists. Why couldn't she stay tucked away, safe in her little cocoon? The thought of venturing beyond her bedroom door filled her with trepidation.

Panic rose. In an instant, she threw the covers over her head and lay shaking beneath the heavy quilts.

❧

Jonesy found himself at a crossroads. If he turned right, the road would lead the wagon home, where his pa waited for him to help with the evening chores. Left would take him back to the Rileys' home, where Eva would either agree to see him or once more jab a knife into his already bleeding heart.

Everything in him wanted to take the road to the left. To plead with her to reconsider, to give him a chance to prove his love for her.

Lily had been silent and shaken on the way back to town. But try as he might, Jonesy couldn't convince her to open up about what Eva had told her that upset her so. Finally he'd given up and allowed her the solitude she seemed to need. Maybe that's all Eva needed, as well. Perhaps if he gave her a little more time, she'd change her mind. It was too late for him to begin the four-and-a-half-month journey back to Texas now; he'd have to wait until after the winter.

If Eva needed time, he had it to give her. He turned the wagon to the right.

❧

"Please, Pa," Eva moaned. "Please don't make me."

Pa's eyes clouded with indecision, but he remained as resolute as Ma. "I'm sorry, papoose. But your ma's right. I'll hold your hand until we get to the kitchen. Then your ma will stay with you while you take your bath. Trust me. You're going to feel much better after you're clean."

Eva stopped fighting. If Pa wasn't on her side, then there was no hope. Her body shook with fear, and she clung to Pa as they walked slowly to the door. A step past the threshold, her knees buckled as fear gripped her throat. "Pa."

"Shh, I'm here." He swept her up in his arms and carried her the rest of the way to the kitchen.

"She'll be all right," Ma's quiet voice assured as Pa set her on her feet on the kitchen floor. He nodded, pressed a kiss to Eva's head, and walked back through the kitchen to the living room and went outside.

Eva glanced at the tub of water, and relief moved through her. Now that she'd left her room, a weight seemed lifted from her shoulders.

Ma helped her undress and get into the tub. Eva closed her eyes and sank down into the warm water. "I'll be okay, Ma. I know you want to get my bedding."

A smile spread across Ma's face. "You sure?"

Eva regarded her mother. Circles darkened the skin beneath her eyes, and her dress hung on her as though she'd lost weight. "Are you all right, Ma?"

"I think I will be now, darling. If you're all right, I will be."

Eva reached out a wet hand and took her ma's. "Thank you for forcing me to do this. I never would have left that room on my own."

When she was alone, Eva closed her eyes once more and allowed the warm water to loosen the dirt caked onto her skin.

Chapter 10

Lady Anne cantered as though she were aware that today was the Lord's Day and she had the distinct honor of carrying Jonesy to the worship service.

A blast of colder-than-usual air whipped up, forcing Jonesy to turn up his collar. He shivered against the wind and glanced at the cloudy sky. It seemed as though Hobbs and the surrounding area might be in for a hard winter. Good thing he'd decided against trying to make it to Texas before spring. He might have gotten stuck in Wyoming.

It had been almost a week since he'd seen Eva, and he still couldn't quite bring himself to believe what she had indicated. She could cook and clean but not share his bed? Hurt burned through him like a branding iron. Did she honestly believe he would harm her the way Pete had? Did she think it would be the same?

The thought that she could even consider such a thing filled him with shame. How did a single man explain to the woman he loved that he wanted to hold her in his arms until dawn? Bring her silky curls to his face and lose himself in the sweet scent of lilac that always seemed to cling to her? There weren't words to explain those things to a young, unmarried woman. Tenderness, adoration, and love were things a young husband had to wait until the night of his wedding to express.

Father, I don't want to lose Eva. How do I convince her that I mean her only good? That I would never harm her?

The answer didn't come in the wind.

As he entered the churchyard, his heart leaped. Eva's pa was helping her from the wagon. Jonesy's throat tightened at the sight of her, frail and pale. She looked as though she might bolt at a loud noise or a sudden movement. She seemed positively terrified.

It took only a moment to tie Lady Anne to a post and meet the Rileys at the door. Eva's eyes were guarded, and she gave him only a cursory smile when he greeted her.

"Nice to see you here, Eva."

"Thank you." She nodded as though to dismiss him.

Mr. Riley clapped him on the shoulder. "We'll talk to you after the service, Jonesy."

"Yes, sir."

Jonesy fought the urge to stare at Eva all through the service. He wasn't sure how many people knew what had happened to her. Certainly her family and friends wouldn't have made it known. But one never knew what the town gossips were whispering about.

Pastor Greg opened the service with the answer to the question Jonesy had asked of the Lord. " 'Charity suffereth long, and is kind.' "

After the reading of 1 Corinthians 13:5, everything else Greg said was tuned out of Jonesy's mind. He zeroed in on that single, short verse that stated charity "seeketh not her own."

Are you trying to tell me I'm selfish? he asked the Lord.

Selfish? Him? Hadn't he left his land to come help his pa? Hadn't he been willing to put his own plans on hold for almost two years in order to honor his father and mother? Selfish? Surely he was hearing the Lord wrong. He'd even been willing to wait until spring so Eva could have a proper wedding. . .before everything happened.

Deep in thought, he would have missed the closing prayer if his ma hadn't nudged him. He stood as they sang the doxology.

The crowded little sanctuary left little room to move quickly. With the Rileys sitting close to the back of the building and his family near the front, by the time Jonesy exited the church, the Rileys' wagon had disappeared. He knew he could easily catch up with them, but he wanted to speak to Eva in private.

"Don't worry, son."

Jonesy turned at the sound of his mother's voice.

"You'll see her tonight. Eva and her parents are coming for supper."

A grin spread across his face.

She slipped her hand through the crook in his arm, and he escorted her down the church steps and to the wagon.

"How do you think she looked, Ma?"

His mother gave him a troubled frown. "Eva seems very frail, doesn't she?"

He nodded. "I can't bear it."

"She's getting better, though. Today was the first time she's been in church in six weeks. Be patient with her, Ben. Eva loves you. She just has to get past the fear."

"I know, Ma. I'm trying. I keep praying that she'll learn to trust me again."

Ma placed a hand on his shoulder. "Maybe it's time to start praying that she'll learn to trust God again. Seems to me all your praying is for your sake, not Eva's."

Jonesy considered her words the rest of the day. Ma was right. So was the Lord. He had been acting selfishly. It was time for him to stop thinking of how her ordeal affected his life and start thinking of how he could help her heal.

During supper, conversation remained lighthearted. Mrs. Riley and Ma discussed the upcoming Christmas dance, while Pa and Mr. Riley talked about the rising price of grain and the rancher who had recently bought land just a few miles to the north. Despite Pa's experience as a rancher, he was a farmer now and worried that ranchers would come in and take up all the farmland with their cattle and horses.

Eva sat pale and still, taking only a few bites of her food in an effort, Jonesy suspected, to be polite. It was obvious her heart wasn't in the meal, though she kept her eyes downcast.

Jonesy kept his own gaze fixed on her, hoping she would look up and catch his eye. She had come such a long way from the dirty, unkempt, angry woman of a week ago. But he could see she had a long way to go.

"Ben, why don't you take Eva out to the barn and show her the new puppies?"

Eva jerked her head up at the sound of Jonesy's ma's voice. Interest flashed in her fawnlike eyes.

Jonesy winked at her. "Lord Byron's a pa. Want to see his young'uns?"

A smile tipped the corners of her mouth. "I'd love to."

Her eagerness sent a sense of relief through Jonesy. His chair scraped the floor as he pushed back from the table.

Eva stood, as well. "Dinner was delicious, Mrs. Jones. Thank you."

"You're welcome."

Eva followed Jonesy outside.

"Trust Ma to ease a tense situation."

"What do you mean?"

"I think she could tell you weren't exactly enjoying the company."

Horror widened Eva's eyes. "Oh my. I didn't mean to be rude. I'd better go back inside and apologize."

Jonesy caught her arm.

"Eva, it's all right. She isn't offended. That's why she offered you a way out of there. To tell you the truth, I was wondering how long I was going to have to sit there and make polite conversation so as not to be rude to your parents. Ma took pity on us both."

Eva gave a soft laugh. Not the throaty, rich laugh that used to come from the depths of her belly. But the sound still sent chills down Jonesy's spine.

Lord Byron gave an excited bark and nearly knocked Eva down when they walked into the barn.

Jonesy laughed. "Seems as though someone's missed you."

Eva ruffled Lord Byron's fur. "So you've gone and found yourself a wife, you crazy mutt."

"Mutt?" Jonesy said with mock offense. "Lord Byron is nobility. Keep a respectful tone in your voice, or we'll be forced to banish you to the tower."

"I'm sorry, old boy."

Lord Byron pranced to the back of the barn, then came halfway back and stood expectantly. Jonesy nudged Eva. "Look. He wants to show off his puppies."

"Well, that is what we're here for. Let's not disappoint him."

The wiggling half-dozen puppies were a mix from a pitch-black mother dog and Lord Byron, whose white, brown, and black patches had no rhyme or reason.

"Ah, so this must be the missus." Eva knelt beside the nursing litter. "And what is her name?" She smiled. "I know she isn't Lady Anne. That name's taken."

"Her name is Beauty."

"Beauty?"

" 'She walks in beauty, like the night.' From the poetry of Lord Byron."

"Ah. Appropriate." She grinned.

One brown-and-white puppy detached itself from its mother and moved blindly on weak, wobbly newborn legs.

A breath of compassion left Eva's throat. "The sweet little thing." She reached down and took the fat, wiggling pup between her palms and cuddled it close. Jonesy held his breath as she rubbed her cheek against the soft fur.

On impulse, he reached forward to brush a curl from Eva's cheek. She gasped and jerked back, her eyes alight with fear. "What are you doing?" she croaked out.

"You had some hair in your face. I was. . .I'm sorry."

She set the puppy down gently next to its mother and watched while it nudged its way in among its warm, furry brothers and sisters. Standing, Eva gathered a shaky breath. "I'd like to go back inside now. I should help our mothers clean up."

"Eva, I'm sorry."

"It's all right, Jonesy." But he could see she was far from all right.

"Just a couple more minutes? I'd like to talk to you about something."

"Please, Jonesy. I said all I have to say about marrying you. Don't make this any harder."

Charity suffereth long and is kind. It seeketh not her own. "Here's the thing." Jonesy summoned the courage to say what he had to say. "I know things have changed. I wish I were the sort of man who could honestly tell you that I could still marry you and never think about taking you into my bed. But that's just not true. As much as I love you, I'm still a man."

"I don't see why we have to have this discussion again."

The sound of Eva's anger spurred him on to explain before she completely cut him off and went inside without hearing him out. "I love you, Eva. And I still want to marry you. But I don't want to lose my friendship with you. I've shared my dreams with you, my poetry, my hope for the future. I miss our rides together and our talks by the river. So if you'll consider it, I'd like us to be friends again. As a matter of fact, I take back my proposal. Consider yourself unasked to be my wife."

An uncertain smile tipped her lips. "You're a little crazy, you know that?"

"Yeah, I know."

"I miss our talks, too, Jonesy. And our rides."

"Does that mean you're willing to take me back into your life as a friend?"

"I guess that's all we were meant to be." She looked up at him, daring him to refute it.

"Maybe so." But he didn't believe that for a second.

"Does this mean you're staying in Oregon until spring?"

Jonesy nodded. "I can't take a chance on getting stuck somewhere because of the weather. I'd rather wait it out here."

"I'm glad."

Eva rode Patches carefully. The horse still seemed to be favoring his left hind leg where the bullet had gone in. Pa's assurance that he needed to work it in order to gain strength was the only thing that could convince Eva to put a saddle on his back and ride him. "He needs to get his confidence back up," Pa had said. "Nothing worse for a horse than to feel helpless."

The early December wind brought with it an icy chill that predicted a cold, harsh winter. Eva shivered and pulled her pa's sheepskin coat closer about her. She cast a sideways glance at Jonesy. They were almost to the river, and neither had spoken more than five words. But it was enough that they be together. Enough that he wanted to be her friend, even if nothing in the relationship went deeper.

"All the geese are gone," she said. "Last time I was here, they hadn't yet flown south for the winter."

"They'll be back."

Eva dismounted and dropped Patches's reins. The horse moved to the river and dipped his head for a drink. "It's still sad to see them go. I know it's silly, but I like to watch them fly away. I always bring bread to feed them. It's sort of my way of telling them good-bye and wishing them Godspeed on their journey."

"I think that's sweet."

"You do, huh?" Eva felt a familiar frustration. Even more unnerving was the fact that she didn't understand where the frustration came from. The old Jonesy would have tugged her long braid and called her a sentimental fool. But this Jonesy was careful. Tender, watchful. Like a man in love, not a friend. It kept her on her guard with him. She longed for their easy camaraderie to return.

Jonesy gave a short laugh as though reading her thoughts. "All right, maybe it's a little eccentric to have a going-away party for a flock of geese."

"Well, it's no more crazy than naming your dog after a poet."

That wonderful, boyish grin spread across his mouth. Eva felt herself relax as she looked out over the water. Jonesy looped Lady Anne's reins around a nearby bush. He walked to their tree and slid down the trunk. "Come sit with me, Eva."

"It's a little cold to be sitting on the ground, don't you think?"

"Cold? This is nothing."

Eva smiled when he shivered and wrapped his arms around himself. Her heart nearly stopped when he opened his arms and legs.

"Come sit against me, and we'll keep each other warm."

Anxiety began to build. "Jonesy. . ."

"All right then. I'll scoot over, and you can sit next to me." He did so and patted the ground. "It's all right. I'll keep my hands to myself."

Eva sat next to him. They stared silently across the water. Eva leaned her head back, enjoying her time with Jonesy. The solid strength of his shoulder pressing against hers surprised her. And the fact that she didn't cringe at his touch.

They sat in silence. There was no need to fill the space between them with empty chatter. The only thing that mattered was being in the open together. Watching the river and listening to the birds in the trees.

Eva closed her eyes. She didn't know how long they remained there, but eventually, despite the cold, her tension faded and peace covered her.

Finally Jonesy's voice broke the silence. " 'He leadeth me beside the still waters. He restoreth my soul.' "

"Do you think that's really possible?" Her voice sounded small, like a child's, but Eva had mustered all of her strength just to gain that much volume.

"What? Having your soul restored?"

Eva nodded but didn't open her eyes. "I don't see how I'll ever be the same person I was before."

"Experiences change us, honey. Some are good experiences, some bad. It's all right to be a little rattled at first, but ultimately it's up to us how we change forever."

Eva gave a short laugh and looked at him. "At least when something good happens, you know the change will be good. How can good come from something bad?"

"I've known fellows who find gold and get rich quick, and believe me, some don't change for the better. It's what's in a person's heart that determines how life's tests and trials will change him or her. The Bible says when believers are tried by fire, we come out pure gold. It's up to us to decide whether to take the tests and become purified or resist the testing and become bitter."

Eva stared, slack-jawed. "You mean to tell me that you think God is testing me by letting this thing happen? How can something like this make me a better person?"

"No," he said. "God doesn't do evil to people to test them. At least I don't believe so. But in the aftermath of that evil, we have some tough choices to make. Do we trust God? Do we allow His still waters to restore us? Or will we fight and kick and wallow in the mire of self-pity until we destroy ourselves?"

Anger flashed through Eva, and she shot to her feet. "That's what you think of me, is it? You think I am choosing to be angry and bitter and wallow in the mud like a pig? All this because I won't marry you and allow you to maul me for the rest of my life?"

Jonesy shoved up beside her, his eyes reflecting her anger and frustration. "You're twisting my words. You know that's not what I meant. And maul you? Do you honestly think I'd hurt one inch of your body? I love you." He reached out to touch her arm.

Instant fear surged inside Eva. A scream started in her belly and shot from her lips.

"Eva, honey. I'm sorry."

But Eva wouldn't hear him. All she could do was scream.

His arms encircled her, and he held her tightly. "It's all right, Eva. No one is going to hurt you. Do you understand? I love you. I love you. I love you."

In the recesses of her mind, the words began to penetrate. Her screams turned to sobs, and her fighting turned to clinging. Jonesy's arms were no longer to be feared, but arms to run to. She clutched at him. "Hold me, Jonesy. Don't let me go. Please don't go."

In a beat, Eva's stomach rebelled. She pulled away just in time to avoid retching all over him. When she was finished, he handed her a handkerchief.

"I'm sorry, Jonesy. I don't know what came over me."

"You can't help getting sick."

"I mean fighting you and screaming."

He stroked her head, and Eva allowed the soft touch. Welcomed it, in fact. "You couldn't help that, either. Now let's get you home so your ma can put you to bed."

Chapter 11

Jonesy stared in horrified disbelief as his mother relayed the news. "How could that be?"

"Son, Eva's been sick every day since shortly after that awful day. Hope finally sent Andy for Doc Smith. There's no question that she's with child."

"And Eva asked her ma to tell us instead of telling me herself?"

Ma nodded grimly. "She can't face you. It was hard enough just having the man she loves know what had happened to her. But this. . .it's too much for any woman to endure."

Just when he was starting to get through to her. Just when she was opening up, allowing his arms to hold her. Now she wouldn't see him again? "When will her suffering end? When?" He leaned forward, elbows on his knees, and buried his face in his hands.

Ma stood behind him, rubbing his back. He heard her softly praying for peace.

"I've been praying that God would allow her to forget so she can heal on the inside and start to live again. Now she's going to have a baby as a reminder for the rest of her life." He took to his feet as a thought entered his mind. "She has to marry me now."

"Son, Eva needs some time to adjust to this. I pray she'll come around again, just like she did before. But now's not the time to press her."

"Don't you see, though? The baby changes things. She needs a husband so people won't gossip."

"People can count the months, son. They'll assume you and Eva fell into sin and had to get married. Either way, Eva will have to bear the burden of public scrutiny. But if you marry her suddenlike, you'll have to bear it, too."

"Not if I move her away after the baby's born. No one in Texas will know anything about Eva or what happened to her. They'll assume we married here and waited until the baby was born and old enough to move. There's no reason for anyone to question whether or not the baby's mine. Eva's reputation wouldn't be in jeopardy."

Jonesy kissed his mother's cheek. "Don't wait supper for me."

His mind churned with the possibilities all the way to the Rileys' home. Eva thought she didn't want to be a wife to him. But once she held that baby in her

319

arms, she'd want another one. And then she'd turn to him. *God, was this Your plan all along?*

Charity suffereth long and is kind. It seeketh not her own.

I am being long-suffering and kind and selfless. I'm taking a woman who is with child by another man and making her my wife!

Eva would know, now, how much he loved her.

Ten minutes later, he stood on the Rileys' porch, looking into the sympathetic eyes of Mrs. Riley.

"I'm sorry, Jonesy. Eva's gone to stay with her cousin Aimee in Oregon City. She won't be home for quite some time."

"But I want to marry her. I'll be a pa to her baby, Mrs. Riley. We can go to Texas, where no one knows."

"Eva will always know." Tears flooded her eyes. "I've never seen her this way. Even after she was attacked, she still had fight in her. Now it's as though all the life has flowed from her veins. I'm afraid for her, Jonesy."

"I have to see her."

Hope touched her fingers to his forearm. "If you love her, you'll let her go. She can't face you right now. Her shame cuts so deeply that seeing you and knowing she can't be yours, pure and untouched, is more than she'll be able to bear. I fear what it might do to her."

All the strength left his legs, and he sank to a wooden rocking chair on the porch. He stared silently into the chilled air.

"I'm sorry, Jonesy. This is for the best. Eva wants to be left alone. I think you need to respect her wishes this time."

Nodding, he rose slowly. "Yes, ma'am." He walked down the steps and mounted Lady Anne. "If you write her a letter, will you please tell her I love her and that I'm praying for her every day?"

"I will, Jonesy. I will."

❧

Eva followed her cousin down a long hallway in the spacious Donnelly home. "This is lovely, Aimes," she said. "Who'd have ever thought when you adopted Georgie that you'd end up living in a mansion with the boy's pa?"

"It's not quite a mansion." Aimee chuckled. "But I couldn't be happier married to Rex and raising Georgie." She stopped before a closed door and turned the handle. With a smile, she pushed the door open. "What do you think?"

Eva drew a breath. A four-poster bed sat against the far wall, covered by a lovely white comforter with lace around the edges. The windows were framed by lacy white curtains that matched the comforter. A lovely maple-wood wardrobe presided over the room and towered above Eva.

"It's extra tall because there's a storage shelf on top," Aimee explained.

"Oh."

Aimee nodded to the carriage driver who had carried Eva's bags up the stairs. "Thank you, Mr. Marlow."

"You're welcome, ma'am. If you need anything else, please ring for me." He bowed out of the room.

Aimee walked to the bed and sat. "Come sit down, and let's talk for a moment."

Fatigued beyond anything she'd ever felt, Eva untied her black bonnet and sank onto the feather mattress.

"You must be exhausted," Aimee said. "Lie back, and I'll take your boots off for you."

Heat warmed Eva's cheeks. "That's not necessary. Really."

"Nonsense. You are here to be taken care of. So let me do that for you."

Eva gave a bitter snort. "I'm not here to be taken care of—just to get out of the way while I have this baby. I think Ma and Pa can't bear to see me. My presence reminds them of what happened to me."

Aimee loosened both boots and set them on the floor. "Eva, do you know why I chose this room for you?"

Eva shook her head.

"I call this the angels' room because it's so beautiful and white. As though the angels needed a place of purity and perfection, so they made this room for themselves."

"Then I shouldn't be here."

"Yes, you should. The white is to remind you that in the eyes of God you are as pure as the day you were born. You are His child, washed in the blood of the Lamb and made pure by His suffering. Now I want you to lie in this bed every night and say this aloud to yourself: 'I am not responsible for what happened to me. It was not my sin that caused this innocent child to exist. I am not to blame.'" Aimee looked at her firmly. "Can you do that?"

"I'll try, Aimes; I promise I'll try." But Eva knew she couldn't. Aimee was sweet and meant well, but some things were just impossible to make someone else understand.

"My ma once told me a very personal story about her past that few other people know. I asked her if I could share it with you, and she gave me permission. Would you like to hear it?"

Curiosity piqued, Eva nodded. "Of course."

"You know I was just a little girl, maybe four or five, when my pa married my ma, right?"

"Yes."

"Well, not many people know that her ma was a saloon girl."

A gasp escaped Eva's throat. "You mean she was a. . ."

"Prostitute, yes." A blush spread across Aimee's already rosy cheeks. "My ma was raised above a saloon, knowing what her ma did to make a living."

Now it was Eva's turn to blush.

"When her ma was killed by the owner of Luke's Saloon, she had to run away or risk being forced into the same life."

Eva kept her eyes on Aimee, riveted by this part of her aunt's life she'd known nothing about.

"Even though her ma was a saloon girl, she was loving and kind. But she had to fight to keep my ma. Luke had demanded she get rid of her."

"You mean put her in an orphanage?"

"Yes. He even threatened to do it himself. But even before she was born, Luke wanted my ma's ma to go to a woman he knew who helped women get rid of babies they didn't want."

Eva's eyes grew wide. She'd never heard of such a thing. "Do you mean there's a way to get rid of a baby before it's born?"

Aimee gave her a sharp look. "It's murder. And even a prostitute who didn't know the Lord knew better than to do such a thing. Don't forget, Eva. The Bible says that God knew us even before we were formed in our mothers' wombs. He knows that child you're carrying. He knows who he or she was created to be. There are no accidents in God's kingdom. He has a purpose for your baby's life."

Once more heat spread across Eva's face. "I'm sure you're right," she mumbled.

"Anyway," Aimee said, "my ma met my pa while she was running away, and he saved her and brought her to Grammy."

"I love the story of how they fell in love."

"What you don't know is that my ma was ashamed to tell Pa about her past. Where she came from. She was afraid he wouldn't understand that she was the daughter of a prostitute."

"But that wasn't her fault."

"You're right. And, Eva, you have to understand that none of this is your fault either. God's grace is more than sufficient to get you through this birth. This baby is as innocent as you are, and Jesus already loves your little one, no matter how he or she was brought into this world. God is forming the little fingers and toes. The mouth that will someday smile at you and melt your heart."

Eva listened halfheartedly to Aimee's speech. She felt no affection for this child whom Jesus apparently already knew. The only thing she could think of was how to find a woman who might help her.

❧

Eva shivered in the dark. From fear, from cold, from the guilt of what she was going to do if everything went according to plan.

She fought back nausea and fear as she walked for an hour to reach the seedier side of town, where the saloons and gambling halls were located. It had taken her a few days to gather the courage to ask one of the maids in the house about it. Reluctantly, and only after payment of a string of pearls Eva's pa had given her for her birthday when she turned sixteen, had the young woman given her directions.

Following the sound of loud, high-pitched laughter, she walked into the first saloon at the end of the street. The raucous laughter receded until finally the room was quiet.

Eva thought she might faint from fear. What had she been thinking? Men who went to bars were not good, God-fearing people. They might be like. . .but she couldn't think about that now. If she did, she wouldn't have the courage to do what she needed to do.

As she walked by a table of men, she felt herself being tugged downward. She let out a scream, and before she quite knew what was happening, she landed in the lap of a laughing, intoxicated man. "Hey, honey, you're a little overdressed to be one of Mike's girls, ain't ya?"

Eva struggled to her feet, shaking in fear. "I'm not one of M–Mike's girls. Now leave me be."

The men let up a roar of laughter.

"What do you want, lady?" the man behind the bar called. "If you ain't lookin' for a job, how 'bout you get on outta here? These men don't want to be reminded of their wives."

"If I had me a wife what looked like her, I would," called a slurred voice. "My wife's fat and bossy."

Eva tried to ignore the suggestive calls and comments. She leveled her gaze at the man behind the counter and lowered her voice. "I need to speak with one of the young women who work here."

"Which one?"

"I–it doesn't matter, I guess. Someone who has worked here for a while."

"Now look here, sister." He poked at her face with a grimy finger. "You leave the preachin' to Sundays. My girls ain't interested in gettin' baptized."

"I assure you, I'm not here to proselytize. I need some information."

Eva had never felt so dirty in her life. She had to close her mind off to what she was about to do, or she couldn't endure it.

"I don't know what you want," the bartender said, "but I'll give you a few minutes. Sally! Get over here."

Eva turned as a young woman with red hair and heavy cosmetics sashayed across the room. Eva's cheeks burned at the sight of her scantily clad figure.

"Whatcha need, Mike?"

"This girl wants to talk to one of the girls."

Sally's eyes went cold as she gave Eva the once-over. "Well, I don't want to talk to the likes of her." She started to turn, but Mike snatched her wrist. She gasped and grimaced.

"I say you're gonna talk to her. And you're gonna do as you're told."

"All right, Mike. I'll talk to her. Don't break my arm, or I won't be able to work."

He scowled and let her go. "You just mind how you're talkin' to me from now on if you know what's good for ya."

"Sure, Mike. Sorry." She turned her icy glare back to Eva. "What's a respectable lady like you doing in a place like Mike's? You crazy or something? Or are you looking for your husband? 'Cause if he came in here, I probably know him." She looked at Eva with smug insolence, daring her to fight back.

Her hostility surprised Eva. She had seen people walk across the street to avoid sharing a sidewalk with a saloon girl, but it had never occurred to her that the feeling might be mutual coming from the other side of the street.

"I don't have a husband, and I couldn't care less how many men you know." She gave Sally a smug look in return. "I need some information. But if you don't want to give it to me, I'll go elsewhere."

The woman's brow furrowed. "What do you mean?"

"I really don't want to discuss it here. Can we go somewhere private?" Fortunately, the men seemed to have lost interest, and the calls and comments had mostly stopped. Still, Eva didn't want to take a chance that someone might be listening.

"Mike, we'll be in your office," Sally said across the bar.

"Hurry up," he growled. "I ain't losin' money tonight so you can go have girly talk."

Sally led her to a rough little room containing a settee and a rough-hewn wooden desk with a chair. Eva sank against the closed door and regarded Sally evenly. Her heart raced.

The other young woman leaned against the desk and shrugged. "So what can you possibly want to know so badly that you'd traipse all the way over to this side of town? And don't say you're not from the rich part of town, because I can tell from your clothes and your manners."

Eva sniffed and raised her chin. "Actually, I don't even live in Oregon City. I'm staying with my cousin and her husband for a while."

Eva felt the woman's scrutiny. She would receive no sympathy from someone who had probably been used by more men than she could count. Eva knew if she had a prayer of obtaining help, she would have to be civil. "I need to know how I can find someone who will help me with a problem."

"What kind of problem?"

"I'm with child."

Amusement crinkled in the woman's blue eyes. "I see. And the baby's father doesn't want to marry you? Let me guess. He's already married. Or maybe you can't let your rich daddy know you fell in love with the ranch hand who isn't nearly good enough for you." She chuckled. "Honey, you're no better than I am, are you?"

Shaking in anger, Eva stomped across the room and slapped the girl's face. "How dare you laugh at me! I'm not like you at all. I didn't give myself to a man. I was accosted. I hate the man who did this to me. And I hate this baby. I want it out of me. And I figure a woman like you must know how to do that."

Sally rubbed her cheek where Eva had struck her. "I don't like to be hit." She strode to the door. "I'm leaving."

Eva clutched her arm. "Please help me! I'm sorry I slapped you. You have every right to be angry with me. But you have to understand. I had no choice in this. I have already lost everything I love as a result of this, and now I'm going to have this monster's baby? How much more must I endure?" Eva sank to the floor and buried her face in her hands.

Sally knelt in front of her. "All right. I'm sorry I laughed at you. But are you sure you want to do this? Don't you have family who will take care of you and a baby?"

"Can you help me or not?"

Sally gave a reluctant nod. "I know someone. But I have to warn you. She's mean. And she'll probably try to force you to stay and work for her."

"But I don't need a job."

Sally gave a short laugh. "Honey, you really are green, aren't you?"

"I don't know what you mean."

"Never mind. You think long and hard about doing this. It's dangerous. A lot of women die from it."

Eva shuddered at the thought of dying in such a manner. She wrapped her arms around herself. "I would rather be dead than have to raise this baby."

"All right. It's your choice. But you'll have to wait until I finish for the night. Stay in here and keep the door locked. Those men aren't even wound up yet." She pointed to the settee, which had a blanket hanging over its side. "Lie down and try to sleep. I'll come get you in the morning."

"In the morning? Why can't we go tonight?"

She gave a short laugh and walked toward the door, her pink satin gown swishing against black stockings. "Honey, I don't get off work until dawn, when the men run out of money and go home to their families."

Chapter 12

Jonesy woke with a start, his heart racing wildly in his chest. Something was wrong. He'd dreamed of Eva, and she was crying and reaching out to him. His body shook as he relived the dream. Her hands dripped with blood. Her lips didn't move, but he could hear the cry of her heart. *Help me. Help me, Jonesy.*

Unable to push aside the image, he shoved back the covers and swung his legs over the side of the bed. He'd never felt so helpless in all his life. Leaning forward, he began to pray.

"Father, keep Eva safe. Please show her Your love for her. Show her Your mercy."

He prayed for an hour. Then he stood and paced and prayed for another hour. When dawn began to break, he knew he had to make the trip to Oregon City. Even if Eva wouldn't see him, he had to see for himself that she was all right.

As silently as possible, he grabbed his saddlebag and stuffed a clean shirt into it, followed by his Bible and extra bullets for his gun, just in case he had need of it.

He carried his boots as he left his room and passed through the living room. He'd wait until he got to the porch to pull them on. He didn't want to wake up Ma and Pa.

Just as he pulled his Stetson off the hat rack, he got the scare of his life.

"Where you going, son?" His ma's voice came out of nowhere.

"You scared me half to death, Ma."

She sat in front of the fire, wearing her robe and a nightcap, rocking in her chair. Her long gray hair was braided and slung over both shoulders. "I asked you a question. Where do you think you're sneaking off to before dawn?"

"Sneaking off? Ma, I'm a grown man."

"Grown men don't sneak off in the middle of the night rather than have to face their parents."

"Oh, all right. I'm going to go to Oregon City and find Eva. I had a horrible dream last night about her, and I need to see her."

"I've been hearing you up there. I imagine you've been praying all night just like I have. But going to Oregon City isn't a good idea. Not until you're invited.

God woke you up to pray. That's all. Now Eva and her parents have both asked you not to pressure Eva. I think you need to honor their request."

"You didn't see what I saw in that dream, Ma. The look in her eyes. She reached out to me."

"And there was blood on her hands?"

Stunned, Jonesy nodded.

"The Lord gave me the same dream, son. Why do you think I'm up at this hour? I've been praying all night, right alongside you. Now do you think God's telling us both to go to Oregon City?"

"No."

"That's right. He's not telling me to go, and you are not to go either. The only thing God is asking of us right now is to bombard heaven with prayers on behalf of that girl. And I'm sure her ma and pa are also praying for her at this moment."

"What does it mean, though? All the blood?"

"I don't know, but it's not good. That's why we have to keep praying until God gives us peace that Eva's all right again."

Jonesy dropped his boots, hung his Stetson back on the hat rack, and slid his saddlebag from his shoulder. "You win. Let's pray."

❧

Eva fought to catch her breath from the rapid pace Sally set. She also fought to contain her nausea as the young woman walked her through the fetid alleyway behind the saloon. "Could you please slow down just a little?" she asked.

"Look, if you want to do this, you'll have to hurry. Bea's been workin' all night, too. If we don't get there soon, she'll be sleeping, and you'll have to wait until later. Maybe even tomorrow."

Eva picked up the pace. "I'll try to keep up."

In a few moments, they reached the back door of what Eva could only surmise was a house of ill repute. It wasn't even disguised as a saloon. Sally knocked, and they waited until a large man answered the door.

"You don't work here anymore," he grumbled. "What do you want?"

"I'm here to see Bea."

The man ogled Eva. "You bringin' her another girl to replace you?"

"No. She ain't like that."

"Then what's she doing with you?"

"That's none of your business. Go tell Bea I need to talk to her."

"Wait here." The door closed, and Eva stood shivering in the cold, foul-smelling alley. Her stomach revolted, and she rushed to the other side of the alley.

When she was finished, Sally handed her a perfumed hanky. "Keep it. I got lots more."

"Thanks." Eva wiped her mouth, fighting nausea once more from the musky scent in the cloth.

The door opened, and the most beautiful woman Eva had ever seen stood there smiling. Eva couldn't take her eyes off her hair, which was just a little too blond to be real.

"Sally, darling. It's wonderful to see you again. Have you finally given up on Mike?"

"No," she said crisply. "And I never will."

The woman sighed and waved them inside. "Ah, well, I had hoped. Who is this?" She pointed at Eva.

"She's in a fix, Bea. I thought maybe you might could help her."

Anxiety began to build inside Eva. She shouldn't be here. How would she ever face her ma again, knowing she'd associated with these sorts of people?

"Honey, you'd better sit down. You look like you're about to pass out." Bea took her arm and escorted her to a kitchen chair. "Now tell Bea all about it."

"She was raped," Sally broke in flatly, without emotion, as though it didn't matter. "She wants to do away with the baby and forget it ever happened."

Do away with the baby? Suddenly Eva saw a fat, pink baby with rosy lips and soft brown hair. Was it a boy or a girl?

No. She couldn't think about that. She'd go crazy if she did. Tears burned her eyes.

The woman placed an arm around Eva's shoulders and clicked her tongue sympathetically. "There, there, we'll have you fixed up in no time. A beauty like you shouldn't be saddled with a baby at this time in your life. Especially a baby conceived in such a wretched circumstance."

Eva's unease increased. She stood. "I—I think perhaps I've made a mistake. I should probably go."

"Well, it's certainly up to you. If you want to see that man's face the rest of your life, every time you look at his child."

Bea walked to the counter and pulled out a cup and saucer. She set the teakettle on to boil, leaving Eva to mull over the words.

How could she carry a child who might look like that man? Bea was right. Eva sank back down into the chair.

"How far gone are you, honey?"

"About two months."

"It's good you came to me when you did." Bea gave an approving nod. "This is the best time."

"What do you mean?"

"Less danger to you. Less mess."

Eva's stomach tightened at the callous words. What was it Aimee had said about God hating hands that shed innocent blood?

The teakettle whistled, and Eva jumped.

"Calm down, little one. You'll likely jump out of your skin."

The woman seemed nice enough, but remembering Sally's warning about Bea's meanness, she resolved to remain on her guard.

Sally glanced at Eva. "Are you sure you want to go through with this? There are worse things in the world than having a baby."

Bea shoved her aside. "Leave the girl alone. What are you still doing here, anyway?"

"Making sure she's taken proper care of. She's a nice girl. Too nice to be held prisoner in a place like this."

Eva started. "Prisoner? What do you mean?"

Bea gave a short laugh. "Sally is always exaggerating. She used to work for me and always complained about my rules. But you aren't that kind of young woman, are you? You came here for help, which I'm happy to give." She set a cup of tea in front of Eva. "Drink this, my dear. It'll help you relax."

Though not fully satisfied with the answer, Eva took the tea, grateful for something to settle her stomach. "Thank you."

"Now I need to ask a few questions before I can give you the help you need. Do you have any friends or family members who are likely to come looking for you?"

"No one will come if I get back home soon. How long will this take?"

Bea looked sideways at Sally, but Eva couldn't decipher the meaning behind the frown.

"The procedure will be fairly quick. But you'll need to rest afterward. I normally keep someone like you in bed for a couple of days at least."

"Oh no. Rex would call on all of his connections to find me if I were gone that long."

Were her words slurring? Eva grabbed hold of the table as the room began to spin. "I—I don't feel so good. Sally? I'm scared." She clutched at the woman's hand. "God hates hands that shed innocent blood. I don't want God to hate me. I love Him."

"It's all right. You don't have to do this."

"Shut up, Sally." Bea's voice rose in pitch. "What connections do you mean? Who is Rex?"

"My cousin's husband." Eva took a deep breath and laid her cheek on the table in front of her. "Rex Donnelly."

"The attorney?"

"Mm-hmm. He fights for the innocent. God hates hands that shed innocent blood." Eva began to sob. Her mind was whirling and confused, but she knew she couldn't kill the life within her. "I have to go. I can't do this. I can't murder an innocent baby." Suddenly she pitched forward, and darkness claimed her.

❦

He'd seen her walk into that saloon last night. But she never came out. Anger burned in his chest. She'd come to Oregon City to taunt him.

Oh, she would pay for this.

❦

Eva woke slowly. Her head pounded, and she was disoriented, in a strange bed, in unfamiliar surroundings. She tried to sit up, but a stab of pain sent her back to her pillow.

"Don't try to get up too soon. You've been out for a while."

She opened her eyes to the voice. "Where am I?"

Soft gray eyes looked down on her with kindness. "My name is Martha O'Neill. My husband is the Reverend O'Neill. We serve the Lord by taking in women like you who are trying to change their ways."

"How did I get here?"

"We found you on the street yesterday morning. At first my husband thought you were dead, but when we got close, we could tell you were just unconscious. Drugged, most likely. We loaded you into our wagon and brought you here."

"Yesterday morning?" Eva sat up quickly, then moaned as pain stabbed her once more. A flash of pink caught her eye, and she glanced down at her dress. "What on earth?" How had she come to be wearing Sally's dress? Not a dress, really; more like a costume. An extremely indecent one at that. She grabbed the blanket and pulled it up to her chin.

"Modesty is returning already. How wonderful. The reverend and I would like to offer you a place to call home if you are willing to end your life of sin and learn to walk in the light of God's love and goodness. If you would prefer to be returned, you may have a good, hearty breakfast first, and afterward, my husband will drive you back to where he found you."

The woman gave her a soft, loving smile and placed her hand on Eva's cheek. "I can see you've been through a lot, child. Perhaps God brought you to us for a reason. Will you give Him a chance to show you true love?"

Eva grabbed Mrs. O'Neill's hand and held it close. "Thank you," she whispered.

"The love of God brought you here. My husband and I are only His hands and His feet."

"Oh, Mrs. O'Neill, if only I could believe in God's love again."

"You will, child. God has led you beside still waters so that He can restore your soul. You may stay with us for however long it takes God to do His work of restoration."

Chapter 13

It was all Jonesy could do not to grab Billy by the front of his shirt and throw him into the wall to make him understand. "We have to go after her."

Billy's eyes flashed, and he slapped his hand down on the desk. "Do you think I don't want to go find my baby sister?"

"Not from the looks of it. It's been two weeks, and I'm tired of waiting."

"Rex has hired four private detectives, and he called in favors at the sheriff's office in Oregon City. Right now I have my hands full with those horse thieves. The circuit judge is going to be coming through any time. I can't leave my post."

Jonesy slammed his fist against the wall. The pain came as a welcome relief against the ache in his heart. His Eva, missing, and no one could find her. What if she was gone for good? What if she was dead? Only the fact that the road between here and Oregon City was washed out had kept him from riding there as soon as he received word that she was missing.

He was about to appeal to Billy again when the door flew open. "Sheriff!" The bespectacled postmaster rushed inside and thrust a letter into Billy's hands. "I would have waited to give it to your pa and ma, but I know how anxious you all are to hear from Eva."

Jonesy's heart leaped. "That's from Eva?"

"Yes."

Billy stared at the envelope. "It's postmarked Oregon City."

"So much for four detectives and the sheriff's office."

A shrug lifted Billy's shoulders. "I'll get this out to Ma and Pa right away. Thank you, Travis."

"You're welcome, Sheriff."

"What are you waiting for?" Jonesy asked. "Open it."

"It's addressed to my parents. I'm not opening it."

Jonesy fought to keep from ripping it out of his hands. "All right then, let's go."

Billy grinned. "Let's."

They raced over slippery, muddy roads the five miles to Andy and Hope Riley's home. Both men reined in their horses at the same time and dismounted in record time. The door opened before they could make it to the porch.

"What are you two up to, tearing into the yard like that?" Mrs. Riley demanded. "Look at the marks you've left. Now the ground is going to dry with holes in it."

"Sorry, Ma. But I think you'll forgive us when you see what we brought you." Billy waved the envelope. "Word from Eva."

Andy stood behind his wife. "Oh, praise You, Lord."

Hope took the letter in shaking hands and looked at Billy with pleading eyes. "What does she say?"

"I didn't read it, Ma. It wasn't sent to me."

"Come inside. We'll open it in there."

In two minutes, they were sitting around the table. Mrs. Riley carefully opened the envelope and pulled out a piece of crisp white paper.

Dear Ma and Pa,

I'm so sorry for worrying everyone. I can only imagine how frantic you've been. Especially you, Ma. I have so much to tell you, and I will, as soon as I return. But for now, I'm staying with an elderly minister and his wife. They help women who need help. I won't go into details about how I came to be with these wonderful people, but please believe me that God brought me here. I'm safe and well cared for.

I need this time. Whether I will stay until the baby's born or even longer, I don't know. But I will write often. Please do not try to find me. Be comforted in knowing that I'm in good hands.

Lovingly,
Your daughter, Eva

P.S. Tell Jonesy he was right. I was led beside still waters, and God is restoring my soul.

Tears misted Jonesy's eyes. "I guess God can take care of her better than I can. I just wish she would have told us where she is so we can at least see her."

"I think that's the point, Jonesy," Hope said softly. "Sometimes we just have to let go and hope our loved ones come back to us."

Andy nodded. "Eva's got a lot of my ways in her. She has to figure things out on her own just like I did."

"Like you, sir?" Jonesy's heart picked up at the look of love that passed between Eva's parents.

"I had my difficult days of trying to understand why certain things happen in life. I blamed God and grew bitter just like my daughter has. I had to go away and spend a winter in the mountains with a mountain man and his Indian wife to find God's purpose for me."

Hope took his hand. "He came back to me just before Eva was born."

"Do you think Eva will come back to me?"

"The most important thing right now is that she's setting her heart back to trusting God's love for her. Whether she'll ever trust yours is something to be determined later."

～

Eva had been at the O'Neills' for less than a month when she was finally able to keep down a full meal. Her energy returned, and she found the routine quite to her liking. Along with doled-out chores, Reverend O'Neill gave a daily devotion in the chapel, tucked inside an arbor of evergreens.

Mrs. O'Neill ended each day's scripture reading by playing a hymn on her organ and allowing the Word to settle into their minds. On Sunday the three families close enough to come to services during the winter made the trip and joined the O'Neills and their girls.

Eva, along with two other women, occupied a spare room in the cozy log cabin. It was a little cramped, but Eva didn't care. She loved the solitude of the cabin. Loved looking outside the door and seeing the snowcapped mountains in the distance.

She felt a little guilty for not admitting to them that she wasn't a prostitute in need of redemption. Some days she felt as though she were taking their kindness under false pretenses.

Millie and Shawna were there for the right reasons. Millie was an old prostitute who had been beaten and left for dead. Shawna had been kidnapped in England when she was fourteen years old and brought over on a ship of white slaves. She hadn't seen her parents in ten years and had no desire to return to England. But her soul was prospering under the kind tutelage of the O'Neills.

She had arrived much the same way Eva had, four months earlier. She'd already given her heart to one of the young men who attended services. Eva could see he shared her affection, but under his mother's watchful eye, the two never seemed to have the opportunity for more than a few cursory words.

Eva's other roommate, Millie, fought a little harder against the restrictions. She'd lived in a drunken fog for so long that facing the clarity of real life seemed difficult for her.

Eva lay in bed, looking at the stars through her window. She was glad she got the bed next to the window. Leaving the house was still a fearsome thing for her, but staring at the stars each night was almost like being outdoors. She longed for Patches and the midnight rides they used to take when the moon was bright and the terrain free from mud or ice. Poor Patches. How was he doing?

"*Psst*. Shawna, Eva."

Eva sat up. "What's wrong, Millie?"

"I'm leavin'."

"What do you mean?" Shawna's hint of an English accent, left over from childhood, always made Eva ache for Jonesy and his penchant for sliding into the accent. Only since meeting Shawna had Eva realized how brilliantly he'd accomplished it.

Millie lit the candle next to her bed. "Listen, ladies. If the three of us started our own business, we could split it three ways and take care of each other."

Leave it to Millie to think of an enterprise. Eva had trouble thinking beyond today. "You mean like sewing dresses? My aunt was a seamstress in her day. I'm sure she'd give us some advice."

Millie chortled. "You're a right funny one. A seamstress. You know good and well what I'm talking about."

"You two can do whatever you want," Shawna said with unaccustomed force, "but I'm never going back to selling myself. I'm living for God now, and I might even be getting married one day."

At the realization of what Millie wanted her to do, Eva's jaw dropped. A gasp escaped her throat, and heat rushed to her cheeks. After living with these women for a month, she thought she was past embarrassment at the mention of their former lifestyles, but judging from her shock, she was far from past anything.

"Millie, you mustn't think of going back to your old life."

"It's all I know. I been in this business in one form or another for thirty years."

"But surely you don't miss it," Shawna said softly. "The O'Neills are so kind. And have you ever in your life heard stories like the ones they read to us from the Bible?"

"They's good people," Millie agreed. "I ain't sayin' they ain't. And livin' here is fine. . .for now. But what about when they need the bed space for another lost soul? Are they gonna let you stay on? I don't think so. And when it's time, where are you gonna go? Is some farmer really gonna marry a woman that ain't untouched? Is Mark's ma really gonna let him marry you?"

"I don't know." Shawna's lip trembled. "But even if it's not him, I hope to marry and have children someday."

A loud snort filled the room as Millie started to laugh. "I've known a lot of men in my day, and let me tell you. Ain't one of 'em any different from the others. They don't want girls like us for marryin'. A man wants a young thing he can take straight from her parents' home to his bed."

"Millie, not all men are that way." Eva's heart pounded in her chest. "There is a man back home who wants to marry me, even though he knows I'm not. . . pure."

"Back home?" The older woman's sharp gaze stabbed into Eva's. "I thought you was from Oregon City."

Swallowing hard, Eva fought for a reply.

Fortunately, a tap on the door silenced the conversation. "Ladies?" Mrs. O'Neill came in. "You're up late. Is there a problem?"

"No, ma'am," Eva said. "Did we wake you?"

She let out a laugh. "I'm looking for the reverend's spectacles. He's laid them down again. That man. If he hadn't married me, he'd be half blind all the time."

The comment brought out laughter around the room. "We were just discussing marriage," Eva said. "You and Mr. O'Neill seem so happy."

A smile spread across the gentle face. "Marriage is the most wonderful relationship God ever created."

"God made marriage?" Shawna's eyes grew wide. "Does the Bible say that?"

"Of course. God saw that it wasn't good for man to be alone, so He took a rib from Adam's side and created a bride for him. It also says that the marriage bed is undefiled. And that a man shall leave his father and mother and cleave to his wife."

"That sounds wonderful." Shawna's eyes grew dreamy in the soft glow of the candlelight. "What's the name of the man who wants to marry you, Eva?"

"Jonesy." A smile tipped Eva's lips at the thought of his handsome face.

"Tell us about him," Mrs. O'Neill encouraged, sitting on the edge of Eva's bed.

So she did. She told them about his silliness. His fake accents. Lord Byron the dog. Lady Anne the horse. His love for poetry. And how he'd asked her to marry him even though she wasn't pure.

The elderly woman patted her hand. "And why did you refuse him?"

Eva looked at her hands, twisting the blanket. "I'm not really ready to talk about that."

"There's no need to. That's between you and the Lord."

Mrs. O'Neill looked at all three. "I want you to remember the scripture we read this morning from 2 Corinthians. 'If any man be in Christ, he is a new creature'—and that goes for women, as well. 'Old things are passed away; behold, all things are become new.' The world may see you as used up. Old before your time. But God wants to give you back the days the devil has stolen from you. You're not impure anymore. God can bring a man into each of your lives who will love you unconditionally, despite past mistakes."

Millie gave another loud snort, turned over on her bed, and pretended to be asleep in moments.

Mrs. O'Neill stood and walked toward the door. "Well, I suppose I'll go back to bed. You girls try to go to sleep now, all right?"

"Yes, ma'am."

In the morning, Millie was gone. And so was fifty dollars that Mrs. O'Neill kept tucked away in a jar in the cabinet. Eva's locket was also missing. As much as she regretted that Millie had stolen the locket Pa had given her, she regretted even more that the woman had chosen to return to her old life.

"Jesus knew that His listeners wouldn't all accept His truth," the kindly reverend said with a sad shake of his head. "We'll continue to pray for Millie until the Lord releases us from the burden."

They bowed their heads and did just that.

Eva had never known such peace.

She had not yet told the O'Neills about her pregnancy. Deep inside, she feared they would turn her out if they knew. She couldn't help but smile at the irony. If she were a woman of ill repute, she could stay. But as merely a wounded soul, the victim of a brutal attack, this wasn't the place for her.

Christmas came and went, and February was now upon them. When Eva lay in bed at night, she could feel her bulging stomach. Soon her condition would be visible through her petticoats and thick skirts. She'd have no choice but to tell the O'Neills. She only hoped when the truth came out, they would allow her to stay and complete the healing God had begun in her.

One night, she was just finishing up a letter to home when a knock sounded on the door. Mrs. O'Neill entered upon Eva's welcome. "Hello, girls."

No matter that Eva was nineteen and Shawna five years older, to Mrs. O'Neill they were mere girls. "The reverend will be going to Oregon City tomorrow morning for supplies. If you'd like to mail a letter, or if you need anything in particular, let him know tonight."

"I have a letter to send." Eva took the addressed envelope from under her pillow. "I—I don't have the price of postage."

"It's all right. You've earned it in the chores you do around here. Always doing more than we ask of you."

"Thank you, ma'am. My ma raised her children to keep up with tasks." Eva took a deep breath. "Mrs. O'Neill, there is something else I'll be needing, but I don't know how to go about asking for it."

"What is it?"

Casting her glance to the quilt, Eva began to tremble.

"What's wrong, dear?"

"I—I need to begin sewing some things for. . .my baby. You see, I—I am with child."

"Oh, honey, I'm so sorry. Imagine you bearing this burden alone for all these weeks. Don't worry. You're not the first girl to come to us in this condition. We have baby clothes in the loft, along with a cradle and some blankets."

Relief washed over Eva. "Thank you, ma'am."

"We can still buy some material for you to make your baby a couple of new gowns, too. Would you like that?"

Eva shook her head. "There's no need to go to any trouble or expense. I'm sure the clothes you have are fine."

"Oh, Eva." Shawna's eyes glowed with the look of a woman who couldn't wait to be a mother. "Imagine having a baby to hold and love."

"I'm not exactly in a position to be a mother," she said bitterly.

"Don't you worry," Mrs. O'Neill broke in. "You're going to be a wonderful mother. I've seen it before. The woman isn't sure until that baby makes his entrance into the world. Then all that matters is that sweet little face."

Eva looked into the woman's smiling eyes and knew she had to come completely clean. "My baby was conceived in rape, Mrs. O'Neill. I wasn't a prostitute. I was a proper girl from a good family. I went riding alone one night when I shouldn't have. I almost died, but Jonesy rescued me."

"A hero," Shawna said breathlessly.

"Oh, Shawna, please."

"But why were you dressed in such a manner when my husband discovered you?"

Tears flooded Eva's eyes. "I had gone to that section of town to find someone who could help me get rid of the baby."

Shawna gasped. "Eva, that's dangerous. I've seen many women almost die from that."

"What happened that you didn't go through with it?" Mrs. O'Neill gently prodded.

"The woman must have slipped something into my tea, because I started feeling strange. I remember telling them I couldn't take the baby's life and risk shedding innocent blood. They asked me about my family. That's the last thing I remember."

"Who is your family, Eva? Is there some reason those people would dump you in the street dressed like a saloon girl? They must have been scared. Otherwise they'd have just killed you."

"My cousin Aimee is married to Rex Donnelly, an attorney."

Shawna shifted on her bed. "He's a famous one, too. Be glad of it. From what I hear, Bea is a rough character. She forces girls to work for her and only lets them go if they're about ready to die or if someone offers the right price."

Eva thought of Sally from Mike's place. If only she could bring her to the O'Neills.

Eva's memory of the conversation between Bea and Sally made sense now. Sally had stayed that morning to make sure Bea didn't try to keep Eva there against her wishes.

"Eva, why did you try to take your baby's life?"

Eva looked at her through eyes blurred from tears. "I don't want to raise a baby who I might resent. Now I have no choice."

"There is always a choice, honey."

It took a moment for Mrs. O'Neill's words to make sense.

"Oh no. I couldn't take him to an orphanage. My aunt and uncle run one. They do their best to take care of all the children they take in. But it never seems as though they can do enough. A baby needs to be held much more than an orphanage can provide with such limited staff."

"What about finding a married couple who might take the baby in and raise him as their own?"

Eva jerked her head up to look at Mrs. O'Neill. "I hadn't thought about that. Do you think. . ." She drew a deep breath. "Do you think it's all right if I do that?"

"Giving your baby to a loving family rather than trying to love someone who reminds you of the agony you endured?" Mrs. O'Neill looked at Eva through eyes filled with compassion. "I think perhaps the Lord brought you here for more than one reason."

"What do you mean?"

"To help heal your pain from the ordeal you've been through, of course. But perhaps also for Lissa and Amos Matthews."

"Who?"

"They've been married for close to ten years, but God hasn't blessed them with any children of their own. They live a little far away, so they don't normally attend Sunday services until after the spring thaw."

A sense of relief filled Eva. It seemed God had provided a way for her to give birth to the baby and yet be free of the constant reminders she would have if she raised the child. In a few months, she could go home and resume her life.

Chapter 14

Dear Pa and Ma,

Every day brings us a little closer to all-out spring. It's hard to believe April has already arrived. The snow is melting, and yesterday I saw a bud on a rosebush. It won't be long now. You know how much I love roses.

I have come to a decision of which I've been trying to inform you for a few months now, but the words just never seemed sufficient. Perhaps they still aren't, but I feel I must go ahead, even at the risk that it will sound callous.

I've decided to give the baby to a childless couple. I believe God brought me here so I could give them the child growing inside me. I know I can't love it the way a child needs to be loved.

I hope you can forgive me for giving the baby away. I do feel that I am making the right decision, and I beg you to understand.

Eva

P.S. Tell Jonesy I saw a flock of geese returning today. I took some stale bread and gave them a welcome-home party.

Jonesy smiled at the memory of Eva telling him she used to send the geese off for the winter with full stomachs. Oh, how he missed their rides together, their talks.

Each time the Rileys received a letter from Eva, they sent for him and allowed him to sit and listen while Hope read. A new letter had arrived at least once a month, and each carried a P.S. for him.

Despite his joy that she'd sent him another personal message, he felt heartsick that she would give away her child. If only she knew that he was willing to marry her and take her away. Be a pa to the baby. Frustration clamped tightly around his middle. How could he prove his love for her if she wouldn't tell anyone where to find her?

He'd missed the April 1 deadline he'd given himself to go back to Texas. Here it was, the middle of May. It always took a couple of weeks for one of Eva's letters to reach them in Hobbs. If she came back late in the summer, they would still have time to leave. Otherwise they would have to wait through one more winter. It would be too risky to leave in the fall, especially with a baby—and that was if he could find Eva before she went through with her plan to give the child away.

Jonesy had been so deep in his thoughts that he hadn't noticed Mrs. Riley lean against Mr. Riley's shoulder. Tears flowed down her cheeks.

"Mrs. Riley," Jonesy said with conviction, "I'm going to Oregon City. I have to find Eva and convince her not to give the baby away. I still want to marry her. I'll raise that child as my own."

Mr. Riley regarded Jonesy evenly. "But she's asked us not to try to find her. She seems to be doing well, and I want to give her time to sort all this out. I think you should, too."

Hope reached across the table and patted Jonesy's hand. "I believe Eva's made a wise choice in turning the baby over to parents who will love him fully."

"But I'd love the baby just as much. There's no need for Eva to do this."

The Rileys remained silent.

He said his good-byes in short order, then rode to his parents' house to relay the contents of the letter to his ma. "I need to find her," he said. "But Mr. Riley believes I have no business trying to."

"He's right," Ma said softly. "Give it some more time, son. She'll come home when she's ready."

"But it'll be too late by then. She'll have already given the baby away."

"Why are you so set on raising this child? Are you afraid that if Eva doesn't keep the baby, she won't need you to marry her and sweep her away to Texas?"

Jonesy cringed at his mother's words. "Of course not."

At least that's what his mind screamed. But as he went about doing his chores, somewhere deep down inside, he knew she was right.

Charity suffereth long and is kind. It seeketh not her own.

He wanted Eva to need him. So much so that he resented her desire to share the baby with a barren couple. "Oh, God. Forgive me."

Peace swept over Jonesy. But the urgency to find Eva seemed to intensify in that moment. He knew that as surely as the earth needs water, Eva needed him. He also knew that God was telling him to go find her.

❧

Pete sat at the bar next to Randy and slugged down another whisky. After being cooped up in this town all winter and spring, he was plenty restless. He made a grab for the nearest woman, a plump but pretty saloon girl.

She gave him a slow smile with luscious, stained lips. "What can I get for you, cowboy?"

A flash of gold around her neck arrested his attention. He frowned. It looked familiar. He made a grab at it and snatched it in his fingers before she could stop him.

"Hey, mister, that's mine. And Mike don't take kindly to us gettin' man-handled. Ain't that right, Mike?"

"Leave her locket alone, mister."

"I want to know where she stole this from. I know the owner."

The prostitute sneered. "I didn't steal it. Eva gave this to me."

"It was a gift from her pa," he growled. "She wouldn't have given it away."

"Okay, fine. Keep it."

"I don't want the locket. I want the girl. Where is she?"

"Why should I tell you?"

"Let's just go," Randy said quietly. "You don't want to start that trouble again."

Pete moved slowly away. Randy was right, for now. He had ways of getting information out of women. This cow would tell him where to find Eva, or she'd be dead by morning.

Chapter 15

Lady Anne carried Jonesy into Oregon City just as dawn was beginning to break. He'd left directly after supper, under protest from his parents, and had ridden all night. Before he left, he'd stopped by the Rileys to let them know he was going. He'd felt it was the right thing to do. After all, Eva was their daughter and they had requested that he not go. But something in Andy's eyes shone his approval when they'd shaken hands. "I'd be doin' the same thing if it were my Hope."

Those words of assurance had been all the confirmation Jonesy needed that going to Oregon City was the right decision.

Mrs. Riley handed him an envelope. "Go to our niece Aimee's house. The address is on the back of that letter. Rex can tell you where to find Eva."

Jonesy stared at the envelope, trying to wrap his mind around the truth of Hope Riley's words. "You've known all along where she is?"

She nodded. "Rex's private investigators found her before Eva's first letter arrived."

"And you never brought her home?" Jonesy said, a bit too harshly.

Mr. Riley had placed a protective arm about her shoulders. "We knew she was safe. And she needed some time away."

"Then why are you telling me now?"

"If you're determined to find her, there's no sense in sending you on a wild-goose chase. What happens between the two of you is something you'll have to sort through. It's not our place to deliberately keep you from her."

Jonesy followed the directions on the back of the letter and by morning had found the place. A servant answered his knock.

"Is this the home of Rex and Aimee Donnelly?"

The stiff male servant nodded. "Who may I say is calling?"

"Ben Jones. I'm a friend of Aimee's aunt Hope and uncle Andy. I have a letter for Aimee from Eva's parents."

He took the envelope and stepped away from the doorway. "Come inside, please." He led the way to an elegantly furnished sitting room and waved Jonesy inside. "Wait here, please. I will inform Mr. and Mrs. Donnelly of your presence."

"Thank you."

In moments, they appeared. The man shook his hand, and the lovely woman with blond curls and blue eyes offered her hand, as well.

"Thank you both for seeing me."

"I read Aunt Hope's letter. Eva is very blessed to have a man who loves her so much."

"I'm the one who feels blessed to know her. I need to find her." He looked from one to the other. "Can you please lead me in the right direction?"

Rex sat next to Aimee on the settee. "She's living with a minister and his wife about four hours' ride north. There is a small community of farmers who gather to worship at Reverend O'Neill's chapel on Sunday. They seem to make a habit of taking in strays like Eva."

Jonesy's ire rose. "Eva's far from being a stray."

Rex gave a chuckle. "Believe me, I didn't mean to insult her. I just meant they seem to take in people who don't have anywhere else to go. If Eva was looking for solitude and kindness, that's why she ended up with the O'Neills and why she's stayed with them for so long."

Mollified, Jonesy let down his guard. "I'm grateful to them for helping her and keeping her in a safe place, but it's time to find her."

Jonesy received instructions on which road to take out of town and how to find the little log cabin and chapel in the woods.

Aimee insisted he join them for breakfast. Jonesy had to admit he felt better and more energized after the meal. His hopes were high as he set out to find Eva.

❧

The sun had already risen by the time Eva opened her eyes and greeted the day. Her back ached before she even moved. She would be so relieved when the next two months were over and her body returned to normal. To have energy again. To be able to sleep all night without visiting the outhouse. To do something as simple as shifting from side to side without effort.

Her bulging stomach rolled as the baby moved inside her. She smiled. "You're just waking up, too, huh, little one?"

Shawna entered the room, smiling brightly. "Oh, good. You're up. Mrs. O'Neill says you should get ready soon or you'll be late for morning services."

Stretching and yawning, Eva heaved up to a sitting position. "I feel as though I haven't slept a wink."

"I heard you get up at least three times." Sympathy sang in her tone. "Don't worry. It'll all be over soon. The baby will be tucked away safe and sound at the Matthewses' home. Then you can forget this ugliness ever happened to you."

Forget? Though the memory had faded and the terror diminished each day as the peace of God reigned in her life, Eva knew she'd never forget the horror of that night. But over the past months, she had come to understand that God was able to carry her through. That every day didn't have to be about what had happened to her. She knew that once the baby was born, she would be ready to go home.

❧

Smoke curled into the air above the little log cabin. From the edge of the woods Pete watched a small dog playing with a fallen branch. He scanned the surrounding area to see if there were any larger dogs that might be a problem.

The door opened, and a pretty young woman appeared. She smiled and stooped down to pet the dog. Pete glanced at Randy. "Looks like there's one for you, too."

"Shut up," Randy snarled. "I like my women willing. I don't force myself on them."

Pete bristled at the accusation. Randy didn't understand the special relationship he had with Eva Riley. He drew in a breath when the door opened again. His dark-haired beauty appeared. Pete frowned. She looked. . .different.

"Aw, she went and got fat. Why would she do that when she knows I'm coming back to her?"

His companion shook his head. "There ain't no helpin' you, Pete. You belong in an asylum somewhere."

"You tellin' me she don't look fat to you?"

"Idiot. The only thing big on that girl is her stomach, and there's only one reason for that."

Pete gave a snort. "Yeah, too much food."

Randy looked away in disgust. "If you don't like fat women, why not just let her go?"

"Let her go? She's been waitin' for me all this time. How would it look if I got this close and then just left without seein' her?"

"Are you crazy?" Randy growled, his voice as angry as Pete had ever heard. "You forced yourself on that girl. She's praying she never sees your ugly face again."

"Shut up!" Pete felt the blackness coming. He didn't like it and tried not to do what it wanted, but usually he couldn't help himself. Pictures played in his head, and he had to do what he saw. He raised his gun and slammed it down on the back of Randy's neck. The man slumped forward with an *oomph*, then slid from his horse.

Poor Randy. He didn't understand how Pete felt about Eva. He'd been a good friend, but Pete couldn't take a chance the burly man would disrupt his plans. Not when he was this close to getting what he wanted.

❧

Eva gathered a deep breath of rain-soaked air as she headed down the path to the chapel. She would be the last one to arrive, as was becoming a habit. Since Mrs. O'Neill had released her from morning chores during the past month, she'd allowed herself those few coveted extra moments of sleep.

The organ music was already playing before she was even halfway up the tree-lined path. Suddenly, above the music, she heard the reverend's voice.

"Fear thou not; for I am with thee: be not dismayed; for I am thy God: I will strengthen thee; yea, I will help thee; yea, I will uphold thee with the right hand of my righteousness."

Eva frowned. How could it be that she heard the reverend's voice so clearly above the congregation singing "Blessed Assurance"?

She heard it again.

"Fear thou not; for I am with thee: be not dismayed; for I am thy God: I will strengthen thee; yea, I will help thee; yea, I will uphold thee with the right hand of my righteousness."

Footsteps behind her made her smile. The reverend must have forgotten his spectacles again. The scripture she heard him reciting was surely his text. Without his eyeglasses, he wouldn't have been able to read a word.

Her smile widened, and teasing bubbled to her lips. She turned to greet him.

Disbelief shot across her mind. Her forward momentum halted midstride, and she backed up. A scream tore at her throat, but no sound emerged.

Him! No! He couldn't have found her.

His eyes flashed with evil intention. "Hi, Eva. Did you miss me?"

He reached out and grabbed her wrist, pulling her to him. Pressing his mouth close to her ear, he whispered, "Don't make a sound."

Hot tears burned her eyes. She knew she wouldn't live this time.

❧

Jonesy heard the sound of singing and an organ playing in the distance. His heart skipped. In moments, he would see his beloved Eva again. All the way from town, he'd tried to imagine what he would say to her. Especially when he knew she didn't want to see him.

He wasn't even sure why he'd come at this point. He wouldn't try to talk her out of giving up her baby. He wouldn't ask her to come to Texas with him. He had decided he wouldn't ask her to marry him until he knew she was ready.

For now, he had every intention of keeping his word that they would go back to their easy friendship. The one they'd shared before admitting their feelings for each other.

Lady Anne stamped her legs and whinnied as they neared a clearing in the woods. "What is it, girl?"

Jonesy heard a man moaning. "Hello? Is someone there?"

"Help," came the feeble reply.

Jonesy halted Lady Anne and dismounted. He walked toward the moaning. "Where are you?"

"Here."

Drawing in a breath, Jonesy recognized the man on the ground. Blood stained his shirt and the back of his head. "Randy? What are you doing here?"

"Pete found her."

Fear exploded in his chest. "What?"

"Eva's in danger. Hurry."

"Where?"

"I ain't sure." Randy grimaced.

"If you've hurt her, I'll kill you!"

"I tried to talk him out of it. That's the only reason I came along. So I could try to protect her for you. But he must have figured it out, 'cause soon as my back was turned, he knocked me in the head." He moaned again. "We saw her come out of the house."

Alarm burst through Jonesy. "Did he figure out that she's. . . ?"

"That dimwit thought she was fat. I tried to tell him, but he couldn't figure it out."

Jonesy blew a relieved breath. He looped Lady Anne's reins around a nearby tree and drew his pistol. "Look out for my horse," he told Randy. "I'll be back to help you as soon as Eva's safe."

Slowly he moved toward the clearing. Several yards of land lay between him and the house where he would be visible to anyone watching. "Lord, please keep me hidden," he whispered.

He traveled swiftly across the open land to the cabin. With his back against the log wall, he made his way around to each window. He could see no one in the cabin.

He forsook the path and used the trees as shields as he headed toward the chapel.

"Fear thou not; for I am with thee. . . ." The sound of Eva's voice reached his ears. "Be not dismayed; for I am thy God."

"Shut up!" Pete's voice sounded wild with anger. "I said, shut up!"

When Jonesy spotted him, his heart nearly stopped. Eva sat beside him, bound to a tree. What could Pete possibly be thinking? If he wanted to kidnap her, he could have been long gone by now. If he wanted to hurt her again, or even kill her, he could have done that, too. But to tie her up not far from the chapel, where people were bound to hear her if she screamed? It made no sense.

"I will strengthen thee; yea, I will help thee."

"Stop it! I can't think." Pete covered his ears and squeezed his eyes shut.

Eva's voice trembled, and Jonesy could see she was fighting to believe her own words. "I will uphold thee with the right hand of my righteousness."

"Stop it!" Pete pointed the gun toward Eva's head. "I mean it. I'll kill you."

346

"No!" Jonesy rushed forward as Pete swung around. A shot rang out.

Pete dropped. Jonesy looked down at his still-cold pistol. He hadn't even been able to think clearly enough to fire. How. . . ?

"Jonesy!" Eva's scream pierced the air. "Behind you!"

He turned just in time to see Randy, gun in hand, crumple to the ground at his feet. His eyes closed, but his chest rose and fell in shallow breaths.

"It's all right, Eva. He saved us." Jonesy quickly closed the distance between them and began working the knots in the ropes that bound her wrists behind the tree. "Pete knocked him out earlier, when he was going to try to save you. He's lost a lot of blood. Only God could have given him the strength to come find us, and just when we needed him."

"How did you find me?" she asked.

"Rex knew where you were."

Once she was free, he held back, unsure if she had digressed to the fear she'd experienced after the first attack.

But she smiled, her eyes shining with what he hoped was love, and threw her arms about his neck. "Oh, Jonesy, God told me He was sending help. He told me not to be afraid. And you came at just the right time."

Jonesy closed his eyes and held her, his heart swelling with love and relief that she was all right, in her soul and in her spirit.

She pulled away slightly and nodded toward Randy's still form. "Is he. . . ?"

"Just unconscious. But I'm not sure about Pete."

Jonesy stood and offered Eva his hand. She lumbered to her feet. His gaze slid across her middle. Her face grew red with shame. There were so many things he wanted to say to her. But for now, he had to attend to the two outlaws lying on the ground.

He slipped his arm about her shoulders. "Let's walk to the chapel where I can get a couple of men to help with those two."

Eva laid her head against his shoulder as they walked. For Jonesy, that small action on her part proved that she trusted him. And for this moment, that was all he needed.

Chapter 16

Eva wiped her damp palms on her dress and paced the room as the hour hand on Mrs. O'Neill's mantel clock turned past midnight.

"Don't worry, Eva," Mrs. O'Neill said softly. "They'll be back soon."

Eva sank into a chair next to the fireplace, but her gaze stayed fixed on the door.

"Your Jonesy loves you a great deal."

"Do you think he still does? Even after seeing me like this?"

Eva's heart nearly burst with love for Jonesy. Love she'd been unable to feel or release for so long. But seeing him again, feeling his arms around her, had made her see everything clearly.

"A person would have to be blind and deaf not to see the love in his eyes and hear the love in his voice."

The instant she heard the rattle of wagon wheels, she flew to the door and flung it open.

Jonesy jumped from the wagon before it stopped and snatched her up in an embrace. They stood motionless in each other's arms. He buried his face in her neck.

Only when Reverend O'Neill politely cleared his throat did Jonesy pull away. They entered the cabin and sat around the table. Mrs. O'Neill poured tea.

"What happened with Randy and Pete?" Eva asked.

"The doctor was able to pull them both through. Billy's been notified, but they'll stay in Oregon City to stand trial. They've done enough thieving in these parts to hang."

"Both of them?"

"I'm going to put in a good word for Randy. But I don't know how much good it's going to do."

"Thank the Lord everyone is all right," Mrs. O'Neill said, smiling.

Reverend O'Neill drained his cup and stood. "Well, I suppose I'll go bed the horses for the night."

His wife stood with him. "I'll help you."

"Help me?"

Her eyes widened, and she jerked her head toward Eva and Jonesy. Eva's cheeks warmed.

"Oh!" the reverend said. "Yes, good thinking. Come help me."

Eva dropped her gaze as the door closed behind them. She stood and began clearing the table. Jonesy's silence compelled her to venture a glance. Her heart sank as his eyes roved over her stomach.

"I didn't want you to see me like this. I was afraid of that look in your eyes."

He stood and closed the distance between them. "Sweetheart," he said, cupping her chin, "the only look in my eyes for you is love and admiration."

"Admiration?" She shook her head. "I'm carrying another man's child. How could you have anything for me but loathing?"

His thumb worked the soft skin along her jaw. "It doesn't matter how. All I know is that I love you more today than I ever have. And if you'll have me, I'll wait forever."

Her eyes misted with unshed tears, and her hand covered his. "Oh, Jonesy. You won't have to wait."

"Are you sure?"

She nodded. "I know I want to be your wife. I've known for quite some time."

"I want to take you and the baby with me to Texas."

Eva felt the blood drain from her face. "But. . .there's a couple here. . .Mr. and Mrs. Matthews. You met them at church today. I—I assumed Ma and Pa had told you I—"

"It's all right, Eva. This has to be your decision. And whatever you decide is all right by me."

"I believe God led me to the O'Neills for more than one reason. For one, I had to clear my head, away from my family. And even from you." Eva gathered in a deep, cleansing breath. "For another, so I could heal. And lastly, because the Matthewses are precious people who long for a child. I have such peace knowing the baby will be loved. And I love the baby enough to know that the Matthewses are the parents God has chosen to raise him."

Jonesy gazed at her with such tenderness that Eva nearly burst into tears of relief. She gave him a tentative smile. "Thank you for coming after me."

"I'll always be there for you. As long as you'll let me."

Eva raised her chin. "Kiss me, Jonesy."

Gently, almost cautiously, Jonesy dipped his head and briefly pressed his lips against hers.

"See?" she said. "No fear."

The corners of his mouth curved upward. "I love you."

Eva smiled and laid her head against his chest. "I love you, too."

❧

On Eva's wedding day, she carried the first roses of spring from her ma's rosebushes. The lace of her white gown trailed the ground as she walked along the path to the river's edge, clutching her pa's arm. Standing next to Gregory, Jonesy waited for her as the water rippled behind him. Handsome and tall, he wore the proudest look on his face that she'd ever seen.

She smiled as her pa lifted her veil and kissed her on the cheek before joining Ma, who stood with family members and close friends who had been invited to share in Eva and Jonesy's joyous day.

Eva's heart leaped at the look of utter delight on her groom's face as he took her hand and stepped forward.

They recited their vows with solemn reverence, and Eva knew as she listened to Jonesy's voice, husky with emotion, promising to love, honor, and cherish her all the days of their lives, that she had no need to ever fear him.

When she promised to love, honor, and obey her husband, and keep herself only for him, she meant it. Every word of it.

When at last they were pronounced husband and wife, Jonesy took her in his arms. His lips descended upon hers with tenderness, and Eva eagerly accepted his kiss. No fear quaked in her belly as it once had at the thought of closeness. Only peace for the life that lay ahead of them in Texas.

A Letter to Our Readers

Dear Readers:

In order that we might better contribute to your reading enjoyment, we would appreciate your taking a few minutes to respond to the following questions. When completed, please return to the following: Fiction Editor, Barbour Publishing, Inc., P.O. Box 719, Uhrichsville, OH 44683.

1. Did you enjoy reading *Oregon Brides* by Tracey Bateman?
   ❑ Very much—I would like to see more books like this.
   ❑ Moderately—I would have enjoyed it more if _____

   _____

   _____

2. What influenced your decision to purchase this book?
   (Check those that apply.)
   ❑ Cover   ❑ Back cover copy   ❑ Title   ❑ Price
   ❑ Friends   ❑ Publicity   ❑ Other

3. Which story was your favorite?
   ❑ *But for Grace*   ❑ *Beside Still Waters*
   ❑ *Hope Everlasting*

4. Please check your age range:
   ❑ Under 18   ❑ 18–24   ❑ 25–34
   ❑ 35–45   ❑ 46–55   ❑ Over 55

5. How many hours per week do you read? _____

Name _____

Occupation _____

Address _____

City_____ State _____ Zip _____

E-mail_____